BAN

CLOSE YOUR EYES
DURING THE EVIL
PARTS.   RKIRBY

P.S. I MEANT ON YOUR
HONEYMOON.

DARK ANGEL

MW01505873

DARK ANGEL

A NOVEL

Robert Kirby

SLICKROCK
BOOKS

Dark Angel
Slickrock Books
© 1990, 1999 by Slickrock Books
First edition published 1990.
Second edition 1999.

All rights reserved.
Printed in the United States of America

No portion of this book may be reproduced in any form
without without written permission from the publisher,
Slickrock Books
P.O. Box 684
Springville, UT 84663

ISBN 1-892936-09-7

10 9 8 7 6 5 4 3 2 1

*For Irene, Christie, Autumn
and Ginny Beth.*

Author's Note

Dark Angel was originally published in 1991 by Cedar Fort, Inc. For reasons incident to production and marketing, I was convinced to heavily edit the manuscript, a task akin to sawing a leg off one of my children. The result was a significantly abridged story and a book I didn't like all that much. Despite this disappointment, Dark Angel soon sold out. Over the years, requests for a second printing were made by readers and local libraries, but it wasn't until the publishing rights were returned to me in 1998 that the possibility was considered. This unabridged volume is the result.

Acknowledgments

Every writer has a string of creditors. For their unflagging help and support during those times when common sense and self-respect might have dictated otherwise, I owe more than I can repay to my wife, Irene, Kim "C" Madsen, Sue Palmer, and Greg Bean.

In those days shall men seek death,
and shall not find it; and shall desire to die,
and death shall flee from them.

Revelation 9:6

Chapter One

On the morning of the day I saw the devil man kill the three soldiers from Camp Floyd, I woke and found my nineteen-year-old sister standing in the middle of the room wearing nothing but a pink ribbon in her hair.

Being sisters, I'd seen Laurel Anne naked often enough so that by now it was only bothersome. After a while, a person's preoccupation with the way they look can sort of wear you down. It was a vision, however, that Henry du Pont, Eldon Bair, or any of the men and boys in the valley would have gladly traded an arm and a leg to share. Me? I didn't even blink.

Laurel Anne didn't know I was watching and so she went right on admiring herself, preening in front of the long mirror Pa had paid dear for in Salt Lake City and given to her last Christmas. First she studied her front, holding her shoulders back. Laurel Anne had a big front and it was clear she wouldn't be bumping her nose on any doors. Satisfied, she turned and studied her bare behind. She was humming a hymn. Even in my fallen state I figured this to be a minor sacrilege. Nothing I'd ever been taught in Sunday School led me to believe that God intended for his hymns to be sung or even hummed by naked girls. Even at the tender age of near enough eleven, I felt it my Christian duty to put a stop to it.

"Your butt's too big," I said.

Actually, if the number of secret looks it drew when it was covered up was any indication, Laurel Anne had a reasonably attractive bottom. Her slender waist bottled out into a woman's set of hips. Not the kind of hips I wanted for myself, mind you. There's nothing like hips for slowing a person down when it comes to sneaking through cracks in the barn and fences when there's chores to be done.

Laurel Anne choked on her surprise, a combination of scream and shout that ended up a strangled honk of indignation. It sounded like our mule, Pilate, the day Pa hit him with a board for kicking one of the twins. She whirled on me with a combination of rage and humiliation. I ducked under the covers while her fists pounded around on the bed, searching for me in the quilts. Mostly she missed. There's an advantage to being small. I kept Brigham tucked under me so she wouldn't squash him by accident. Brigham's my frog and there was no reason he should pay for what I'd said.

Laurel Anne's fists found me once or twice and I let out a howl. She didn't hit me hard enough to hurt—she couldn't—but I had to put a stop to it before she mashed Brigham. If she discovered that she'd been sleeping in the same bed with me and a frog, there would have been hell to pay. There was also the added danger that she might be mad enough to work up a sweat. Then we'd have to wait while she took another bath before we could leave for Provo. Folks go gray in the time it takes Laurel Anne to bathe.

When the pounding stopped, I peered back out. Laurel Anne was wearing a pair of bloomers and a chemise. Red-faced, she was trying to jam her legs into a petticoat. She gave me a scathing look over her nose. It was a look that, had it been turned on any of them, would have reduced her many beaus to tears and pleas for forgiveness. Unimpressed, I stuck out my tongue.

"Some people think they're mighty smart spying on others," Laurel Anne said.

"And some just like spying themselves in the mirror," I replied. Before I said it though, I made sure there was enough space between her and the door. There was such a thing, I knew, as pressing one's luck too far.

Laurel Anne chose not to pursue me or the matter any further. "You just get out of that bed, Rose Lee Merrell. We need to leave soon or the sun will fry us crispy. Hurry up."

I slid out of bed and gathered my clothes, pulling a gingham jumper over my head. Brigham went into the pocket and I scuffed on my Indian moccasins. I headed for the door, glancing back to where Laurel Anne continued to struggle with yards of frilly unmentionables. It would be at least an hour before we could get in the buggy and leave. Time enough for me to eat breakfast, catch a hopper for Brigham, and see my ma.

When I peered through the kitchen door, my sister-ma, Alva, was bent over taking a pan of biscuits from the oven. I sneaked past her, knowing that if she saw me she would interpret my presence as an offer of servitude. Alva was big on the two things I hated most in the whole world: chores and Red Jacket Bitters, her prime cure for general ills and laziness. Fortunately, Alva's butt was a blind and dumb sentry, though two-year-old Aaron spotted me. He gave me a red grin from the floor where he was eating jam and trying to touch the side of the stove. Aaron was a true Merrell and as such the more absolute rules of life came hard to him. He touched the stove at least once a week. Alva, like Laurel Anne, was humming a hymn and missed me altogether. I shook my head. Anyone who had ever been ambushed had probably walked into it humming a hymn and showing off their behind.

On the porch of the brick house Pa built for Alva, I paused and surveyed the wide promise of the summer morning upon which the rest of my life would turn. Thus far, 1869 had been an enlightening year. Mainly because even though we lived on a farm stuck midway between Salt Lake and Provo in the Territory of Utah, Pa was ever piling us into a wagon and tearing off in the direction of something to see.

In May, Pa loaded his two wives, a third hopeful candidate, and all his children into wagons and drove us two days to a place at the very top of the Great Salt Lake, so we could watch two fat men in stovepipe hats pound a gold spike into the railroad that linked the continent East and West. Even though the two men missed their first swings at the spike, everyone whooped and fired guns, generally acting as if they'd lost their minds. Even Ma applauded. She said the joining of the railroads was the biggest thing to happen in the United States since the vision of God and Jesus to Joseph Smith. Maybe, but I was bored by the whole affair.

I wasn't bored in June when Pa loaded us into the wagons again and took us to Salt Lake City to see Dan Castello's Circus, Menagerie and

Abyssinian Caravan. Without a doubt it was the best day in my life. We gawked for hours at knights, acrobats, clowns, tigers and monkeys. Pa's pockets seemed as large as his determination to make sure that his family had a good time. I ate cotton candy, ice cream and popped corn until I vomited it all up in the back of the wagon. Getting sick was no fun, but I definitely was not bored.

Since the circus, I'd been in love with elephants and tigers. Mostly though, I was infatuated with Signorita Clarinda Lowanda, the beautiful Portuguese bareback rider of the Brazilian tropics. Signorita Clarinda stunned the Salt Lake crowd with her equestrian abilities, proving to me at least that being born a girl was not as serious a setback as I had previously thought. She did tricks on the back of a galloping horse that astonished even the men. Pa said she had to be part Indian or part leech, judging from the way she rode. But considering the comments of some of the other men, they mostly liked Clarinda's riding outfit, a gorgeous pink and gold affair that clung to her body like an extra skin. Silla Van Orden, one of Alva's friends who hung around our house in the hopes that Pa would lose his mind and marry her, said the outfit was so snug it was positively a sin. Her son, Josh, said it was so tight that if Clarinda farted she would've blown her boots off. This observation earned Josh a slap from his ma. Silla was desperate to impress my pa with how well she controlled her son in the absence of his own pa, who had deserted them four years ago in favor of California and sanity. I laughed out loud at what Josh said. This plainly peeved Silla, who scowled and waited for Pa to wallop me. Pa didn't because he never hit his children and because he was too busy trying to hide his own laugh in his beard. Mormon bishops aren't much for letting people see them laugh about such stuff as farts.

Dan Castello's circus was a turning point in my life, being both a wonderment and a curse. It's strange how you can see things like trained monkeys and coal-black swordsmen and realize with despair that everything about the world has changed but yourself. I saw things in the circus that threw wide the doors in my mind. Dan Castello showed me what a double-edged promise life was. The burden was on yourself to choose between excitement and drudgery—and the price you had to pay for both of them.

Ever since the circus, Alva had complained to Pa about the effect it had had on me, pointing out in her usual grim manner that I was more disobedient, less inclined to work and increasingly more profane in my observations. The first two Pa didn't much care about, although he handed out a goodly share of chores when I was in sight. He was death on the cussing, though. I could sometimes squeeze by him with a "hell" or a "damn," but "shitaree" and "sonuvabitch" invariably meant a trip to the rain barrel with a bar of store soap. As kind and tolerant as my pa was, he had his limits, and I couldn't even stand to think what he'd do to me if he ever heard me take the Lord's name in vain. There probably wasn't enough soap in the whole world.

My own ma, Pa's second wife, said cussing was just a creative phase I was going through. All I know for sure was that what came out of my mouth was nothing compared to what ran around loose and limber inside my brain. Nights I dreamed of riding an elephant to school or standing calmly on the back of a galloping horse circling my awe-struck friends. In those dreams, the boys who teased me got the seeds squeezed out of them by my faithful elephant while the girls all turned green at the sight of my pink and gold costume.

I shook off the memory of the circus, knowing that it would only depress me. I thought instead about the pending trip to Provo and the two things I hoped to accomplish there. First was to get as many ice cream sodas as possible inside of me. Second was the covert purchase of several dime novels, the reading of which was looked down on by my family as a waste of money and contrary to the order and spirit of God.

My plotting was interrupted by the bright ring of Pa's blacksmith hammer. I looked down the lane at the barn. Having identified another potential source of work, I decided to steer clear of the barn until it was time to leave. Down by the river, toward the road that went around the mountain to Salt Lake City, I spied the solitary figure of Cletus, our negro hired hand, returning for breakfast from his morning work. He was riding Pilate and at that distance, man and beast, colored in equal shades of tar, blended into the fantastic figure of a centaur. I liked Cletus even though he talked more Bible than Pa and was widely believed to be crazy for having agreed to Pa's proposal of single-handedly digging a canal from the Jordan River to a series of half-finished irrigation ditches on our farm. The proposal had sent our other hired hand, Mr. Stubbs, packing. But not before he had taught me how to cuss in fine style. Cletus didn't mind digging Pa's ditch, saying he had dug so many ditches for free while a slave in Georgia that digging one now for pay seemed like a blessing from God.

Across the distance, I saw a white flash of teeth. I knew Cletus was praying over his unseen breakfast, a sign that he still didn't trust Pa's polygamist prayers. Cletus was a wandering minister of the Baptist sort and held Mormons in high regard, claiming we were the nicest folks God would ever send to hell. Late evenings, he and Pa would sometimes argue scripture. Cletus was a mediocre canal digger, but he was a damn marvel at arguing scripture, which everyone knew was the real reason Pa kept him around.

I glanced up the slope toward the trees where my mother, Colleen Merrell, and I lived. Blue smoke curled from the chimney of the log house. It made me feel good to know Ma was up and waiting for me and that she didn't mind that I sometimes slept in the brick house. I shook back my hair and breathed in the cool, minty smell of the morning, the last morning of my childhood. Beyond our cabin, desert mountains stretched broad and distant under the morning sun. Out there lurked Indians, cougars, bears and other hurtful things. Eight years ago, Bishop Samuel Woodbury had disappeared into those mountains with Brigham Young's gold. The ghost of the murdering Indian, Squash Head, was said to wander the canyons and the draws. It was dangerous out there, I knew. But here in the valley, with the smell of Alva's biscuits, the ring of Pa's hammer, and Cletus' interminable prayers, I believed we were safe from all of that.

I was still thinking about how safe it was when a clod exploded on the post above my head.

I wheeled off the porch under a shower of dirt and ducked behind the rain barrel. Cautiously poking my head up, I saw the twins, Lehi and Nephi, hoeing weeds in Alva's vegetable garden. Heads low under straw hats, they were perfect models of hard working innocence—except that I could see their round shoulders shaking with suppressed laughter.

I ducked down and circled the house, keeping low under the kitchen window where Alva still hummed her insensible hymn and Aaron finally touched the stove. His screams fell behind me as I rounded the corner. The woodpile was a perfect blind and I used it to screen my approach, gathering rocks from the yard as I went. Snow, Alva's pet duck, came over to have a cursory look at me before waddling off to hunt for hoppers in the garden. I hunkered down behind the raspberry bushes and glanced up at the house for possible witnesses.

Laurel Anne smiled down at me from a window. Decked out in a pale green dress with a lace collar, she looked like a princess in a castle. She winked and smiled when she divined what I was up to, our own squabble forgotten in the face of a common enemy. The twins were two years older than me and boys in the bargain. They had range on me when it came to rocking, but I had accuracy and speed in my camp, potent weapons in a feud that had existed as long as we had. I transferred Brigham to my left hand and put the rocks in the pocket of my jumper before standing up.

The twins were still going through the motions of hoeing, but their bovine attention was now riveted on the porch where they'd seen me last. They were understandably having difficulty believing that I wasn't going to retaliate.

Nephi stooped and picked up another clod. "Where'd Mutt get to?"

"Dunno," Lehi replied, looking around, "But I got a bad feeling."

I started throwing.

The first rock was the biggest and it hit Lehi in the back of the head with a hollow, gourd-like sound. He went down on his face like it was God's idea. Nephi spotted me and let fly, a clumsy throw that sailed wide and harmless. The next rock struck him square in the knee and he sat down abruptly on his brother. I peppered them some more, conscious of Laurel Anne laughing and clapping behind the window. She had no sympathy for the twins, who only yesterday had rocked the privy while she was in it.

Screams rent the morning air. Out of rocks, I turned and ran, knowing Alva would soon put in an appearance; like as not with Pa's musket. Alva was terrified spitless of Indians. Anytime her children screamed, she was sure they were being carried off. Pa insisted that Indians had better sense and kept the musket unloaded.

Across the road, I climbed the fence and waved at Cletus. He waved back, his smile an approving light in the dark night of his face, his voice slow and warm as noon.

"You's a caution, Miss Budge," he called to me. "Bless you..."

The rest of Cletus's words were lost in the rush of my flight from the brick house. I ran through the fields, jumping milkweed and rock piles left by the spring plowing. Hoppers and quail scattered at my swift approach and a fat deer bounced into the woods. Killdeer scurried wide, whistling their shrill lies while dried thistles caught at my jumper. A raven circled the woods and fell low over me, gliding in black silence toward the house where I lived with my ma, healer and seer, and second wife to Bishop Lee Merrell, captain in the Nauvoo Legion.

Ma was waiting for me at the door, her beautiful face lit with a smile. She caught me up and I buried my face in the softness of her hair, inhaling lemon verbena and mint. The house itself was wild with a licorice tonic bubbling on the stove.

"Good morning, sweet Rose," Ma said, hugging me tight. Ma always hugged me tight whenever I returned from sleeping in the brick house. It was as if she feared I wouldn't return from down below where her younger sister primly reigned as Pa's senior wife.

"Did you see me rock the twins?" I said, trying to catch my breath.

Ma laughed and I kissed her. Ma rarely scolded me for the things I did. She had her own way of explaining the wrong side of your crimes, a gentle way of making you feel small and miserable for something unchristian. Rocking the twins wasn't one of those things, however.

"You need to eat," she said suddenly, putting me down and shooing me to the table. "This is a big day."

I sat down next to the framed daguerreotype of my brother John, who had died two years before. Johnny was feeble-minded and lived only twelve years before his affliction claimed him. He lay a hundred yards away from our cabin in a family cemetery that included Pa's folks, Bumpa and Nanna Merrell; Pa's first wife and Laurel Anne's mother, Alice; a cousin named James who I'd never seen; three of Alva's babies; and a hired hand killed by Indians during the course of an argument over a bucket.

I turned the daguerreotype of Johnny around to face me. Together we were my mother's sole contribution to the family of Bishop Lee Merrell, and there were people in the valley cruel enough to remind her that she had done poorly by him. Choosing to live on the slope above the family farm where she brewed her tonics and doctored folks with things learned from books and Indians had earned Ma the whispered accusation of "odd" and, in a few extreme cases, "witch." The collateral effects of this made these same people suspicious of me as well. I didn't care. In the immortal if intemperate words of Mr. Stubbs, they could all whistle up their asses for luck before I paid them any mind.

Ma put my breakfast in front of me and waited while I said a few breathless words of grace, none of which were heartfelt since countless other prayers had yet to secure me a single elephant from God and Jesus.

Then she started combing my hair. Across the room on the bed, my church clothes were laid out: a white apron and a broadcloth dress, both were drab and heavy, and would make me look like even more of a field mouse next to Laurel Anne. I hated my church clothes, considering them to be little more than a portable prison. Church clothes, however, were the non-negotiable conditions of accompanying Laurel Anne to Provo. Laurel Anne was big on appearances. I saw town little enough as it was and so I wasn't going to balk out loud. I'd get even with her later.

Brigham chose that moment to wriggle out of my pocket and make a bid for freedom. He hit the wooden floor with a rubbery slap. Down below in the brick house, Alva would've had a conniption at the sight of a frog on her stone floor. Instead, Ma bent over and popped him into his box full of wet moss before putting him on the table next to my plate. I tapped his green-brown head and he blinked slow, stunned by what had to be the human equivalent of belly flopping off the roof of a barn. Brigham was a hardy captive if a poor pet. Which was fine. I didn't want another real pet, certainly not the sort you get attached to. Not a dog.

I finished the bread and cider before getting up and stripping off my jumper and the cotton pantaloons I wore underneath. Ma bustled about getting my church clothes ready. While she did, I took a peek at myself in the mirror. What I saw wasn't very encouraging. Where Laurel Anne looked like a woman, I looked like a shaved gopher. With my dun-colored hair, large eyes and feet, and all the robustness of a famine victim, I looked exactly like what the twins called me when out of Pa's earshot: Mutt.

For a moment, and just for a moment, I found myself wishing I had big pillows in front and graceful hips like Laurel Anne's, as well as her honey-colored hair. I considered what it would be like to have every man stop and stare goggle-eyed at me when I passed by, pretending not to notice. I shook the thought out of my head. Laurel Anne couldn't climb trees, skinny dip with her friends, and she had probably never caught a bug or a frog. She spent half her life getting fixed up to receive a caller or to go to one of the dances in Lehi City or Provo. No, I liked being me despite what Alva and some others said. Ma liked me, Pa liked me, and before he got snake-bit and died last summer, my dog Hercules had liked me. I was fairly certain that Laurel Anne liked me despite what I said about her butt. Jesus liked me, but then he was stuck doing it because he was Jesus, so it probably didn't count. Still, that was plenty enough.

When Ma finished dressing me in the smothering folds of my church clothes, she kissed me again and gave me my spending money, a handkerchief with sixty cents in real coin, not church script, tied up in it. Then she handed me a list of herbs and things she needed, which I could charge to Pa's account at the big Zion's cooperative. Finally, she handed me Brigham, who had never been further from our farm than the creek where I caught him.

"You do well and see that you mind Laurel Anne," Ma said. "Cooperating with people is very important if you expect them to treat you right."

I looked up at my ma. She was a tall woman with hair the color of Merlin, the raven whose wing we had mended two winters before and now wouldn't leave. Ma had dark eyes and a cameo face that filled with intensity whenever I read to her at night from the books lining the walls of our tiny home. She was beautiful, and not just because she was my ma. I'd seen the way men looked at her, too.

"I love you, Ma," I said. My throat grew thick and clumsy. For some reason I felt like bawling.

"And I love you, sweet Rose," she replied. "Go now. Have fun, and hurry home to me."

Merlin tried to light on my head when I went out into our flower-filled yard. I batted him away and ran as fast as I could in my clumsy church shoes, which felt like two bricks strapped to my feet, all the way back down to the big house.

Laurel Anne waited on the porch for me. Cletus had the buggy pulled up in front, the canvas sun bonnet in place. The twins were nowhere to be seen. Their hoes still lay in the garden like abandoned pikes on the field of battle. Alva had probably already dosed them with Red Jacket Bitters. If they hadn't been the twins, I would have felt sorry for them. I'd tasted Red Jacket Bitters before and, frankly, would rather drink a tonic of coal oil and cat piss. I clambered up into the buggy.

Alva came out of the house holding a tear-streaked Aaron, whose hands were wrapped in buttery bandages. She gave me a level look but said nothing. Alva was a humorless woman, much shorter than her sister and considerably broader through the beam. Although younger than my ma, there were wisps of gray in Alva's dark hair and pursed lines around her mouth. She still hadn't forgiven me for calling her "pumpkin ass" to her face last summer during an argument over something Herc had done and for which I was attempting to defend him. Fair was fair. She had called me a "worthless brat" and I responded with the first thing that came to mind, which unfortunately turned out to be something I'd learned from Mr. Stubbs. It was a verbal slip that earned me her undying enmity as well as a trip to the rain barrel, where Pa calmly lectured me yet again on the evils of bad language while feeding me large slivers of store soap.

It was clear that Alva was angry with me now for having incapacitated the twins. I didn't much care. I glanced back toward our house. Ma waved to me from the doorway. I turned and crossed my eyes at Alva, who tightened nonexistent lips and looked away. She was a great one for getting even later, too.

After conferring with Alva—probably about selling me to the first group of slavers we came across—Laurel Anne gathered her skirts and accepted Cletus's helping hand into the buggy. She picked up the reins and flicked them across the horse's rump. Waving, we started off on the three-hour trek to Provo.

We made one more stop, pulling up in front of Pa's shop. My father was a blacksmith, horse trader and a sometimes puller of teeth. He had broad, iron-hard shoulders and a generous mouth set in the middle of a gray-shot beard. A lifetime of swinging a hammer had given him forearms the size of hams. I'd seen him twist horseshoes in two with those arms. I loved my pa and near about everyone else in our ward did, too. I liked to think he looked a little like Arthur in that king's latter years. Grinning, Pa dusted off his hands and plucked me out of the buggy as easily as taking a cup from a shelf. He smelled of cedar smoke and hot iron from his forge. His beard billowed across my face as he kissed me and stuck me back on the seat.

"You take care and leave some of Provo standing, Budge," he boomed. Pa called me Budge. It wasn't the prettiest name I'd ever heard but it was special between us and a damn sight better than Mutt. He patted my leg and turned to his oldest daughter. Laurel Anne was the only survivor of Pa's first family, who had all died while he was off on a church mission to Great Britain. I knew and didn't mind much that Laurel Anne was special to him in a way that none of the rest of us could ever be. She was too big to haul out of the buggy and so Pa took off his hat, bowed elaborately and kissed her hand. Laurel Anne blushed. No man ever bowed to me, probably because I was just a kid stuck on the ugly edge of becoming a woman. I don't know why, but it bothered me.

Pa fixed us with a stern look. Going off to Provo alone was something we'd never done before, and despite the fact that we'd be hooking up with two more families along the way, he worried.

"Mind that you wait for Brother Clark and Brother Willoughby at the crossroads. I won't have you traveling the whole way alone." He was smiling when he said it but you could tell he meant it just the same. Of all the things I was sure of about my pa, the first was that he loved us without reservation and the second was that he expected to be obeyed when he talked serious.

"Yes, father," Laurel Anne agreed. She blew Pa a kiss which he pretended to catch and hide in his beard.

We were full of smiles when Laurel Anne started the buggy again. I turned and looked back at the snug farm the Merrells had carved from the wilderness. It looked peaceful there in the hollow of the trees. Like a piece of heaven.

Along the way we passed the homes of our nearest neighbors. There was the smaller and less prosperous farm of the Knight family, the immaculate dairy farm of Otto Hoffenstetter, and the cluster of buildings which marked the cooperage of William Pettus & Sons. Off in the distance, where green trees trailed the Jordan River, I saw the farms of Floyd Jackson, Harvey Stoddard and Leo Poulsen. Plowed fields spread a distinctive checkerboard against the silver-green of the desert. Down in the narrows, where the trees and the river made a turn under the bluffs, I could even see the roof of the shanty saloon belonging to Slobber Bob.

As we passed the Pettus place, I kept a special lookout for Josh. Though he was only twelve, he worked long hours at the cooperage to support his ma. Lately, despite the fact that most girls did whatever it took to avoid him, it had become important that Josh Van Orden notice me. I wanted him to see me dressed up and going to town like a lady, although I couldn't have said why such a thing mattered.

I spotted Josh carrying a heavy bundle of staves into the shop. His hat was off, his hair dark and damp with sweat. Pleased as I was to see him, I made sure not to wave. Studying Laurel Anne's behavior around her beaus had educated me to the fact that it was the responsibility of young men to notice young ladies and not the other way around. But Josh didn't wave, or otherwise acknowledge our passing. Still, I know Josh saw me because I suddenly felt run out of air. Then we were gone, Laurel Anne oblivious to my discomfiture, and me wishing I could twist around and yell to Josh that we should go swimming or fishing when I got back.

After that, there was nothing much left between us and Provo but time and road dust. Birds sang in the trees and the clip-clop of hooves soon made me sleepy. Because I didn't want to miss any of the trip by falling asleep, I picked a fight with Laurel Anne.

"Henry du Pont says he's going to marry you before Christmas," I said off handedly.

Laurel Anne sat a little straighter in the seat. "Oh? And just when have you been sharing confidences with Lieutenant du Pont? I wasn't aware the two of you were so close."

Actually Henry had said nothing of the kind, at least not to me. He barely knew I was alive. The center of his universe was Laurel Anne. Pa said Henry could be run over by buffalo and the matter would completely escape him if Laurel Anne was anywhere in the vicinity. Henry was an army lieutenant at Camp Floyd and although a gentile and the product of a refined Eastern family, he attended many of our Mormon dances and social functions. He was a nervous boy in a man's uniform who tried in vain to mature his appearance with wispy sideburns and whiskers. Besides Henry du Pont, widely considered to be the most exotic of Laurel Anne's beaus, there was Jack Clayton, Jason Butterfield, Lester Knight, Eldon Bair and about a million others, each of whom would have gleefully murdered the rest.

I shrugged. "He must have said something about it at the dance."

Laurel Anne paused, unsure whether to believe me or not. I had a reputation for pulling legs, sometimes damn near off.

"Is this the same dance that you spent sitting in the buggy because you poured punch on Eddie Hoffenstetter?" she asked.

"He pulled my hair. And, yes, it is the same dance." Inwardly I fumed. I couldn't have a simple conversation with anyone, even if it was a pack of lies, without them bringing up my faults.

"And what else did Lieutenant du Pont have to say? Not that I'm the slightest bit interested, mind you."

"Well," I said, knowing I had her hooked. "He said if you married him, you wouldn't have to worry about him marrying some other gal. You'd always be his only wife." I paused to examine the tapestry of my lie. It didn't sound half bad considering that I was making it up as I went along. "We talked for a long time. He was mad because you danced more with Jack and Eldon than him."

"How interesting."

I glanced at Laurel Anne out of the corner of my eye and shifted Brigham from my left pocket to the right. Laurel Anne touched her hair and looked over the tip of her nose like she did whenever she mulled over the management of her beaus.

"Was he quite angry or just annoyed?" she asked after a moment.

I put my chin in my hands and pretended to think. "I'd say a smidgen annoyed with maybe a dab of murder thrown in. He said Eldon couldn't dance any better than a pig." I thought about that for a second and a giggle crawled up my throat. I pushed it back down. "He said Eldon would have been kicked out of West Point for just his dancing alone."

Laurel Anne sniffed. "For your information, Eldon Bair is an excellent dancer. Not that you or Lieutenant du Pont would know anything about it."

"I'm just telling you what he said. He said you'd have servants and a big house in New York."

"Massachusetts," Laurel Anne said with a new air of distraction. Her head was so full of the notion of having a houseful of servants that she let this obvious mistake go by without further challenge.

"Right. He did speak of his concerns about taking you back east to meet his family."

"Oh?"

"Maybe I better keep my mouth shut. After all, it wouldn't do to share confidences. Pa says gossiping is a sin."

We rode for another mile or so while Laurel Anne pleaded with me to tell her everything. She worked herself into a considerable lather and I started to worry that maybe I'd gone too far.

"It's because we're Mormons, isn't it?" she lamented. "Oh, I just know it is. You don't know those Eastern society people, Budge. His parents would never understand."

"So?" I demanded. "Just last Sunday you told me that you never wanted to see Henry again."

"Well, that's before I knew he seriously wanted to marry. Besides he's taken to smoking."

I snorted. "He's only asked you fifty damn times to marry him. And he hates smoking. He just does it because he thinks it makes him look mature."

"Don't cuss," Laurel Anne said. She made little fists around the reins and stamped her foot, too upset to castigate me further. "I didn't know he was so serious. Oh, I wish he'd just let Pa baptize him and be done with it. He claims to admire Brigham Young and the church."

I rolled my eyes. Henry du Pont stood about as much chance of converting to Mormonism as I had of becoming an Indian chief. He hinted about it but never got any closer than waiting for Laurel Anne outside the meeting house on Sundays. "He never said anything about you being a Mormon," I said. "Besides, I think he's got other worries."

"Worries? What worries?" It surprised and concerned Laurel Anne Merrell, inarguably the most beautiful woman in the territory, that any of her beaus might find the slightest thing wrong with her.

I swallowed hard. "He, ah, told me he didn't know how he could break the news to his folks that he was marrying a girl like you. Before he left home his parents made him swear a holy promise that he wouldn't marry a girl with a butt as big as yours."

It took Laurel Anne maybe a full minute to realize what I'd said and that I'd been pulling her leg all along. With a snort of fury, she swung a cuff at my head. I weaseled down and around behind the seat, knocking over the basket of food Alva had packed for us.

Although Laurel Anne is nineteen and I'm only almost eleven, and despite the fact that she continually tries to teach me manners, it's always easier for me to bring her down to my level than it is for her to raise me to hers. I have to pay for doing it, mind you, but it's worth it every time.

We were traveling in a shaded area where the trees were thick enough to prevent the horse from wandering off the road. Laurel Anne let go of the reins and turned in the seat to box my ears. I would have escaped if laughter and my church shoes hadn't slowed me down. As it was, Laurel Anne caught me on the backseat and pretended to strangle me. Then she started tickling me, something she knew I hated worse than church. It took my breath away and I saw spots.

When the spots cleared, the buggy had stopped and soldiers were blocking the road.

I sat up and knew instantly that we were in serious trouble. Laurel Anne knew it, too. When she turned around and saw the men, she trapped a scream in her throat.

Camp Floyd was to the west of our farm and mostly deserted. Ma said it had been founded by the government in 1857 to keep an eye on us Mormons and eventually was almost abandoned during the War between the States. It had been renamed Camp Crittenden on account of how

Secretary of War John B. Floyd, for whom the camp had originally been named, had embarrassed everyone by running off to become a Confederate. But everyone around here still called it Camp Floyd. To Mormons, the name would always be synonymous with government bondage, something akin to a curse. Most of the soldiers were now at Fort Douglas in Salt Lake City, their cannons pointed in the direction of the growing temple. There was still some cavalry at Camp Floyd to protect stage and mail routes from the fractious Utes though. Except for Henry, the soldiers there still didn't mix well with the Saints.

Sergeant Bukovski was just one of those. Although an evil legend in our valley, I had only seen Bukovski twice. A barrel-shaped man with sloping shoulders and arms knotted with muscle, he possessed all the physical appearances of a stupid bear. Once, he bought a horse from Pa with money he'd earned at Slobber Bob's trading punches with valley men who were either ignorant of his prowess or had drunk enough to lessen the importance of it in their minds. Rumor had it that the sergeant had crippled a Salt Lake boy during the winter, breaking his jaw and neck with a single blow.

Bukovski was no admirer of Mormons. He liked to brag about having ridden with the mobs back in Illinois when he was a boy. He even claimed to have been at Carthage with the Grays when they killed Joseph and Hyrum Smith. These were not the sort of boasts one made in the Territory of Utah without the strength and the ferocity to back them up. No one knew for sure whether Bukovski had a hand in killing the Prophet, but it was widely held and hoped that sooner or later he would run afoul of Brigham Young's bodyguard, Porter Rockwell, who would send him to hell. In the meantime, Bukovski loafed around Slobber Bob's and taunted the Mormons who dropped in or passed by.

Two weeks after he bought the horse from Pa, Bukovski rode the poor animal to death during a drunken spree. He came back to our farm to accuse Pa of cheating him. Pa refused to return the money and finally ordered Bukovski off at musket point. I still remember Bukovski standing at our gate, shouting curses and ugly threats through his beard. Seeing him now, I had an idea some of those things were about to come true.

The other two soldiers were smaller than Bukovski but cut from the same bolt of nasty cloth. One had the pointy face of a rat while the other sported two dirty yellow stripes across the sleeves of his faded shirt. All three were grinning.

"Well, well," Bukovski said, his voice husky and full of dirt. "I reckon there is a God after all." He bobbed his head at Laurel Anne. "Howdy to you, Missy Merrell." He slid heavily out of the saddle and caught the reins of our horse. "You two fillies are a little far from home."

Laurel Anne did her best to recover her wits. I could see she was badly frightened by the surprise appearance of Bukovski and friends. She straightened her dress and picked up the reins. Red spots high on her cheeks overlaid the nervous white of the rest of her face.

"Y-yes," she stammered. "We're on our way to Provo. If you will turn loose our animal please, we'll continue."

"Can't do that," Bukovski said. He chuckled, a low sound in his barrel chest like far off thunder headed our way. From where I sat in the back of the buggy, I could smell the sour odor of beer and sweat on him. I glanced behind us for help but the road was long and empty.

"And why not?" Laurel Anne asked. She was becoming more frightened.

Bukovski removed his cap and scratched his sweaty head, searching for a reason. "Well, you know, it seems there's Injuns about, missy," he said finally. "I couldn't go off and just leave women and children alone. It's the army's job to protect civilians. Have to do my duty, y'see."

Laurel Anne mulled this over and then attempted to pull the reins out of the sergeant's hand. He just grinned and held on to them. She gave it up and put her hands in her lap. Clearly she didn't believe the sergeant's claim of marauding Indians.

"I'll have you know, sergeant," Laurel Anne said, her bottom lip beginning to tremble, "that I am almost the fiancee of Lieutenant Henry du Pont. You can be sure he will hear of your behavior."

Bukovski showed bad teeth when he laughed. He winked at his companions. "You hear that, boys? This here's the fiancee of Prince Dither. Mr. High and Mighty is gonna marry hisself a Mormon."

Rat Face leaned on the pommel of his saddle. "I reckon that makes this little meeting double lucky then, eh, sarge?"

Bukovski turned back to us and all the feigned merriment left his eyes. They turned flat and ugly like the eyes of a wild pig. "That it does, Leroy," he said softly. "That it does."

"What do you really want?" Laurel asked.

Bukovski's grin widened, huge and yellow. "I reckon I want my money back for that sickly horse your Pa sold me. That horse up and died on me not even a week after I paid good money for it. Your Pa's a cheat, missy. I think it's your Christian duty—provided you damn Mormons really are Christians—to make good on your Pa's debt."

Ma always said the greatest cross I would bear in my life was having an Irish temperament hitched to a Merrell mouth. When Bukovski claimed Pa was a cheat, the blood drained out of my face, leaving me weak with fury. I crammed Brigham in my pocket.

"That horse cost me fifty dollars," Bukovski was saying. "And it was a poor horse. But since I'm a fair man who don't like being cheated by lying Mormon bishops—"

"You're full of frog shit!" I shrieked, leaping to my feet.

Prior to this outburst I had been ignored. Now, however, every pair of eyes swiveled in my direction. Bukovski blinked stupidly, Laurel Anne's mouth fell open, and the other two soldiers paused in the act of climbing off their horses.

"My pa's no cheat," I ranted. "That was a good horse and you ruined it. Fat sonuvabitch."

Bukovski blinked a couple more times in surprise. Then his heavy face darkened with fury. Carefully, he motioned to his friends.

"Bob. Leroy. Haul that ugly little nubbin out of there. She needs some manners taught her."

"I'd like to see you try, you puffed up cat turd." I continued to rage. "I'm not afraid of you."

Truth was, I was petrified by the mere thought of Bukovski laying his grimy, walnut- knuckled hands on me, but reason and I had parted company. He had no call to talk like that about Pa.

Laurel Anne turned and grabbed my arm. "Rose Lee Merrell, you just sit right down and be quiet this instant! Good heavens, ladies don't talk like that."

Bukovski laughed, an ugly grunt in the hot silence of the road. He looked at Laurel Anne, straight at the swelling front of her dress as she tried to catch her breath. "Except you gals ain't exactly ladies, are you? Just a couple of Mormon sluts is all."

That did it fine. I snatched up a hard-boiled egg from the basket Alva had packed for us and pitched it. It struck Bukovski full in the face, knocking off his cap. He staggered and momentarily turned loose of our horse. Laurel Anne slapped the reins down in an effort to drive away.

The next few moments were a wild blur of images and shouts. Being an accomplished brawler, a boiled egg thrown by a skinny girl wasn't much of a blow for Bukovski to shake off. He recovered quickly and hauled our horse up short while his two accomplices rode their own horses along either side of the buggy, reaching inside for me.

Out of the corner of my eye, I saw Bukovski yank Laurel Anne out of the buggy. Her hair came loose and she screamed. I tried to kick at Bukovski while at the same time reaching for another egg, but someone seized the back of my hair and the next thing I knew I was hanging over the road, my church shoes kicking in the air.

"Now," Bukovski said to me, holding on to the struggling Laurel Anne with one hand and doubling up the other. "It's time for a lesson in manners."

Bukovski's fist landed on my side like a knobby meteor. All the air in me went out my nose and mouth with a whoosh and a fair amount of slobber and snot. The one holding me dropped me on the road where I lay waiting for Jesus to come and get me. Hot sparkles of light swam in front of my face and a green nausea washed over me. If I didn't die first, I vowed to sick up my breakfast just as soon as I got a breath.

The soldiers didn't wait for me to catch my breath. Rat Face jumped off his horse and yanked me up by my hair again. He locked a cruel arm around my neck and I dangled there, toes barely brushing the ground. Through a silver blur of tears and a cloud of sweat and tobacco, I glimpsed Bukovski push Laurel Anne up against the side of the buggy, pressing his huge body along the length of hers.

"Looks like I'm going to ride one of Bishop Merrell's fillies again, boys," Bukovski chortled. "Reckon I'll have to take the price of that horse in swap."

"Go it, sarge," the corporal cheered. "Only save some for your men."

"Don't worry," Bukovski grunted, rubbing his hands over Laurel Anne. "She's got plenty for all of us."

The corporal was holding the reins of their horses, glancing up and down the highway for signs of interference. At that moment, Brigham made another untimely leap for freedom from my pocket. He flopped into the road and paused to gather his wits. With a whoop, the corporal stamped on him. Blood and frog juice squirted in a sunflower pattern from under his boot. I screamed and kicked. The arm around my neck tightened until I thought the top of my head would pop off.

"Hold still, nubbin," Rat Face growled in my ear. "Else I'll bust your skinny damn neck."

I closed my eyes and started praying. I'd prayed for a lot of things in my almost eleven years. Ever since the circus, I had prayed for a elephant but hadn't got one. Ma told me prayer didn't work like that and that I should only pray for things I truly needed. This particular prayer was exactly that kind of prayer. It bolted straight from the very center of my soul, the words a strangled, "Oh God, Oh God, Oh God," over and over again. Inside my head though, the prayer was a plea for Jesus to command an angel to rescue us from Sergeant Bukovski.

"No!" I heard Laurel Anne weep, and then she screamed, high and terrible in the warm morning. My eyes shot open.

Sergeant Bukovski had his hands on Laurel Anne's pillows, squeezing and twisting them. Her jacket was torn and her hair hung down across her face. She struggled and pounded his heavy chest with her fists, an inconsequential fluttering against the massive bulk of the man. One of the sergeant's big hands cracked across her face, changed into a fist and bludgeoned her on the back swing. Long tresses fanned out as Laurel Anne's head recoiled under the blow. She sagged in Bukovski's arms. The sergeant began pulling at the front of her dress, ripping the lace collar and opening the front. All the while he was laughing. I realized with a sick feeling that for the second time that day I was going to see my sister naked.

"Hold still, missy," Bukovski was saying. "We're just going to have us a little polygamy is all." Laurel Anne screamed again and the soldiers laughed louder. I closed my eyes again and increased both the urgency and tempo of my prayer, knowing full well that it wasn't going to work. Except it did.

A piercing whistle froze everyone. I opened my eyes and looked. Instead of a golden angel hanging in the air above us, I saw a devil standing at the side of the road.

The devil man seemed to have come from nowhere, as if a harried Satan had cracked open hell and kicked out someone he couldn't manage. Dust drifted from his shirt like sulphur smoke in the warm breeze. A brace of pistols hung from a wide leather belt around his hips, one low on the right side and the other strapped across the front of him. The wide brim of a hat wrapped a shadow around his face while a ragged blue scarf covered his mouth and neck like the mask of a highwayman. But it was the eyes that riveted my attention and put a piercing weakness deep in the pit of my stomach. The devil man's eyes were flat gray dead things in the shadow of the hat, like the lifeless button eyes of the dolls Ma made for me. Seeing those eyes on a man made my skin crawl up in gooseflesh. If Rat Face hadn't of had such a fierce hold on me, I would have fled screaming from the very sight them.

Sergeant Bukovski let go of Laurel Anne as he turned to face the devil man. Half-conscious and bleeding from the mouth, my sister sank to the road. Rat Face tightened his grip on me.

Bukovski cleared his throat, troubled by the intrusion. "Don't know who you are, mister," he said, breathing hard. "But this here's army business. You best be on your way."

The devil man didn't move. Something heavy seemed to swell and press the air around us, making it hard to breathe. The soldiers must have felt it too because they started to fidget. I saw the corporal touch the flap of his holster with anxious fingers.

Seeing that the bluff of authority wasn't working, Bukovski tried another course. He too had noticed the scarf across the devil man's face. "Like I said, partner, this don't concern you none, but if you want to wait, you can have what's left." Bukovski rumbled another of his laughs, except this one didn't sound quite so confident. "Less of course you want the kid."

The corporal and Rat Face laughed nervously. For a minute, I was afraid they actually might hand me over. My throat felt lined with chalk. All I could think of was that if the devil man turned those hideous eyes my way, if he so much as glanced at me, I might pee right in my church clothes. Instead, the devil man pointed at Bukovski and friends and indicated with a short gesture that they should get on their horses and leave.

Bukovski shook his head and tried a grin, some of his bravado returning now that the initial shock of the devil man's sudden appearance was wearing off. I could see the sergeant studying the situation, weighing his options. He was much bigger than the devil man and there were three of them to his one. Bukovski shook his sweaty head, confident now.

"No, we ain't leaving. But I think you are. And if I have to make you, you might just find out this is the most unlucky day of your life. You better scat while you can, road tramp."

"Sarge," Rat Face hissed above me. "Looky that hat of his."

I looked. The devil man's hat was a battered, dirty gray affair with a faded red cord running around it. A brass badge made up of two tiny swords was pinned to the front. There was nothing special about it except to Bukovski.

The sergeant squinted and his yellow grin widened. "A reb," he gloated. "Two Mormon sluts and now a goddam Johnny Reb. This is getting better, Leroy. There ain't nothing I like more'n stomping rebs again, 'less maybe it's riding Mormon gals." To the devil man he said, "I'm giving you one chance, grayback. Skedaddle now, like you chicken-gut bastards did at Shiloh, and I'll—"

My heart stopped as the devil man's fallow eyes came to life. They blazed with an unspeakable malevolence. One hand jumped as if it had been burned. When it stopped again there was a pistol in it. Thunder blasted across the road as a white lance of fire stabbed Bukovski. The sergeant clutched his big stomach, stumbled, and abruptly sat down. Stunned, Rat Face and the corporal made tardy grabs for their pistols.

I jumped at the hot slam of another shot. Over my head came a thunk! sound, like the time Pa dropped a melon on Alva's stone floor. Rat Face's arm fell away from my neck as something wet and hot spattered down on me.

I peeked and saw the corporal, his pistol half out of its holster, backing away from the devil man. He threw up his hands while his jaw worked crazily, as if he wanted to get a lifetime of talking done in a few seconds. "Hold on," he gobbled. His voice climbed into a reedy screech. "It was the sarge. Swear to God, I never laid a finger on them!"

With a terrible casualness, as if he only wanted some peace and quiet, the devil man shot the corporal in the mouth. The corporal's hat popped straight in the air as a red gout of blood jumped out the back of his head.

Silence filled the road.

Carefully, the devil man turned and thumbed back the hammer of his big pistol again. I saw it all as if it had been slowed down for my benefit, as if God wanted to make sure I remembered it forever. The cylinder rolled over with a series of oiled clicks and the smoking barrel swung around to Bukovski. The devil man waited until the sergeant looked up in soundless agony. Then he pulled the trigger. Bukovski's brains sprayed across the road like March slush. His feet kicked a couple of times and he was still.

I closed my eyes, knowing full well that I was next.

The evil smell of sulphur tickled my nose while my face twitched in rebellion. When I dared open my eyes again, the soldiers' riderless horses were galloping like mad back up the road. A curtain of powder smoke drifted through the dappled shadows while the soldiers themselves lay sprawled in the dust like sacks of blue rags. Bukovski had a look of won-derment on his face, along with a big red hole in the center of his broad nose.

The devil man was no longer standing at the side of the road. He had crossed over to the buggy and was pulling out a coverlet. With a quick motion, he used it to cover Laurel Anne's torn clothing. Her pillows were half out of the ruined bodice of her bloody dress. She glanced up at the devil man and then away again, her cornflower eyes huge with shock.

The devil man turned and looked at me over the scarf that still cov-ered his lower face. My mouth felt full of ants and I got more colored spots in front of my eyes. Without warning, my knees buckled. The next thing I knew, the devil man had scooped me up and was carrying me to the buggy. He smelled of horses and sage smoke as he laid me on the backseat.

When the spots cleared I sat up and watched as the devil man lifted Laurel Anne into the buggy. She clutched the coverlet around her shoul-ders and turned away from him with a moan.

I started to say something, but the devil man bent over in the road. When he straightened he had Brigham wrapped in a bandanna. He handed him up to me. For a moment, the devil man's covered face leaned out of the shadow of his hat and I saw a twisted scar rising out of the mask, curling up under his left eye and into his sideburn like an old rope. He looked and moved like he might be a young man, but the scar and the emptiness in his eyes made him seem as ancient as the mountains.

"My name's Rose," I whispered.

Winter eyes flickered, surveying me as if I were a strange bug on the toe of his boot. A hand touched the kerchief covering Brigham and the starkness in his eyes changed, arranging themselves into a silent ques-tion.

"Brigham," I replied. "He's—was—my frog." My eyes blurred with tears and I felt a rage so thick it threatened to blind me entirely. The devil man saw me glance at the soldiers. His right eye drooped in a sly wink, as if confiding to me that an eye for an eye was the same thing to him as a corporal for a frog. He reached in and cautiously touched Laurel Anne's hair. She flinched and he snatched his hand away quick, turning those sickening eyes back to me.

"Laurel Anne," I said. "My sister."

From down the road came a shout. With another glance at Laurel

Anne, the devil man took a quick step back, his hand going to the guns at his waist. Spotting help coming at a gallop, he turned to leave.

"Thank you," I called after him. It sounded weak and pitiful. I wasn't sure he heard me until he stopped and turned around in the middle of the road. In cavalier fashion he swept off his hat and for the first time in my life, a grown man bowed low and graceful to me, like something right out of a storybook.

Then he was gone. I caught a glimpse of Laurel Anne's pink hair ribbon trailing from one hand as he vanished into the trees. In the hush of the woods, backed by the soft sound of Laurel Anne's sobs and the drifting, sulfurous smell of gunpowder and hell, it was almost like Satan had taken him back.

Lester Knight and his brother Jeremiah reached us first, with their ma and pa not far behind. I learned later that the Knights had been hunting for their milk cow when they heard the screams and the shots. Being the kind of folks they were, they naturally came running.

Although not as well to do as some, the Knights were among the steadiest people around. Skinny and morose looking, John Knight was my Pa's first counselor at church. Ophelia was John's only wife. She was also one of the few church women on whom my own Ma was on friendly terms. Seeing Brother and Sister Knight instead of someone who might have only added to our misery with a lot of useless hollering and fretting caused a wave of relief to spill over me. I looked down at my hands and saw where my nails had peeled up little half-moon flaps of skin in the palms. There was drying blood from Rat Face all over the front of my dress.

Lester and Jeremiah skidded their horses to a stop beside the buggy. The horses shied away from the smell of the dead soldiers and I saw Jeremiah, who was my age and a sworn enemy of the twins, staring at us with wide eyes.

Lester appeared at the side of the buggy flushed and out of breath. He touched Laurel Anne's shoulder and she cringed away with a dull moan, hiding her torn dress under the coverlet. He looked at me.

"Rose, what happened?"

"They killed Brigham," I croaked.

Admittedly, a frog was the least of our worries, but at that moment it was the best I could do by way of explanation. I couldn't summon the right words to tell what Sergeant Bukovski had been doing to Laurel

Anne and there were no words in the entire universe to describe what I'd seen the devil man do to the soldiers. Everything was a bunch of flitting, batlike images.

Sister Knight rode up in the wagon with her husband, looking both alarmed and purposeful. She climbed out of the wagon, shooed the boys away from our buggy and heaved her bulk inside. She first tried to see to Laurel Anne. Laurel Anne fought her for a moment and then seemed to recognize her as a friend. Then she let her peek under the coverlet. Sister Knight had been a young girl during the Clay County troubles. Once, when I was spying, I listened to her tell Ma about those black days, about what Missouri mobs had done to some Mormon women. I came away feeling sick and frightened by what bad men will do. When she looked at me, Sister Knight's brown eyes were huge with an unspeakable question.

"Did they—?" she asked.

"No'm," I said. "They tried. But he stopped them."

Sister Knight looked around but saw only her sons and husband scratching their heads over the dead soldiers. She turned back to me, frowning. "Who, Rose? Who stopped them?" she asked. When I didn't answer right away, she put a hand on my shoulder and shook me gently. "Honey, who stopped them?"

"The devil," I said, shivering violently when I remembered his eyes. Full terror finally caught up with me. "The devil came and killed them." And then, like a cloudburst, I started to cry.

"Merciful Lord," Sister Knight breathed. She leaned over the seat to give me a hug.

Other wagons and riders, attracted by the sounds of the shooting, began to gather. Otto Hoffenstetter, Rolly Howard and Bill Pettus and his sons. There were some people from Lehi, too. Everyone paused to gawk at us and peer pop-eyed at the dead soldiers. They had a hundred questions and concerns, but all I heard was a buzz of voices. Sister Knight yelled them all away. She gathered up the reins of the buggy, and with a motherly arm around Laurel Anne, she turned our buggy around and started back for the farm. Lester galloped ahead to fetch Pa.

The ride home lasted an eternity. Sister Knight tried to talk to me several times, but I couldn't muster the strength to answer. I just sat in the back with my flat frog wrapped up in the devil man's kerchief, wondering why I wasn't dead, too.

When we got closer to home, Pa appeared, riding hard on a lathered horse. His hat was gone and his beard flew in the wind. He swung off before the horse came to a complete stop and was inside the buggy and touching us. A look of barely concealed terror was on his face, one I hadn't seen since Johnny died. His throat made scared noises and his words fell all over themselves as he tried to ask a hundred questions all at once.

"I believe they're all right, Bishop," Sister Knight said. She continued to drive and Lester caught up the reins of Pa's horse. Pa gathered me in his arms and I cried some more into his shirt front. He held me until we reached the farm.

Sister Knight turned the buggy into our lane and drove around the barn. Following Pa's directions, she headed straight for the log house where Ma and I lived. I was alert enough to know he'd done this in spite of the fact that it would cause him trouble later with Alva. It made sense though because there was nobody in the valley better at fixing folks than my ma. I looked up and saw her rush out of the house, skirts flying.

Pa handed me out to Ma, who clamped onto me until I couldn't breathe. I started to whimper all over again. All told I think I cried maybe a bucket of tears since our ordeal but they somehow seemed better spent in the arms of my ma.

Over Ma's shoulder I glimpsed Pa carefully lifting Laurel Anne out. Beyond him I saw Alva lumbering up the slope from the brick house with Aaron in her arms. Close behind came Silla and the turban-wrapped twins, all clumsy as heifers.

In the instant before Ma whisked me into the house, I caught whirlwind glimpses of our farm. Cletus riding up on Pilate and staring around at all the commotion, chickens pecking in the yard, the neat rows of corn in the fields. I smelled the river and the heavenly odor of fresh bread. Down at the well, one of the barn cats chased a butterfly. It was home, still home, but somehow it had all changed. I couldn't get the smell of blood and gunpowder out of my nose. I felt weary beyond words and I shuddered when Ma laid me on my bed and started taking off my bloody clothes. She was talking in a soothing voice, trying to calm me, telling me I was home and safe. But I didn't feel safe anymore. I didn't think I'd ever feel safe again. It seemed like centuries had passed since I rocked the twins.

Chapter Two

When I opened my eyes again, the day had passed into late afternoon. Golden bolts of sunlight streamed through the window and lit up the picture of Jesus on the wall above my bed. I said a quick, silent prayer, thanking him for saving me and Laurel Anne. Just when I said "amen," I remembered the devil man and wondered if maybe I hadn't thanked the wrong person.

The house was quiet but I heard angry voices in the yard. I peeked out of the blanket and saw Ma sitting beside the bed where my sister lay, dabbing Laurel Anne's bruised face with a wet cloth. I smelled comfrey and marigolds.

"Hello, Ma," I said, wanting her to know I was alive and needing her, too. She gave me an anxious look and tucked the blanket around Laurel Anne before coming over to me.

"How are you?" she said, kissing my forehead. Her own brow was turned down in worry. Wisps of hair wreathed her face and her bottom lip was puffy like it got when she bit it from too much fretting.

"I'm fine." I looked around. "Where's Brigham? He's worse than me."

Ma got up and fetched Brigham's box, now a coffin, over from the table. She put it beside me on the bed and went to get some water. On a chair I saw my shoes, still splattered with dried blood. In my head I heard the shots and the splitting melon sound. My stomach rolled over.

"There are some people who need to speak with you, Rose," Ma said when she returned with the water and a cup of herb tea. "They would like to ask you some questions about what happened."

I swallowed hard. The back of my throat still hurt from all the crying I'd done. I didn't want to talk to anyone but her.

"Who?"

"Henry du Pont, the sheriff and your father. Someone who knows what happened needs to tell them about it." She glanced at Laurel Anne. "I don't think your sister is ready to talk about it yet. Will you?"

"If you'll be there," I replied. I could probably muster enough gumption to talk to Henry or Pa. Sheriff Jewkes was a different matter. He was a blowhard gentile who hated Mormons, especially polygamists. Once, at an Independence Day parade in Lehi City, I saw him kick Josh Van Orden for spooking his horse. I think Jewkes hated kids more than polygamists. If you happened to be a polygamist kid, well that was double unlucky for you. He just hated you twice as much. I hated Sheriff Jewkes right back. Being the fallen spirit Alva said I was, and a Merrell, I figured him for a kid-hating, tin-coated, horse apple-eating sonuvabitch.

"I'll be there," Ma promised. "Every minute."

"Pa, too?"

"Of course."

"All right."

Ma got me up and wrapped a blanket around me. With her arm around me, we walked out onto the porch, passing a wooden tub where my church clothes soaked in pink-tinged carbolic. Ma sat down in her rocker and lifted me onto her lap. There were soldiers in our yard, at least a dozen of them. I started to shake as soon as I saw them. Ma noticed and held me closer. "You don't have to do this. Do you want to go back inside?"

"No'm."

Peeking out of the blanket, I surveyed the men in our yard. Henry, dressed in his uniform and wearing a pistol, was talking earnestly with Pa. The balding figure with high boots and a cigar, laughing nastily with some of the soldiers, was Sheriff Jewkes.

Pa saw us and said something to everyone. Sheriff Jewkes looked around and his angry eyes fell on me. He stalked immediately for the porch. Merlin flapped in and tried to land on him. He struck at the bird with a curse. Merlin skipped up to the roof of the house and cawed.

"Well," Sheriff Jewkes said curtly when he reached the porch. "Now that we've wasted enough time on beauty sleep, I want some information so's me and the army can catch this bunch of killers."

Ma's voice was cold and clear. I felt her arms tighten protectively around me. "You seem to have forgotten not only your manners, Sheriff," she said, "but the fact that this is the Territory of Utah, not Prussia. Lower your voice and alter your tone, sir, or leave my yard. Rose has had enough bullying for one day."

Sheriff Jewkes clamped fleshy lips down on his cigar and glowered. He looked at us the way Sergeant Bukovski had. While their behavior differed, it suddenly occurred to me how much the two men were alike. Both seemed to be looking for control and dominion over other people for their own purposes.

Henry cut into the silence. "We're very sorry, Mrs. Merrell. But we are quite anxious to locate the gang that murdered Sergeant Bukovski and his men. May we please ask Rose a few questions?"

"Certainly," Ma said, but her voice carried a clear warning.

Sheriff Jewkes tried a false smile and took over. "Come on then, girlie," he said, bending forward, hands on his knees, as solicitous as if I were an idiot. "Tell us what happened. Who killed them soldiers?"

I told what happened in the most simple terms I could find. I faltered once, when it came to telling what I'd seen Bukovski doing to Laurel Anne. When I said it, Henry went white. Pa's face turned such a deep red with suppressed fury that I feared his head would explode. Only Sheriff Jewkes looked skeptical. I finished as quickly as I could.

"And you say one man shot all three of them?" Sheriff Jewkes said. "Before any of 'em could bring a gun into play?" He slapped his gloves across a knee. "Hell, I don't believe it." He looked around at the other men. "Three against one and this fella a clean winner? It ain't possible, Henry. Leastways not the way she's telling it." He looked back at me, squinting. "My bet is she's hiding some secret Mormon doings."

That started an argument between Pa, Henry and the sheriff. I stopped listening to them. I turned and put my face on Ma's neck like I'd done when I was little and tired. As far as I was concerned, what happened to Laurel Anne and me on the road to Provo was over. It was enough for me that we were safe and back with our family. In my heart I harbored the secret and unchristian pleasure of knowing that somewhere the bodies of Sergeant Bukovski and his two friends were getting stiff and cold while their souls roasted in hell. Henry interrupted my evil reverie with another question. He got down on one knee so he could look me in the eye.

"Rose," he said. "Tell me more about the man who shot Sergeant Bukovski."

"He was the devil," I said, remembering the dust drifting off his shirt and those blank, soulless eyes.

Sheriff Jewkes got a big grin out of that. "Ol' Beelzebub hisself, huh?" He laughed shortly. "Just popped up with a revolver and kilt them all." He shook his head and spat something brown and nasty into Ma's herb garden. "Makes about as much sense as that gold Bible stuff you folks spout."

Henry ignored the interruption. He reached over and took my hand. "What did he look like, Rose? Have you ever seen him before?"

I shook my head. "He wore a scarf around his face. The soldiers told him to leave and he wouldn't. They made fun of his hat and he shot them."

Henry looked perplexed. "He killed them because they made fun of his hat?"

"No. It was mostly 'cause of the fat one squeezing Laurel Anne and for stomping my frog. But he shot them when they called him bad names."

"He was a Mormon," Sheriff Jewkes insisted. "One of them crazy Danites you folks got riding around getting into mischief. This time they went too far. They'll swing for it sure enough. Just as soon as we find 'em."

"He wasn't a Mormon," I said.

Sheriff Jewkes snorted. "And how do you know that? You said he wore a mask. He could have been Jesus Christ hisself and you wouldn't have knowed it."

I was suddenly tired, weary of being badgered about something I wanted to pretend had never happened. It wouldn't have done to try and explain why I knew the devil man wasn't a Mormon. I would have to tell them about those bleached, lifeless eyes, and I would have to try and explain the perfunctory way the devil man took life. All the Mormons I knew were farmers, wheelwrights and millers, simple, industrious folks more handy with hammers and hoes than guns. They didn't have eyes like the devil man and they didn't shoot men like rabbits.

Henry stood up straight. "I pray Laurel Anne and Rose will recover fully, Mrs. Merrell," he said politely to Ma. There was a quiet agony in his voice. I guess he really did love Laurel Anne.

"Thank you, Henry," Ma replied, hugging me. "I expect they will. I don't know when Laurel Anne will be receiving again, but I will tell her you called and of your concern for her."

Ignoring this exchange, Sheriff Jewkes started for the waiting soldiers, who began climbing onto their horses. Merlin skimmed off the roof in silent ambush and deposited a streamer of runny shit across the sheriff's back. Jewkes bellowed a hideous oath, fumbled for his pistol and would have shot at Merlin had Pa not stopped him. Cursing Pa, Merlin and all Mormons, the sheriff stormed away. Henry did his best to suppress a smile. He turned to include Pa in what he said next and his youthful face grew grim.

"We're going to track this man down," he said. He held up his hands to block a protest from Pa. "Please don't misunderstand, Bishop Merrell. It's not that we don't believe Rose. But we need to investigate the matter as thoroughly as possible. We'll want this man's statement, although he has only made it worse for himself by running off." He turned to go and paused, looking back at me. "Is there any more you want to tell me about your devil man, Rose?"

"Yes," I said. I gave Henry the best advice I could think of. It probably didn't make much sense to him, his being a gentile and all, but it came right out of my heart and soul. My voice broke when I said it.

"Pray you don't let him find you, Henry."

That night I had a nightmare. I was playing down by the river when a mossy bank split open and Satan reached for me with hot, lizard-skin hands. He tried to drag me down a burning hole in the ground. Down inside the fiery earth, I spied Bukovski being pitchforked by demons. He still had a bullet hole in his nose. His eyes rolled white when he saw me. Flaming hands clawed at my legs. "Get the nubbin," he boomed. "Get her." I tried to run but my feet wouldn't move. Rat Face, his head looking like shattered crockery, helped grab and pull me over to the hole.

I screamed and jerked awake to find Ma bending over me in the night, touching a cool cloth to my face. She got me up and I realized only then that I had peed the bed. Humiliated, I stood there shivering while she changed the linens. I heard Laurel Anne whimpering in her sleep. The moon was up, the curtains open. Silver light filled the cabin, making magic out of the smells of lavender and chamomile from the compresses Ma had put on our heads. I slipped into a clean nightgown and drank a couple swallows of clove tea before climbing back into a dry bed. Ma sat beside me, her hand a blessing on my neck until I drifted off again.

By morning the terror of the night was a dim memory and I felt some better. Merlin appeared at the window in the gray light of dawn, pecking at the glass and waiting for someone to come outside, no doubt so he could practice shitting on them.

I crawled out of bed, stepping over the sleeping form of Ma who had spent the night on a pallet between the beds. Laurel Anne's back was to me. I crawled under the covers with her and snuggled up close. She stirred and a hand snuck over her neck and touched my face.

"Morning, Rose." Her voice sounded muffled and strained.

"Morning," I replied.

"You don't have that frog...?" She faltered when she remembered what had happened to Brigham.

We were quiet for a spell and then she rolled over. I gasped when I saw the right side of her face. It was bruised and lumpy. A crust of blood clung to the corner of her mouth, and her eye was swole up. The herb paste Ma dabbed on her face had dried and flaked, giving her a leprous look. Laurel Anne saw me staring at her and she tried a smile, wincing at the pain it caused.

"I must look a sight."

I nodded. "Looks like Pilate stepped on your face." I snuggled closer, feeling bad. "I'm sorry for what I said about your behind yesterday."

Normally Laurel Anne would have seized this rare, penitent moment to lecture me about hurting people's feelings along with my other spiritual crimes. Instead, she lay there looking empty and sad. "Every time I think about what happened I get sick."

I thought about mentioning that if the devil man hadn't come along, her memories might be a sight worse. In fact, if my nightmare was close to true, I was pretty sure the soldiers were feeling a whole lot worse than sick. Although I wanted to put it all behind me, to return to normal as quickly as possible, I was afraid that it would be a long time before Laurel Anne was her cheerful beautiful self again, long after the bruises were gone. She was accustomed only to worship from men. What happened on the Provo road had changed that. I didn't know what to say and so I kept my mouth shut until Ma woke up.

While Laurel Anne stayed in bed, Ma and I went through the motions of breakfast. Afterward, Ma put a compress of Solomon's seal and beer on Laurel Anne's face. It smelled awful but made noticeable progress in reducing the swelling and bruises. Me, I hung around the house playing with my dolls and arrowhead collection, content to be near Ma where it was safe.

After a time, I put on my jumper and went out to bury Brigham. Ma came along as a mourner. We dug a hole under the same tree where Herc was buried and put the box down in the damp ground. It seemed a minor sacrilege to bury a frog next to Herc who had saved me from a snake last summer by jumping in and killing it. The snake bit Herc instead. The poison had killed him with some ugly strangles, the memory of which still gave me shivers.

Ma suggested we offer a prayer for Brigham. I knew it was just an effort on her part to get me to settle the matter with God and Jesus. But since I figured them both for cheaters, I shook my head. I didn't feel like asking them to take care of Brigham now since they'd done such a poor job of it while he was alive. It had been my experience that praying to God and Jesus was dangerous since they almost never gave you what you asked for, instead choosing to send you something that only compounded your misery. I sure didn't want them to send me another frog. I wanted the one I had. Ma picked some daisies and bluebells from her garden and laid them on the grave. I found a rock to mark the spot.

Because of what happened and because she wanted to tend Laurel Anne, Ma let me off my morning chores. So rather than carry water to her herb garden and fetch in wood for the stove, I got to mope around, useless and out of sorts. I spent most of the morning in a tree behind our house, watching the twins work in Alva's garden. They picked dejectedly at it when she wasn't watching and hacked in a frenzy whenever she put in an appearance on the porch. While I watched, I gave some thought to a new pet.

I was quits with frogs. Brigham had been forever trying to get away. A dog would be nice but I agreed with Pa that good ones like Herc only came around once in a millennium, and I didn't feel like settling for seconds. We had Merlin but he was no pet at all, just a hang-around freeloader too lazy to forage with the rest of his kind. Besides, he was always shitting on folks, something that didn't set well even within the narrow circle of my ill-mannered friends. In rapid order I also eliminated cats as too independent and self-serving, rabbits as too timid, chickens for comestible reasons, and a duck because Pumpkin Ass already had Snow tethered around her garden to eat hoppers. Snow had gotten so fat on hoppers that Pa gave him an axe-sharpening look whenever Alva wasn't around. He had described the various ways of cooking Snow so often that my mouth watered every time I heard a bossy quack. But Alva was set on Snow and we stood about as much of a chance of eating him for supper as he had of ever leaving the ground again under his own power.

What I really wanted was a pet that could take care of me as much as I took care of it. Something along the order of an elephant or a tiger. I'd even settle for a horse like the ones Signorita Clarinda Lowanda rode, but only as a last resort. Horses weren't exactly handy at this stage of my growth when there had to be a fence or a rock handy for me to climb on one.

No, an elephant would be the perfect pet. As usual, praying for one hadn't done me a damn bit of good. I had tried to explain to God and Ma both that I truly needed an elephant, one exactly like Dan Castello's famous performing Jenny Lind. I needed it to start a circus because no one would pay to come to a circus that didn't have a performing elephant. I wasn't greedy, I argued, both over the supper table and at night on my knees. I would have gladly settled for an untrained one. Ma just smiled and said prayer should be for something God and Jesus wanted us to have. That didn't pass for logic in my book because God and Jesus have lots of elephants and it wouldn't have hurt for them to part with one. I also pointed out that she had prayed for them not to take Johnny, just as I had prayed for Herc, but both died anyway. I concluded by saying that prayer didn't do anyone a lick of good since God and Jesus were probably cheat-givers. Ma looked sad and I felt bad.

Dejected, I gave up on pets and watched the farm through the leaves in my perch. The tree provided me with an excellent view, in addition to making me difficult to locate when the idea of chores occurred to someone. I watched Pa climb the slope to our house and eavesdropped when he told Ma how the soldiers had failed to find any sign of the devil man. This came as no surprise since I was already beginning to think of him as a spirit—a dark one, but a spirit. Not someone real, like a person I might ever know. Pa's voice drifted up through the branches of my perch.

"Not a single track," he said, scratching his head. "But there he was, right when he was needed the most. If I didn't know better, Colleen, I'd claim some divine intervention in all of this."

Pa didn't know better. If he'd seen the devil man, if he'd looked into those eyes he'd know that God didn't have a thing to do with it. Pa glanced back at the brick house to see if Alva was watching and gave Ma a quick, fierce kiss before heading down to his lunch. If it hadn't been midday and Laurel Anne hadn't been staying with us, Ma might have invited him for lunch and maybe to make squeaks afterward. As it was, they tore themselves away from each other. Pa scuffed on down to the brick house where his life was more or less a misery. Knowing Alva as I did, Pa would get a fine lunch but no squeaks, at least not until dark.

After Pa had gone, I entertained myself with what I thought I knew about making squeaks. I'd thought about it a lot in the last year, more because it seemed an eventuality for myself than because I was interested in it. Girls only five years older than me were getting married and doing it. All I knew for absolute certain about what went on between men and women inside a closed up room was that it produced babies and was accomplished with a great deal of squeaking, both from the bed frame and the participants themselves. Some nights down at the brick house, I would lay awake next to Laurel Anne and swear the floor above was going to drop flat into our room and mash us. Occasionally I heard Alva groan as if someone had punched her. I know Laurel Anne heard it, too, but she never let on. The one time I broached the subject to her, after we'd seen our bull Samson clamber up on the back of a heifer, she got red-faced and snippy.

I could have asked Ma the exact particulars about making squeaks and she would have answered me straight out. I didn't ask because I wasn't sure I really wanted to know all about it yet. I knew that when I did, it would be because I was ready to be a woman. But from what I had seen around our farm, I certainly wasn't in the market for that.

News of the killings on the Provo road must have hit the community like a double clap of thunder. In the space of the next two hours dozens

of folks came by in wagons and on horses. They came to offer support
and sympathy, to maybe catch a glimpse of the tragic princess, and to hear
the particulars of the event firsthand from the biggest gossips in the territory: Alva and Silla.

Silla Van Orden showed up as usual and stayed most of the day. She
was Alva's best friend and the two of them, despite Silla's pinched face
and skinny frame, were a matched pair of busybodies. Silla's husband
had run off a couple of years ago, leaving her and Josh to fend for themselves. Josh, who was only a year older than me, worked a man's job at
the Pettus's cooperage to support his ma. Silla was prowling for a new
husband and it bothered me a lot that she had set her narrow sights on
Pa. Alva was burden enough, even for a bishop.

Alva and Silla had steady hands in the kitchen but loose jaws everywhere else. The transcontinental telegraph line had arrived in Salt Lake
City almost eight years before, eventually continuing on to California. I
personally figured whoever was in charge of the telegraph line could have
saved a pile of money by stopping in Utah and turning all the news over
to Pumpkin Ass and Pinch Face. Within twenty-four hours the entire territory would hear of it, they were that bad. I once overheard Sister
Knight, who suffered more than most from Alva's viperous tongue, tell
Ma that every time Alva opened her mouth, her butt fell out.

Alva and Silla met each caller at the door and invited them in for a
glass of something cool. The callers left a few minutes later without coming up to the log house, although I saw all of them glance up the slope.

Laurel Anne's beaus came, all ten thousand and a dozen. Each
fetched along flowers or some token of their helpless devotion. I saw Jack,
Eldon, Lester, Fred Dirkin, the two Pettus boys, the Lehman brothers
and others who rode the thirty or so miles from Provo and Salt Lake City.
One by one, Alva shook their hands, accepted their gifts and watched
them ride off. I could tell it was giving her and Silla fits not to have Laurel
Anne down there where they could pick the story out of her.

I watched Eldon Bair and Lester Knight stop and have words down
where our lane met the road. Lester brought flowers and was leaving
when Eldon arrived. Of all Laurel Anne's beaus, Eldon Bair was my least
favorite. He was tall and handsome but had a smug look about him and
a sarcastic wit that rankled all but his closest friends. What Laurel Anne
saw in him was beyond me. As I watched, Eldon said something to Lester
that made Lester's face burn even at this distance. Lester turned and rode

off on his family's only saddle horse. I surmised then that Eldon had said something about the condition of Lester's clothes and his farm pony. Eldon himself wore store clothes and rode a fine chestnut gelding, all provided for him by his pa, who owned a grist mill down in the Narrows. Eldon was also in the recent habit of wearing a fancy pistol on his belt and rumor had it that he was a fair shot. After inquiring with Alva, he turned a long look up toward our log house and then rode away. I watched him go, thinking that if Sheriff Jewkes ever wanted to arrest a real Danite he might look Eldon's way. There was something sly about the way the miller's son carried himself.

Eventually, I grew tired of sitting in the tree and so I climbed down and wandered around in the woods behind our cabin. Then I sat beside the creek for an hour, trying to interest myself in fishing or swimming. When nothing caught my interest, I gave it up as a lost cause and trudged back to the cabin.

Laurel Anne was up and dressed. Ma was dabbing another wicked smelling salve on her bruises. Ma figured that if I was spry enough to climb a tree, I was also strong enough for chores. "Rose, please run down below and tell Alva to send up some bedclothes for your sister."

Going down below on an errand was something I put right up there next to soap and church. It wasn't the actual going that I minded. An errand usually meant that I had to deal direct with Alva, which made such a trip risky at best. Still, I couldn't very well argue with Ma considering the shape Laurel Anne was in.

"Yes'm," I replied and turned to go.

"This afternoon I'll bake some gingerbread," Ma said. "And we'll read a wee bit before bed."

My heart took a sudden lift. As far as I was concerned, books and gingerbread were the reasons God made smiles. I went off with a bounce in my step, bad and improper thoughts pushed to the back of my mind. I skipped all the way down the slope.

The twins were still weeding the garden. Lehi still had a bandage wrapped turbanlike around his head. He looked like one of Dan Castello's genuine African native elephant trainers, only white and stupid. "Hey, Mutt," he called as I passed.

I stopped and turned toward them. I cooed as sweetly as possible. "I'm sorry. Were you addressing me, Mr. Pig Fart?"

"There isn't nobody else," Nephi replied. He grinned and his eyes narrowed until he looked like a crafty boar. "We heard you and Laurel Anne got raked yesterday." He snickered a mean chorus with Lehi.

There were times when the lack of lucid thought on the part of the twins could actually catch a person off guard. I puzzled out what they were after and rolled my eyes. "The word is 'raped', you ignoramus," I said. "And if you must know, it wasn't even close to that."

"Ma said they tore sister's dress," Nephi retorted, "and did"—here his mind visibly labored—"some stuff." He paused, waiting to see if I might be forthcoming with an explanation of this "stuff."

I wasn't. Mostly because the images dredged up by the probing made me slightly nauseous. For a thin slice of a second, I smelled gunpowder on the afternoon breeze. I took a deep, shaky breath and said, "Well, it's none of your beeswax. That's for sure."

Lehi proffered the obvious. "Anyways, some soldiers got killed. Ma said so."

"That's right," I said, turning to go. I had no intention of discussing the matter further, least of all with the twins.

"What for?" Lehi called.

An idea came into my head, pushing aside my annoyance. I approached the fence cautiously, as if I was about to share a secret. The twins' eyes grew round and their jaws relaxed in anticipation of a confidence they had no intention of honoring. I smiled to myself. They really were their mother's sons.

"If you must know," I confided in a whisper. "They were shot by a devil gunman."

"Criminy," they whispered. "How come?"

"Because they were bothering us. You know?—throwing clods and calling us names? And because they stomped Brigham."

So it began. This would not be the last time I used the reputation of the devil man for my own purposes.

The twins, like a yoke of matched oxen, exchanged sidelong looks as they mulled over this unsettling revelation. The part about the soldiers being killed for bothering Laurel Anne and me seemed to sink in most because Lehi opened his hand and let a clod slip to the ground. He glanced furtively at the trees surrounding the farm.

Snow waddled over. The green legs of a hopper kicked spasmodically from his orange bill. A length of red yarn tethered him to a porch post. He gave me a dubious look out of one button eye, as if to say he didn't believe any nonsense about a devil gunman. Being a duck he was singularly unimpressed with the doings of humans. He studied me for a minute and then moved on in search of something more interesting, oblivious, as we all were, to the fact that he only had a single day left in his gluttonous life.

When I looked back at the twins, they were hoeing the garden with uncharacteristic fervor. I spun around and found Alva watching us from the porch, her mouth turned down in familiar disapproval. She had a bottle of Red Jacket Bitters in one hand and a spoon in the other. Silla stood behind her.

"Rose Lee," Alva said, sounding concerned, but her mouth a flat line of suspicion nonetheless. "What brings you down from the cabin?"

I swallowed several biting retorts and relayed what Ma wanted. I watched my sister-ma toy with the notion of refusing, something she wouldn't dare do to her sister without considerable forethought.

"I think Laurel Anne should be down here with the family," Alva said finally. "That old cabin is so drafty." She gave me a level look. "She's had visitors asking about her all day. I think…"

Normally I wouldn't have traded a chicken turd for the entire contents of Alva's mind. Her opinions were a matter of supreme indifference to me and I frequently told her so to both our consternation. But I was on an errand for Ma and so I kept my mouth shut, even though the force of my irritation made the hinges of my jaw ache. Eventually, after she held forth on a variety of subjects aggravating to her and therefore to God, Alva shooed me toward the barn.

"Go and tell the bishop his dinner is near ready to burn. I'll see about putting together a clutch of things for Laurel Anne. But only a few things, mind you. I'll not have her moving up to the cabin for good. You go on down to the shop while I think on it."

"Don't hurt yourself," I muttered.

"What was that?"

"Nothing."

I skipped off toward the barn. Alva, Silla and the duck were still glaring at me when I looked back. The twins whined and tossed their hoes aside as she commanded them to come and take their bitters. They had no choice. Alva was hot on Red Jacket Bitters.

Pa's blacksmith shop was a place of wonder for me. He shoed horses, doctored animals, fixed wheels and provided a hundred other services to anyone requiring an expert metalsmith. He even pulled teeth when folks were ailing with bad ones. He also passed out Ma's tonics and potions since most folks would rather be seen knocking on the door of a saloon Sunday morning than visiting my ma. The shop was a smokey dragon's lair, a place of easy magic, full of noise and flying sparks. Sometimes I'd sit off to the side and squint my eyes while Pa worked, pretending that I was a beautiful princess locked in a dungeon, waiting for a prince to rescue me. It was a special fantasy, one I used to comfort me during those times when I was feeling low because I wasn't pretty and certainly no prize a prince would risk his life over. There was, however, a genuine danger in letting my guard down while doing this. The danger was Pa, or rather his un-bishoplike sense of humor. One time he pulled a sack over his head and snuck up on me. He popped up in front of me, like the king's own executioner, and scared me out of a certified year of my life.

On the coldest of winter days Pa's forge was the only place a body could get truly warm. Some mornings I'd wade through the snow with my breakfast just to sit in a roasty corner and watch him work. Summer days though, the forge was a piece of hell itself and a dangerous place for Pa to work. There were days he would stagger out at noon dripping with sweat and drink buckets of water. Terrible headaches sometimes gripped him in the evenings. In July and August, Pa would begin work in the cool hours of morning, long before the sun was up. Later, after I was grown and Pa had gone to his celestial reward, summer never seemed quite the same without the cathedral sound of his hammer in that dark spell before dawn.

I couldn't find Pa at the forge and so I looked through the rest of the barn. Just when I had decided that he had gone off to check on how Cletus was coming with the ditch, I heard voices in the direction of the stock pens.

"Can't nobody be knowing who you are with that rag and all." I recognized Sheriff Jewkes's harsh, nasally voice. Curious, I pushed through the heavy doors.

I think my heart recognized the devil man long before my eyes did. I went rigid with shock. The sight of him on our farm swelled up my chest with a numbing fright.

The devil man stood in the middle of the yard holding the reins of a tall, long-legged horse the color of a rocky creek bed. This horse was no beast of burden, no pack animal with a lackluster spirit. He turned and looked at me with a black eye crammed full of smarts. I'd never seen a horse that sparked off that kind of spirit, as if it was your equal and knew it full well. Behind the devil man's horse was another sturdy looking animal loaded down with packs.

It was silent in the yard for a long moment while everyone looked at me. Pa motioned for me to come alongside of him. He was holding several pieces of paper in his hands, frowning with thought. I pressed up against his side, my tongue stuck fast to the roof of my mouth.

Pa's big leathery hand cupped my jaw protectively. "Rose," he said, motioning at the devil man, "do you know this gentleman?"

I nodded, too afraid to look the devil man in the eye. He was no gentleman and it frightened me badly that he had found my home. It was one thing for him to help us on the Provo road and another to have him come to a place I associated with safety. My skin started to twitch in odd spots while my kneecaps squirmed and jumped.

"Is he the man who saved you from the soldiers?" Pa asked. When I hesitated, he prodded me gently. "Don't be afraid. Nothing's going to happen."

I wanted to tell Pa that he couldn't know that. If he had seen what the devil man did, if he knew how fast and easy and eager it had been done, he wouldn't be making rash statements. I tore my eyes away from the pistols wrapped around that lean waist and ducked my face against Pa's side.

"Budge, listen to me," Pa said, trying to turn my chin out. "Sheriff Jewkes needs to know if this is the man who saved you from the soldiers."

"Murdered is prolly a better word," Sheriff Jewkes grumbled. "Ain't nothing been proved about him saving no one."

I peeked and saw no change in the devil man. His hands rested lightly on the front of his legs, not far from the pistols. Mercifully, his hat was pulled low enough to hide his eyes.

I nodded again and swallowed hard. My heart ran all over itself when I squawked, "Yes."

In response to this accusation, the devil man said nothing. He didn't pull his pistol and shoot me. He didn't even act like he cared much. He simply waited.

Sheriff Jewkes cleared his throat, spat and shifted the pistol belt around his thick middle. "I knowed something was wrong the minute I clapped eyes on this one," he said to Pa. "Good thing I come out here today to get my horse looked after. Damn lucky I'd say. I'll take it from—"

Pa stepped forward, dismissing what Sheriff Jewkes was saying. He put out his hand to the devil man, just the way he did to the brothers and sisters who went to church. "I want to thank you, sir," he said, "for what you did for my family. I owe you a debt that can never be repaid."

It didn't seem rude when the devil man ignored Pa's offer of a handshake. He nodded his head and backed up half a step, as if Pa had pressed too close. Pa didn't look offended either. He simply dropped his hand and hugged me tighter to him with the other. He glanced at the papers clutched in the hand near my face. "Says here your horse needs shoes," he said. "And that you know something about a forge. I'm sure we can—"

"Now just a damn minute, Merrell," Sheriff Jewkes interjected. He took a step forward and I saw the devil man's posture change, smooth and liquid as hot wax. The shaded eyes under the hat narrowed and he turned to face the sheriff. "This man here is a wanted killer," Jewkes said. "Well, prolly wanted. Like as not I got me some official flyers on him back at the office. Let's get that rag off'n his face and we'll see what's what before you go shoeing his animals."

Pa and Sheriff Jewkes started to argue. Neither saw the subtle change in the devil man's eyes when mention was made of the scarf he wore. They filled with an evil light that I remembered well. I pressed my knees together, hoping my bladder wouldn't shame me.

"He came here looking to trade me some work for shoeing his horses," Pa was saying. "I believe he'll still be here by the time you check with the army. You can't go hauling him off to jail for what he did. We'll hold an inquest and take depositions. A man's innocent until proven guilty." He looked at the devil man and then back to the sheriff. "I'll vouch for him. You get Henry du Pont out here and we'll be waiting."

Sheriff Jewkes crumpled up some note papers and tossed them aside. He plucked a pair of hand nippers out of his pocket.

"That ain't good enough, Merrell," he said. Stepping forward, he reached for the devil man's hand. "You're under arrest, buster, for murder. We'll find out soon enough if you're a Danite or what. And I'll damn sure be taking a look under that rag, too."

The devil man flicked away the sheriff's blundering paw.

My throat squeezed shut. That heavy something that had swelled and tightened the air on the Provo road returned in a flash, only this time it came with a name. Death. In those few seconds when the angel of death considered us all in the hot yard of our barn, I understood in my heart that killing was an art to some dark men, that blood also had its Michelangelos and Shakespeares.

All of this escaped the sheriff. With a curse and a red face, he reached for his pistol with one hand while still reaching for the devil man with the other.

Have you ever seen a cat move on a mouse? It's a fluid ballet of lovely murder, something the cat doesn't even know it has. That's what it was like watching the devil man move. He hooked the sheriff's arm under his own and trapped the fat man against the side of the barn. Before the sheriff could react, the devil man whipped out a long, wicked-looking sword knife from the scabbard at the middle of his back, pressing the needle point deep in the fleshy bags under one of Sheriff Jewkes's eyes. It took about one-tenth of a second.

"Wha—?" Sheriff Jewkes gasped, looking cross-eyed down at the knife point. What he saw caused his voice to break.

Carefully, so Sheriff Jewkes wouldn't get the idea that maybe he was just fooling around, the devil man turned the knife ever so slightly. A thread of blood ran down the sheriff's sweaty face. The sheriff gave a whine of fear.

"Hold on now," Pa stammered. The devil man flashed him a threatening look so full of black promise that whatever Pa was going to say dried right up. Pa thought for a small eternity. He collected his wits and set about trying to save the sheriff's miserable life.

"Harv," Pa said feebly. "I don't think this man really wants to kill you."

I agreed, since if he did Sheriff Jewkes would already be dead. Still, I kept my face scrunched up in anticipation, in case the devil man changed his mind and decided to change the sheriff's with the blade of his knife. Sheriff Jewkes moaned in reply.

"That being so," Pa continued quickly, "I think we should talk some more and see if there isn't some other way of handling this situation. Surely we can put our heads together and reach a common ground, a compromise. There's no call for a killing here. The good Lord knows we've had enough killing." He looked at the devil man. "Isn't that so, sir?"

I could see Pa was going to get nowhere quick by trying to appeal to the devil man's sense of brotherly love. It was like asking a catfish to rely on its legs.

I saw the devil man flick a cold, distracted look at me and realized with a burst of understanding that Sheriff Jewkes was still alive because I was standing there watching. For some reason, the devil man didn't want to knife the sheriff in front of me. Killing soldiers set on rape was one thing, but killing a sheriff was another. He was working up to it anyway, though. You could see it plain in the half of his face visible above the scarf.

The thought of being indirectly responsible for saving Sheriff Jewkes rankled me, but I also knew that killing him would surely cause the devil man more trouble. And the Merrell family owed this man a lot. I personally owed him more than it was possible to measure.

"Pa," I said, tugging on the leg of his trousers.

"Not now, Budge," he said, flashing me that peeved look he got whenever Cletus got the best of him in their scripture talks.

So I just went ahead.

"Sir," I said tentatively to the devil man. His response was to give me a carnivorous look that froze my insides. I swallowed hard and pressed on. "If you hurt the sheriff, you won't be able to stay and do any work for my pa. The soldiers will come and we'll get blamed for helping you. They'll put my pa in jail."

I saw the devil man mull this over. His eyes flicked from me to Pa and back again. He never once looked at the sheriff. In his own mind, I think the sheriff was already dead. The knife pinning him to the barn never wavered. In truth, I don't think the devil man worried much about soldiers. He probably welcomed the notion that there would be more of them to shoot.

"If you let the sheriff go," I continued, "my Pa will see that you don't get blamed for anything. He's a bishop and folks listen to him. We'll tell them how you saved me and Laurel Anne."

At the mention of my sister's name, I saw something new in the devil man's eyes. It looked like indecision, as if he was changing his mind and finding such a thing a troubling experience.

Sheriff Jewkes had the bad sense to try and shift his weight just then. The knife pressed deeper into his face and the thread of blood became a bright ribbon against the sweaty white of his skin. He warbled another shrill whine of fear.

I tried to think fast, to come up with a way to save Sheriff Jewkes from the devil man. Except my brain wasn't working very well. All my shortcomings seemed to swell up and block my best intentions. Like Pa, I was foundering and it was looking like the devil man was going to just go on and stick his knife in Sheriff Jewkes's eye. He might get a vote of thanks out of it from the Mormons, but more likely he'd get himself hung by soldiers. Just when things looked like they were going to get bad again, God and Jesus finally broke down and sent us some help. Not a devil this time, but a genuine, bonafide golden angel.

"Father?"

The sound of Laurel Anne's voice brought a new element into the ugly drama being played out in our barnyard. Contrary to good sense and the way she'd been carrying on about the marks on her face, my sister had ventured down from the log house to talk to Pa. She had always been like that. The only surviving child from Pa's first marriage, she generally confided her deepest feelings to him. She should have stayed in bed but nobody complained because her sudden appearance stopped cold another killing. We heard her call a few more times inside the barn. She must have glimpsed us through the cracks in the wall because she skirted the stalls and pushed on the big doors leading into the yard.

At the sound of Laurel Anne's voice, I saw a remarkable change come over the devil man. The catlike grace receded and his eyes mellowed, dropping a notch from murder to something resembling a cornered wariness. He loosened his hold on the sheriff a fraction. As soon as the barn door creaked open, he stepped away from the sheriff completely and the knife vanished into the sheath behind him. Sheriff Jewkes swayed and would have sprawled flat had Pa not caught onto his arm.

"Oh, dear," Laurel Anne exclaimed when she saw blood on the sheriff's face. "What happened to him?" Her gaze kept traveling between the sheriff and the devil man. I could see her studying the devil man, trying to connect where she might have seen him before. Eventually she would connect the sheriff's bloody face with the devil man and come to the wrong conclusion, even if maybe it was the logical one.

"He bumped into a nail," I lied, pointing to a rusty hook on the side of the barn.

Being a good liar is not a talent of which I am particularly proud. It has, however, served me well in the past and it served me well now. If lying is a sin, it's a mighty useful one.

The devil man shot me a glance that was both surprise and something else. Gratitude? He pulled off his hat in the presence of Laurel Anne and stood bareheaded in the sunlight, his clean yellow hair wild and uncombed.

Without the shadow of the hat obscuring his upper face, it was easy to see that the devil man was young, not yet thirty—and handsome, at least from the nose up. The blue scarf stayed wrapped around his lower face. He nodded politely to Laurel Anne and dropped his gaze when her eyes remained fixed on him.

Laurel Anne smiled tentatively. The pain it caused reminded her of her own bruised features. She quickly put a lace hanky to her mouth and held it there, hiding some of the marks left by Bukovski's fist. We all stood there looking dumb while Pa helped a wobbly Sheriff Jewkes in the direction of his horse.

"I suggest you get that cut looked at right away, Brother Sheriff," Pa was saying, "You don't want lockjaw setting in. As for this other matter, well, why don't you tell Lieutenant du Pont to drop by?" He guided Sheriff Jewkes's foot into the stirrup and boosted him up. "I'm sure everyone will be happy to answer to an official inquest."

"Yeah," Sheriff Jewkes wheezed, dabbing at the cut under his eye. "R-reckon I'll do that, Merrell. Be seeing you." He glanced fearfully at the devil man, then turned his horse and socked his heels into it. By the time Sheriff Jewkes reached the bottom of the lane, his horse was in a big ol' hurry.

"Well," Pa said, rubbing his hands together. "I'm glad we resolved that."

"Resolved what, Father?" Laurel Anne asked.

"Oh, ah, just some questions the good sheriff had, dear," Pa said. It sounded mighty weak but it was as close as Pa could get to steering around the truth. Bishops aren't much for lying, useful or not. He motioned to the devil man and said to Laurel Anne, "Have you met my new hired hand? Mr. Lorings?—this is my eldest daughter, Laurel Anne. Laurel, dear, this is Mr. Lorings, late of California. He's agreed to stay and work here for a spell, if what I make of these notes is correct." He looked at the devil man. "Did I say your name right? Lorings?"

The devil man—Mr. Lorings—nodded. I could see that he was still as nervous as a wild animal, trembling almost invisibly as he wrestled with the instinct to attack us or run away.

Laurel Anne had the presence of mind to try a curtsy, although it was obvious she was still trying to sort out where she had seen Mr. Lorings before. From the look on her face, I guessed she was getting close. She took in the pistols around his hips and the rifles on the horses and I saw her expression change, becoming unsure.

"But I thought we already had enough help," Laurel Anne said. "You told the Lehman boys just last week that—"

"I've decided we need another hand," Pa hurried to say. "There's plenty of work around this old farm, and Brother Lorings claims to know a forge. We could double our smithy business."

In response to Laurel Anne's doubtful look, Mr. Lorings turned slightly to one side. I saw him touch the ragged scarf on his lower face, checking to be sure it was in place. He was hiding something there and it was plain he was more worried about Laurel Anne seeing whatever it was than me or Pa.

Things got sort of clumsy then. Two minutes before, we had been close to a murder, and now Pa and me were trying to act as if nothing had happened. Mr. Lorings was dying an inch at a time under the scrutiny of Laurel Anne.

"We'll see to your horses in the morning," Pa said to Mr. Lorings. "You can put up in the barn. Let's get washed up for dinner." He motioned us toward the house. "Brother Lorings, you're invited up to the house. Our help eats with the family."

Mr. Lorings shook his head. He took out a pencil stub and scribbled fast on a scrap of paper. He handed it to Pa, who read it with a glance and frowned. "Are you certain? We'd be most pleased to have you."

The devil man shook his head again and gathered the reins of his horses. He tipped his hat to Laurel Anne and—in a move that earned him a friend—to me as well. He turned and led his horses into the barn.

Walking back up to the house, we discussed our new hired hand.

"I don't know, Father," Laurel Anne said. "He gives me a fright. He's so—so dark." I think she had finally guessed what really happened to Sheriff Jewkes's face. "Are you certain?"

"Not everyone has had the best upbringing," Pa said. He wrapped an arm around Laurel Anne. "But we can't hold that against him. Besides," he said in his bishop's voice, "I think this family owes that man quite a bit."

I glanced back over my shoulder and saw the devil man watching us from the dim interior of the barn. He was back in the shadows, trying not to be seen in case one of us turned around like I did. I couldn't see him well but I knew he was there because his gaze on us was as chilling as cold water down my back. I also knew those dead eyes were watching Laurel Anne most of all. It scared me and I shivered in the afternoon heat. Pa put his arm around me and I saw Mr. Lorings's note stuck in his big hand. I took it out, unfolded it and read. Disturbed, I stuffed the note in the pocket of my jumper. I still have it to this day, pressed between the pages of my first clumsy journal. Written in an educated, cursive hand were two words, the only lie the devil man ever told us: *Not hungry.*

Maybe. But from the looks the devil man was giving Laurel Anne from the barn, I wasn't so sure.

That's how the devil man came to us in the summer of 1869, a soul-blistering season of terror and love. In the days that followed, I learned not to think of him as the devil man, or any of the other names men called him, names that made people stupid with fear. Whispered around a campfire, those names brought stories bloody and terrible enough to scare the sleep out of you.

But all of that came later. Right then it was good that we were so ignorant about Mr. Lorings, oblivious to exactly who and what he was. Good because as much as he needed us, and as much as we needed him, we would never have let him stay. That summer the monster who could freeze a human heart with a single glance became my best friend.

As I dozed off in my own bed that night, while the moon lofted itself over the mountains like one of Bishop Woodbury's lost coins, the notion seized me that everything had changed for my family. Somehow I knew that those few fiery minutes on the Provo road would be the hinge upon which the rest of our lives turned. It was an unsettling thought and I murmured a prayer as sleep claimed me, hoping that God was listening high up in his heaven as I asked him for the only thing I could think of that could truly help any of us.

"Please, God," I prayed into my pillow so Ma and Laurel Anne wouldn't hear. "Please bless the devil man."

Chapter Three

Pa was as good as his word. A week after the near murder of Sheriff Jewkes, the army came down from Fort Douglas and held an inquest into the killings of Bukovski and his friends. The officers accepted Pa's invitation to set up shop in our church. The inquest lasted most of one day and was closed to civilians except for witnesses.

I didn't go to the inquest and neither did Laurel Anne. Ma refused to let us have anything more to do with soldiers, so we stayed put at home and waited it out. By way of testimony, Pa turned over our written statements describing the events leading up to the killing of Sergeant Bukovski. Ma made me write mine twice, saying it wasn't proper or necessary to call dead people so many names. Judge Parkins came out to our farm in his rickety buggy and read our statements before having us sign them. Then he sealed the pages in a big envelope with a gob of blue wax and gave them to Pa to take to the inquest.

That evening, Pa returned with news of Mr. Lorings's exoneration. Pa said our statements had sufficed mostly because the army had determined that Bukovski and friends were in the process of deserting when they got themselves killed. There was even some speculation that

Bukovski was on his way to our farm to settle his score with Pa that day, so I guess we owed Mr. Lorings double.

Even though the verdict undoubtedly galled him, Sheriff Jewkes let the matter of Mr. Lorings drop. After the inquest, Mr. Lorings became something of a local hero. Nobody ever got the chance to mention it to him direct, but he was talked about approvingly by people who, if they weren't grateful for Bukovski being killed, were at least thankful that Laurel Anne and me were spared. Also, I think being rubbed up against the sides of his own grave had demoralized the sheriff.

Although he had been officially cleared of any crime, you couldn't have told it by Mr. Lorings's behavior. The fact that he was now a certified hero didn't change him a bit. Pa said the only emotion Mr. Lorings displayed during the inquest was an ill-concealed inclination to kill more soldiers. Mr. Lorings, Pa said, watched the soldiers with the same intensity a starved wolf studied meat. There was a note of worried wonder in Pa's voice.

"He was a man sorely tempted," Pa said. "He fairly shook from it, like a drunkard tempted by drink. I wouldn't have wanted to be in the guard detail that tried to hang that man." Pa shook his head. "It doesn't figure, though."

"What?" Laurel Anne asked.

"It doesn't make sense that a man like him would let himself be examined by any court. He could have ridden off and never answered a word to anything. Since it was obviously so contrary to his nature, I wonder why he did it?"

I didn't say anything. One look at Laurel Anne and I knew I was lots closer to the answer than Pa.

Mr. Lorings never said a word about the inquest. In fact, he never said word one about anything to anybody. He bunked down in the barn and kept to himself, doing whatever chores Pa assigned him. Pa said Mr. Lorings probably was mute because he answered questions either with a gesture or a hastily scrawled note.

"He keeps track of everything," Pa said, that first evening after the inquest. "He watches with those eyes of his and never says a word. I expect there'd be an interesting story there if someone ever decided to write it down."

Alva sniffed. She was sewing and listening. "Well, I'm just thankful he's mute and will never make mention of his sordid past around here. I wouldn't want him corrupting our sons, like someone I know."

She meant me, of course. I let her know that I knew who she was referring to by sticking out my tongue. But I waited until Pa wasn't looking.

Most of the rest of the family, including Silla, agreed that the best thing would be to give Mr. Lorings lots of space. While at the same time filling me with nervousness, the subject of Mr. Lorings fascinated me. My self-appointed calling in life was to study people. I spied on everyone and everything. I didn't look at it as something to be ashamed of, even though everyone said I should. It was simply the only way to learn what I wanted to know since adults never told me a word about the subjects that interested me. If spying really was a sin, at least it was my salvation from boredom.

There was nothing on God's earth more boring than our farm. The only happenings prior to the arrival of Mr. Lorings concerned who was trying to kiss Laurel Anne and who she would eventually agree to marry. Thus far, only Henry du Pont and Eldon Bair had managed the former. I knew because I watched them from my self-assigned station in the bushes at the end of the porch. It was perfectly nauseating. Laurel Anne acted the disgusting coquet while Henry and Eldon fretted and fawned over her in turn. If Laurel Anne knew I'd watched, she would have strangled me. If Eldon or Henry knew they were indirectly kissing each other, there would have been a murder. Eldon hated Henry and no doubt would have sliced off his own lips and thrown them away if he knew Laurel Anne had kissed Henry before him. Theirs was not a graceful competition. Deep down, I think that's probably why Laurel Anne let them both kiss her. She was bored, too.

If life on our farm was akin to a prison sentence for me, the arrival of Mr. Lorings was like a pardon from the governor. Overnight, drudgery and boredom—both of which had been perfected by my family until they were routinely confused with spiritual experiences—vanished. I knew mysteries when I saw them and I committed myself to the insane goal of getting as close to our hired hand as possible, no matter how hard or dangerous it was. The physical prospects of doing it were difficult because Mr. Lorings never came anywhere near the family. He refused to eat with us or, most of the time, even eat what we gave him. Once, when I carried a plate of Alva's roast beef down to the barn, he barely touched it.

The only people Mr. Lorings had any sort of regular traffic with were Pa and Cletus. He worked for Pa and slept in the barn with Cletus who, being a nervous and God-fearing man, wasn't exactly happy about the arrangement. Cletus made no pretense that he considered Mr. Lorings anything other than a devil's curse wrapped up in skin. Eventually, after Cletus's jittery behavior made their situation intolerable by him jumping every time Mr. Lorings made a sound or a sudden move, Mr. Lorings moved to the other side of the barn, preferring to sleep on feed sacks in the tack room.

The move disappointed me because I had intended on soliciting Cletus' help in spying on Mr. Lorings. Also because it raised a question about Mr. Lorings' character. In spite of the awful things I already knew about him, Mr. Lorings didn't seem small enough to hate someone because of the color of his skin. I expressed this concern to Cletus.

"No chile, I don't reckon it were on account of I'm African," Cletus said. "Man like that don't bother with hatin' just color. I 'spect he hates near 'bout ever'thing and ever'body."

There was, however, some good in Mr. Lorings's presence. He did know something about blacksmithing. Pa was able to turn over a lot of farrier work to Mr. Lorings, work that didn't necessarily involve him mixing with people. Mr. Lorings stayed back in the shop where the bellows wheezed and the sparks whirled. Cletus dryly pointed out how it was a lot like hell back in there and so Mr. Lorings probably felt right at home.

Also, Mr. Lorings's big horse turned out to be an Appaloosa stud, a product of the Nez Perce who bred, said the men who did business with Pa, the best horses ever sent to earth by God. Which was probably true because Mr. Lorings's horse was as fine an animal as any I'd ever seen, if possessed with more than the normal amount of meanness. Pa offered Mr. Lorings some money to turn the stud loose in our north pasture with a dozen mares fixing to come into season. For the first few days the frightened mares gave the rocky-colored stud a wide berth, crowding themselves into one corner of the pasture like a ladies' tea circle caught in a holdup. For his part, the stud ignored the mares. Instead, he set about the serious business of making sure that no man or beast came within a hundred yards of the pasture. He half-killed Poulsens' big, chicken-stealing dog, Joe, one afternoon by kicking it over the fence. I saw it happen. Joe flew so high that it seemed to take him forever to come down, and he walked sort of folded in half ever after. The result of that, plus a few poles kicked loose from the fence, was that everyone steered clear of Mr. Lorings's horse and his harem. Even Samson, big and cantankerous as he was, shied away from the fence that separated his pasture from the stud's.

After about a week, I settled in on the serious business of spying on Mr. Lorings without Cletus's help. I knew it was going to be difficult if not a little dangerous. The folks I had spied on previous to this—mostly my family and members of our church ward—weren't serious threats. The most that would have happened to me had I been caught was the assignment of some loathsome chore or, worse, a lecture. I considered these consequences serious punishments to be sure, but nothing at all like what Mr. Lorings might do if he caught me being nosey around him.

The biggest problem was that I didn't know exactly how to sidle up next to someone like Mr. Lorings. He hovered on the periphery of our lives like a distant storm, a blue-black threat of fury that made sensible people close up their shops and homes. But approach him I did, and to this day I am never certain if my actions were an answer to my own prayers or because I was too dumb to know better. I'd like to think God and Jesus had a hand in it because to think anything else still scares me.

The first killing on our farm took place a week after the inquest. I was up before the sun that day, even before Ma. Dressing silently, I let myself out of the cabin and into the cool half-light. I ran through the morning dew, kicking diamonds out of the grass all the way down to the shop where Pa was firing his forge. Outside in the pens, nervous from the noise, horses waiting to be shoed milled around steaming piles of manure. I climbed through the fence and slipped inside the cavernous barn.

Mr. Lorings was stoking the forge with coal. His arms showed through ragged holes in a threadbare shirt. They were slick with sweat and knotted with muscle. Despite the building heat, he still wore the scarf wrapped around his face, and belted around his narrow waist, looking like they had grown roots there, were the omnipresent guns and the huge knife. In the lurid flames, backed by the dimness of the shop, he looked both reassuring and monstrous. He glanced my way once, stone-colored eyes alert and penetrating over the top of the mask. I hiccupped in surprise and scrambled up on some boxes where I crouched, watching him ready the forge. Pa came in from outside and saw me, which was easy since I wasn't actually spying yet. This was only an official reconnoiter.

"Morning, Budge," he boomed.

Pa had a loud voice, the result of too many hours working at his anvil. He used it to good effect on Sundays, when some folks said his sermons were loud enough to make God pay attention. I waved and saw him glance sidelong at Mr. Lorings. Pa was slow on some things, but he was no idiot. He knew the reason I left my bed so early that morning was the gunman stoking his forge. Pa blew me a kiss. I caught it and stuck it on my cheek.

When Mr. Lorings had the forge going, he lugged in some water and spread out Pa's tools.

"That'll be fine, Brother Lorings," Pa said, wiping his hands on a rag. Pa called everyone brother or sister, whether they were Mormons or not. "Go on up to the house with Budge. Alva will have your breakfast waiting."

Mr. Lorings just stood there. Pa wasn't entirely oblivious to the strange habits of our new hired hand, but he waved us on anyway. "I know you like your privacy, Brother Lorings. You can take your meal out on the back stoop and eat there if you've a mind to. Nobody will bother you. Budge, be a good girl and show Brother Lorings the way. I'll be along directly."

I expected Mr. Lorings to refuse, but this time it was different. He followed after me. It was a little like having a tiger at your heels. The skin 'twixt my shoulder blades squirmed around and I kept looking over my shoulder to see if he was sneaking up behind me with his sword knife.

We walked up to the brick house, where Alva and Laurel Anne saw us coming and were waiting on the porch. Alva's eyes positively shone when she saw Mr. Lorings coming up to be fed. His exploits on the Provo road were still something of a mystery to everyone in the community, mostly because neither myself nor Laurel Anne talked about it. This bothered Pumpkin Ass, who couldn't stand not knowing important things. She didn't have to understand them, mind you, only know about them. Details are more important to gossips than any real understanding.

Despite the unkind things she'd already said about him, Alva introduced herself graciously to Mr. Lorings when we arrived at the porch. She was obviously mulling over what she should do by way of inviting him in for breakfast when Snow wandered over and blocked our way. Snow was proud of the fact that he had slipped his yarn tether this morning and wanted to brag about it. He puffed up his chest at us, flapped his wings and quacked bossy and loud.

"Oh, he's such a bother," Alva said. "If someone would only wring his neck for me, I'd cook him for supper this very afternoon. I'm sure he'd taste fine, but I just can't bring myself to mess with the killing."

It probably didn't occur to Mr. Lorings that Alva was only joking. After all, killing people was about as easy for him as blinking and Snow was just a duck. The sword knife flashed in the morning sun, and with a tiny bell-like ring of steel on bone, Snow's head flipped into the garden. The rest of him just stood there, blood squirting from the hole in his long, empty neck.

Alva's mouth went round with shock. She couldn't tell who to settle her bulging eyes on—Mr. Lorings, who was calmly putting away his big knife, or her headless pet. Laurel Anne blanched and turned in the doorway, a hand against her bruised mouth. Even I was surprised. My mouth got suddenly weak in the hinges.

Snow was having an equally hard time coming to terms with what had happened to him. He waddled aimlessly before deciding the situation was permanent. That's when he got excited and began thrashing around in blind search of his head, making a mess all over Alva's clean stoop.

Mr. Lorings put a boot on Snow's neck until he ran out of blood. Then he picked Snow up by his twitching leathery feet and handed him up to Alva. He'd done her the politeness of killing Snow and now it was up to her to cook him. After all, the whole thing had been her idea.

Alva's response was to scream like a steam whistle. It made my hair shoot up on my skull and brought Pa straight out of the barn carrying his hammer. Inside the house, I heard one of the twins ask in a bored tone if Alva wanted the musket. Alva jumped back, stepped on her skirts and went down on her heavy rump with a blow that punished the entire length of the porch. Still holding her bloody pet, Mr. Lorings went up the steps to offer his hand.

"Get away from me!" Alva screamed, kicking frantically. "Oh, you get away. Murder! Murder!"

Bewildered, Mr. Lorings dropped Snow and backed down the steps. I could see confusion in his eyes. Alva, however, chose to act as if he was still coming after her with his knife. She continued to kick and scream, making an interesting display of her petticoats while eventually walking herself all the way into a corner of the porch on her hams. Laurel Anne came to her rescue with a broom.

"Get back," Laurel Anne snipped at Mr. Lorings, as if shooing one of the barn cats. "Get back. Just get away from here, you." The ludicrousness of swatting someone like Mr. Lorings with a broom would have made me laugh had I not been so completely astonished by the events. The blood, the noise, the possibility that Mr. Lorings might kill us all, everything was better than I could have possibly hoped for.

Mr. Lorings wasn't of the same mind. He retreated further, holding up one hand in defense. The other never got very far away from the guns. I guess he was trying to figure out what he'd done wrong and if shooting someone might help solve the problem. Laurel Anne took another swipe at him with the broom. It landed on his shoulder and he shrugged it off. The overwrought reactions of Laurel Anne and Alva started to make me mad. When my sister raised the broom for another swipe, I came to Mr. Lorings's rescue. After all, fair is fair.

"You leave him alone," I cried. I got between them and seized one end of the broom, precipitating a furious tug-of-war. I managed to wrestle the broom away by kicking at her legs. I would have laid into her with it had Pa's firm hands not snatched me up from behind.

Laurel Anne retreated. She helped the still-shrieking Alva to her feet and they scrambled into the house, slamming the door and dropping the bar behind it.

"You can let go now, Pa," I said. "They're gone."

When the hands didn't put me down, I looked up—straight into the gray, lifeless eyes of Mr. Lorings. The broom fell out of my nerveless fingers while my heart plunged straight to the cellar of my stomach.

Mr. Lorings put me down. There was an uneasy moment while I tried to gag up my tongue, which had somehow become lodged in the back of my throat. I saw Mr. Lorings's expression arrange itself into something that didn't fit him at all. He motioned at the mess that used to be Snow and gave his shoulders the almost imperceptible lift that I would eventually learn passed for his apology.

I straightened my jumper and surveyed the massacre. Snow's blood covered the brick walk and the lower porch steps. A single feather drifted off in the breeze, following the duck's departing spirit. The rest of the family was inside the house, glued to the windows, wailing and waiting for me to be dismembered. Pa came running up, still carrying the hammer and looking mighty concerned. It took a few minutes for me to explain what had happened. When I finished, Pa relaxed and toed Snow's blood-smeared carcass away from the porch.

"We can get Alva another duck," he said, although it was plain from the look she was giving us through the window that Alva wanted Pa to shoot Mr. Lorings, or at the very least fetch him a wallop with the hammer.

Mr. Lorings made another of his silent, apologetic gestures.

Pa shook his head. "No matter. It's done." He scratched his beard, thinking. "See here, Brother Lorings, why don't you go on back down to the shop. There's some wood out back that needs cutting. I'll have Budge fetch down your breakfast directly."

As soon as Mr. Lorings was gone, Laurel Anne appeared on the porch with the twins. Everyone gaped at Snow and the departing Mr. Lorings. The twins squatted and began stirring the blood pools with sticks, goggling at the massacre.

"Father," Laurel Anne said, sounding remarkably like a peeved Alva. "I don't know what's come over you, keeping a man like that around here. He's a villain, a blackguard! Just look what he did. What's going to happen next?"

Pa would have come to Mr. Lorings's defense, except Laurel Anne rushed on, listing our hired hand's faults, both known and surmised. Standing on the porch with her arms folded and the toe of a shoe tapping under the hem of her dress, she looked like a mother scolding errant children. It didn't make sense that she was running down the man who saved us. Later I understood that she was afraid of Mr. Lorings, or, more accurately, afraid of herself and Mr. Lorings.

"We need Mr. Lorings," I said hotly. "And he—" I was about to add that Mr. Lorings needed us, too, but she cut me off.

"We most certainly do not need him around here, Rose Lee Merrell. We're Latter-day Saints. Good heavens, what possible need could we have for a gunman? What will our neighbors and friends think?"

I started to say something, but Pa clamped his hand over my mouth and kept it there. Dammit, no one ever let me finish having my say. Laurel Anne shot me a venomous look and continued her attack on Mr. Lorings's character.

Pa and Laurel Anne blabbed some more about it, debating what we owed the mute gunman and the corresponding dangers of keeping him around. I ignored them both, peering over Pa's stonelike hand to the barn. Mr. Lorings came outside with an ax. He glanced our way once and disappeared around the back. The rhythmic sound of the ax knocking into wood drifted up to the house.

"And another thing," Laurel Anne said. "What kind of influence is he having on the children? Last summer, Rose Lee learned to curse from our last hired hand. Because of Mr. Stubbs, she now has a vocabulary that would shame a freight driver. Just last month you caught her trying to smoke a cigar butt she found down by the barn. All that from loitering around the shop and spying on bad company. So you just ask yourself, Father, what bad habits is she going to learn from this one?"

Enough was damn well enough. I swung another kick at my sister, intending to give her some shin bruises to match the ones on her face. I would have, too, only Pa's hand tightened on me. I must have caught him by surprise because he squeezed too hard, painfully clamping my lips against my teeth. I tasted blood.

It hurt and I would have complained about it long and loud except at that moment, like the sun coming up, I figured something out. The smell of bread from the house and the scarf Mr. Lorings wore, coupled with his refusal to eat with us, the untouched roast beef—it all suddenly made sense.

Mr. Lorings wouldn't eat with us because he couldn't. Not our kind of food anyway. There was the owner of the shanty saloon by the river, Slobber Bob, who was born a harelip. Bob couldn't eat regular food either. There was something wrong with Mr. Lorings's mouth and that's why he wore the scarf. Was he a harelip, too? I sincerely hoped not because Slobber Bob wasn't a pretty sight. I'd seen him a couple of times in town, the front of his shirt wet with spit, causing widespread revulsion whenever he tried to get his name out. "B-b-bobert," he would spray. Folks would grin and sometimes laugh right out loud. I felt sorry for him.

I motioned for Pa to let me go. He made me apologize to Laurel Anne first. I did it even though it galled me fierce. Because I wanted to get away with a minimum amount of fuss, I made the apology sound as piteous as possible. It seemed to mollify her, although she continued to glare at me. I scrambled up the steps and into the house, turning once to make a face.

Alva was in the parlor weeping and carrying on like she just found out that Jesus personally hated her guts. She was hoping Pa would come in soon and comfort her. Breakfast was off, cancelled by the murder of her kindred spirit, a fat, bossy duck. Fanning herself and leaking snot and tears, Alva looked perfectly useless, a waste of flesh and bone that God and Jesus could have used making an elephant for me since they were so damn stingy with the ones they had.

"Did you see it, Rose Lee?" she sobbed. "Oh, did you see what that awful man did to poor Snow?"

I ignored her and went into the kitchen. Fortunately the stove was already heated up. I cracked four eggs into a frying pan and scrambled them. Then I sliced up half a loaf of bread and cut all the crusts off.

Finally, I poured a jar full of cool milk from the pitcher in the stone cooler box. Loading everything into my arms, I snuck out the back door and took a circuitous route down to the barn. I passed Pinch Face, who was walking up the lane to the brick house, wondering what was causing all the commotion. Normally I might have asked about Josh, but I was on important business now.

I found Mr. Lorings still swinging the axe against the woodpile. He saw me coming but kept right on chopping. I put the plate and the jar down on a block of wood and backed up. I kept backing up until he stopped swinging the axe. If my presence annoyed him, I wanted a good head start for the house.

Mr. Lorings' cold eyes glanced at the plate. It was obvious that the soft food appealed to him. The look on what was visible of his face made my own mouth water. He chopped through the log and then swept up the plate and the jar. Carrying them to the other side of the woodpile, he squatted down with his back to me. Pulling down the scarf and keeping his face averted, he went to wolfing the food. He reminded me of the wild dog that crept into our yard one winter morning looking for a stray crumb. Mr. Lorings was just like that dog, all exposed nerve and humming sinew, taut ties that kept him together in an environment he didn't trust but couldn't quite do without.

I eased down to the woodpile, careful not to put myself in a position where I might threaten his privacy. He kept right on eating, but I knew he was watching me, as if he had eyes in the back of his head.

"You don't have to worry about killing Snow," I said to his back. "The only person fierce mad is Pump—Alva. She'll blab it around for a while, but she'll get over it."

No answer. If not for the fact that his senses were so alive that I could feel them on my skin, it would have been easy to figure Mr. Lorings for deaf as well as mute. He continued to eat. I pressed on, fighting a nearly overwhelming desire to run back to the house where it was safe.

"I wanted to say something else," I said. My voice trembled, making me more angry than frightened. It was worse than the time I got up in church and said my testimony of the gospel in front of everyone. "I hope you won't take it wrong." I swallowed hard. It was the first time I ever had to express my gratitude to someone like him. "I only wanted to thank you for saving us from the soldiers. I was real scared when...they were doing those things. I didn't know what to do so I said a prayer. I asked for an angel, but got you instead. I figure maybe God and Jesus sent you and that it means you're supposed to be here."

It all sounded mighty stupid and so I shut my mouth before my butt fell out.

Mr. Lorings paused and adjusted his scarf. Then he turned his head and gave me a long look out of one cold eye. It wasn't a mean look. He looked confused, like he was wondering if he'd heard right or if I was joshing him.

"I wanted you to know I was thankful," I added hurriedly.

He turned back around and finished his breakfast. As soon as he was done, he secured the scarf and stood up. He put the dishes on a stump and turned to go into the barn. He hesitated and looked at me again with those terrible eyes. The scarf twitched. His voice was raspy, garbled and broken, as if from disuse.

"My name is Fulton."

He disappeared into the barn. I was so astounded that a hopper fart would have knocked me right over.

I don't know how long I sat there dumb as a toadstool; long after he went into the barn anyway. When I sufficiently gathered my addled wits, I picked up the plate and jar and carried them up to the brick house. Suddenly I felt like Magellan, Columbus and Cortez, like anyone who had ever stepped ashore on an unexplored continent, made contact with a dark race and lived to tell about it. Mr. Lorings could talk. The possibilities were breathtaking. I kicked up my feet and ran for the house, hugging the secret close to my heart.

Alva lay on her bed, suffering, she said, with a grand megrim. Laurel Anne and Silla were trying to put a breakfast together for Pa. The house was sheer pandemonium. Pa, unable to take feminine confusion of any sort, grabbed a slice of bread and headed back down to the shop. Silla, holding a pan of burned eggs and ham, looked stricken.

Following Pa, I ran into Laurel Anne washing blood off the front porch with a bucket of soapy water and the broom. When she saw me, she started in on Mr. Lorings again, how he had killed poor Snow and insulted the lady of the house. How he obviously didn't know manners enough to be around good people. She worked herself into a sizeable steam. I realized then that my sister was working on blocking from her mind the horrible memory of what had happened to us on the Provo road. She was trying to make herself feel safe by making things be the way they were before that day, by fretting over things that were once important but now should pale in comparison. As cruel as it was, she needed reminding.

"Was shooting the soldiers bad manners, too?"

Laurel stopped scrubbing and stared at me, suddenly pale in the morning sun. Her wet hands went to the front of her dress. The look in her eye told me she was feeling Bukovski's hands on her pillows again. Before she could say anything, I turned and ran for the barn.

I followed Pa. He seemed preoccupied with the killing of Snow and so I kept my distance, wondering what he planned on doing with Mr. Lorings. I caught up with him at the shop, where he dispatched Mr. Lorings to the canal to dig with Cletus. He didn't say a word about Snow.

Alone, Pa looked at me and sighed. I started first, a giggle that came out like a hiccup. He snickered in his beard, causing me to laugh outright. In an instant we were both roaring. I tucked my thumbs under my arms and squatted down, waddling around the forge and bumping into things, pretending I couldn't see without a head. Pa laughed so hard I thought he'd seize up. He fell down and kicked his feet, tears leaking out of his eyes and wheezy gasps coming from his mouth, in general acting more like a Saturday night drunk than a bishop. He got me going and after a few minutes I was pretty sure I was going to go blind from the strain. I started to gag. Gradually, our laughing fit coasted into weary giggles, snorts and finally a groan or two.

Pa sat up after several minutes of recovery and picked the straw out of his beard.

"I think people of the nosey sort might have to be careful around here now," Pa said, meaning me. When he saw I didn't understand, he said, "Some people are like a tar pit, Budge. You touch them and you can't get back out so easy. Also, Mr. Lorings strikes me as a man fussy about his privacy. He might find it bothersome to have someone around him all the time."

I understood. Pa didn't come right out and tell me not to spy on Mr. Lorings. I took it as neither permission nor restriction. It simply meant that I had to be careful. When I assured him that I wouldn't trouble Mr. Lorings, Pa kissed me and I went off to play.

✾

While it was hard on Alva, Snow's untimely death had some merits to it. The duck tasted mighty good when Ma cooked it up the next day. It also gave me a lot of genuine pleasure to see Alva so discomfited. But the killing of Snow started the gossips talking in earnest. It was, many said, a bad omen. Alva's flapping mouth fueled most of it. God's chosen or not, the people in our narrow corner of the world were a herd, and herds—even Christian herds—get mean when confronted with the out of the ordinary. The herd was to teach me an important gospel lesson that summer—that virtue for most people consists of little more than severity to others.

I wasn't the only one with a developing interest in Fulton Lorings. My twin half brothers had also marked our dark hired hand as a subject of study.

Although Alva continually lectured Nephi and Lehi about Fulton, telling them that any evil habits they picked up by even a chance encounter with him would follow them forever and keep them out of the Celestial Kingdom, they loitered around Fulton whenever they could.

I think it was the guns. Not just the guns, but the fact that they were pistols. Most of the men I personally knew had shotguns and rifles, weapons that spent much of the time on pegs above a door or fireplace. Few had pistols and fewer still ever wore them anywhere. Pa had one that he wore when the Nauvoo Legion was called out to fight Indians, but I'd never seen him shoot it. Fulton was the only person we'd ever known who wore a pistol like most men wear pants. He kept two of them belted around his lean waist no matter what he was doing for Pa—forge work, cutting wood, grooming horses. The world probably would have seemed off kilter had he shown up without them.

From what little I knew of pistols, Fulton's were unremarkable in their appearance. Since that day on the road to Provo, I'd never seen him shoot or even take one to hand. I couldn't have told you anything about them beyond the fact that they were loud. But Nephi and Lehi speculated on the pistols constantly, calling them this caliber and that make and insisting that they, themselves, could shoot expertly if only Alva would allow them the chance to prove it. Their constant bragging got under my skin.

One morning, as I watched Fulton from the safety of the brick house porch, the twins came up to stand behind me. "I could shoot just as well as him if I had a pistol," Nephi said. "It ain't hard at all."

"Me, too," Lehi said, shoving me away from the porch rail. "Eldon Bair has a pistol. He let us shoot a bullet once. I hit a big rock."

Nephi leaned next to his brother. "I shot a bottle. Bet I could do it again."

My own mental images of shooting had nothing to do with rocks and bottles. They were all screams and the smell of blood. "Guns are nothing to be fooling with," I said.

Lehi smirked. "A lot you know about guns. You're just a girl."

"Girls know just as much as boys," I shot back.

"Do not."

"Do too."

The argument degenerated to the point where I dared them to prove how much they knew about pistol shooting, which was precisely the wrong thing to do under the circumstances.

I watched Nephi and Lehi muddle the dare over in their heads. Plainly, the problem was where to get a pistol. Sneaking Pa's pistol was out of the question. He kept it in a locked box under his bed and had told us that if he ever caught us messing with it, he'd wear the hide off of us, which was a lie. Pa never beat us. But he sometimes lectured us until we wished we were dead.

Things turned dark when I saw Nephi's face sharpen with interest. He was looking off in the direction of the pastures. I turned and saw Fulton and Pa far out in the fields, walking among the horses.

"I know," Nephi said and whispered something in Lehi's ear. They gave me a smug look and tramped off in direction of the barn. I immediately knew what they were up to.

"You better not," I called after them. "He won't like it, you messing with his stuff. He might..."

I fell silent. He might what? Kill them? Part of me knew it was a distinct possibility, but it would sound stupid to say so. I stayed on the porch, watching the twins walk down the lane and disappear into the open doors of the shop. I waited as long as I could stand it and then went after them.

I found my brothers where I expected them to be—in the tack room that doubled as Fulton's sleeping quarters. Giggling, the twins snooped around, touching this and poking that, settling finally on some saddle-bags beside the bed.

"Don't," I said, half pleading, my insides squirming around.

Nephi shoved me away and sneered. "You dared us. Anything happens, that makes it mostly your fault."

I watched with morbid fascination as they undid the buckles and opened the leather bags. Nephi pulled out a shirt, two leather pouches containing what appeared to be pistol cleaning items and battered copies of books my ma sometimes read, including Maturin's *Melmoth the Wanderer*, and Bronte's *Jane Eyre*. And, finally, a pistol. He held it up so Lehi and I could see.

I didn't know if it was the gun Fulton had used to kill Bukovski, but just the idea that it was one of Fulton's guns filled me with a familiar dread. "You better leave that alone."

"It's just a gun," Lehi snorted. "Don't be such a sissy."

Nephi pointed the gun at me. "Yeah. We shoot sissies." He reached up with a thumb and cocked the hammer.

At that exact moment, Fulton walked into the tack room carrying a saddle.

It was one of the things about Fulton that I never got used to—his ability to materialize as if right out of thin air. Despite his spurs and guns and full-grown size, he moved like a warm breeze. He was forever scaring the barn cats silly by nudging them with the toe of his boot when they didn't even know anyone was around.

I reckon all Fulton saw out of the corner of his eye was someone with a gun. He dropped the saddle and spun to the side. His own pistol was out, pointed and cocked before the saddle hit the ground. I doubt Nephi even saw Fulton move. One instant my brother was turning his porky head in surprise at being caught messing where he shouldn't have been, and in the next, the cold muzzle of a gun was pressed directly under his right eye. Probably nobody but Fulton and me ever knew just how close Nephi came to having his brains blown out. I saw Fulton catch the descending hammer of the pistol with his thumb, a hair away from snapping the cap that would have sent a bullet through Nephi's thick head. I don't know where my spit fled to, but my mouth was suddenly so dry that I couldn't even muster a swallow of fear.

In the instant that Fulton realized the nature of the threat and halted his reaction to it, I saw the reptilian cast in his eyes change to one of alarm. Just a flicker and it was gone. His eyes told me, however, that despite how effortless it had been for him to kill three soldiers, he would have regretted shooting Nephi.

"Gah," Nephi gagged when the gun muzzle touched his face. His skin went parchment white and his mouth fell open. The pistol dropped out of his nerveless hands.

I suspect Fulton was more mad about nearly shooting Nephi than he was about catching us in his stuff. He snatched his gun away from Nephi's face. At the same time, a flat hiss of fury came from behind the mask. The gun against his face must have scared Nephi bad. It did me. But it was the sound of Fulton's anger—evil and snake-like—that undid Nephi's nerve so completely that the front of his pants suddenly darkened as pee flooded over the tops of his shoes. Lehi, who had come nowhere as near to meeting Jesus as his brother, fled the tack room, leaving Nephi and me to face the wrath of Fulton.

I figured the least we'd get would be a flogging, or threats so bad they gave us nightmares for the rest of our lives. Instead, Fulton reached down and picked up the gun Nephi had dropped. He wiped off the dust with a rag and put it back in his bedroll. While he was occupied arranging his things, I reached over and got hold of Nephi's arm. Carefully, I steered him toward the door. It was hard because he acted like he was blind and his knees kept buckling.

"I'm sorry," I said to Fulton when we reached the door and some margin of safety. "They don't listen very well. I won't let them come around again."

Fulton didn't say a word. Except for the time he told me his name, I hadn't heard a peep out of him. He stood there watching us, waiting for what I don't know. Later, I came to understand that his behavior came more from not knowing what he should do in a given situation than from being indifferent. Rather than fidget or fret about what to do, he just waited to see how things developed. Just like after killing Snow, now he was waiting to see what calamity would befall him for nearly shooting Nephi.

I made sure nothing did. I didn't tell anyone what happened in the barn and neither did the twins. When we got back up to the brick house, I helped Nephi take a seat on the porch steps. Then I fetched a full bucket from the well and poured it into his lap, drenching him. Alva saw what I did and came out and yelled at me. I took the yelling because I couldn't think of anything to offer in my own defense. Things might have gotten out of hand if she'd seen that Nephi had wet his pants and went to pecking at him to find out why.

The soaking jarred Nephi more or less back into an operable frame of mind. At the very least, he was able to grasp that I'd saved him—both from Fulton and from at least a dozen extra doses of Red Jacket. He didn't do more than side with Alva, berating me for my plain meanness, when he could have really torn into me. I saw him look funny at me as Alva sent him into the house to change his drawers, like he didn't really know who I was anymore. It wouldn't be the last time someone looked at me like that, trying to figure out what connection there was between me and Fulton Lorings.

It had been nearly two weeks since he came to our farm, and despite the killing of Snow and the near murder of Nephi, our family still didn't know exactly what kind of a man Fulton was. If you didn't count shooting the soldiers, trying to knife the sheriff and bobbing Alva's duck, he had behaved admirably. We knew he was a rough sort, that he could be violent when pressed, even that he had dark secrets better left untouched, but we didn't really understand the dangerous extent of the man. We stayed blissfully ignorant until the day Pa asked Fulton to go to the freight depot and pick up a bucket of Dr. Tyler's Extraordinary Hoof and Horn Balm.

When Pa sent him, Fulton didn't act put out at being asked to do such a menial chore. He saddled up his wicked horse and rode off north toward town three miles away as calm as you please. To our knowledge, it was the first time he'd been off the farm since the army inquest. I think he was happy to go, although with Fulton it was hard to tell. Happy or sad, he only had one way of showing it. As I watched him ride off, grim as a one-man funeral, I wondered if it pleased him to get away from us for a while. Things had been a little strained lately.

Picking up some hoof balm was a common enough errand, but this time it had very uncommon results. Nothing was the same after that. There was no escaping it. After his errand to the freight office, news of who and what Fulton was swept the quiet valley like a hot wind full of poison. Men who saw and recognized our new hired hand that day must have felt their bones turn rotten with fear as death slipped, gray and mangy, past them.I didn't personally witness what happened, but I heard enough about it over the next few days to form a clear picture. Parts of it I pieced together from the things people said later.

Leaving our farm, Fulton followed the road past the Hoffenstetter dairy and along the Pettus cooperage. If not for the mask he wore, few of our Mormon neighbors would have paid him any mind. As it was, the ones Fulton did pass recognized him as Bishop Merrell's new hired man, the one who had saved Laurel Anne and me from the soldiers. If not grateful for the actual dispatching of Bukovksi, our neighbors were at least pleased with the rescue of Laurel Anne. They greeted Fulton politely, in some cases making it clear they wanted him to stop and accept their thanks. They got no reply for their troubles, not even the courtesy of a glance.

"He rode right by us like we weren't good enough to speak to," Sister Pettus complained later. "Plain rude, if you ask me."

"He knew I vas der," Otto said. "He chust didn't care to say hello."

"Peculiar," said the laconic Brother Knight.

Sister Pettus and Brother Hoffenstetter might have grumbled more over being snubbed if Fulton hadn't also passed Mr. Pinkerton's road gang. The fretting over his manners stopped when the gentiles got a look at him. After that, nobody in their right mind wanted Fulton even so much as glancing in their direction.

Most of us knew Mr. Pinkerton even though he was a gentile and didn't have much in the way of use for Mormons except when it came to making money. An Eastern-trained engineer, Mr. Pinkerton had finagled a contract with the army to keep the freight road graded between Traverse Mountain and Provo Canyon. We had all passed his road gang at one time or another, fifteen or twenty sweaty men—most of them gentiles needing a quick stake on their way to California or some other sin-ridden spot—swinging picks and shovels in the middle of the road.

Two miles from the depot, out where the Salt Lake road turns to start its climb over the Traverse Mountains, Fulton passed Mr. Pinkerton's gang like a bad dream. As with Sister Pettus and Brother Hoffenstetter, he didn't acknowledge the presence of the men in the road gang. I guess there wasn't anybody there he knew or cared to know. But there were men who knew him. Lord, yes.

Rupert Wicks, a Mormon, was part of the gang. He later spelled out what happened. At first, none of the men gave Fulton so much as a look when he rode by. Mr. Pinkerton's foreman was a man who liked to get as much work as he could out of his men and letting them wave at passing traffic wasn't the best way to get it.

Rupert said it was the foreman whose behavior stopped the work. He took one look at Fulton and turned the color of spoiled milk. Then he crossed himself like the papists do—not once but three times. "Mother of God," he squawked.

Without another word, the foreman moved off in a trot, leaving the survey gear and the crew. Rattled by the foreman's break in routine, the rest of the road gang followed after him, wanting to know what the trouble was.

The foreman kept trotting while he told them. "Boys," he said, "things have gone bad around here. You'd best pack it in and draw your pay. I hear they're looking for diggers out on the Humboldt."

"Leave? What for?" one of the men demanded. He was a new man, not yet comfortable with the foreman's authority. "This is a prime job. It'll plumb fix me for the winter."

The foreman looked cross but kept on walking fast. "There ain't no job that'll fix being dead."

"What's that supposed to mean?"

The foreman stopped. As the rest of the gang gathered around, he fixed the new man with a bleak look. "It means, Tulley, that you're so damn dumb you couldn't tell if it was raining rocks. I'm talking about the rider on that Injun horse."

"What of him," Tulley spat. "He the king of England or something? Looked like some road bum is all."

"That road bum," the foreman said with a deep breath, "was Red Legs."

A shiver ran through the road gang. The man named Tulley actually jumped, dropping his shovel. The foreman nodded sadly at the reaction. He looked west, toward California, or maybe China, someplace far away where it was safe. "I was a policeman once," the foreman said. He seemed in a trance. "More of a night watchman—back in Abilene, when they started bringing the big herds north in '67." He took a deep breath. "August the twenty-third."

"Damn, I heard tell—-" one of the gang started to say.

"That's right," the foreman replied. "I was in the Fat Dog Saloon the night Red Legs killed the Bar D crew."

Some of the gang, the well-informed ones, milled around. They flashed nervous looks up and down the road, trying to spot the fifth horseman of the Apocalypse who had casually trailed their personal eternities so close to them in broad daylight.

"I just stopped in to get out of the rain for a minute," the foreman continued, talking low. "I saw that fellow at the bar, wearing his mask and them reb cannon britches with stripes down the legs. I didn't guess it was Red Legs until it was too late. These four drovers were riding him for wearing a mask, laughing and squaring off like they wanted him to try and do something about it. They were just kids, fresh off of herding, full of whiskey and meanness. It was plain they were looking to have sport with somebody, only they didn't know who it was. One of them started it. Said if a man needed to wear a mask in a saloon, he must have a face like the ass-end of a steer." The foreman shuddered. "His back was to 'em when it was said, and them drovers had their hands on their pistols, but they were pressing him too close and so it didn't matter a damn. When Red Legs come around to face them, it was with that busted saber. "

"What happened?"

The foreman's face grew pale and sweaty with memory. Rupert told us later how the road gang could almost smell the blood in the foreman's words.

"It was like watching someone mow wheat," the foreman said in a whisper. "The first two boys went down with their throats open like water pumps. The third tried pulling his pistol, but got it tangled up when Red Legs let out his guts. The fourth one, a towhead boy, took it low and hard in the side. He screamed for his ma until morning. Not a shot fired by anyone."

"Lord," someone breathed.

"You was the law," someone else pointed out. "Didn't you do something?"

The foreman looked tired. "Yeah, Pete, I did. I watched it happen. Then I messed in my pants when Red Legs looked my way. He come close past me, the blood on him steaming from the cold. He went straight out into the rain and gone. The only people he left alive in that butcher shop was me and the barkeep and I've spent the last two years wondering why he bothered."

That evening, most of Mr. Pinkerton's road gang quit, the foreman included. They drew their pay, snatched up their belongings and disappeared into the night for parts unknown but far away. Mr. Pinkerton cussed plenty and offered double wages to the ones who stayed. The ones who did were the ignorant ones, men who couldn't bring themselves to believe the horrendous things they'd heard about the man with the ragged mask. But Mr. Pinkerton couldn't hang on to the smart ones, the ones who had sense and years they still wanted to enjoy.

The spread of fear might have ended there except that when Fulton stopped at the freight depot someone else recognized him. It was Mr. Bowthorpe, district manager of the Bunce & Edwards Freight Line. He was sitting at his desk doing the company ledgers when Fulton walked in to collect Pa's hoof balm. The clerk, a young kid, said Mr. Bowthorpe peered up, spotted Fulton at the counter and aged ten years in a single moment.

"Started shaking and sweating like he had the palsy," the clerk said later. "I filled the order and the feller left. But Mr. Bowthorpe, he just kept right on sitting there looking like he was fixing to die or something. I brought him some water and asked him was he all right."

Mr. Bowthorpe was not all right. A Union quartermaster sergeant during the war, he'd seen things that he could never forget while hauling army supplies through a burned-out Virginia. When he regained his power of speech, Mr. Bowthorpe clutched fearfully at his clerk's shirt and choked out two words that added speed to the spread of terror:

"Stuart's Wolf."

That was all the clerk got from him because Mr. Bowthorpe quit Bunce & Edwards that same afternoon, but not before he passed on the name of his nightmare to several freight drivers. An hour later, six drivers and three hostlers walked away from their jobs. Some of them passed our neighbors' places on their way to anywhere but here.

"It were him at Dinwiddie Courthouse in '65," a driver told Brother Pettus. "He brung down a railroad bridge and drowned nearly a whole New Jersey regiment when their train went into the river. Then he stood on the trestle and shot at the heads of the swimmers. He killed more'n two-hundred men that day."

"He was a one-man guerilla operation," said another. "Made Mosby and Quantrill look like schoolteachers. They say Yankee cavalry wouldn't patrol except in regiment strength when he was about."

"He killed General Pierpont in his own headquarters tent," an old hostler added. "Snuck past the pickets in a snowstorm and slit his gullet."

While us Mormons tried to sort out what it all meant, news of Red Legs and Stuart's Wolf became a runaway grass fire among the gentiles. It sped through the herder camps and the stock pens outside of town and descended like a stray curse of Moses on the tramp shanties and the huts down along the river where the squatters lived. Men coming into the valley heard the news and turned around, putting frightened miles between themselves and the place where hell had bobbed too near the earth's surface. In town, saloons emptied seconds after the name Stuart's Wolf was spoken aloud on Main Street. Men who knew of Stuart's Wolf and Red Legs babbled what they knew to those who didn't, glancing nervously over their shoulders as the did. Much of the legend was secondhand, bits and fragments of a horror too enormous and bloody for the average human being to comprehend.

"He killed Lee Jackman over them Sand Creek scalps," another said. "Red Legs put four balls in his face before Jackman even hit the ground."

"The Sioux call him Ghost Smiler. Fought with 'em against the Blackfeet in '68. Killed Chief Strong Mountain and ate his heart."

"Down Mexico they call him Sonria del Diablo, the devil's smile...could kill Mexes just by looking at 'em."

"He's butchered women and children. Little babies..."

If only a tenth of the things people said about him after that day were true, Fulton Lorings wasn't just a devil, he was the Devil. Those other names were just different ways of saying Beelzebub. It wasn't hard to believe any of it. If Jesus could come to Earth and walk around like a man, why not Satan?

The word eventually reached us Mormons. It was understandable that it reached us last. Gentiles were wiser to the ways of the outside world than we were. By and large they came to our valley from the goldfields, buffalo camps and rail yards, rough places where news of men like Fulton Lorings got passed word of mouth as a matter of survival. Mormons rarely heard of such things because we kept mostly to ourselves. We had little truck with gentile doings, believing we were safe enough here in the mountains if we just closed ourselves off and minded our own business. We liked to think we knew a lot about God, and maybe we did. But we were about to get an education in the devil.

Things were in a fair lather by the time Fulton returned home with the hoof balm. Gentiles were stampeding out of the valley like the Exodus of the Israelites while Mormons were gazing about in confusion at the dust. If Fulton knew the impact his presence had had on our community, he didn't let on. He passed over the hoof balm to Pa and went straight back to hammering away at the anvil in front of the forge as if nothing had happened.

Pa was some put out when he heard the news about Fulton and finally got around to understanding what it all meant. He wasn't about to ask Fulton to leave, though. No matter what he heard in the way of evil, Pa felt he always owed people a fair shake. And he owed Fulton more than fair for saving Laurel Anne and me from Bukovski. And aside from nipping Snow's head off, Fulton had behaved himself admirably. As long as he wasn't a clear danger to the family, our home would be open to him.

Alva thought different. She took in every black rumor, every shred of indecent information about people, and then made up her mind based on the worst of it. She told Pa straight out to get rid of Fulton. There was nothing Pa could say to change her mind. The bishop had little choice, Alva claimed. It was only a matter of time before Fulton either killed us all in our sleep or God revealed the truthfulness of her revelation to everyone in a dream. Either way, Alva said, Fulton had to go. The sooner the better.

"He's trash," Alva said. "What are people going to think if you keep that beast here? He's no longer welcome in my house and I want him gone from our farm altogether."

Pa said no. But it wasn't hard to tell that he was worried. That evening, he walked up to the cabin to talk to Ma. I just happened to be sitting inside an empty barrel nearby and so I heard the whole conversation. In spite of telling Alva that he wouldn't, Pa asked Ma if she thought he should run Fulton off. Even with my limited understanding of what kind of man Fulton was turning out to be, it seemed I had the dilemma figured more clearly than the grown ups. Namely, would Fulton go if Pa tried to run him off? I'd seen what happened to three men who tried to make the masked gunman leave when he didn't want to go.

Ma pointed out how Fulton hadn't done anything wrong. She said he was a good worker and honest and we should treat him accordingly, no matter what everybody else said. She pointed out how Pa already knew this himself.

"Confound it, Colleen," Pa said "You've heard the things they're saying about him. It's not what he's done but what he could do that's got me worried."

Ma sounded nonplussed. "And why does that only apply to people like Brother Lorings?"

Pa knew he was in for it because I heard him groan. "What are you talking about now?"

"Why doesn't that same logic apply to people like us? We're so worried about what he might do that we never get around to what we should be doing ourselves."

Pa groaned, knowing Ma was now going to put him through her brain wringer. When it came to talking to Ma, I don't think Pa minded being proved wrong nearly as much as he minded how hard it was to keep up with her in order to find out that he was.

"I'm saying that when it comes to being Christian, people seem more interested in the possibility of getting hurt themselves than they are in the possibility of hurting someone else. Brother Lorings deserves more from us than that. Except for the duck, Brother Lorings hasn't hurt or threatened a single member of this family. He's a good worker and he's polite. You'll notice that I haven't troubled you for wood in weeks."

"What's wood got to do with all this?"

"Brother Lorings cuts it for me. I go out every morning and the wood box is full. I expect Alva's is too. My advice is that we should be kind to him, treat him with respect instead of running him off. It just may be that no one has ever done that for him before. Remember, it wasn't Brother Lorings who attacked Laurel Anne and Rose, it was Bukovski. And none of the busybodies talking about running Brother Lorings off ever tried running Bukovski off."

"I suppose," Pa allowed. "But I'd feel better if there was some way to talk to Brother Lorings about all this. I sorely wish he could speak. I'd like to know exactly what his intentions are."

"There's something else," Ma said.

"What?"

"Johnny's vision."

"Colleen, please," Pa said, exasperated. "You can't mean that Brother Lorings is—"

I plugged my ears and started to hum. There was no way I wanted to listen to them talk about my dead brother right now. It hurt too bad to think on it.

When I finally unstopped my ears, Ma and Pa were done talking. Pa had gone off to wrestle with whatever it was that his strange Irish wife had said. It must not have taken long because he went back down to the brick house that evening and told Alva that Fulton was staying and he'd be obliged if she'd stop caterwauling about it. Alva went up to her room in a huff, leaving Pa to get his own supper.

The next couple of days were uneventful. Fulton minded his own business down at the forge. He was polite when approached for good reason, but his general demeanor left you with the clear impression that he'd much rather be alone. He remained as cold and gray as a winter day.

Fulton's effect on me was odd as well. While I was a committed and unrepentant cynic on nearly everything else, I was entirely optimistic about our wicked hired hand. I figured that given time, Fulton might get to where he didn't mind being around us. Eventually, he might even want to open up more and be our friend. But I was young and stupid. I didn't yet realize that the one thing good people never give men like Fulton is time.

Like it says in the scriptures: there has to be opposition in all things. I guess that's why that even though reasonable folks were stampeding their way out of our valley because of Red Legs, there were men with feverish eyes who would come slouching down into it for the very same reason.

Blood.

Chapter Four

Two days later, Fulton killed a man named French Pete. Pa, Fulton and Cletus were working on the stock pens behind the barn when it happened, short-tempered and sweaty as they dug new post holes to expand the pens. It was pick and shovel work under a blazing sun. I lugged buckets of water for them.

Although it was a chore to haul water, I did it this time without my usual complaining because it was the best way to stay close to Fulton in case he said something else. He hadn't uttered a word since the day I took him his breakfast. But now that I knew he could talk, I wanted to be there if he did it again. I didn't want to miss whatever secrets were locked behind that blue scarf.

Pa worked with the studied pride of ownership. Everything he did was built to last and so he was careful and deliberate. For Cletus, who had been a slave before the war, work was something that had to be done. Although he worked hard and earned his pay, he talked a constant stream while he worked, paying little real attention to what he was doing. For Fulton, work was just another way to do battle. He furiously attacked every job placed before him, knocking out more work than both Cletus and Pa together.

"I reckon I ain't been this warm since before the war in Georgia," Cletus was saying. He dipped the cup in the bucket and handed it to Fulton who took it and turned away. Shielded from our eyes, he took a long careful drink, adjusted the scarf and handed the cup back. Cletus studied it for fang marks or something before giving it to me to refill.

"No, suh," Cletus continued on. "That Georgia sun be a man killer. I sho' be reminded of Mistuh Sun right now..."

Cletus sort of trailed off because nobody was listening to him anymore. Fulton had stopped digging and was staring down our lane. I followed his gaze to where the lane intersected the town road. A dark man sat on a horse in the shade of some trees.

I put my hand up to shield my eyes from the sun. It wasn't unusual for people to loiter at the end of our lane. Folks coming and going from Pa's shop often stopped under the trees there to pass the time. Laurel Anne's beaus frequently waited there, hoping to catch a glimpse of her picking flowers, brushing her hair or even just going out to use the privy. In fact, many of them volunteered to do extra errands that led them past our farm on the off chance they might spot her. But this wasn't the case today. For one thing, the man was older than any of Laurel Anne's beaus—except for Wilbur Nielsen who was sixty-five and in the market for a fourth wife. Also, I'd never seen this man before. Finally and worst of all, he was wearing a gun in the same casual yet prominent way Fulton wore his.

Pa apparently sensed something was up because his own gaze traveled back and forth between Fulton and the waiting man, trying to put a connection together.

"You know him?" Pa asked.

Fulton nodded. His hand came up and a thumb casually touched a pistol.

"Lawd, I just got me some bad feelins," Cletus said. He dropped his shovel. Then he reached over and collared me, dragging me behind him.

When it became apparent to the waiting man that we were watching him, he put his heels to the horse and came up our lane slow and cautious. An involuntary shiver went through me as I watched him move along. It was like watching a snake sew its way through dry grass toward you. I was becoming more in tune with the emotions that accompanied these stormy meetings and I had to almost physically resist the mental image of a dark and safe place under my bed.

The man who rode into our pens wore a charcoal gray suit over a
starched white shirt. Sunlight sparkled from a large ring on his hand. His
boots were polished to a high buff and a silver buckle flashed sunlight
from his belly. He looked more dapper than even Eldon Bair, and infinitely more dangerous. He drew up, eyes black as anthracite flitting to
each of us in turn.

"Good day," he said, his accent thick but understandable. He leaned
forward and made a poor attempt at a smile. "Do you peoples know who
I am?"

"Don't you?" I asked. I wasn't trying to be smart. It just sort of leaked
out. Cletus squeezed my shoulder, cautioning me.

The man gave me a look containing all the warmth of a glance from
a buzzard. "She makes good joke, *non?*" he chuckled coldly. His smile
disappeared as he indicated Fulton with a long finger. "I have some business with zees man. The sheriff in town he tell me where to find him."

Pa cleared his throat. "What kind of business?"

The cheery facade faltered. The man turned his oiled head to Pa. "Are
you his moth hair?"

Moth hair? It took me a minute to understand the man's crazy accent.
He was really asking if Pa was Fulton's mother.

Pa shook his head. "This is my place. What goes on here is my concern. Who are you and what do you want?"

"I am French Pete," the man said, obviously expecting us to recognize
the name. "And zees farm will be your grave if you interfere. I am a ver'
dangerous man, *n'est-ce pas?*

"We're all Christians here, Brother Pete," Pa protested. "We don't want
any trouble." I rolled my eyes behind closed lids. Pa was a good man, but
he had a hard time with some things. I was only ten but already knew that
trouble never needed anyone to want it in order for it to pay a visit.

"Chreestians?" French Pete scoffed. He threw back his head and
laughed, a dead sound in the bright afternoon. "No, no. What would
Chreestians be doing with him?" He indicated Fulton with another flick
of a finger. "No, Red Legs is no Chreestian. He is the *diable*. He stabbed .
a look at our hired hand, a look so black it killed hope. "Hey, Hash Face,
are you going to hide behind thees big bastard?"

Hash Face?

"You kill my brother, Hash Face," French Pete continued, all the false
merriment gone out of his voice. "Now I kill you, *non?*"

Fulton didn't reply. He continued to stare impassively at French Pete, waiting. Despite the sun, ice gathered around my heart.

"I am growing impatient with you, Hash Face," French Pete spat. "I hear about the soldiers, eh?" He made a pistol with his thin finger. "Boom, boom, boom. So I come on the train." He indicated the tree-lined creek with a slight nod of his groomed head. "We go there, or we stay here where the neegar and the *fille* can watch. But we do it now, ugly man. Today you die."

I looked at Fulton. His lifeless eyes had come alive again. The malice in them made me sick to my stomach. French Pete beamed and jumped off his horse with the sinuous grace of a weasel. He tossed the reins at Cletus and straightened his coat.

"*Bon*, I am ready."

"Now wait just a minute," Pa growled. He reached out to catch Fulton's arm, but our silent hired hand was the devil man again. He shook Pa's big hand off. The look he gave us sent me ducking back behind Cletus.

When I dared peek around, Fulton and French Pete were walking side by side in the direction of the creek. Pa opened and closed his big hands in silent frustration as he watched them go. Cletus was muttering something. I recognized a prayer.

"Lord Jesus, amen," he finished. He looked at us with enormous eyes. "God o' mercy, Brother Merrell. Don't know 'bout you, but I always believed there be only one Lucifer."

"Pa?" I said, wanting him to do something. "Pa, you got to stop them."

"Hush, girl," Cletus said, putting a hand on my head. "Ain't nothing to be done now."

Fulton and French Pete disappeared, swallowed by the trees.

We waited for a small eternity, helpless as three people could be. The flow of time slowed to a numbing syrup while my heart fluttered high in my chest like a trapped sparrow.

From the direction of the creek came the sound of three shots—two close together and one off by itself, almost a lazy afterthought—each punching a hole in the warm fabric of the afternoon. I had some experience with that horrible, breathless pause between shots. I had a pretty good idea that if I ran down into the trees I'd find French Pete with a new hole in his face.

Fulton reappeared, walking toward us. He kept flicking his left hand in a distracted manner. I let out my breath, unaware that I'd been holding it. Our dangerous hired hand came up through the hoppers and the black-eyed Susans with a loose stride, never looking back toward the creek. When he reached us he stopped and waited for Pa to pronounce sentence on him. There was no apology in his eyes, no remorse in his bearing. He was what he was and didn't care who knew it.

"You're hurt," Pa said, finally.

It was then I noticed a bright web of blood clinging to Fulton's fingers. I followed it up into the cuff of his shirt to a small, soppy patch of red at the top of his shoulder. Fulton looked at it and shrugged, as if to indicate it wasn't much by way of bullet wounds. If ever there was an expert on that sort of thing, I guess it was Fulton.

Pa shook his head, struggling to cope with things beyond his pale. He motioned to me. "Budge, take Mr. Lorings up to the cabin and have your mother tend to him. Cletus and I will take care of"—he glanced wearily at the creek—"everything down here." Sadly, he beckoned to Cletus and together they headed toward the creek, French Pete's horse ambling along behind.

I didn't know what to say. After some hesitation I motioned for Fulton to follow me. We silently climbed the slope up to the cabin. Fulton was as docile as a dog now, his eyes bleak and empty like pond ice, all the venom in him temporarily spent.

Ma had heard the shots and her keen Irish intuition told her that it wasn't hunters potting sage hens in our fields. Water was already heating on the stove and her doctor stuff was laid out on the table. A rainbow of apothecary jars filled with tinctures and herbs waited to be pressed into service. Fulton took off his hat and bowed his head in respect. Ma glanced at his bloody shoulder and motioned him inside.

"Sit there, Brother Lorings," she said, indicating a low stool. Taking down clean rags from the shelf above the stove, she began tearing them into strips. Instead of sitting down like Ma said, Fulton paused and surveyed our crammed bookshelves.

"After we've taken care of your shoulder," Ma said, "you may look at the books. Now, please, sit. You're much too tall for me to do this otherwise."

Fulton sat and Ma moved around behind him. Watchful as a wolf, gray eyes swiveled back and forth between the corners of Fulton's skull. I went to the stove and fidgeted, pretending to take part in the doctoring but in reality just sticking close in order to indulge a morbid curiosity.

"You shall have to take off your shirt," Ma said.

Fulton didn't like that and he started to stand up. Ma tried to get him to stay seated by putting one hand on his uninjured shoulder, too near the blue scarf covering his face.

Fulton jerked away with a hiss. The air in the room grew thick and hard to breathe again. My heart scrambled around my insides as I backed up against the table. Ma lowered her hands. She took a deep breath and stared a furious Fulton straight in the eye without flinching, the first person I'd seen do that.

If she was afraid, Ma didn't show it. She spoke calmly. "Brother Lorings, listen to me. I'm the closest thing we have to a doctor. I'm also a married woman. I've seen quite a bit of the male anatomy, sir. Your shirt is filthy and I cannot work through it. It will have to come off or the wound will become infected. Please sit down. I assure you, we won't move the cloth around your—neck."

Cautiously, not liking it a bit, Fulton sat back down. He hesitated and then began unhooking the buttons on his shirt. Ma helped him out of it, careful not to let her hands stray anywhere close to his scarf.

He was appalling. Ma may have seen quite a bit of the male anatomy, but judging from the look on her face it had never been anything like this. Fulton's chest, back and most of his left shoulder were cross-hatched with vicious scars, as if he had once earned a living sorting bears and wildcats. The marks were deep, slick furrows and rips in the curly hair on his upper chest. They angled unnaturally across the ropey muscle of his shoulder and up where they disappeared under the scarf. It hurt my insides to imagine what that ragged blue cloth was hiding. His ribs looked like slats in a fence while his lean belly was all sucked in like a starved dog's. The bullet hole was a black-rimmed pucker in the twisted skin at the very top of his shoulder. Eventually it too would be a scar, stacked on top of the others. More than a dozen of these healed puckers speckled his chest and back.

Ma recovered first. It was only after I saw Fulton gazing steadily at me that I realized my own mouth was hanging open. I shut it with a click of teeth and he lowered his brutal gaze to the floor.

Ma worked quickly. Using one of her knitting needles boiled in water on the stove, she poked a scrap of cloth soaked in a comfrey tincture straight through the hole in Fulton's shoulder. He didn't even flinch as the needle skewered him. He continued to stare at the floor as if the bloody shoulder belonged to someone else. With his scarf-wrapped face he looked like a cross between a sinister circus freak and a visiting sultan.

Though not a regular doctor, Ma had fixed or cured hundreds of folks. Most recently she had saved Minnie Fletcher's baby when it was born backwards, something everyone agreed was near enough a miracle. She also doctored Solomon Pope after his leg got mangled in a thresher. Brother Pope still limped, but at least he could walk on it. When she couldn't save a freighter's foot after it turned black and green and started sending angry streaks up his leg, Ma had even helped old Doc Babbitt saw it off. But the most interesting cure she performed, at least of the ones I got to see, was extracting a fishhook from the inside of Willie Hofenstetter's nose. How Willie got the hook up there he never said, but he sure enough had a lot to say about it coming out. You never heard such howling in your life. There wasn't much Ma couldn't do when it came to afflictions of bones and innards and birthing. And although many thought her odd, plenty of folks came from miles about to have Bishop Merrell's second wife take a gander at their ailments.

This time, Ma skipped her usual attempts at comfort. I reckon she knew the most comfortable thing for Fulton was to finish quick and stop touching him. She was almost done when a shadow fell across the floor. I looked up and saw Laurel Anne standing in the doorway. "Father said Mr. Lorings was injured."

At the sound of my sister's voice, Fulton, whose view of the door was blocked by Ma, looked stricken. His gray eyes blossomed with distress. He would have gotten up, knitting needle through his wound or not, but Ma pushed his good shoulder down, gently but firmly. Trapped, Fulton clutched the ragged shirt to his scars and peered at Laurel Anne out of the corner of one eye. She stood behind him and helped Ma prepare a poultice to stick on his new bullet hole.

Since whacking on him with the broom for killing Snow, Laurel Anne hadn't said two words to Fulton. And since everyone had started talking about him being the infamous Red Legs, she avoided him completely. She stayed away from the barn and never carried Cletus's lunch down to the dig when Fulton might be there. Part of it was that ladies like Laurel Anne didn't associate with the likes of Stuart's Wolf, not if they wanted to hang on to their reputations. However, I think it was Fulton's own reputation that mostly did it. When it came to matters of men, Laurel Anne was accustomed to the high advantages of her beauty. It made men weak and foolish. But those were normal men, rational creatures whose worlds turned on the whims and moods of my sister.

Fulton was anything but normal. Certainly Laurel Anne had little experience with his kind. It was one thing to coyly torment idiots like Henry Dupont and Eldon Bair and another to try it with a man so unconcerned about killing folks as this one. Of course no one, least of all Laurel Anne, yet understood the effect she had on Fulton. We certainly didn't know that his bloody deeds of late, while alarming to us, actually constituted remarkable restraint on his part. There were some people still alive for no other reason than my sister's blue eyes and the sound of her voice.

Perhaps her thinking was that a wounded Fulton was a more manageable Fulton. After all, bullet holes tend to slow most people down. It's the only reason I could imagine why Laurel Anne would come up to the cabin. But standing there looking down at Fulton's vast experience with bullet holes, Laurel Anne must have been having second thoughts. Her eyes grew wide at his scars. She held the bandage while Ma applied the poultice.

"Another man is dead," Laurel Anne said to no one in particular, but solemnly, as if the world suffered intolerably from the loss of French Pete. "When will it stop? The holy scriptures say—"

I cut her off. "He called Cletus a nigger and Pa a bastard." Both, according to the law of Rose Lee Merrell, were excellent reasons to be shot and I said so.

Laurel Anne reached over and boxed my ears. She was distracted enough so that it didn't hurt much but it made me mad as hell. I started off to kick her a good one, but Fulton put out a hand and shook his head. Laurel Anne continued, unaware that her shins had been spared by the same man she was bullyragging.

"I suppose that's the way things are in other places," she continued, "but we're Mormons. We don't hold with violence. People who know anything about us know we came out to this wilderness to be free from just that sort of thing."

Fulton didn't say anything. He sat with his shirt covering his scars as best he could and let the women fiddle about some more on his shoulder. Whereas he had been as indifferent as a statue when Ma rammed her knitting needle into him, a thin sheen of perspiration had now broken out across his brow. Every few seconds his fingers would stray up to the scarf on his face, reassuring himself that his secret remained safe behind the faded cloth.

"There are other ways to resolve differences," Laurel Anne said, cross because she wasn't getting any response from Fulton. She was used to men paying attention to her. It galled her not to be able to steer this one around with her opinion. "Civilized ways. Good heavens, everyone knows violence never solves anything."

I curled a lip in disgust, wanting to point out that violence settled some issues just fine. Unless he met up with some in hell, Bukovski wouldn't be bothering any more fillies—horses or Mormon. Laurel Anne gave me a warning look and continued her naive lecture. I sat on a chair and fumed. She had no call to lecture Fulton. Ma remained silent, tending to her business, a faint smile on her face as if amused by Laurel Anne's peevish lecture.

Finally, they finished doctoring Fulton. Uncoiling from the chair, he carefully drew on his shirt. The collar brushed the scarf causing it to slip a little bit. I saw another inch of scar below his left eye. Laurel Anne saw it, too.

"Oh, your..." she started to say, reaching out to touch the scarf.

If God blinked he wouldn't have seen Fulton move either. Common mortals, we never even came close to seeing it. Laurel Anne yipped with surprise when an iron hand trapped her wrist. Menace danced in the room again like a crazy witch. While I couldn't say for sure about Ma and Laurel Anne, I now had the idea down just fine that the tiniest peek under that scarf would be worth a person's life. Fulton let go of Laurel Anne's hand and backed up a step.

"Well, I never," Laurel Anne said, unnerved. "I was only trying to help." Furious, she whirled and went to the door, pausing to get in a last shot. "Sorry to have troubled you." she said, her face white with anger. She waited for him to apologize or fidget the way other men did when she spoke that way to them. When he didn't, she flung herself out the door and stormed down the slope to the brick house.

Fulton watched her go as he buttoned his shirt. Then he looked at Ma and nodded his thanks.

"You're most welcome," Ma said.

Fulton glanced once at me and started for the door. He was almost through it when Ma called to him.

"Brother Lorings?"

Fulton paused without turning around.

"It's a hard thing, to be sure," Ma said gently, "but some people can be trusted."

Fulton didn't reply. We watched him walk catlike through the field back to the barn, with the sun banging fire out of his yellow hair.

"Such a hurt man," Ma said.

Personally, I didn't see it that way. All the things I'd seen Fulton do were injurious to others. He'd been cut up some himself, judging from the scars, but in the short time he'd been with us he had definitely given better than he got. Except maybe when it came to Laurel Anne.

"It doesn't figure, Ma," I said as she cleaned up the bloody bandages and jars. "Laurel Anne was so mean to Mr. Lorings and he never did anything about it. He just sat there and let her rag him. If anybody else said those things to him they'd sure be sorry."

Ma smiled knowingly. I asked her why Fulton had let Laurel Anne boss him around without killing her or at the least beating her senseless.

"He's starved for the attention of a woman," Ma said. "So much so that he was willing to have one yell at him rather than ignore him. Laurel Anne was paying attention to him, dear, even though she was hard on him. Sure and I think Brother Lorings has been alone for so long that he can't tell the difference anymore."

It sounded farfetched. What would someone like Fulton care about an empty-headed valley princess? Even though I loved her, Laurel Anne was the most spoiled person I knew. I went over and sat down on my bed.

Through our window, I watched Fulton. He reached the pens and began furiously driving the pick bar into the ground again, a cyclone of effort oblivious to his wound. By the time Cletus came back from helping Pa deliver French Pete's corpse to town, Fulton would have the rest of the holes dug and the posts lugged out from the side of the barn. Any evidence of the killing had been pushed into the shadowy wings of his mind. Cletus told us later that the bullet wound didn't slow him down a bit, as if Fulton was incapable of feeling pain.

Ma made me stay inside the rest of the day. Although she was firmly on Fulton's side, she wanted to keep an eye on me until things settled down. So, while she fussed with her remedies and tonics, I read to her from a new book titled *The Innocents Abroad* by a man named Twain.

Reading was my special gift from Ma. I would later be grateful for the grace of her looks and the sharpness of her mind, but it was the reading that I was truly thankful for as a child. She unlocked the world to me by giving me books. My favorites were those penned by burning imaginations: *Beowulf, Jason and the Golden Fleece,* Sir Thomas Malory's *Le Morte D'Arthur* and Walter Scott's *Ivanhoe.* They all kept me from dying of boredom on our farm.

Mr. Twain's book was good, but I wasn't feeling particularly humorous tonight. I asked Ma if we could switch instead to Shakespeare. I opened the big book at random. The luck of the draw was Othello.

What I read to Ma next might have been simple coincidence. I like to think not. I believe it was Jesus who put me on to Othello that night, even though there are parts of it that old William will have to do some fast explaining for come the Judgement Bar. The "beast with two backs" part always got me thinking about the unattractive and disturbing human mechanics of making squeaks. Described that way, it didn't sound nice at all.

While Ma filled her jars and brewed her tonics, I skipped ahead and read aloud. Eventually I came to a part that puzzled me.

"Base men being in love have then a nobility in their natures more than is native to them." I looked up, confused. "Ma? What does that mean, 'base men'? Is it evil men?"

Ma nodded through the toil-and-trouble steam of a dandelion tonic. "Or perhaps men who don't know any better," she said.

I thought for a minute. "Like Brother Lorings?"

"Maybe. It wouldn't be right to judge him just yet, in spite of what we've heard. He might be better than any of us know." She smiled at me. "It's possible for people to make men base, dear. If Brother Lorings is a bad man, I don't think he was always that way. Someone helped make him bad."

"You mean people like French Pete and Bukovski?"

"Perhaps. But even people like our neighbors can hurt others. Good people don't always do good things. They become frightened or confused and they do harm to others in the name of good. Brother Lorings doesn't know how to behave around us and that tells me he doesn't trust us yet. People like us have hurt him before, I wager. Maybe without meaning to."

People like us. That got me thinking harder. I considered Josh Van Orden. Everyone knew that his ma beat him awful. Pinch Face said Josh had the natural inclinations of his absent pa, and it was her job to see that he didn't succumb to them. So I guess strapping him was her way of trying to make him behave so that he could make it to the Celestial Kingdom, though I had serious doubts about the effectiveness of such a routine. Strapping people didn't make them behave better any more than tormenting them in other ways. Kids at school liked to poke fun at Josh. At that moment, something else occurred to me. What was the name French Pete had called Fulton? Hash Face?

Just then, I remembered a song we sang at school while skipping rope, a mindless ditty serving no purpose other than to mark time while you jumped. Elizabeth Crenshaw taught it to us when she moved here from Wyoming. There were several verses, most of which recounted the activities of a bloodthirsty killer.

Hash Face, Hash Face has two guns.
He shoots people just for fun.
If you see him you will cry;
Oh, dear Lord, I'm gonna die.
Hash Face, Hash Face has a knife
For to take your precious life.
He comes creeping in the night
To give the ladies such a fright.

I suddenly wanted to cry. Was Fulton that Hash Face? I didn't know for sure, but I thought so because sitting there on the bed with the heavy book in my lap, I felt ashamed for every time I'd sung it without thought. Like Ma said, it was possible to hurt people without meaning to. What was it that had hurt Fulton so bad?

Along about evening, I went outside and sat in my tree. I saw Pa come back with Sheriff Jewkes. They talked briefly with Fulton, no doubt trying to settle the latest killing. Apparently it was a case of self-defense because Sheriff Jewkes rode away a short time later. I wondered how much it bothered him to see Fulton alive, considering that it was him who pointed French Pete in the direction of our farm. I stayed up in my tree until the sun went down and Ma called me in for supper.

That night before bed, I told Ma I had to use the privy. It was only half of a lie. I finished my business quick and then crept down to the barn where I really spied on Fulton for the first time. Normally I wouldn't have dared venture such a thing in the night with someone like him, but I was desperate to see his face and learn more about the black prince who loved and feared my sister.

I climbed the ladder and made it to my perch before he returned from shutting down the shop and seeing to the stock. High above him, I huddled close in the dry embrace of the hay and waited. Mice skittered in the loft, making me jump.

Fulton came in presently, carrying a lantern. In the flat harsh light he looked sharp and bone thin, honed down by years of living on death's razor edge. He stripped off his shirt and unbuckled his guns. Ma's bloody bandage was still stuck to his shoulder. His eyes went around the tack room and I held my breath, certain he would see me in my elevated roost and maybe come for me with his sword knife. Instead, he sat down and leaned back against some feed sacks. One of the barn cats came over and hopped into his lap. Fulton rubbed its ears until it curled up and began to purr. From his pocket Fulton removed a bit of string or something and twined it reverently through his fingers. A look of naked yearning filled his dead eyes. It took me a minute before I recognized the pink ribbon he took from Laurel Anne's hair on the Provo road. He held the ribbon up to the light of the lantern and regarded it for a long moment. Then he touched it to his nose and closed his eyes. A gentle humming filled the silent barn, a remarkably clear waltz, soft and sweet and full of longing. For a scant second, a bare flicker of my young brain, I could almost see Fulton in a ballroom full of taffeta and lace and violins, liquid eyes watching every move of his straight shoulders. It was an intimate moment, as if our hired hand had opened his heart like a purse and spilled its cryptic secrets all over the floor. After all my hours of mystery spying, after all the scolding I'd received for violating the privacy of others, I felt ashamed for the very first time. I crept away from the loft silently, considering the extent of my violation and what it had done to me.

When I reached the bottom of the ladder, I heard a noise. From inside the barn came a guttural sound. I fancied it the cough of one of Dan Castello's tigers. My hair stood on end as I waited to be eaten. There in the smothering darkness of the night, with my heart leaping hysterically against my ribs, I learned two things that I have never forgotten. They were hard burdens for a young girl.

The first was that the sound I heard from the tack room was the suppressed sob of a tormented beast, not the snarl of a killer. The second was that hell is not like they say in the Bible: a fiery, noisy place where sinners get tortured eternally by shrieking demons. No, sir. Hell is a silent place, as black and deep as night, as cold as the lean belly of winter, a place where the damned wrestle against the embrace of an eternal lover called Hopelessness.

I took my first conscious step toward womanhood that night. With my innocence slipping away from me there in the dark, I realized that beneath his invulnerable exterior, and despite the weapons of destruction he wore as instinctively as most people wear their noses, our dreadful hired hand was dying one night at a time of loneliness.

Sheriff Jewkes couldn't leave well enough alone. Not all of it was his fault, however. After hearing the awful things going around about Fulton, folks were in a fair lather to have him gone. They started pestering Sheriff Jewkes, saying they didn't want Fulton's kind around. I have to admit that I didn't entirely blame them. The things I'd already seen and heard about Fulton had cost me a lot of sleep.

On the other side of things, Sheriff Jewkes now had Pa furious at him for sending French Pete in the direction of our farm. Although Pa claimed he was a peace-loving Latter-day Saint elder who bore no man except a Missourian any ill will, he was still no one to have mad at you. I once saw him knock our mule Pilate clean off his feet with a punch to the side of his hammer-shaped head after the mule kicked the spokes out of a buggy wheel for nothing more than the pure sake of orneriness. Afterward, Pa's hand swole up big and red. Ma had to wrap it in a poultice for him. But it took our dumb mule an hour to regain his feet and the better part of a week before he stopped shivering whenever Pa came near him.

I guess that's why Sheriff Jewkes took it to heart when Pa said that if he sent anymore gunmen out to our farm looking for Fulton, he'd personally come into town and work the sheriff's fat neck like a rusty pump handle. The sheriff blustered a lot and told Pa that laying hands on the law would only get him locked up in the territorial prison. Maybe, Pa replied, but his being locked up wouldn't fix the sheriff's neck.

All this really meant was that Sheriff Jewkes had to be crafty about getting rid of Fulton. He wasn't up to facing Fulton straight on himself, not after what had happened when he tried to arrest him the first time. As much as I didn't like Sheriff Jewkes, I didn't blame him for being afraid of Fulton. Nobody was willing to be his deputy when it came to arresting Fulton or running him off.

It probably would have been easy for a sheriff to find a reason to arrest Fulton. It wouldn't have taken anything more than a telegram to someplace where he was wanted for something. But if Sheriff Jewkes ever tried to find out if Fulton was wanted, he never let on. I personally think he didn't even bother asking around. If he had, he would have been duty bound to arrest Fulton—and get killed in the process. Sheriff Jewkes was a coward but he was no idiot. It would have to be something sneaky and low.

That something came the very next day when two strangers arrived in Lehi City and started asking about Fulton. Josh Van Orden saw them. He told me later that the two men were bearded and rough looking. They carried rifles and saloon-hopped around until they picked up what they wanted to know about Fulton. Then they went to see Sheriff Jewkes.

Mindful of what Pa had said about his neck, Sheriff Jewkes craftily pointed the men in the direction of Slobber Bob's saloon. It was sound reasoning. Those infrequent times that Fulton left our farm, Bob's was the only place for miles around where he stood even a remote chance of being welcome. Rumor was that Fulton and Bob had even forged a kind of kinship, which, if everything that was said about Fulton was true, probably meant that Fulton didn't kill Bob for just talking to him or getting in the way of something he was looking at.

Rowley Washburn saw what happened at Bob's that night. So did a dozen other men, but Rowley was the only one willing to talk about it. He blabbed it around Pettus's cooperage the very next day, speaking in a hushed, strangled voice you'd expect out of someone who'd seen something incomprehensible and terrifying. Josh Van Orden passed it on to us.

Following the sheriff's advice, the two men went to Slobber Bob's and camped in the trees next to the ramshackle brewery. At the time, no one knew they were looking for Fulton to kill him. Judging from their rough appearance, some of the other saloon-goers worked out the theory that the two were part of Hash Face's gang, come to perpetrate some foul deed with their infamous leader. Except for the foul deed part, it wasn't even close to the mark.

Two nights later, Fulton went to Bob's and sat alone at a table as he always did—which wasn't odd seeing as how his presence was usually enough to empty a place. A few men, the suicidal ones, crowded the other half of Bob's, keeping their distance from the man who sat alone and tinkered with his pistols or stropped his sword knife on a piece of soft leather. No one ever saw him drink any of the liquor Bob fetched to him or heard any of the things Bob and he communicated to each other through vague mutterings.

On this particular night, however, the Carters were waiting for Fulton. They'd been sitting at a table and drinking beer, coldly surveying the regular crowd. They kept their rifles on the table, which more or less gave everyone the idea that they weren't interested in company.

The person they were interested in arrived as they knew he eventually would. Nor was it hard to recognize him when he did. Fulton was the only man who wore a highwayman's mask the way most men wore a hat, except that he never took it off. He came into the saloon and sat down at his table. Bob fetched him over a glass of liquor and then left him alone. Fulton sat there stropping his knife, waiting.

He looked up when the two men got to their feet, dragging their rifles with them. They took a couple of steps toward him, pointing their rifles at him. The big one said, "We're the Carters, you murdering sonuva—."

Nobody ever learned why the Carters thought Fulton was a sonuvabitch, or what it was he'd done to cause them to come hunting him. Before Carter Number One finished his announcement, the brass handle of Fulton's half-saber was sticking out of his right eye socket, the red cord hanging down over his stunned face like some crazy wattle on a turkey. The rifle in his hands went off, the bullet plowing a splintered hole in the table as he fell on his back.

Carter Number Two stood no more of a chance than Number One. With a feminine shriek, he tried to bring his rifle to bear. Too slow. Fulton snatched out a pistol and shot him in the center of his terrified face. The muzzle flash set Carter Number Two's beard afire. He slammed down onto the floor next to his brother, both dead as a couple of Romans.

Keeping his pistol ready for anyone else who wanted to challenge him, Fulton put a boot on Carter Number One's face and yanked his sword knife out of the dead man's eye with a wet, popping sound that made Lucas Durrant, a hard-rock miner and former soldier, faint like a schoolgirl. Rowley said Lucas spilled out of his chair as loose as Saturday's linen, banging his head off the table and chair on the way to the floor.

Fulton cleaned his sword knife on one of the Carters' shirts, waiting through a dozen heartbeats to see if anyone was going to object. When nobody said a word, he stepped over the dead men and walked through the door. He nodded once to Slobber Bob and put some coins on the counter.

"I ain't never seen nothing like that," Rowley said. "Didn't matter a speck that them two had guns ready on him. Hash Face killed them Carters like me and you'd swat bugs."

Sheriff Jewkes disappeared as soon as word spread about the killing. The next morning, when someone stopped by the sheriff's office to complain about a missing cow, Sheriff Jewkes's badge was on his desk and all his personal things were gone. He wasn't about to wait around for Fulton to come looking for him. We never saw him again.

As much as I disliked Sheriff Jewkes for other things, I had to admire him for his common sense. Even though he was roundly condemned by the folks in Lehi City for running off, I personally thought Jewkes's midnight flight for distant parts was one of the most sensible things I had ever seen anyone do.

But there were still a few people around too stupid or too stubborn to know any better, people who insisted on pushing the limits of Fulton's scant tolerance, people who thought they were special or bulletproof. People like me.

Chapter Five

The next day was a smother of wet heat. To the west, over the Oquirrh Mountains, a storm slowly gathered dark skirts. The valley lay flat and sweaty, waiting. Pa sent Fulton off with Cletus to dig some on the canal.

With Fulton absent, boredom returned full force to our farm. Feeling oppressed, and with nothing better to do, I skipped barefoot down to the barn to watch Pa lance Sheldon McDermott's boil.

I climbed the outside ladder into the loft and crept over to my usual perch. Pa's victims were already present, Sheldon and Fred Dirkin who needed a tooth pulled. A half dozen men formed an audience. Most of them had left chores to follow Sheldon out from town, his agony visible in the dirty poultice glued to an infected neck. There's nothing like a good boil lancing to get folks together and give them a reason to put aside work.

While Pa got ready, the topic of conversation centered naturally around our hired hand. Understandable, since the unexpected death rate of our community had more than tripled. Brother Hoffenstetter was there with two of his sons. The burly German dairyman was questioning

Pa's judgement in letting Fulton stay on our farm.

"I fault no man just for vanting the use of a goot stud horse or a ditch to be dug," Hoffenstetter said, watching close as Pa positioned Fred's terrified head under one arm. "But it seems dangerous to haf this man about, bishop. The killings are not goot. Dots vot I say."

Fred squirmed, looking like he might want to change his mind. Pa motioned for Brother Pettus and Hoffenstetter to hold Fred's arms. Realizing the situation had progressed to a point beyond his control, Fred composed himself.

"I expect his being here is making everyone a might nervous," Pa said, poking around in Fred's mouth. This rummaging produced a low whine of fear from Fred. "But I won't put him out. Every time I think about it the Spirit reminds me of what I'd be feeling if those soldiers had gone and had their way with my girls." He pointed a spit-wet finger around at everyone. "That's something the rest of you should be thinking about, too. It could have been your wives or daughters. Brother Lorings didn't only do me a favor, he did one for this whole valley. That Bukovski was an animal."

A respectful silence followed while the men considered this. Even though it happened long before I was born, the church as a whole wasn't so far removed from the black days of Nauvoo and Missouri that any Mormon could talk easily around the subject of rape. Pa bent over his victim again, maddeningly blocking my view. Fred's skinny legs thrashed as Pa went to work and everyone leaned forward for a better view. A gargled cry announced Fred's growing concern. When the gargle turned into a nerve-wracking screech, Fred's tooth popped up through the circle of watching heads. There was a mutter of appreciation as Brother Pettus caught it.

"You do goot work, Bishop," Hoffenstetter said. He tugged aside Fred's bloody lip for a quick perusal before sitting back down. "You haf goot hands."

Fred, who might have been a voice of dissent had he been able to speak, leaned over and spit a load of red slobber into the straw between his feet. Pa handed him a clean rag and a blue bottle of Ma's mouth tonic and waved him aside.

"It's my second wife's talent," Pa said, wiping his hands on a towel. "I just do what she tells me. If some of you weren't so pigheaded, you'd be better off letting her tend to this sort of thing." He motioned a stricken Sheldon to the chair.

"We haven't got anything against Sister Colleen," Pettus said. "I just trust what I know more than that magic stuff she believes in. My eyes, Lee, she gets some of it from the Indians, not to mention those trashy Eastern books. I say not everything that comes out of books is good, and darn little from Lamanites." He waved a tattered copy of the *Deseret Evening News*. "Says in here the Swedes are starting a medical college for women." He shook his bald head. "Women doctors. Can you beat that? The Second Coming's not far off, I'll bet."

"You just hate change is all," Pa responded. "That's a sight different than whether or not the Second Coming is close. Don't mix up what God wants with what you're afraid of."

"I'm not afraid," Pettus insisted, tugging irritably at his beard. "I just think change is better if it comes slow and natural. Some change shouldn't ought to happen at all."

"Maybe that's the real problem here," Pa said, trying to pull the poultice away from Sheldon's neck and not having much luck. Sheldon acted as if the dirty plaster was the only thing holding his head on. "This hired hand of mine isn't like the rest of us and so he makes everyone skittish. You sound like a bunch of old nellies."

"He's a killer," Hoffenstetter insisted. "Dot's vot makes me nervous. Who vill he kill next, yah? Ve chust don't know. Maybe he is cuckoo in der head, bishop. Vot den?"

Pa succeeded in getting the poultice off Sheldon's neck with only a modicum of howling. Sheldon's neck was swole up like a hog's. Just under his jaw was a knot that looked as if a live coal the size of a hen's egg was trying to push its way through the skin. The group winced in pity.

"As far as I know," Pa said, fishing hot, soapy rags out of a bucket and gently laying them against Sheldon's boil, "Brother Lorings hasn't killed anyone who didn't come looking for it."

"That doesn't make it good or proper," Pettus said. "And it doesn't make me feel any better about having him around. He's a killer, plain and simple. It's his nature. He can't tell the difference between someone like that fellow French Pete and me. It's only a matter of time before he hurts an innocent person." He looked around for support and saw Otto and some of the other men nodding in agreement.

"Look here, Lee," Pettus continued. "I've heard plenty of tales about this Red Legs fellow. Most of 'em I wouldn't want repeated around my wife and young ones. You can't change a fellow like that just by showing him a little gratitude and charity. He doesn't understand it."

"Why do they call him Red Legs, Brother Pettus?" one of the Hoffenstetter boys asked.

In a voice that spoke authority on the matter, Pettus said, "Well, boy, that name comes from the habit he has of wiping his hands on his trousers after slitting throats. He kills for hire with that sword knife. They say that's his specialty." He leaned forward to take everyone into his confidence. "Sure it is. You could offer him twenty dollars gold right this very instant and he'd slit the throat of anyone you pointed your finger at, woman or child, just as easy as you please. I hear he's called Stuart's Wolf as well. Probably for some other bloodthirsty reason."

I was disgusted. If there'd been something heavy in the loft I might have pushed it down on Pettus's bald knob. I'd never met anyone outside of Alva who had so much to say about things they knew so little about.

"Heck," the Hoffenstetter boy gulped.

Rolly Howard spoke up then. Rolly was a corn farmer and hog breeder whose place bordered the Pettus cooperage. He and Pettus were of the same stamp, hardworking church goers but dumb down to the bone, though Rolly advertised it considerably less.

"I was talking yesterday with some freighters," Rolly said. "They told me this Red Legs feller has killed more people than cholera." He paused for effect and then went on. "One of them freighters was in Fort Bridger two winters ago when Red Legs killed the Barlow brothers. Said he watched him shoot Big Frank and the little gimpy one—I forget his name—anyway, both of them in the left eye just as cool as you please from thirty yards. And all the time they was shooting at him."

"Der vas fife of dem Barlows," Brother Hoffenstetter mused, bushy eyebrows raised in consideration. "Dey robbed us ven vee vas coming out mit de wagon company." He shrugged and slapped his hands on his knees. "Goot riddance to dem. Dots vot I say."

"Well, sure, Otto," Pettus said. "The Barlows in Fort Bridger and them Carters down to Bob's is fine. That's just scum killing scum. But Red Legs isn't the sort you want around your family." He paused and studied Pa. "Lee, you wouldn't by chance be more interested in getting some use out of that Nez Perce stud of his than you are in protecting your women?"

Pa gave Pettus an annoyed look while stropping a thin knife on a piece of strap leather. "I owe him, Pettus," he said shortly. "And I pay my debts."

He tested the knife with a thumb. "I'm not entirely ignorant about bad men. I was ten years old when I watched a Clay County mob horsewhip my father right down to his bare spine just for being a Mormon. My father never walked proper again, but he never turned anyone away from our home who needed help, Missourians included. As long as Brother Lorings needs a place to lay up, he can stay. He's been nothing but courteous to my wives and daughters. Which is more than I can say about some folks we sit with in church."

Pa was speaking, of course, of the snippity way some of the sisters treated Ma. He turned to Sheldon, but paused and looked back around at the group. "And another thing—as long as you're on my farm, I'll thank you to call him Brother Lorings, not Red Legs or any of those other names."

"He's no brother of mine," Pettus muttered under his breath. Pa chose to ignore that.

After several more applications of hot rags, Pa leaned over Sheldon with the knife. There was a grunt of sympathy from the group and an ear-splitting screech from Sheldon, worse than the time one of our barn cats got run over slow by a wagon. A yellow ribbon of pus spurted across the barn and struck the wall with an audible splat. A bloated smell wafted up into the hay loft and one of Hoffenstetter's sons went outside to throw up.

"You haf goot hans, Bishop," Hoffenstetter said again, admiring the reduced circumference of Sheldon's neck.

"But not such good sense," Pettus said, cleaning dried mud from his boots with a stick. He pointed the stick at Pa. "I still say you're asking for trouble keeping trash like that around. If you can't see it for yourself, I'll have to remind you there's others around who don't like it any more than me." He paused and shook his head, as if he was trying to explain something to an exceptionally dull child. "You can't tame a rabid animal, Lee. That's exactly what this fella is. If you feel like you owe him something, give him some money and send him packing. Say thanks very much but so long and good riddance. He strikes me as the sort who'd appreciate a few dollars more than he would your Christian charity."

Pa helped a woozy Sheldon over to some feed sacks and sat him down. He carefully applied another poultice and wrapped Sheldon's bloody neck with a clean cotton bandage. Finally he tossed some wet cedar chips in the forge and the smell in the barn got better.

Pa surveyed the group before sitting down on the stool and picking up a newspaper. "The Savior wouldn't turn him away and I won't either. If Brother Lorings worries you fellows so much, you can take your smithy business over to Leo Poulsen. I reckon he can use it. "

"Christ never met up with Stuart's Wolf," Brother Pettus observed wryly.

Pa lowered his newspaper and stared at Brother Pettus. "He stays."

I recognized a hard note of finality in Pa's voice. I was proud of him, proud to be his daughter. Sometimes he let Alva and Ma push him around so much that it made you wonder if there was any personal resolve in him. But my pa had steel and it showed just fine at times like this.

The men started talking horses, how Fulton's stud was faring with our mares and what price the colts would fetch. Horses didn't interest me. As soon as I realized the subject of Fulton had been dropped for good, I slipped away from the loft opening and climbed back down the ladder.

Outside, the storm was a lot closer. Lightning stabbed at the mountains and thunder rumbled a final warning across the valley. A cold bullet of rain struck the back of my hand, chilling me. I sprinted down to the brick house and made it just as the storm washed over the farm in silver sheets. I waved at Ma standing in the door of our cabin. She waved back and went back inside, satisfied that I was under cover.

Alva and Silla were in the parlor sewing on a quilt and hatching another plan to get Pa to notice Silla. I thought about suggesting to them that Pinch Face might fare better if she would practice smiling more and maybe whittle a few inches off her nose. Maybe, but I doubt it. Unless Ma told him to, Pa wouldn't pay Silla Van Orden any mind even if she stood up in testimony meeting stark naked. Pa wasn't big on having another wife. He could barely keep up with the two he had. Instead of stirring them up, I sneaked past them.

Laurel Anne was in her room brushing her hair and studying herself in front of the mirror again, which meant that one of her ten thousand beaus was going to pay a call. The bruises on her face were almost entirely gone now and her social life had picked back up. My own, on the other hand, was as empty as Sheriff Jewkes's heart. I flopped down on the bed and let out a death sigh.

"You're bored," Laurel Anne said, a statement of fact. "Well, don't start a fight with me. I've been vexed enough for a year. And mind you, don't muss the bed."

I sat up and looked at her. She had these little notches in her brow, just above and between her eyes, which meant she was still mad about the way Fulton had treated her yesterday. I felt sorry for whoever was coming by tonight. She'd wrap and twist them around her finger until they were ready to bark at the moon or kill themselves.

"You're being mighty bossy," I said.

She paused and gave me an arch look. "Just because a person reminds someone of their obligation to manners does not mean they're being bossy."

"You going to kiss Eldon tonight?" I asked, changing the subject.

"That's none of your business."

I tried to bait her into a fight with a number of other insensitive probes, but for the most part she just ignored me, continuing to brush her hair. I did notice that the strokes were becoming more harsh. I looked at her face and saw that she wasn't annoyed anymore, she was worried.

"Are you all right?"

She put the brush in her lap and looked at me in the mirror. She shook her head. A couple of times she started to say something but stopped, as if the words wouldn't come. She blinked hard like she might start crying. When she did get it out, I wished she hadn't.

"I've had night visitors again."

I sat up straighter. More than three months had passed since anyone had come prowling around the window of Laurel Anne's bedroom. Most everyone figured it to be the riff raff hanging around Slobber Bob's. The ramshackle saloon and brewery was just a mile or so through the woods, down in the river bottoms. Beginning last year, someone, maybe even more than one, had paid frequent night visits to Laurel Anne's window, hoping to see in while she bathed and dressed. One summer night, she awoke to the sound of her window sliding open. Her screams fetched Pa, who ran outside and blistered the unidentified intruder with a load of salt as they scrambled off into the night. We never found out who it was or even how many, but the visits tapered off after that.

Laurel Anne looked genuinely frightened. It occurred to me again how much of a cross it sometimes is to be beautiful. For some folks, a woman's beauty is a possession just like a pretty blanket or a fine piece of furniture. If you have it, there's some folks who want it and you for them- selves. You'll never know when they might just try and take it like Bukovski did.

"Did you tell Pa?"

"No."

"Why not? Somebody needs their butt salted again. Want me to tell him?"

"No, I don't. And please consider your language."

"Are you going to tell Pa?"

She shook her head.

"That's dumb," I said. "That's real dumb. You should tell. Pa would put a stop to it right fast. I'll tell him. I bet he—"

Laurel Anne flung herself around on the stool, dropping the brush on the floor. "Don't you dare." Confused, I started to protest again but, she cut me off with a swipe of a hand. "Rose, no!" She sagged against the back of her chair. "I'm afraid of what will happen."

"Pa shot at the last ones," I pointed out. A perfectly logical response and where was the harm in that? It had kept them away until now.

"That's what worries me. I'm afraid if I tell, he'll wait up with his gun again." She gestured at the window where the curtains billowed against a wet wind. Outside, the afternoon was black with rain. Her voice faltered. "And, Rose, I'm afraid of what will happen to Father if it's who I think it is."

"Who?" Immediately, I wished I hadn't asked.

She gave me a stricken look. "Mr. Lorings."

It was like being shot in the stomach with a cannonball. The very thought of Pa trying to scare Fulton off with a gun made me sick. At the same time, I had a mental image of what it would be like to be stalked by someone like Fulton. It made my knees twitch and my mouth dry up. I knew then why Laurel Anne was so near tears. If it was Fulton trying to peek in her window, he wasn't your normal trespasser interested in getting a peek of my sister wearing nothing but soap suds. And he definitely wouldn't be frightened off by a load of salt.

"Rose," Laurel Anne said. "I don't know that it's him, but I want you to swear that you won't say a word to Father. I'm keeping my windows locked and the curtains drawn tight. So far, whoever it is hasn't tried to get in. I just hear them out there at night." She turned back to the mirror. "Ever since he came here, things have been changing. Terrible things. If it is Mr. Lorings, I'm afraid of what he would do to Father. You know what kind of man he is. Please? I couldn't bear what might happen if you told."

Eventually I swore I wouldn't tell Pa. Laurel Anne cheered up a bit. She let me brush her hair and help pick out what she would wear to receive Eldon Bair that evening.

I knew Laurel Anne didn't love Eldon any more than she loved Henry, certainly not like Ma loved Pa. But she felt like she had to choose someone, and the rest of her options were considerably less attractive. There weren't but maybe three men within a hundred miles that wouldn't give a lot to marry her, and that included some men who already had plenty of wives. Important men.

Last summer, in a move that stunned her associates, Laurel Anne told a particular apostle of God who came courting one day that she plain wasn't interested in becoming wife number fourteen. Alva and Pinch Face were still in a lather over that. Such a thing would have guaranteed Laurel Anne a prominent spot in heaven, not to mention making her mark in Salt Lake society. Being a sister-wife-in-law to an apostle wouldn't have been bad for Alva, either.

While some women married themselves into a batch of sister-wives because they happened to love the same man, plenty more did it because they calculated it to be less work at salvation than all the bother of keeping the more common commandments.

Laurel Anne wasn't sure. She told Pa later that she only knew that she couldn't get married unless she loved a man more than her life and that such a man simply hadn't come along yet. Plenty of her suitors were handsome and engaging, to be sure, but none had moved her heart.

But that didn't slow Alva down when it came to helping Laurel Anne find the right man. After the visit of Apostle So-and-So, she kept a steady stream of polygamist brethren coming out to our place on one errand or another. The list included another apostle, two seventies, a couple of bishops, and even one poor idiot who dragged along his first dozen wives to examine and vote on candidate number thirteen. It was awful. But then I only remember the first half of this visit. In a move that forced Pa to side with Alva, I spent the last half of it standing in a corner for pegging one of the higher number wives with a dried horse apple.

By my way of figuring, falling in love wasn't something you did in a crowd. 'Course I knew little enough about falling in love. I was born loving Ma and Pa and Johnny, and although I learned to love Herc, it wasn't quite the same thing as loving a man. What I was learning about it, I was learning from Laurel Anne. But she was damn slow about it, to be sure.

It was the darker suitors who were the problem right now, men too twisted to announce their interests out in the open. After Pa salted them, I figured we were done with such things. Worse, after Bukovski, I understood what some men really wanted from a woman. Hearing that such men were back scared me.

I didn't bring up the subject of her night visitor again because I didn't want to argue with her about it and I didn't want to spoil her evening. But my own mind whirled with the possibilities.

I didn't believe it was Fulton, though part of me wondered. You could never be sure what secrets people hid. It was bad enough trying to read people when they were normal and behaved in a predictable fashion. With someone like Fulton it was impossible, in large part because I had no experience with anyone like him. There was nothing to base a prediction on. He was quite simply the most closed person I had ever met.

I stayed with Laurel Anne until the thunderstorm passed. On the outside, we behaved reasonably cheerful. On the inside though, I was all squeezed into a turmoil. Pa was the bravest man I knew, a captain in the Nauvoo Legion, a bishop and husband to not one but two Irish sisters. All my life he had protected us from Indians, wild animals and rowdy men. It made me fearful now to think that being brave might not be enough, especially if he tried to run Fulton off when Fulton didn't want to go.

Laurel Anne got ready for her bath. I volunteered to haul buckets of hot water to the tub. Then I stayed and watched her undress, wondering how much my own life would change when I got pillows and hips like hers. Would men want me bad enough to hang around my bedroom window at night and scare me? We were quiet while I washed her back. Next to Ma and Pa, I loved Laurel Anne the most. I'd do anything to protect her.

After Laurel Anne was finished with her bath, I went out past the kitchen where Alva and Silla wrestled stuffing into a turkey. Ever since Silla had set her cap for Pa, we'd eaten like royalty, with Pinch Face taking all the credit. While I hoped Pa wouldn't marry Silla, I knew that if he did, we could at least stop all the nonsense of pretending and get down to regular family behavior of tormenting each other near to death.

Outside, the tail end of the clouds were disappearing over the ramparts of Timpanogos Mountain. The sun was out as bold as a Spanish doubloon. Rain dripped from the eves and the green smell of grass and washed earth hung wine-heavy in the air. Birds sang from the trees and I breathed it all in. I'll tell you, there's no place like our valley after a summer rain. I considered hiking over to the cooperage and waiting for Josh Van Orden to finish work so we could go swimming. I'd about made up my mind to do it when I heard voices coming from the side of the house. Immediately, I recognized Cletus and Pa.

"No, suh, I cain't do that," I heard Cletus say stubbornly.

I crept over to the corner and peered slowly around. Cletus stood at the bottom of the steps, worrying his hat with rough hands. He looked fretful and put out about something. Pa just looked grim.

"Can I have a reason, Cletus? You've been a good man and I don't want to lose you."

Whatever it was, Cletus didn't much want to talk about it. He scuffed his feet and squinted up at the clearing sky. Then he scratched the back of his neck and looked down at the ground. Finally, he looked at Pa. I think he saw me, too.

"You got yourself a bad one, Brother Merrell," Cletus said. "Mistuh Lorings, suh. I cain't be working next to him." He nodded toward the pasture where Fulton's Appaloosa grazed with the mares in belly-deep grass. "The good book say death rides on a pale horse and desolation be the dark angel." He shuddered visibly. "Suh, I seen him this afternoon when the storm come over. I told him we should git to cover, but Mr. Lorings, well, suh, he hops up on the bank, laughing and making hissy noises through that rag of his, like he daring God to fotch him with a thunderbolt. One or two even come close but that din't shake him none. No, suh. He kep' right on daring God." Cletus shook his head in amazement, unable to comprehend what would drive a man to such a one-sided duel with God. "I've seed some bad things in my travels, suh, things that would make Jesus weep, but I never seed nothing like that. That crazy white man is the right hand of death. I know you're beholding to him and all for what he did for Missy Merrell, but I'd much appreciate it if you'd just pass me my pay, suh. I'll be on my way. I can get me some work up north."

I thought Cletus had some nerve calling Fulton Lorings a dark angel, considering that his own skin was blacker than the inside of a stove. Still, I liked Cletus and was going to miss his brilliant smile and laughing stories. He'd worked for Pa for most of a year and was undeniably the best hired hand we'd ever had. Pa tried to talk him out of leaving, but Cletus remained adamant. With a sigh, Pa went into the house for his receipt box. He came out and paid Cletus.

"You've been a good worker, Cletus," Pa said. "Take the bay down there. She's old but she'll get you where you want to go. It's my thanks."

Cletus apologized some more before heading down to the barn to pack his things. Pa watched him go, a strange look of loss on his face. Laurel Anne was right, things were changing on our farm. What worried me the most, however, was the nagging feeling that the biggest changes still waited in the wings with sly grins and hidden gifts. I think Pa suspected it, too. Seeing that worried look on his face made me nervous about our future.

I waited until Pa went inside and then I ran down to the barn to say goodbye to Cletus in case he didn't come back. I dallied outside, afraid Fulton might be in there with him. I didn't want to see Fulton after the things I'd heard from Laurel Anne and Cletus. I was afraid he'd be able to read them on my face and I wouldn't know what to say.

Eventually Cletus came back out through the door carrying his bedroll and a busted out old grip filled with his meager belongings. He tousled my head, knowing I'd eavesdropped on him and Pa.

"You take care, purty Rose," he said. He led me a short distance away and lowered his voice. "And you be cautious 'bout hanging around the barn and down by the dig now. I know you be a spying girl, but they's some evil afoot in these parts and you don't want to get caught too close to it."

"Do you really think he's evil, Cletus?" I asked.

"He a dangerous man," he replied. "And he doan care 'bout nothing or nobody. That's almost worser than evil, chile. It mean anything can happen and cain't nobody say what or even stop it."

"But is he evil?"

Cletus stopped and gave me a solemn look. He shook his wooly head. "Lawd, but you ask fierce questions for a bitty girl. Questions even growed folks don't never think of asking." He took off his hat and wiped his shiny face with a bandanna. He thought for a long moment. "No, Missy Rose," he said, replacing the hat. "I don't believes he be exactly evil. But he gots no love in him. It all been killed out of him, by the war I 'spect. He's hurting bad, and when folks be hurting that bad, they just gots to hurt back. It might have somethin' to do with his face. He hurt there behind that mask, that fo' sho'. I got me a peek the other night when I was washing up." Cletus shivered.

104

"Was it really bad?" I asked, holding my breath.

"Din't see much," Cletus said. "Jus' enough to know I don't want to be here when it come off all the way. You mark what Cletus say, they be more killing long as that hoodoo man's 'round."

"What if he had a friend?" I asked. "What if he made friends with someone who cared about him? Maybe someone he cared about. Wouldn't he be better?"

Cletus gave me a sober look, wise as any prophet. "That someone be you, I 'spect." he said.

I nodded. Laurel Anne, too, but I didn't say so. In my heart I firmly believed that all Fulton Lorings really needed was someone to be his friend. If he had a friend, maybe he wouldn't need to hurt folks like Cletus said.

"He isn't as bad as people think," I said. I tried to think of some redeeming qualities for a man whose mere name frightened people into stunned whispers. I brightened when I thought of how Mr. Lorings had stood up to Sergeant Bukovski. "He saved us from the soldiers. And he's very brave."

Cletus made a face. "He got no hope. That ain't 'zactly the same thing as brave. Folks get the two mixed up. C'mon now. Let's get on up to the house so's I can say my fare-dee-wells."

I walked hand in hand with Cletus back up to the house where everyone waited. Alva gave him a package of food and shook his hand formally, the only time I think she'd ever touched a black man. Ma gave him some root tonic for his gums and a kiss on the cheek. Pa pressed on him another two dollars. Laurel Anne hugged him and everybody got leaky. My throat hurt from squeezing sobs back down it.

"Y'all take care of yo selves," Cletus said when he had climbed on the horse. "Like as not, I'll be back this way again. The Lord don't never let me rest when his word needs spreading. Lots of misbeguided souls up to Salt Lake. I just may call on that Brigham Young and bring him 'round to Jesus Lord."

We laughed and cried and waved, watching Cletus go until he disappeared into the trees at the end of the lane.

"What're you bawling about, Mutt," Lehi demanded as the family separated, heading back to our boring chores and our boring lives. "You act like you're in love with him."

I wiped my eyes, feeling my hackles rise. "He's my friend and I don't want him to go."

Nephi snorted. "Figures your only friend would be some dumb darky. Who cares? He talked too much. He's gone and we won't have no more windy prayers over supper."

I reached down for a rock and the twins scrambled up on the porch where the window glass evoked sanctuary. They started in with the name-calling so I chose a handy direction and fled, not intending to, but heading down the lane to the barn.

When I reached the stock pens, I put my head against a fence post and cried out the hurt in my heart. While I cried, I banged my head on the post, punishing the only person handy for my misery. Except for that day on the Provo road, I hadn't cried since Herc died. Now, the more I thought about Cletus and Herc, the harder I cried. And the harder I cried, the madder I got.

They said in church how you were supposed to pray when the world weighed you down. But God and Jesus and me had a contrary relationship. I held them personally responsible for all the things weighing me down. I didn't believe any of the stuff taught in Sunday School about answers to prayers and such. It never happened the way they said, no burning in my bosoms and no ministering angels. I wanted it to, but it never did. I even pressed Ma about it once, asking her while she was giving me a bath one night if I had to wait until I was older and actually had bosoms for the burning to begin. It must have been a difficult question to answer because she paused a long minute to compose herself and then pointed out how the prophet Joseph Smith was a man and how he still got a burning in his bosom when he prayed in the grove even though his bosoms were, for all practical purposes, no bigger than my own. God and Jesus didn't leave the job to no ministering angels either. Not by a damn sight. They showed up right smart themselves. Ma said she doubted the burning had anything to do with my age and the state of my bosoms, and I should keep trying until I got it right.

But I wouldn't. Not if God and Jesus were going to cheat me out of Cletus, too. Ever since Herc and Johnny died, misery had been piling up around here faster than bull turds at an auction, and I didn't see God and Jesus helping out one stingy, measly bit. I was getting ready to tell them I would never pray again when I remembered something that made me feel ashamed, as if I'd been selfishly hasty in my estimation of things. I had gotten an answer to a prayer once. It wasn't a burning in my bosoms or a sneaky whisper to my spirit either. No. This one came with fire and smoke and with pieces of hell stuck to it. It hadn't resembled one bit the thing I had asked for, but it was an answer that worked undeniably well. And it also came with an account.

My heart leaped and I threw myself away from the post, wiping my eyes and staring at the barn. If Fulton had been the answer to a prayer once before, maybe he still was. I had promised Laurel Anne with a hope-to-die vow that I wouldn't tell Pa about her night visitors. And I wouldn't. After all, a vow was a vow and I nearly always tried to keep the ones that I'd made to people I liked. For the time being, Pa would have to remain ignorant.

But I never said anything about telling Red Legs.

I crept down to the barn like a horse thief. The big door creaked when I leaned into it. Dust, like spun gold, drifted on beams of sunlight piercing the gloom. Without the noisy presence of Pa and the hiss and belch of his forge, the barn seemed an ominous place, as empty as a crypt. I considered turning chicken. Nobody knew what I was doing. There would be no shame in backing out. I could just walk up to the house and act normal, steal some cookies or get even with the twins. I could go looking for arrowheads or wait for Josh to finish work and go skinny-dipping. I shook my head at the temptations. I would know, and that was enough. I let the door swing shut behind me.

In the absence of Pa, the barn was big and dark. A mouse thrashed in the corner and I almost came out of my skin. The further into the barn I went, the more sensible the idea to turn and run seemed. I didn't and that was probably less because of courage and more because I was a Merrell and not bright enough to know when I was in serious trouble. Later, in bitter retrospect, I'd wish I had followed my instincts.

I slipped past the stalls and picked my way through dusty shadows to the tack room. Inch by inch, I approached the door. It resembled less our tack room now and more the lair of some brooding beast who would seize and devour me as soon as my presence was detected. Finally, when I couldn't put it off any longer, I leaned around the corner.

Fulton sat on a long row of feed sacks that served as his bed. A lantern burned feebly on a barrel beside him, cutting black shadows across everything. In his lap were several guns. One hand held a cleaning rod, the other rested on his leg not far from another gun that was obviously loaded and waiting for someone to bother its master. Fulton's alert gaze locked on me as soon as I poked my head around the corner, almost as if he'd been expecting me.

My throat closed down to a pinhole. My palms got sweaty and my feet kept trying to turn themselves around. But I was still stubborn enough to try and bring this off.

"Hello," I said.

The only response was a single blink of the stone-colored eyes above the cloth. I put my shoulder against the edge of the door, not yet willing to venture into the same room with him.

"Cletus left."

No reply. I might as well have been talking to the feed sacks. But I knew he could talk and so I kept after him, letting some of the bitterness I felt leak into my voice.

"He left because of you."

Still nothing.

"Pa paid him and gave him a horse." I took a deep breath. "He told Pa you were crazy."

I was less afraid now than I was mad, sick of having almost no say in the way my life was going and tired of being ignored by God and Jesus and now Fulton. Just when I figured talking to him was pointless, he spoke.

"I am."

I blinked. It was a simple admission, two words whisper soft and devoid of apology, like the track of a snake through dry grass. I blinked some more and tried to decide on how to proceed. It was hard because I'd been expecting him to defend himself, or at least try and prove me wrong.

"Now you'll have to do more work," I said lamely, trying to make him see that running Cletus off was going to affect him adversely as well. "Pa won't be able to get another hired man because everyone is afraid of you."

The eyes above the scarf changed hues, softening into a less dangerous shade. He put the guns to one side and wiped his hands on a rag. He nodded at the corner where his saddle and packs lay.

"Go?"

I shook my head, for two reasons. First was because I really didn't want him to go, and the second was because the sound of Fulton Lorings actually talking was so unsettling, like the squeak and groan of hinges on an old treasure box. Like everyone else, I'd been locked into the notion that he couldn't talk. Now that he was actually participating in a conversation, it felt a little like I imagined it would to teach a tiger to jump through a hoop—proud but uneasy, as if the tiger might someday mistake your throat for the hoop.

"No," I said. "Don't go."

He shrugged, eyes silently asking me what he should do.

I didn't have a ready answer. I knew I was tired of my life being out of control. I wanted the threats of change to stop. I wanted my family protected from the bad things I felt were coming our way at breakneck speed. I knew Fulton could help me. For some reason, it never occurred to me that he might be any of those bad things. I thought of Laurel Anne and remembered the way he held the ribbon. It couldn't be him outside her window. Could it? There was only one way to find out.

"My sister's scared. She's scared of someone."

Fulton's eyes changed. I was never certain afterward if it was that change itself or his voice that said, "Who?"

I shook my head and shrugged. "We don't know. Somebody sneaking around in the dark."

In a halting voice, I explained the night visitors, what had happened in the past and what was happening now. Fulton listened intently. I watched his eyes, looking for any sign that it was him: uneasiness, shame or even open defiance. I saw nothing but a predatory interest. I felt better for it.

Still, there was no physical response to my tale of woe and I wondered if maybe he was going to refuse to help me. Irritated, I thrust my hands into the pocket of my jumper and found a small comb Ma sometimes put in my hair. The moment I touched it I remembered the pink hair ribbon fluttering over the dead soldiers on the Provo road—and knew exactly what I had to do. I brought the comb out and held it in my open hand.

"Laurel Anne asked me to give you this," I lied.

I held it up and saw his eyes follow it, glowing like pirate ship lanterns in the night.

"It's a lady's favor," I explained. "Like in the olden days when there were knights? Anyway, I'm supposed to give it to you and tell you that she needs your help." I was laying it on pretty thick, but in my ignorance I wanted to impress on Fulton how much we needed his help. Later, I would find myself wishing God had struck me dead the minute I lied.

Instead, the devil held out his hand.

I leaned forward and, quick as a mouse, dropped the comb into Fulton's palm. It was just an old battered hair fancy made from a shell, but he treated it like it was covered with diamonds. From the look in his eyes, I think he would have gladly swapped his soul for it.

"Could you watch over her?" I concluded. "Make whoever it is that's bothering her stop coming around?"

When Fulton shook himself loose from the sight of the comb and looked up at me, he nodded. Oh, yes, he could most certainly do that. Whatever life had taken from Red Legs, the devil had filled him back up with an enormous talent for "stopping" people.

"You have to swear," I said. "I'm supposed to get a promise from you."

What I really wanted was for Fulton to promise me that it wasn't him lurking around out there in the dark under Laurel Anne's window.

Fulton seemed amused. What happened next was right out of the story books. He slipped off the feed sacks and lowered himself to one knee in front of me, just like in *Ivanhoe*. He touched a fist to his chest and his eyes danced above the scarf as he bowed his head. The word came soft and eager, as gentle as the whisper of a knife from a sheath.

"Promise."

There wasn't much to say after that. Fulton sat back on the feed sacks and studied the comb. I felt better, believing now that it wasn't him under the window. He fussed with his guns some more and I got the impression that he wanted me to leave. I did, bidding him good-bye. Totally absorbed with the comb and the guns, he seemed oblivious to my departure.

I was halfway to the door when I heard him say something. A trite phrase most people never put much thought or feeling to, it struck me as being out of character for someone like Fulton. It must have been the intensity with which it was spoken that sent a cold spider of fear scurrying down my back. His voice seemed to fill the dim interior of the barn.

"Thank you."

That night, after Eldon Bair had made a fool of himself begging two hours on our porch for a kiss he never got, I crawled into bed with Laurel Anne. She seemed to welcome the company, although I doubt she would have been quite so grateful if she knew I'd kept her and Eldon company by hiding in the bushes at the end of the porch.

Sleep came hard. I tossed fitfully next to her on the feather mattress. I don't think my restlessness bothered her much. If she was sleepy herself, she would have been vexed by all my thrashing. Truth was, I guess, we were both waiting to hear something outside her window. Several times I thought I did. I held my breath, but nothing ever came of the night sounds that startled me. Along about morning, I finally drifted off to sleep.

Although sorely tempted, I never told Laurel Anne what I'd done to ensure her safety and vindicate Fulton. Several more nights passed without a visitor to her window. After a while, she seemed happy. Part of me wanted to think I could take credit for it, but for once I was glad I kept my mouth shut. It wasn't until the next week when I learned just exactly what I'd done by trying to make a champion out of Fulton Lorings.

On that night, another storm rolled over our farm. The rain made Pa happy because our crops needed the water. The rest of us were glad because the storm swept the heat out of the valley. It was pleasant to sit on the porch without the bother of the heat and bugs. I snuggled in Pa's lap and watched the lightning pop and flash. When it was time for bed, I begged a spot next to Laurel Anne again, rather than risk a dark tromp across the fields where I suspected the ghost of a murdering Indian called Squash Head lay in evil wait for me.

Laurel Anne drifted off immediately, wore out no doubt by the sleeplessness of previous nights. I swore myself to alertness, but the warmth of her body and my own weariness conspired against me. I dozed.

I wasn't sure what woke me up, but it must have been something bad because I came awake fully alert, my feet and hands tingling. Whatever I heard must have sounded like a threat. I listened harder, my heart thumping. The air was stifling. Out in the dark front room, Alva's German clock chimed the hour.

I slid out of bed, careful not to wake Laurel. The room was an oven. I went over to the window and peered through the curtains. There was nothing out there but the rain. A drop of sweat ran down my back. Carefully, I opened the window partway. The cool night air and the wondrous smell of the rain rushed in. Outside it was pitch black. I leaned against the crack and let the breeze dry my sweat-soaked hair. Just then, lightning flashed.

A wild face leered at me from the night. Hands pushed through the crack, throwing the window open. "Where's your sister?" the wet, gargoyle face laughed. "Give her to us."

My scream peeled paint.

Upstairs, I heard Pa exclaim, "What in the—?"

Laurel Anne sat up. Her scream joined mine when she saw the intruder trying to climb in the window. She threw herself out of bed and rushed to help me. Together we tried to close the window. Outside, someone yelled encouragement to the man clambering in. In a flash of lightning, I saw the second man laugh and raise a bottle to his lips. The window shattered and wood splintered as the first man tried harder to pull himself inside.

The cursing intruder was stronger than the two of us. Chances are he would have gained entrance if Laurel Anne hadn't brought her water pitcher down on his head. Suddenly the window was vacant except for the rain and blowing leaves.

Pa thundered down the stairs with his musket, spilling powder and bullets as he tried to load in the dark. Alva hung close on his heels, carrying Aaron. "Is it Indians, Bishop? Is it? Oh, do be careful."

As politely as he could, Pa told Alva to shut up so he could hear to think. Holding his musket at the ready, he ventured out onto the dark porch.

We waited inside while Pa poked around in the bushes. I remained by the bedroom window, trying to get my legs to stop shaking. Laurel Anne went into the front room to comfort Alva. I was still standing by the window when she came back carrying a candle and a broom. Her face was white.

"It wasn't Mr. Lorings," I said.

She shook her head. "No, it wasn't."

"Do you know who?"

She began sweeping up the broken pieces of her water pitcher. "There were two of them. They were drunk. Are you all right?"

I nodded.

Pa came back in and Laurel Anne went into the front room to tell him what happened. I stayed by billowing curtains, gazing out into the darkness and the slanting rain, trying to come to terms with what would have happened just because I opened the window. I started to cuss myself when lightning rippled along the edge of the world, far off over the mountains.

I gasped.

Hatless in the rain, Fulton stared up at the house from the middle of Alva's vegetable garden. Soaking wet, his eyes were wild with the rain-swept night. He glanced in the direction of the trees. In those wobbly seconds it took the lightning to burn itself out, I saw blue light gleam along the sword knife in his hand. With a final look at the house, he turned and loped for the trees. Blackness returned.

I whirled and tore through the front room, past everyone and out onto the porch.

"Rose Lee," Alva cried. "You get in here right now. The Indians—"

Pa caught my arm as I tried to run down the steps and into the wet yard.

"Hold up there, Budge. What did you see?"

"N-nothing," I stammered, staring at the trees. I was only just beginning to realize what I'd done, and I couldn't bring myself to tell. "I thought—"

From the trees in the direction of the river came an unearthly scream. It rose and fell and eventually tapered off into a blubbering sob. My scalp shriveled up into a scab.

"Merciful heavens," Alva said, latching onto Pa. Aaron started to cry.

Another scream pierced the night, this one more terrifying than the first. It went on and on and then ended abruptly, as if the author of it had ended too.

The screams robbed us of reason. I couldn't even muster enough spit to swallow. We stood rooted on the porch, staring into the night like dumb animals. The twins started to sniffle.

"Father," Laurel Anne whispered. "What—who was that?"

Pa shook his head. "I don't know. But I think it would be best if we all got inside and barred the doors." He motioned for Alva to lead us in. Without waiting to see if we complied, he disappeared in the direction of our cabin, his musket ready. He was gone to check on Ma.

Alva took over. When we were safe inside behind locked doors, she insisted on leading us in a long prayer asking Heaven for protection from mobbers, outlaws and most of all Indians, who, she warned God in a frightened voice, would take us away and make us have their babies.

"Even us?" Nephi and Lehi queried from the corner behind her chair. Alva told them to hush and started in on her prayer.

With Fulton outside, I was pretty sure nobody would get within a hundred yards of the house. While Alva beseeched God for help protecting our collective chastity, I said my own prayer. I prayed for whoever it was that Fulton had run to the ground out there in the woods, for whoever it was that I had helped kill.

Pa returned in a few minutes with the news that Ma was fine. In typical fashion she refused to come down to the brick house with the rest of the family. Pumpkin Ass muttered something under her breath about Ma's poor sense. Not wanting to start a fight right then, Pa said nothing in Ma's defense. So I stuck out my tongue.

We waited together in the front room until morning. Alva held Aaron, and the twins dozed in their corner. I slept with my head in Laurel Anne's lap while Pa rocked impassively in a chair positioned between Laurel Anne's bedroom and us, the loaded musket across his knees. We looked like a family besieged and I guess in a way we were. We didn't know that it was just the beginning.

Morning dispelled most of the night's immediate fears. Alva trudged into the kitchen to make breakfast. The rest of us yawned and tried to stretch out the kinks in our bones. I followed Pa out onto the porch and around to Laurel Anne's window.

Broken glass littered the wet ground. I found a brown bottle that wrinkled up my nose when I picked it up and sniffed it. Pa took the bottle and pointed out a couple of soggy cigar butts.

"Looks like there were two of them," he said, showing me boot tracks leading away from the house. His eyes turned toward the trees. "I suppose they ran down to the river when they couldn't get in the house."

"You figure it was them screaming?" I asked.

Pa shook his head. "Don't know who else it would be at that time of night. Running through the dark like that, they might have fallen over some log and broke their legs. Either that or they were just playing mean tricks to scare us." He sounded mighty doubtful.

We went back inside and ate a listless breakfast. Pa said grace and thanked the Lord for seeing us safe through the night. After we ate, he went down to the barn and brought up a new pane of glass to replace the broken one. I held the nails while he stripped the case apart and pulled out slivers of broken glass.

"Didn't see Brother Lorings down at the shop," he said. "I guess he's gone off to the dig."

I nodded. "Probably."

Crouched there beside Pa, I could feel him look at me from time to time. I kept my own eyes on the handful of nails.

"You're awful quiet for the Budge I know."

"Yessir."

"Got something on your mind?"

I shrugged.

"Want to talk about it?"

I shook my head.

He didn't press me further. When the window was done, I climbed the slope to see Ma. Even though it was broad daylight, she stripped off my clothes and got me into bed. Normally this would have caused me serious aggravation, but right now the quiet safety of my own bed sounded good. I told her what happened. I even told her about seeing Fulton in the garden. I didn't, however, say a word about commissioning Fulton as Laurel Anne's champion. Ma sat beside me smoothing my hair with her hand.

"Ma, do you reckon it's possible for people to change?"

"Yes, Rose, dear." She leaned over and kissed me. "But it takes wanting to change bad enough."

"What if somebody else wanted it bad enough? Would the person who needed to change still change?"

"No, dear," she said, and it broke my heart just a little bit to hear that. "You can only show them how. You can't make them want to."

"Can God and Jesus?"

"Yes," Ma said. She told me then about Jonah, the apostle Paul, young Alma and the rotten sons of Mosiah from the Book of Mormon. God and Jesus, she said, had helped plenty of folks change, mostly by torturing them with guilt or letting angels clobber them until they begged for the privilege. "You see, dear," Ma said. "With God and Jesus, all things are possible.

It was a small patch on my heart, but it helped me get to sleep.

I slept hard, with none of the dreams you might expect after such a night. When I woke up, the sun was sending shadows the other way. I crawled out of bed with a headache. Ma fed me some lunch. Afterwards, I mentioned that I was going down to the shop.

"Mind you come home in time for your bath," Ma said. "Tomorrow is worship."

Inwardly, I groaned. The bath I could tolerate, but long meetings filled with boring people were something else. Not only did they annoy me, but deep down they worried me. Since God commanded us to attend them, did that mean he was boring as well? Weighted down with this horrible thought, I left the house and trudged down to the barn.

I located Pa in his shop, talking to a couple of boys from the ward. Fred and Earl Lehman were frustrated beaus of Laurel Anne's and infrequent hired hands of Pa's. Fred and Earl, known to the valley as Big and Dumb respectively, were a couple of harmless oafs forever hatching one scheme or another to see the world and get rich. Their widowed father, a humorless and hard man, had a sheep ranch up against the mountain that Big and Dumb found particularly tedious. Six years hence, one of their harebrained schemes to see the world and get rich, probably Big's, would take them up to the Black Hills goldfields where it was said they saw the world, got rich and scalped in the space of an hour. Right now, however, they were alive and the bearers of some ugly news. They were talking earnestly to Pa and didn't see me as I slipped in behind a pile of boxes to listen.

"You wouldn't believe it, Bishop," Big was saying.

I peeked through a bundle of burlap. Pa, busy trying to fit a shoe on Dumb's skittish horse, grunted. "I won't if you never get around to telling me what it is, Fred. Spit it on out."

Big and Dumb exchanged looks. "Well, it's like this," Big said. "Me and Earl was out riding and we stopped to, ah...water our horses. You know, down to Bob's?" Here Pa gave Big a stern look, knowing exactly why they had stopped at Bob's. Big hurried on. "Anyway, that's when we saw them. We were the first ones," he added with a trace of nervous pride.

Pa straightened up, a nail in his mouth. "First ones to see what?"

"Well, sir," Big said nervously." Last night someone nailed a couple of ears to Slobber Bob's front door."

My blood froze. Pa stared at them. "What?"

Big nodded vigorously. "People ears. I ain't never seen nothing like it in my life." He glanced at his brother. "It made Earl sick." Dumb nodded, still a little green around the edges. He showed Pa where he'd puked on his boots.

It took Pa a minute to digest the news. I could see him putting it together with last night's screams from the woods and I think he knew the answer before he asked the next question. Me, I felt all queasy in my stomach remembering the lightning reflecting off the sword knife in Fulton's hand.

Pa took the nail out of his mouth and pointed it at Big. "Anyone see who did it?"

"Nossir. Bob told us he heard somebody pounding on the door early this morning. Said he paid it no mind cause he thought it was a drunk." Big peered around and leaned on the pommel of his saddle, lowering his voice. "But I hear they think it's your hired man, Bishop. That Red Legs feller."

Pa bent back to his work, filing the shoe to fit. "No one knows that for sure," he said. "I haven't even talked to my man this morning, so don't you boys go spreading rumors."

Big and Dumb paid Pa and left. Pa watched them go, put down his file, came over to the pile of boxes and shook me out of my hidey-hole. His broad face was full of worry.

"What have I told you before about spying on people?" he growled, which was about as angry as he ever got with me. "One of these days you'll hear something you don't want to hear."

I already had. For a moment, I considered telling Pa what I'd done. But he didn't look like he needed to hear anything bad from me. He turned and stared after the departing Lehmans. I kept my mouth shut.

"Go on now, Budge," he said, shooing me out of the barn. "Run and play. I've got to get some work done."

I left, but not without pausing at the door to give him one more look and one more chance to get me to open up. But his face was full of something that confused me. It took me several long moments to understand what it was. I was halfway back to the brick house before I realized that my pa, a captain in the Nauvoo Legion, Indian fighter and husband to two Irish sisters, was scared.

I could have gone straight into the brick house when I arrived on the porch. I didn't because I saw a parasol leaning against the door and knew it belonged to Pinch Face. Skirting the door, I ducked under the window and eased around the back to where the kitchen curtains waved over two pies.

Thoughts of stealing one of the pies entered my head, but sweets wasn't what I was after. Besides, Alva would know who to blame and come looking for me. I sat my butt down on my heels and ooched along the house. As I got closer to the kitchen window, I heard the sound of Silla's whiny voice and smiled to myself. I hunkered up in the hollow formed by the back stoop and the woodpile.

"The whole town is just in a state," Silla was saying. "And I have the most dreadful news—"

"Oh, it was perfectly awful here, too," Alva said, interrupting. "I just knew we were going to be killed. But I prayed, Silla, and you should have felt the Spirit of the Lord settle over this house." I could almost see Alva's self-satisfied smile. "The bishop told me that I have such a special way with prayer."

"Did you see...him?"

"Oh, no. The bishop had his musket. He wouldn't have dared approach the house. My husband is a crack shot."

Silla went on to tell Alva about the ears nailed up at Slobber Bob's. Her account, which generally followed the Leeman brothers' narrative, was punctuated by frequent gasps of horror from Alva.

"Blood was just everywhere," Silla said when she finished.

"Did anyone find the bodies?" Alva asked in a voice that was barely audible with the weight of expectation. "Don't tell me, Silla. I don't want to hear. I couldn't bear it." A dramatic pause. "Were they terribly mangled?"

"They came into town to get sewn up," Silla said simply. "Leo Poulsen brought them in his wagon."

"They weren't dead?"

"Oh, no. They were howling and going on something awful, though. He just cut off their ears. I was on my way here—I knew you wanted to get an early start on Sunday supper with this ham and all—when Brother Poulsen fetched them in. Why you never saw so much blood, Alva. They were covered with it."

"Who?"

There was a long moment of silence. I didn't have to look to know that Silla was rolling her watery eyes in order to properly prepare Alva for the news.

"Who, Silla? I'll just pop if you don't tell me this instant."

"Philo Hooper and Gilbert Bair."

"Phil...Gilbert Bair!"

My own breath caught in my throat. Handsome and as sophisticated as people tended to get around these parts, Gilbert was the older brother of Eldon Bair and favored son of their father, Josiah Bair. Brother Bair owned the biggest mill in the Narrows. His oldest son was married to a pretty, quiet girl from American Fork who, rumor had it, started to swell up like a dead puppy right after Gilbert began courting her. They got married and directly had a baby, which explained why Gilbert wasn't courting Laurel Anne with the rest of the men. The Bairs had a house next to the mill where Gilbert was preparing to step in for his father someday. Philo Hooper, on the other hand, was a known hanger-on at

Slobber Bob's and a shiftless sort who worked at the mill those times when he wasn't too drunk to tell corn from barley. I knew immediately that it was Philo who tried to force his way into Laurel Anne's bedroom last night. The bigger question was who stood outside calling encouragement to Philo? I swallowed hard because I knew—like I knew that it was Philo who broke the window—that it was Gilbert Bair. I closed my eyes and could see him standing in the rain, bottle in one hand and a sloppy grin on his face. I looked toward the river at the trees. Drunk and mean, Gilbert and Philo had paid the devil for whatever stupidity it was that they intended out here in the dark. Fulton cut off their ears and nailed them to Slobber Bob's door as a warning for anyone else who wanted to come creeping around for a peek at the woman he had sworn an oath to protect. I felt sick.

"Brother Bair came into town in a terrible state," Silla was saying. "Cursing and swearing. Oh, Alva, you should have heard him. He wanted Sheriff Jewkes to raise a posse and ride out here and hang the bishop's hired man. But the sheriff is gone now."

"I told the bishop that Mr. Lorings was trouble," Alva replied. "I prayed about it and got my answer. Here, just put that bread over here out of the way. I counseled him but he wouldn't move on it. This is what happens when he doesn't listen to the strong spirit I get through prayer."

"Oh, Alva, I feel so much safer in this house. Do you suppose we might say a prayer now for Gilbert Bair?"

I snuck away from the window. In a daze, I wandered up the slope to the cabin and climbed up in my tree.

Watching long shadows steal out across the land, I thought about repenting. After some consideration I decided I wouldn't. Most of what had happened last night was God's fault. I only asked for help. I never asked for Gilbert Bair to get his ears cut off. It seemed every time I asked God for help he shoved Fulton Lorings my way. It wasn't my fault the gunman only followed his instincts. God was just lucky that Gilbert and Philo weren't dead.

I wiped my eyes. Tomorrow was church. I suspected that Red Legs would be a major topic of discussion. Knowing the people of our ward like I did, I had a pretty good idea that it wouldn't be an easy experience, nor a prosperous one. Cutting Gilbert and Philo's ears off was sure to set people against Fulton. Nobody would pause long enough to realize that in spite of how cruel a thing it was, it could have been much worse.

Fulton could have killed them as easy as you and I draw breath. That he didn't kill them was an indication that he was capable of showing some restraint. No one would ponder on that, though. Like Bumpa Merrell used to say, what most people called deep thinking was really just an energetic rearrangement of their ignorance.

I climbed down from the tree and went into my bath. Sleep came hard that night. As I lay in my bed, I thought about the presence of Red Legs and our combined future. I didn't see anything but bad.

Whatever else it accomplished, all night visits to Laurel Anne's window ceased from the moment we heard the screams. Life began to change for us Merrells. No more cigar butts and liquor bottles turned up under Laurel Anne's window. All shortcuts through our woods stopped, and social visits to our farm began to taper off. I think if Pinch Face hadn't wanted Pa to marry her so bad, she would have stopped coming over, too.

Most noticeable of all the changes was the fact that Laurel Anne's callers thinned out. The valley boys stopped coming to our farm and hanging around her like nervous dogs. Whether right or wrong, they must have deduced that a courting visit to our farm might be worth their lives. It was, I supposed, a typical doglike response to the wild message quickly spreading through the valley: the wolf is loose on Bishop Merrell's farm.

Chapter Six

In the morning, we loaded up in the wagon and went off to church. Pa drove the team. Alva, as senior wife, sat next to him. The rest of us—me, Ma, Laurel Anne, the twins and Aaron—rode in the back. Sunday was the one day when it was safe to get all us Merrells together. We behaved tolerably polite, out of fear of God if not each other.

Church services were held in a solid rock building that had served more than once as a fort against the Indians. Inside were two hours of the cruelest, butt-punishing pews you've ever seen. I didn't know much about other faiths and the way they conducted worship, but I knew Mormons inside and out. I privately figured that if heaven had any similarities to our Sunday services and the people who attended them, I'd just as soon go to hell. Since whatever waited for us in the next life had to last forever, I'd rather be tormented by demons than bored by saints. At least demons didn't drone and whine about their lot, and they stood a good chance of keeping your interest up with all those pointed forks and screams.

We rode to church in silence. Each of us must have been trying to come to grips with the problem of Fulton Lorings. Fulton himself stayed behind, watching us from the doorway of the barn as we loaded ourselves into the wagon and drove away. From the back, I snuck a tiny wave at him. No response. He was holding something in his hand and I guessed it was the comb.

"Probably steal us blind," Alva muttered under her breath.

I bristled at the insinuation that Fulton was a thief. I felt like asking Pa to turn around and go back so Alva could call him a thief to his face. But she had already started in on Pa, pecking her words at his head like a spiteful hen.

"Well," she said primly, "I hope we have something reassuring to tell them, Bishop. After all, you're their leader and they'll be waiting to hear what we plan to do about it."

"I don't plan on doing anything," Pa said.

"That's not very wise," Alva replied. "Gilbert Bair is the son of a well-respected man. It won't do to pretend like nothing happened."

Pa frowned over the reins and looked like he wished Alva would fall out of the wagon. "Gilbert Bair didn't deserve what happened to him," he said. "But it wouldn't have happened if he hadn't been drinking and peeking in windows," he said.

"We have responsibilities, Bishop," Alva said. "We can't let this go on. What are people going to think?"

Lord, but Pumpkin Ass did love being senior wife to a bishop. It was evident in the routine and frequent way she said "we" when she really meant the bishop. I decided to ask her if "we" meant she had a rat in her pocket, but Ma saw me start and shook her head.

Pa did his best to ignore Alva. She stopped giving him the benefit of her spiritual guidance only when we pulled up at the church. Everyone piled out. From other wagons and buggies, I saw people giving us steady looks. Leo Poulsen, Joe Spafford and his loony wife, the Bairs, the Knights, the Hoffenstetters and Pettus with his lunkhead sons. One-arm Floyd Jackson and his pretty wife and daughters came over and greeted us. I noticed that not many of the other men came over to shake Pa's hand, and none of the women came over to suck up to Alva except Pinch Face. Josh Van Orden was there with his ma, looking as aloof and unreadable as always.

We clumped into the church and got ourselves seated on the benches. Pa, Brother Knight and Brother Stoddard sat up behind the lecture stand, looking spiritual and official and long-winded in their Sunday meeting suits. I got into my favorite seat, a spot where the stovepipe rising up in the center of the room more or less interrupted Pa's view of me. I had to pinch Lehi to get it, but I needed the pipe. There were things a person sometimes had to do to keep from being bored to death, things that person wouldn't want their pa to see. The stovepipe had saved me countless lectures and chores.

When we all got settled, Sister Knight cranked up a howling hymn on a pump organ old enough to sport a bullet hole and Illinois militia spur scars from the Nauvoo days. We all sang, our voices carrying the substance and timbre of lowing cattle. Then came a prayer by Leo Poulsen who, predictably, asked God for the three things all Mormons are born wanting more than life itself: protection from enemies, more rain, and would he please get on with the Second Coming of Jesus.

Pa, who had marched in the Mormon Battalion with Leo years ago, told us how Leo once got lost in the Mexican desert for a few days. When they found him, Pa said, the sun had cooked old Leo darn near down to jerky. He was never really the same after that. It showed up mostly in his choice of words and the way he sometimes forgot things or mixed them up. The meeting might have been your typical slice of tiresome except for what Leo said at the end of his prayer.

"And please and thank you don't let nothing more bad happen to us, Father," he prayed. "Protect us from weevil spirits and the like that might come among us in the skies of rescue. Keep Jesus ever in our mines and the good wrong arm of your destroying angle close by where it might be needed to ride us of evil. Same of Jesus, Amen."

The amens following Leo's prayer carried more than the normal enthusiasm. Leo noticed and looked pleased with himself. I peered around the stovepipe at Pa, who remained expressionless. He got up, cleared his throat, and proceeded to give us a medium-to-good sermon on forgiveness. The subject set well with me as long as I didn't have to include the twins and Bukovski. Where the subject of forgiveness was concerned, I sided with my grandfather, the long-dead Bumpa Merrell, whose school of thought ran more or less to the idea that God never really intended forgiveness to be wasted on sons of bitches. I snuck a look around Ma at the Bair family. Forgiveness obviously wasn't on their list of things to do today either. They looked mighty grim and didn't say amen when Pa finished.

After Pa's sermon we had the sacrament. A couple of elders passed around a plate of tore up bits of bread and a single brass goblet of water.

By the time the water got to me, I could see crumbs floating at the bottom.

After the sacrament, Pa surprised everyone by opening the meeting up to the bearing of testimonies. It wasn't testimony meeting time and inwardly I groaned. I reserved a particularly intense brand of hate for this part of our worship, when any jackass could get up and proclaim personal revelation from God about this or that. Last month, Bill Pettus testified that God had told him to stop doing business with a certain Chicago nail manufacturer because his barrels kept falling apart. Before that, Edwina Spafford testified that Satan had turned up in her yard one day looking remarkably like Poulsens' mangy hound and proceeded to urinate all over her freshly washed bed linen. It was a sign, Edwina claimed, that Satan was seeking to destroy the purity of her daughter, Chrissie. I didn't think so. The natural consequences of being born a Spafford had already botched Chrissie's looks enough to where she wasn't in any danger of becoming impure, unless it was by accident. It was an opinion I wisely kept to myself. Likewise, I said nothing the time Pinch Face testified that God had shown her in a vision where her wandering husband had drowned excruciatingly slow in a river faraway so she could now legally and morally wed another. Everyone knew Pinch Face was after Pa, so I don't think even the most gullible among us believed her.

No, I wasn't big on testimonies. Personal revelation mostly seemed to come from people who didn't have the sense God gave geese. My own meager personal revelation held that testimony giving was a time for simple minds to brag about things no one could prove wrong. The fact that folks like Edwina Spafford, Bill Pettus and Alva took such fervent advantage of it confirmed it.

This particular Sunday, however, would go on record somewhere as the Sunday when testimony time wasn't boring at all. But that was later. First, we had to wade through a couple of average spoutings. The first came from Alva, twenty minutes about the righteous line of authority among plural wives as explained to her by a heavenly messenger in a dream just last week. Ma sat through it quietly, making me wish I had her tolerance for hogwash and the people who thrived on it.

Then we heard from Big Lehman, who said God had finally answered his prayers about going off to find a lot of gold somewhere with his brother, Dumb. They would, Big assured us, hasten directly back and share their wealth with everyone just as soon as God showed them where to dig. Since Big also testified once that Jesus was saving Laurel Anne for him, no one started mentally adding up their share. Which was just as well since even though they really did find gold a few years later, the Sioux found them about the same time. Rupert Lehman, a cousin who accompanied Big and Dumb to the Black Hills, came home safe except for most of the skin on his head and all of the fingers on one hand. He said Big and Dumb had more feathers in them than a couple of Christmas gobblers. In later years, I often wondered if God hadn't hedged his bets a little that day by answering both the Lehman and the Lamanite prayers.

Echo Stoddard, oldest daughter of Pa's second counselor, got up after Big sat down. Echo muttered along for a bit about the truthfulness of the Book of Mormon. Of the three testimonies, Echo's was the most boring but the least self-serving. It made me feel a little guilty for being so lazy where the scriptures were concerned. All in all, it was a pretty typical testimony time.

And then Sister Spafford got up and changed everything.

Edwina Spafford was an ample woman with an equally well-fed opinion of herself. She was married to a long-suffering boot- and shoemaker named Joe, who everyone felt sorry for. Edwina could have been on good terms with Alva if not for the fact they both figured themselves God's chosen on certain things, mostly the same things. Then there was the subject of personality and will. Where Alva was just irksome and overbearing, Edwina was maddening and tyrannical and probably crazy. Even Joe said so, only not within earshot of Edwina.

Edwina drew her shawl closer around her shoulders. She took a deep breath and turned her porky face beatifically in the direction of the ceiling. I saw Joe roll his eyes. Chrissie dropped her head in quiet agony.

"Goozle-dee-gum," Edwina said in a loud voice. "Goozle, goozle, iffum goop. Goozle."

Everyone got still. Some studied their fingernails, others looked around embarrassed. I bit my lip and hid my face against Ma to keep from laughing out loud. Edwina was speaking in tongues, something she specialized in and inflicted on the rest of us at least a dozen times a year. When I asked him about it once, Pa told me people spoke in tongues when they were full of the Spirit of the Lord. With Edwina, however, being full of shit seemed to work just about as well. Up behind the lectern, Pa bowed his head and pinched the bridge of his nose like he was in mortal pain.

Edwina pointed her finger at the bishopric and said something ominous like, "Rooty dooful pifful hum," or gibberish to that effect. She went on in a similar vein for several minutes, gradually building up a head of steam that was impressive if not a little frightening. Toward the end, she started to yodel and shake her bulk from side to side.

"Rickety-rack, fluffer-doo," she cried in a screechy voice, whereupon she collapsed back on the pew, which let out a few cracks of protest. She was panting and sweating buckets. Alva went over to fan her solemnly, like it was a spiritual calling.

I shook my head. Pa told me that speaking in tongues was supposed to be something special, a needed message from heaven that God could only send through a really righteous person. Maybe. I'd never personally heard anyone I considered righteous do it. It was always somebody like Edwina, somebody who used church as their very own stage show.

According to Pa, the gift of tongues was also supposed to be followed by someone who would interpret what the person said to the rest of the congregation, who generally wished God had put it in English in the first place or, as was the case here, at least picked someone to blab it around who had a reputation for being normal, if not a genius.

After a few minutes of nervous waiting, Leo Pouslen stood up. All heads cranked around his way and we waited for him to decipher Edwina's gibberish, a little disappointed because Leo never made much sense either. We had to wait while he composed himself. Hands folded and head bowed, Leo acted like he was trying to wrestle the message out of God and finding the Creator more than a little obstinate today.

"Brothers and misters," Leo intoned solemnly, "Mister—Sister Spafford has been blessed by the spurt of the Lard. Through her earthy voice chords, God is warming us of a great and bombable evil on this land."

"Hoppers?" queried Brother Hoffenstetter—who up until Edwina's tirade had been asleep. It was loud enough for everyone to hear and the congregation snickered. Otto hated hoppers. They were particularly fierce this year, wreaking havoc on his forage crops and nerves.

"No, not hoppers, Mother Hoffenstetter," Leo said. "The devil hisself. He's close by and already hatching us with our gord down. Night before fast, he stuck down one of our brightest spurts—Bilbert Gair."

Either because they believed Leo, or because they owed the Bair family money, most of the congregation nodded their heads. Sister Bair put a hanky to her eyes in grief for Gilbert's ears. Eldon and his father looked stormy. There was no mention of Philo who, since he wasn't even an irregular church goer, probably didn't count.

I felt irritation rise in me like lava. Gilbert Bair hadn't been struck down by Satan. He had his ear sawed off because he made the mistake of prowling around our house when it was being guarded by Fulton Lorings. Then there was the nasty reason for Gilbert's nocturnal visit in the first place, plus the fact that he was drunk as a lord at the time. I would have said something about it but no one would have listened to me. Besides, Leo wasn't done.

"The Lord has commanded us through Mist—Sister Spafford to do sun thing about this curse," Leo was saying. "It's a test, brothers and misters. He wants us to mumble ourselves and rid the valley of this weevil." Here Leo snuck a worried look at Pa behind the lectern. Pa showed no emotion, waiting for Leo to finish up so maybe he could haul him out back of the church and punch on his head until he got his thoughts and words straight. "Anyway," Leo said lamely, "that's what God tells us through Mister Spafford." He gestured at Edwina. "We pray these things, amen." He sat down quickly.

I saw the Bairs nodding. Edwina was bobbing her sweaty head in agreement with Leo's interpretation. I suspect she would have agreed with it even if Leo had said God wanted us to bail out our privies with tin cups.

Everyone waited for Pa. He in turn seemed to be waiting for anyone who might want to add their testimony to the meeting. A long silence passed. When it became apparent that no one had any more advice for God, Pa got up and said we'd close the meeting with a song. He motioned for Sister Knight to play the organ. Sister Knight started to oblige, but Brother Bair leaped up to block her, his face red and boiled looking. He was a big man in a black suit with a yard of gold chain anchoring a watch to his belly. He was the richest man in the area and an infrequent church goer.

"Now hold on a darn minute here," Bair shouted. "We got some business that needs settling."

The outburst in the middle of church made everyone sit up and take notice. Pa didn't bat an eye. He motioned for Sister Knight to start playing.

"We'll talk about it as soon as we close out the meeting, Brother Bair," Pa said.

Josiah Bair shook his head. "There's no time like the present, I reckon," he said stubbornly. "I want it talked about right now."

"Let us close the meeting first and—"

"No, Merrell," Bair said, shaking a finger at the lectern where Pa stood flanked by his counselors. "It's time you faced up to the danger you've put us all in. If you can't talk about it, or won't, I will."

Pa stayed cool as ice. "No, Josiah, you won't," he said. "What you will do is plant your fat hams back down next to your wives and hold your tongue until we finish the Lord's meeting with a hymn and a prayer like always."

I guess it was the fact that Pa appeared to be talking as Captain Lee Merrell—Indian fighter and guerilla chief against the U.S. Army— instead of just a bishop that made Josiah Bair wealthy miller and self-important blowhard think it over and sit back down. He plainly didn't like it but the grim look on Pa's face convinced Josiah that it just might be the best idea he would have all day. Eldon looked some surprised that his pa had backed down to mine.

Disoriented and fidgety, we muddled through "A Mighty Fortress," after which a skinny stage driver named Phillips ran us through the fastest prayer in the history of the church. Normally there was a scramble for the door at the close of a meeting. This time, however, nobody moved when Phillips said amen. He leaped back into his seat like he was an hour off schedule and there were Utes on the horizon. Pa sat motionless, waiting.

Bair stormed a glance at the congregation. "Well, are we going to talk about this or aren't we?"

"Another minute, please, Brother Bair," Sister Knight said. With several other sisters, she went around the chapel, gathering up children for an impromptu Sunday School outside. I didn't want to go but Ma said I had to. Scuffing my feet along the floor, I permitted Sister Knight to shepherd me out the door with some thirty or forty other sets of ears deemed too sensitive to hear what the adults were going to talk about. Outside, the sisters broke us up into smaller groups for instruction. My group consisted of the twins, Sarah and Fannie Gormann, Joey Leeks, Coyle Morgan, Josh Van Orden and a half dozen others. Except for Josh, I had overdue accounts with everyone there. The worst were Sarah and Fannie. Our running feud had gotten me stood in a corner at school more than once. We gathered under a tree and prepared ourselves to be fatally bored by Squawk Martin. Squawk was fresh back from a mission to the Sandwich Islands and about as exciting as cold toast.

"Today, we're going to talk about Adam and Eve," Squawk said, opening his dog-eared Bible.

Who cared about Adam and Eve? I glanced back at the chapel where the subject of the decade was being hashed over. Beyond the chapel I spied the double-hole privy set back in the trees. An idea sprouted up in my head and I raised my hand before Squawk could build up spiritual momentum.

"Yes, Sister Merrell?" Squawk asked.

"I have to go to the privy."

Fannie and Sarah snickered at this but, I maintained an urgent, imploring look on my face. There are two kinds of boring people: boring and smart, and boring and dumb. Fortunately, Squawk was of the boring and dumb tribe. If he really knew me, or even kids my age, he would've seen through my request and made me sit through his lesson on how Adam and Eve got fooled by a snake. Instead, he glanced at the privy and nodded once before turning back to his Bible.

I ran, gradually angling my line of travel until I got a corner of the chapel between me and the rest of the grown-ups. Then I detoured and cut around to the back. Our congregation had enough kids that I wouldn't be missed, unless someone took a moment to try and figure out why things seemed to be running so smoothly.

On the back wall of the chapel an iron grate hung over an opening into a shallow cellar beneath the building. Formerly where the stock had been run in and out of the fort during the Black Hawk War, it was now closed up to prevent exactly the sort of thing I intended to do. Rust and neglect had loosened the bolts fastening the grate to the stone wall. I lifted the crossed metal bars and let them fall, then ran like hell as a dozen mad wasps whirled out looking for a fight. After the wasps drifted off, I returned and scrunched inside and up under the cobwebbed cross beams of the floor. Angry, ghostlike voices settled around me in the half light. Praying there were no snakes or badgers of similar minds as the wasps, I duck-walked my way through the gloom to the corner underneath the lectern. I peered up through a narrow ventilation grate and into the chapel.

"He's your man and it's your farm, Merrell," Josiah Bair's voice boomed. "You encouraged him to stay and I hold you responsible for what happened to Gilbert."

"Gilbert's a grown man," I heard Floyd Jackson say in Pa's defense. "I'd like to know what business he had on the Merrell place in the middle of the night? Seems to me he was up to no good."

"That's not the point," Bair growled. "Gilbert may have misbehaved, certainly. That isn't exactly a crime. You probably sowed some wild oats of your own when you were younger, Jackson."

"Never had to sew my ears back on," Floyd said dryly.

"My son was mutilated by an outlaw," Bair roared. "This isn't a joke and I want something done about it."

I heard Sister Bair start to weep. The next voice belonged to her son Eldon, recognizable by it's smooth, superior tone. I shuffled to the other side of the vent and spotted him still sitting beside his mother.

"The question is, what are we going to do about it?" Eldon said. "This hired man of the bishop's is a vicious killer. It's only a matter of time before someone else gets hurt, maybe one of your children. Someone has to send him packing. It might not be easy, but I'm sure it could be done. I guess what I'm saying is the bishop might need some help doing it."

I made a face. Eldon was sucking up to Pa to impress Laurel Anne. His argument, however, seemed to sway the congregation. I heard muttered assents.

"And who's going to do that, Eldon?" Floyd asked. "You?"

An elaborate silence followed and then Eldon said, "If I have to. There's people I care about out—around here."

Floyd chuckled and said, "I bet there is."

Although she was out of my line of sight, you could almost feel the warmth of my sister's blush.

"Brother Lorings hasn't hurt anyone who didn't somehow deserve it," Pa said. "Everyone in this room knows I had trouble in the past with night visitors. Bob's brewery is just off through my back fields, and it's common knowledge that I dusted some trespassers with salt the summer before. That should have been warning enough to stay away. I'm not saying it's right what Brother Lorings did, but it wouldn't have happened if Gilbert had been behaving properly."

Everyone started to talk at once. Argue was more like it. Eldon leaned back and put his arms up on the back of the bench. The butt of his shiny pistol protruded from his coat. He made sure everyone saw it.

"Who's next is what I want to know," Rolly Howard called out.

"He doesn't belong here," someone else said.

"I don't want him around my Chrissie," Sister Spafford bawled. "I know he's after her."

"I reckon I side with her, Bishop," Bill Pettus said. "I don't want him around my family, either. The way I see it, as our bishop you got to settle this for us. You got to get rid of him."

"And if I don't?"

"We'll get someone to do it for you."

"Who you got in mind, Bill?" Pa said, his voice cold. Bill seemed to shrink. I could see him calculating things, namely that Pa was a Merrell and forever was a damn long time to have a Merrell mad at you.

"Well, the church authorities, I guess," Pettus said lamely. "Or maybe the sheriff."

"The sheriff," Josiah Bair scoffed. "Nobody's seen that bag of wind for days. I went straight to Judge Parkins over to Battle Creek. He claims there's no legal proof Red Legs cut up my son, at least not so it could be proved in court."

"That happens to be true," Pa said. "It was dark. Gilbert and Philo can't identify who attacked them. There's no proof Brother Lorings had anything to do with it."

"Ridiculous," Bair snapped. "Of course he did it. Who else? He goes around with that big knife of his all the time. He's killed hundreds of men. And another thing, Merrell, he's no brother of ours. He's an animal. I say call him what he is—Stuart's Wolf or Hash Face."

"I've said it before," Pa replied. "I owe that man. He saved my two girls when I guess no one else could. I won't repay him by sending him off just because you're all scared. He hasn't hurt anyone who wasn't asking for it. I reckon this is the first time he's been around our kind of people and he needs a chance to adjust. I'm sorry about your boy, Josiah, but he plain wouldn't have got hurt if he'd been behaving like he should."

"We could still get someone else to run him off," Pettus said again. "If you won't do it, Bishop, we could sure get someone else. I even got somebody in mind."

Pa's tone said it plain: Bill Pettus should never make the mistake of crossing Lee Merrell's path when he was done being bishop. "Who might that be?" Pa asked sternly.

"Porter Rockwell."

The temperature in the chapel dropped ten degrees. Porter Rockwell was a gunman and a bodyguard to Brigham Young. Crouched in the damp cellar, I shivered. I'd seen Brother Rockwell a few times. He came out to our place whenever he needed good smithy work. His pale eyes never seemed to rest and I don't ever remember him smiling. And just like Fulton, he always had a gun close to hand.

"That's right," Brother Bair said, eager now. "If it doesn't come under the law, then we could pay Porter to get rid of this Red Legs. Porter'd send him flying, I bet."

Everyone started talking loud about Porter. Pettus was fair certain that Brigham Young's bodyguard was up in Salt Lake. Rolly said he thought Porter was out in the Tintic Mountains chasing horse thieves unfortunate enough to have attracted his attention. Sister Spafford said she was certain Porter was drunk at his tavern in Lehi City and she wouldn't let her Chrissie within a block of the place.

"Are we talking here what I think we're talking?" Pa asked, interrupting. "Is that what you folks want? To settle this with more killing?"

"If we have to," Pettus said, fuming.

"Oh, Bishop," Eldon cried harshly. "With scum like him, we'd be doing the territory a favor. Why, I'll do it myself if it comes to that. I owe it to my brother. I owe it to all of you."

"We'd be planting you like seed corn five minutes later, youngster," Floyd laughed. "What pieces we found."

"Watch it, Jackson," Eldon warned.

"Gonna shoot me, are you, Eldon? I see you brung your shiny pistol to church."

"I just might."

"Snot-nose, you wouldn't have lasted ten seconds at Fort Donelson."

"There's still Porter," Pettus cut in. "Who's in favor of Porter...talking to this killer?"

"I am," Josiah said, gruffly. "I'd rather he was swinging from a tree all legal-like, but one way or another, I want him to pay for what he did."

Pettus tried to organize a vote. Several hands started to wave in the air. They came down quick enough when Pa stood up.

"You folks won't be running anyone off my land," he said. "And you won't be sending anyone out to do it for you."

"This ain't just a church affair," Pettus said. "We don't have to listen to you." He pointed at Sister Spafford. "What about her warning?"

"What of it?" Pa snapped. He gathered up his books and headed for the door. In the back, Alva, Ma, Laurel Anne and Silla came into view as they stood up.

"Where are you going, Merrell?" Josiah demanded.

"I'm taking my family home."

"Home? We haven't settled this."

"And we won't. Not this way." Pa turned and looked at the congregation. "I would advise you all to think twice before you go hatching any plans to try and run Brother Lorings out of this valley. He's not a man who runs. The mess you stir up may be worse than the one you think you're trying to solve."

Pa didn't wait for a reply. He stormed out of the chapel. Red-faced with fury, Josiah muttered a word at Pa's back that brought a gasp from Edwina Spafford. She slapped her hands over her ears, changed her mind and clamped them over Chrissie's.

I scooted my butt back over to the grate and slipped out past the wasps. I made it around the front of the chapel just as the rest of the family was loading up into the wagon. Pa and Josiah were shooting murderous looks at each other. Everyone else was clearly put out by the fact that the bishop was leaving church early. I boosted myself into the wagon as Eldon Bair came over and spoke to Laurel Anne.

"I'll be dropping by tonight to check on your safety, Laurel, dear," he said, holding his hat in his hands like a dinner plate.

"I'm sure that won't be necessary, Eldon," Laurel Anne said, thanking him just the same.

"Nevertheless, I shall. I would never forgive myself if I didn't take extra precautions where this matter is concerned."

Pa didn't wait for Laurel Anne to tell Eldon to bring some iron earmuffs. He slapped down the reins and we were wheeling out of the churchyard in a cloud of dust.

We didn't slow down for more than a mile. Pa ran the team hard, letting his temper do most of the driving. Ma finally got up and went up behind him, putting her hand gently on the back of his neck. Pa gave her a look of surprise as she bent and whispered something in his ear. When she finished, all the anger suddenly ran out of him and he backed the horses off to a slow amble, looking foolish. I breathed easier. We all did. Pa's fuse was hard to light, but once it was lit you hunted cover, preferably underground somewhere far, far away. Ma was the only person who dared approach him when he got like that. She never once failed to calm him down. Likewise, Pa never failed to pay close attention when she talked quietly in his ear. As usual, Alva was some put out, but she didn't say anything. Ma's power over Pa was Alva's cross to bear in life. I added a few extra nails of my own by grinning openly at her.

We arrived home and unloaded. Pa put the team away and we tromped into the brick house for the dinner Alva and Pinch Face had put together. Josh was there and he sat next to me. We faced the twins but I knew with Josh beside me, I'd get through the meal without any teasing.

At twelve, Josh Van Orden was a serious, silent boy. Unless you knew him well, you'd think he'd never laughed in his whole life. I'd only seen it a couple of time myself. He had thick hair the color of walnut stain, a shotgun scattering of freckles and bottle-green eyes. Lately the deep green of those eyes sometimes put a funny weakness deep in the pit of my stomach. Josh almost never went to school. Instead, he worked hard at the Pettus cooperage to support his ma. In turn, Pinch Face was hard on him. She'd never really forgiven her husband for running out on her, and I think she took it out on the product of their failed marriage, which is why Josh almost never accompanied his ma to Sunday dinner at our place. He must have worked a miracle or found a treasure to be allowed off their place for the day.

You had to give Alva and Silla credit. They set a fine table. After Ma said grace, we plowed into buttered corn, baked beans, squash, cucumber salad, biscuits so light and fine they needed anchors to keep them on the table and a baked ham roughly the size of a small child. We ate like a gang of ravenous wolves. No one said anything about what happened at church. I think we knew Pa wasn't in the mood to discuss it. He kept looking at Ma. Ma repeatedly complimented Alva and Pinch Face on the dinner. After a few minutes, Pa got the idea and complimented them as well. Pinch Face gave Pa a look so full of naked gratitude that it squeezed her plain face up into a pucker. She looked as if a toad had found its way into her bloomers. Alva merely nodded, alternating her glum look between Ma and Pa.

After dinner, Silla and Alva brought out three kinds of pie. We polished them off and shoved back groaning, a family of well-fed ticks. Ma offered to help with the dishes but Alva was in a surly mood and turned her down flat. She helped with clearing the dishes anyway and then excused herself, walking back up to the cabin. After a minute, Pa got up and followed her. Alva went into the kitchen and began slamming her pots around, scaring Pinch Face. I collected a plate of food and motioned to Josh. Together we slipped out of the house.

Halfway to the barn, I stopped and showed Josh the plate of food I'd fixed up for Fulton. Beans, corn, two biscuits and the softest bits of ham I could find. There was also a big slice of cherry pie mixed in for good measure.

"Want to come with me while I feed him?" I asked, making it sound like I had a wild animal chained up in the barn.

Josh shrugged. I led him in the direction of the barn. Up on the slope, I saw Ma and Pa go into the cabin and close the door. It didn't take a genius to figure out that our cabin was going to be full of squeaks in about one minute. I made a mental note to stay away until Pa came back down. When he did, I knew he'd feel better about what happened at church. Ma, for her part, would probably sing me to sleep tonight. The one bad spot about Ma receiving Pa so openly was Alva. I hoped her pots and pans could stand the strain of our family being set to right.

Fulton was in the tack room. A small book he'd borrowed from Ma rested in his lap. A gun lay close at hand. After all the times I'd fetched his meals, I'd like to think his eyes had some kind of greeting for me. It was hard to tell, though. I put the plate on top of a barrel and backed away. His eyes sized up Josh and came back to me, waiting.

"Mr. Lorings," I said, sounding extra formal but not knowing how to do it otherwise. "This is my friend, Josh Van Orden. He's twelve."

Josh nodded. Fulton did likewise. A long period of silence followed as they took each other in. Josh didn't seem a bit nervous and it occurred to me then that he and Mr. Lorings were big and small versions of each other. Neither of them said much and both seemed about as fearless as God.

"Anyway," I said, "we'll just go so's you can eat." I started to turn but Josh remained fixed in place. His eyes were on the guns hanging in their holsters behind Fulton. He looked down at the man whose mere presence panicked an entire territory and said, just as casual as you please:

"Did you cut off their ears?"

My mouth hung open, a haven for stray flies. In spite of all the talk on the subject, no one had ever asked Fulton if he'd done what he stood accused of. We had better sense and lives we still wanted to live.

Fulton didn't kill us. He didn't leap to his feet with an oath and threaten our miserable lives. He didn't even fire up those terrible eyes of his. He just sat there staring at Josh. After a long, breathless minute, he gave a little nod.

"Good," Josh said solemnly. Then he turned and walked out of the tack room. I caught up with him outside.

"Are you crazy? What did you do that for?"

"Gilbert Bair beats his wife. He got what was coming to him."

I didn't know what to say to that. Rather than argue, I asked Josh if he wanted to go swimming. He said yes, looking more approachable than usual. We headed off toward Indian Rocks, even though it was the Sabbath day and therefore supposed to be kept holy and boring.

The swimming hole was in a thick grove of overhanging willows where the shaded creek backed up against two enormous boulders covered with old Indian writing. Nobody knew what the writing meant, including the Indians we had the infrequent occasion to ask. Mostly it was just lines and whorls and squiggles edged with lichen, but also some pictures of buffalo and wolves and people. Some of the people were men fighting with spears and arrows. It was easy to tell which of the etched figures were men. They had long tallywhackers stuck on them, as if the ancient artists themselves were enormously proud of such a ridiculous thing. The only time Alva had been to the rocks, she took one look at the tallywhacker men and forbade me to ever come back to such an evil spot. Of course I ignored her. Partly because it was my job, but also because Indian Rocks was the only swimming hole around deep enough to dive into without cracking your head on the bottom.

Arriving at the rocks, Josh and I split up in the bushes to undress. Girls went to the left, boys to the right. Actually, I only knew that it was me who went to the left. I was the only girl bold enough to swim naked with boys, and even then only with a few male cousins, my late brother, and occasionally with Josh.

I snatched off my church clothes behind a bush. Two hops and half a skip and I plunged deep into cool water. A second later came the sound of another splash. Josh swam up next to me.

We swam for an hour, during which Josh said a total of two words. The first was in response to me asking if he was ever coming back to school: "No." The last, when it came time to leave. He simply said "chores" and swam to the edge of the pool. I turned my head as he climbed out, but not before I glimpsed the marks of a dozen raw cuts across his thin back, as if someone much bigger had waded into him with a rose cane. Although I had seen marks like that and worse on Josh before, the sight still made me cringe.

Everyone knew Silla Van Orden beat her son. However, I doubt anyone but me, Josh and her knew just how bad the beatings got. Josh certainly never let on. He worked for Brother Pettus, did his home chores and minded his own business. And it was plain from the way he carried himself that he expected others to mind theirs. I kept quiet about them because I knew that if I said anything, Josh would disappear out of my life.

Walking together back to the house, I understood that there was the way things were supposed to be and the way they are. Good people sometimes lived the way they ought to so blindly that they were never much good to those caught in the clutches of the way things really are. I remembered how casually Josh had approached Fulton, as if there was nothing the killer could do that would possibly worry a boy who carried those kinds of marks under his shirt. I knew then that if anyone could ever reach Fulton, it would have to be someone like Josh, someone able to wade across a horrible moat of misery because the consequences of such a trip no longer mattered.

Around dusk, Eldon rode up to our farm. I was sitting on the porch and watched him ride up the lane. He wore a new shirt and enough pomade on his hair to make it look like a Chinaman had lacquered his head.

Eldon's arrival signified that the road leading to our farm hadn't been blown up or otherwise blocked. Usually on Sundays we had lots of visitors. This Sunday, after the mess at church, nobody had come by. Eldon's visit today was no surprise, to be sure. Word was that Henry du Pont was off on a patrol in the desert and Lester Knight had gone back up into American Fork Canyon to work on his gold mine. Eldon wasn't going to let all that free time with Laurel Anne just slide by. He would have come calling if it had been hailing anvils. Besides, he wore his pistol in a new holster on his leg and it was obvious that he wanted Laurel Anne to see it.

Laurel Anne received all her callers on the east porch, away from the evening sun and prying eyes. Close enough though, so that Pa could check on her from time to time. As usual, she hadn't reckoned anyone would be curious enough to crawl through the dirt under the porch, squirm up under the boards and tear their jumper in order to peek out through the bushes. It was a good lesson for me. Being an accomplished spy has less to do with your own craftiness than it does with the moronic oversight of those you intend to spy on.

Eldon was smart enough to begin the evening's courting by apologizing for Gilbert's behavior. As might be expected, though, he laid it all off on Philo, claiming that he had infected Gilbert with gentile ways. Things would be better now that Gilbert had foresworn liquor of all kinds. Laurel Anne accepted the apology graciously enough, although she managed to get it dragged out to half an hour. In the end I guess it was hard to stay mad at someone with one ear.

Laurel Anne fetched out a tray with a corked bottle of a juice she called Ladies Quiet Cherry Comfort. She made it herself, and from personal experience I can tell you that it's just plain awful. Pa calls it "Hairy Discomfort." Laurel Anne's beaus lapped it up by the quart, though. They'd guzzle a bottle of weasel spit if Laurel Anne served it.

"I see you're wearing your pistol, Eldon," she said, handing him a glass of her juice. He took it, sipped, coughed discreetly and nodded.

"Yes, I am," he replied. "These days, a man should be prepared for every eventuality."

"I don't like pistols," Laurel Anne said.

"Yes," Eldon said. "However, I'm wearing it for you. And for my brother."

"And why, pray tell, would you be wearing a pistol for me?"

Eldon stroked his chin, wanting Laurel Anne to know he was thinking deep on the subject. "I guess you might say I consider it my duty to defend those who are unable protect themselves from the villainous behavior of others."

Horse piss. Eldon wore his gun because he wanted Laurel Anne to see it, plain and simple. There was something else there too, but I couldn't quite tell what it was yet.

"Guns are a necessary fact of frontier life, dear," Eldon said condescendingly. "As civilized as most of us are, there are still those who only respect the law according to Colonel Samuel Colt. The .44 caliber objection is all that stands between the genteel and the savages. I'm prepared to do just that." He looked down at the barn and took another sip of Laurel Anne's red nausea. He was determined, if irritating. "You shouldn't worry. I target shoot at least twice a week and, modesty aside, dear, I have become quite proficient. The other day, I actually hit a bottle tossed in the air by one of my fellow practicing pistolsmiths. Shattered it completely to pieces. So, you see, you wouldn't need to fear a thing in my company."

In the bushes, I pretended to throw up.

"Well, you certainly don't need a pistol to court me, Eldon Bair," Laurel Anne replied.

"There are those who feel otherwise," Eldon said. "Your father's farm is not as safe as it once was, dear."

"Because of Brother Lorings?"

Eldon shook his head. "Don't call him that," he said. "He's no brother. You know what he did to mine. He's not even a fit subject of conversation for mixed groups, but now that you bring him up, yes, your father's generosity toward this—individual—seems to have gotten the better of his judgement."

"That may be," Laurel Anne said. "And I don't doubt our Mr. Lorings is a dangerous man. As you know, he came to our rescue."

"Gratitude is an honorable emotion," Eldon conceded gravely. "Even to one such as he. However, considering more recent events, I feel compelled to say that care should be given that gratitude not place one in bondage or unnecessary danger. As you say, he is a dangerous man."

Laurel Anne nodded. "I gather Rose thinks quite highly of him."

Hearing my name, I perked up.

Eldon snorted. "She would. The child's obsessed with riff raff and the like. She's far too free with her wanderings and comments, if you ask me. It's the Irish blood. Thankfully, you don't have any."

"No, I don't," Laurel Anne said reproachfully.

Eldon realized then that he had overstepped his prerogative and set about apologizing yet again. No easy task with Laurel Anne. She exacted a heavy toll from those who paid homage to her beauty.

"What I meant to say, dear," Eldon stammered, "is that you are certainly graced with your own mother's beauty."

"You never knew my mother, Eldon. And you couldn't find two men in this entire world who would tell you that Colleen Merrell isn't beautiful."

Eldon fumed. "Blast it, Laurel Anne, you know what I mean. Sister Colleen is...attractive. So are you and I've expressed my feelings for you several times. Why do you persist in making me feel badly."

"Oh, Eldon," Laurel Anne cooed, happy that she was able to get a rise out of him at last. I wriggled closer, hoping we were getting around to the kissing part. "Silly. You know I'm only teasing." She got up and sat beside him, letting him briefly take her hand. "Would you really fight a duel to defend me?"

"Why I most certainly would. I prize honor above all things, and your honor above heaven itself. I'd fight a duel with Satan himself for you."

"That's sweet, but unnecessary."

"Well I would. Eventually, I'll have to fight one for my family's honor."

"Oh?"

He nodded and stood up. He began pacing the porch. "This Red Legs fellow needs to be brought to justice. For some reason, Sheriff Jewkes doesn't seem up to it. There's even a report going around that he's run off. But I can tell you that myself and a number of the church elders are discussing ways to handle it, if it comes to that."

"You don't mean force."

"Laurel, dear," Eldon said patiently. "It's the only thing his sort understands."

"And what sort is that? None of you have said so much as a word to him. Has anyone around here tried communicating with him? He can't speak, of course, but I've seen him write notes to Father."

"Of course not. It wouldn't do any good. Everyone knows he's mute. He's probably incapable of human reason as well. Some terrible birth defect that affected his mind, I hear. They say he got it from his mother who, well, if you must know, was a—woman of the street in St. Louis." He paused. "I'm sorry I said that in front of you, dear."

Laurel Anne stood up and walked to the rail. She looked down the lane to the barn, down to the lair of the wolf. "What else do they say about him?" she asked.

"Oh, I don't know," Eldon replied, impatient that the conversation had turned away from himself. "It's not really a fit subject for the Sabbath. Or for ladies. Please come and sit down."

Laurel Anne persisted. "Your father thought it was fit enough to interrupt services. Why do they call him Red Legs and—what was the other?—Stuart's Wolf?"

Eldon sighed. "Yes, Stuart's Wolf. I don't know about that one but I have it on good authority that the name Red Legs comes from the time he massacred some homesteaders in Colorado. He did it for money. He even shot the innocent little babies in their cradles. They say he was wading in blood when it was over. That's where he got the name."

"Oh, dear," she said. "Does anyone know why he hides his face?"

Eldon's impatience was clearly visible. "He's ugly. I heard he was born with a harelip or a disease. They say he takes the mask off when he goes out to kill, so he can shock his victims with his appearance before he slashes them to pieces."

"How perfectly horrid."

Eldon got up and stood behind her. "Now do you understand why I wear a pistol? The thought of you so close to this animal makes me feel I must do something. If I thought it would make you feel safer, I'd go down there right now and settle this."

I nearly groaned out loud at this. It was bold talk for the pampered son of a miller who only recently started sporting a pistol. Bolder talk still for someone who in another ten minutes would have his life saved by a ten-year-old girl.

It was growing uncomfortable there under the lilacs. Now that darkness had fallen, mosquitoes hummed around my ears and bugs skittered over my legs. Fortunately, it looked like Laurel Anne and Eldon were getting around to the kissing part. Eldon knew that Pa wouldn't let Laurel Anne stay out on the porch much longer. If he wanted a kiss, he'd better hurry it up.

"I wish," Eldon started to say, turning Laurel Anne around to face him. "I wish I could talk reason to you, dear."

"And what kind of reason is that?"

"That we should be married and end this nonsense. Henry du Pont is not the man for you. He's not even a Mormon. You'd spend years wandering from one shabby army post to the next with him. Marry me, Laurel Anne, and you'll never have to leave this valley. I'll buy you anything you want."

The offer sounded like a straight up bribe to me. I think Laurel Anne thought so too, because she smiled and tried to slip away from him. "I haven't received a witness about marriage yet, Eldon," she said. "I've told you, I can't agree to any man until I do."

"A witness?" he said, holding on to her. "Are we still stuck on that? Well, what if you've had a witness and just don't know it?"

"I'd know it," Laurel Anne said. "Now please turn me loose. You're being forward. Father will see and then—"

Funny thing about guns and some men. Having one makes them feel they have a leg up on everyone else, that they can do what they want and everyone has to like it. I guess it was the pistol on Eldon's leg that made him do what he did. He would have been too afraid of Pa otherwise.

"A witness," Eldon said. He sounded a mix of angry and stupid. "If what you're looking for is a witness dear, try this."

Before Laurel Anne could budge, he was kissing her. He got his arms around hers and kissed her good. It looked like more of a mad thing than a romantic thing. Laurel Anne managed to get her face loose for a second.

"Eldon! Stop it. Stop it right now."

But Eldon didn't stop it. He wrestled another kiss while Laurel Anne struggled to get free. There was a brief scuffle on the porch and then Laurel Anne was loose. Eldon was doing a little jig on one foot. He leaned against a post, rubbing his shin.

"You didn't have to do that," he protested.

"I didn't—? Eldon Bair, you get off this porch and leave right now. I mean it."

"No you don't," he said, trying to placate her. "It's just that you got me so mad with that witness stuff."

"And now you've got me mad. Good night."

"Don't take on so," Eldon said. "You needed that and you know it. It's high time you understood how deeply I feel for you. You're the woman for me."

"I am not the woman for you," Laurel Anne said hotly. "Why, I'd rather marry someone as ugly and disgusting as Lorings than have another thing to do with you."

"Now, look..." Eldon started to say.

Laurel Anne didn't bother arguing with Eldon any further. She marched straight for the house. He tried to catch her arm but she yanked free of him, went inside and slammed the door.

Eldon waited for minute, I guess trying to figure if he ought to knock on the door and get her to hold still long enough to apologize. But Pa was in there and Eldon, despite his bragging ways, wasn't going to face Pa after the mess at church. He shook his head and straightened the pistol on his leg. He moved to the other end of the porch and peered in through the window, careful so he wouldn't be seen.

Although he said it to himself in a low voice, I heard him plain as day. "Go ahead and get mad, you little hussy. I'd like to do more than that. And I will, too. Just you wait." Whistling, he cut down the steps to his horse.

I was getting ready to move when I heard another sound. It came from behind and off to the side of me—the soft whisper of leaves over cloth. I turned my head and peered hard, hoping it wasn't Squash Head. It wasn't, but I wished it was. In the shadow of Alva's raspberry bushes, little more than a black shape cut against the evening stars, was Fulton. A thin rim of light reflected off his knife in his hand. I almost shrieked with fright.

Fulton didn't see me. He was too busy concentrating on the departing Eldon Bair. I knew that he had seen Eldon force a kiss on Laurel Anne and heard what she had said about him being ugly and disgusting. He'd probably also heard what the miller's son said about the woman he'd sworn a holy oath to protect. Eldon wasn't going to make it home in one piece tonight. Lord, no. When Stuart's Wolf caught him along the lane, Eldon was going to pay for insulting my sister. They'd find bits and pieces of him from here to California.

Oblivious to his impending doom, Eldon climbed on his horse and turned it out of our yard. When I looked back to where Fulton had been, he was gone. I jumped up and fought my way out of the bushes.

Don't make any mistake about it. I ran that night not for Eldon Bair, but for Fulton Lorings. I knew what would happen if he killed Eldon. Even though he didn't deserve dying for his rudeness, the world wouldn't have missed Eldon. On the other hand, I would have missed Fulton terribly. That's why I ran with my lungs bursting, no thought for Squash Head or other demons of the night that normally terrified me. Around the house and down past the privy, through the bushes and the weeds.

Twice I fell full length. I scrambled up, knees on fire, and pushed on, knowing that I wouldn't make it, that I would arrive to find Eldon butchered up like a hog.

Somehow I did make it, though, and when I thought about it later, it's the part that scared me the most: those few seconds when there was doubt that I could keep Fulton Lorings from crossing the bleak line between killing and murder.

Wheezing like the bellows of Pa's forge, I pulled up at the bottom of the lane. Thankfully, my shortcut through the field put me there before Eldon. I clambered up on the rails of the fence just as he came riding by.

"Howdy, Eldon," I cried.

Actually, it was more of a screech. Eldon's horse did a few frantic crow hops while Eldon cussed and tried to get to his pistol. He got it out fine but dropped it in the road.

"Rose?" Eldon exclaimed when he finally brought his horse under control. He was breathing hard. "What in the devil are you doing out here at night? Does your mother know where you are?"

"I reckon," I said, still breathing hard myself but trying to sound casual.

Climbing off his horse to hunt for his pistol, Eldon bawled me out. I
ignored him, my eyes searching the darkness for Fulton. I finally spotted
him standing back in the shadows where the lane met the road. I talked
fast so Eldon wouldn't start looking around, too. If he saw Fulton, Eldon
was stupid enough to make an issue of it and get himself killed.

"You scared the blazes out of my horse," Eldon snapped at me, finally
locating his pistol. He jammed it back in its holster. "If you were my
child, you'd be getting a good whipping right now. Fact is, I've a mind to
give you one anyway."

I got mad and thought about daring him. He'd be dead three seconds
after the first whack and I knew it. But that wouldn't do at all. Somehow
I had to get him moving.

"Sorry, Eldon," I said. "I'm waiting here for Pa so we can go look for
one of our colts. He'll be right here in a second. He got called back up to
the house to talk to Laurel Anne."

That put a burr under Eldon. He didn't feel like hanging around any
longer than necessary in case Laurel Anne told Pa about him being rude.
He muttered a few dire threats and put his heels into his horse, trotting
safely past the spot where Fulton had been waiting.

I stayed on the fence until the sound of hoofbeats faded in the night,
satisfied that Eldon had made it away safe.

Fulton wasn't happy about missing his opportunity with Eldon. Off
in the pasture I heard a musical note of metal on metal. I turned and saw
the dim shadow of him striding through the star-lit field back toward the
barn, swinging his knife at black-eyed Susans and fence posts that got in
his way. His knife found a nail or something in one of the posts and
sparks flashed.

I climbed down off the fence. It was me who had started all of this and
it was up to me to put a stop to it. I had to tell Fulton that I lied to him
about Laurel Anne.

Being a coward, I couldn't very well face him straight up. Not after
the furious way I'd seen him move through the field. Keeping low, I crept
up to the barn and around to the loft ladder. Out in the stock pens I heard
the horses moving around as Fulton checked the gates. I climbed the ladder into the loft and crouched above the tack room, waiting for him to
finish his evening chores.

He came into the barn carrying a lantern. I hunkered low behind the
hay. There was something about the way he moved this time that fright-

ened me, as if he had slipped the bonds of reason. He paced like the tigers I'd seen in the cages at Dan Costello's Circus. Then he went to checking his things and getting ready to throw himself down on the feed sacks for the night. He glanced up at the loft and I turned to ice. But he didn't seem to notice me and went straight back to doing what he was doing. After a minute he went out of my view, leaving the lantern as if he expected to come right back.

But he didn't. I waited for the longest time and he didn't return. I started to get worried. He wouldn't have gone off for good leaving the lantern burning in the barn. Maybe he'd gone to the privy or something. It didn't matter. He wasn't in the mood to be approached tonight.

I turned to go and my blood froze. There was something in the loft with me. I sensed it more than I saw it, some weird animal-like intuition that let me know I was close to death. With a frightened whimper, I peered hard into the shadows. A black form took shape, hunkered in the shadows between me and the ladder. Dim light from the loft opening played across eyes so cold they snapped my veins like a blast of frost.

"Oh," I squeaked.

The black shape shifted and light gleamed along the edge of a familiar huge knife. My knees gave out and I plopped down in the hay numb with terror. It was the worst thing imaginable. While I was distracted, a furious, vengeful Fulton Lorings had come up the ladder behind me as soft and silent as death itself and put himself between me and the ladder. The only other way out was the long drop behind me.

"What you want, girl?"

Fulton's voice was raspy and full of mush, heavy with S's and soft consonants, as if God had handed a snake the gift of speech. It didn't sound at all like the first times I heard it. It wasn't nervous and fretful. This time it was an eager voice, full of pending cruelty.

I tried to say "nothing" but it came out a series of stuttered Ns. My tongue and lips kept trying to crawl off my face. Pa had told me about a thousand times that spying would get me in trouble. His nagging prophecy had come to the fullness of times, even as my own time ran down into a few worthless seconds.

"You been scoutin' me?" Fulton asked.

A fever of fright swept over me and I shivered. Jesus, please. No, no, no, no.... I gave my head a violent shake.

"I think so," the shape said. "You good. Hear you before. Hearing you for a couple of nights. Didn't catch you till now." The ruined voice paused in absent reflection. "Want see me?"

My heart skipped a half dozen beats. I shook my head again, afraid if I opened my mouth, a scream might come out.

Fulton laughed, a sour cough scoured free of amusement. The voice grew eager. "Come see the freak, huh? Come get peek at my face?"

"N-n-no, sir," I lied.

The black shape shifted and something soft dropped on the hay in front of me. When I recognized the scarf Fulton wore, terror wrapped my own face in a smothering hood. The loft grew darker as my vision narrowed.

"Sure you have. Everbody want see it. 'Course it usually—" his voice faltered over a difficult word "—costs 'em. Costs 'em their worthless life!"

A long arm swung out of the blackness. The sword knife, like a lightning strike, buried itself in a roof beam between us. It hummed there, a live thing telegraphing something unspeakable in the stifling air of the loft.

I didn't speak. I couldn't. There were a thousand things I wanted to say, begging and weeping things, but they all sped around the inside of my skull and refused to get in any kind of sensible order. I had a paralyzing image of my family, hunting through the barn for my arms and legs. And my ears. I was unable to stop my hands as they snuck up to cover the sides of my head.

Fulton's voice was mushy and liquid. "What you pay see face of the wolf, girl?"

I shook my head. "I don't want to see anything, sir," I managed to croak. "Please. I want to go home."

"Yes, you do. Smart, nosey girl like you. What you give see the freak?"

"N-nothing." The last thing in the world I wanted to see now was Fulton's face. I didn't like the way he said the word "freak," a mocking promise that my worst imagination wouldn't be disappointed. But I wanted to be disappointed. God and Jesus, yes. More than anything I wanted to be disappointed by what the devil kept hidden under that ragged scarf. I wanted my Pa to come and get me and I wanted Ma to hold me. I wanted God to—.

"I know," Fulton said with another dry, breathless laugh that made me whimper. "You got no money. Your life isn't worth much. How about your dreams?"

"What?" I asked, surprised even through my terror. "My dreams?"

"What you dream when you sleep? Puppies? Angels? Candy?" He shifted towards me and a scream scratched its way up my throat. I trapped it in my teeth and fought it back down.

"Boys. You ever dream about boys?"

"N-no."

"Bet you dream about kishing."

Kishing? What was kishing? My mind tried to hurry itself with rescue while at the same time trying to decipher the last words I would hear on earth.

"Kishing? I don't know——."

"Kishing!" Fulton snarled. "With boys. Kishing. Kissing!"

He saw that I finally understood. The black shape of him seemed to smile. I heard the devil snicker, coming for me. "Bet you never dreamed of kishing boys who look like—this!"

The face that leaned out of the shadows and into the wan light from below wasn't human. In the extremity of my terror I saw the hideous visage of a slavering wolf, all teeth and wet snarl. It was something from a nightmare, and the scream that finally ripped its way out of me sounded as if my soul was unraveling. I fell backwards through the opening of the loft.

The last thing I remember was the wolf man lunging for me, seizing me in midair. In that instant, when Fulton Loring's cruel hand closed on my throat, the snarl on his ruined face softened into something less carnivorous, something considerably less than murder.

I saw apology and I saw fear.

Chapter Seven

Now I have to tell you about my brother, Johnny. Mostly because in the end it was the memory of Johnny that kept Fulton Lorings on our farm long after everyone wanted him gone.

My brother was born John Lee Merrell, and he was touched in the head. I don't just mean that he was feebleminded, although that part of his trial on earth was obvious to everyone, particularly those who took a perverse pleasure in reminding him of it. Mostly I mean he was touched in the sense that he was blessed. I wouldn't swear to it in church, mind you, but there were times while Johnny was alive that I believed he had been touched by the finger of God, just like the Jaredite stones in the Book of Mormon.

Ma said Johnny was a special child. Most people would have agreed with her if "special" meant bark-at-the-moon crazy. At the time of his death, Johnny was the eldest son of Lee Merrell. Pa's first family, a wife and three children had died of the fever while Pa was off tramping around creation with the Mormon Battalion and later on a church mission in England for Brigham Young. Only Laurel Anne had survived , taken in by Bumpa and Nanna Merrell. The rest of us were Pa's second try at a family. After all he'd been through, it seemed an additional cruel tragedy that his eldest son was a feeb.

In spite of all his shortcomings, there was indeed something special about Johnny. He possessed an unearthly ken that both eluded and annoyed the rest of us. All except Ma. She actually encouraged my brother, mostly because she possessed some of this weird intuition herself. The best way I can explain it to you is to tell what happened the summer he died—the summer he predicted the dark angel would come to us.

It was Independence Day and Pa had taken us down to Provo to visit my Uncle Moyle, younger brother of Alva and Ma. Moyle Bryson was a backslid, Irish Mormon who lived just north of the center of Provo on a big apple farm and distillery. Uncle Moyle owned acres of orchards and a nice two-story house with flowers and an iron fence. I was nine that summer. My cousin Perle was exactly my age, and she had a collection of store-bought dolls I would have cheerfully murdered her to own.

In between dinner and the fireworks, Perle and I carried the dolls into the backyard for a tea party. We were engrossed in our play when Johnny lumbered up and stood over us. He was twelve that summer, but his huge size made him seem older. He blotted out the late afternoon sun with his stuporous presence and I think he frightened Perle.

"Know something?" he queried that day in a voice deep beyond his years. "Hey, Rose, know something?"

What Johnny actually said was "know suffing." He seldom spoke and not very well when he did. "Know suffing?" was a favorite phrase of his whenever he had something particularly unbelievable to tell you. And I mean stuff that would make you tear your hair.

Irritated, I looked up at Johnny. I wanted to play with the dolls and not be bothered by a brother everyone knew was crazy. Perle gave me a speculative look. I knew she would tease me as soon as Johnny tired of bothering us and moved on to amble after a butterfly or stare off into the distance for an hour or two.

"What?" I said impatiently, knowing full well that two "know suffings" in a row meant Johnny wasn't going to give up easily. Three "know suffings" meant he would keep at it until you answered him, lost your mind, or the Second Coming rolled around.

"Know suffing, Rose?" he said, growing excited. "Their shoes has teeth."

This ludicrous revelation brought a giggle from Perle. I heaved a sigh. It was obvious our afternoon of dolls was over thanks to my brother. There's nothing like the antics of a feeb to take people's minds off really important things.

Johnny ignored Perle, holding a blunt hand down to me. "Show you."

With a sigh, I took Johnny's hand. He hoisted me up like a rag and lurched off. With little choice, I followed him down to the edge of Uncle Moyle's orchards where he stopped and pointed into the trees.

"See," he confirmed. "Their shoes has teeth."

I looked and didn't see anything but an orchard. It was getting on into afternoon. The shadows had grown longer back in amongst the apple trees and it was hard to pick out details, but I certainly didn't see any shoes with teeth.

"Whose shoes?" I asked.

"The blue mens," he replied, as if the blue men were standing around us and I was a dolt for not seeing them. "And the red mens," he added. "All the mens with numbers."

I heaved another sigh. "Blue and red men. You mean soldiers and Indians?" I asked, squinting up at him.

John shook his head. He peered at me with infinite patience from under a heavy brow. "No," he said. "They has a ball with points." He gestured into the orchard again. "They kicks it. See?"

I looked. There was nothing in the orchard except a mangy cat looking for a nest to loot. I looked up at Johnny and marveled at the strange things that went on inside his misshapen head. He was my brother and I loved him, but I couldn't understand the images produced in his malformed mind any more than he could grasp even the most rudimentary bits of normal logic.

"They throws 'em high," Johnny murmured, obviously entertained by what he thought he was seeing.

"The ball?"

He shook his head and smiled shyly. "No. They throws the girls high." He pointed. "Up in the sky."

I rolled my eyes. Lord, now we were talking about the sky. It could only get crazier from here on. Johnny was notorious for making up stories about things he claimed he'd seen in the sky. Back home he would sometimes rush in from outside and sit next to Ma while she worked. Eating warm bread and molasses, he would regale her with endless and clumsy fabrications about the "shiny whirly bugs" he said he'd seen in the air over our farm. Once he even told her he'd seen "mens on strings and blankets" in the sky.

Ma never scolded Johnny and never gave him anything less than her full attention. Under her loving patience, Johnny would unfold completely. Some of the things I was personally around to hear him say were nothing less than sheer lunacy, things that would have made even Jesus flinch. Pumpkin Ass told all her friends that Ma encouraged Johnny to fabricate and that this only prodded "an addled mind deeper into sin."

Eventually, Johnny stopped staring into the orchard. He grew listless and confused. I noticed that he'd broken out into a sweat. He usually did when seeing things. Sometimes he got the chills and peed his pants. Once he even fainted. Worried, I took his big hand and started leading him back to the house where the adults were sitting around talking. I knew Ma would give Johnny a tonic and make him lay down. He plodded along next to me, as huge and indifferent as a milk cow.

"Are the blue men gone now?" I asked, wanting him to know that I didn't think he was crazy even though he was.

Johnny ignored me. He looked fretful, as if concentrating on something rhythmic far away, like the black swell of wind before a storm. Abruptly he stopped. His thick shoulders bunched and he turned back to face the empty orchard where his pretend blue men were.

"Third down," he said softly, listening to something huge and beyond me. His voice was normal now, as if it belonged to someone with a full load of smarts.

"Johnny?"

"Bootleg four," he whispered.

Johnny opened his mouth and paused, waiting for the silent and invisible tide to reach him. Suddenly, he bellowed:

"Touchdown!"

It wasn't an exclamation of fear, but more of a war cry. It didn't make any sense and it scared the hell out of me. I got ready to bolt for the house on the off chance that Johnny would have another of his fainting spells.

Too late. When Johnny swung back around to me, blood was spurting from his nose. His eyes fluttered like lanterns in the wind. Perle had followed us. She took one look and fled shrieking. Pushing and pulling and crying, I steered my reeling brother back to the house and Ma. She saw right off that it was his worst spell yet.

Later, when we were sitting in a darkened room where Johnny dozed fretfully with a wet cloth on his forehead, I asked Ma why God let Johnny be the way he was.

"Why does God let him be feeble and go around telling windies?" I demanded. I was still frightened by what had happened and more than just a little annoyed with the unfairness of it all. I wanted a normal brother and felt cheated because I didn't have one. It was one of the many grudges I held against God.

Ma was the smartest person I knew, including Pa. If she couldn't answer a question, it probably couldn't be answered outside of heaven. Still, I had enough experience with her answers to know that I might not want it once she gave it.

"God didn't let your brother be anything," Ma said quietly. "He made John this way for a reason." She paused and looked at me. In the dim room she was an amorphous shape, a spirit hovering in the gloom as she tended Johnny. Johnny muttered something in his sleep. It sounded like "yards." Ma patted his hand and looked at me over her shoulder. "Your brother's not feeble, Rose. Not in the way you think. He's very special."

I curled a lip at that. If Johnny was special, the rest of us ought to get down on our knees and thank God for making us just plain old ordinary. I didn't know anyone who would have traded places with John Merrell. It bothered me that Ma couldn't see this.

"Ma," I said aloud. "He tells lies and embarrasses me in front of my friends. You, too. Remember when he came home with Pa that day from the lake and said big canoes were dragging naked ladies around in the water on little boards? And he said it right in front of Silla. She told everyone who held still for five seconds that he was possessed of an evil spirit." I sat back and folded my arms in a pout. "Bet she's right."

"Rose, dear," Ma said, reproaching me. "Sure and now maybe we're the feeble ones." She rearranged the cloth on Johnny's brutish face and then came over and took my hand. She was a rainbow of comforting smells: lemon, sage, cinnamon and roses. "Stop and think. Life is not always made up of simple equations and logic. That's why God has given us both a heart and a brain. Your heart will tell you that certain things make sense when your brain can't."

I sat there wrapped up in my own selfishness, grinding my molars down. I knew better than to argue with Ma. Not because she would strap me or because she made me feel small, but because she was invariably right and the rightness of her perceptions were often painful to the pride of those around her. She was a baptized Mormon, the second wife of a bishop and a captain in the Nauvoo Legion, but still very much that dark-eyed girl from an emerald land who had crossed the sea when she wasn't much older than me. Colleen Bryson had brought with her from Ireland a frightening acumen, handed down over a thousand dark years of Druid torment. Her ability to see things so clearly was injurious to some. I took it for granted and loved her, and Pa, well, I would never say this out loud, but my father worshipped my ma in a way that was almost a sin.

"There are lots of ways of being special," Ma said. She looked at me and I felt those soft eyes visit the rooms of my heart. "John's not a perfect boy to our way of thinking, Rose. He's better. Remember the needle?"

I didn't want to remember the needle. It was a secret between Ma and me and Johnny, although he couldn't have remembered it to save his life. He could barely find the privy from one day to the next. I didn't always remember the needle story myself and suspected it was because there were things about it that didn't make sense to me and would never make sense no matter how hard I tried. There were things about it, too, that scared me a great deal.

It happened on a rainy night when I was eight. Ma had sent me down earlier in the evening while it was still light to fetch back a needle from Alva. I dawdled, visiting with Laurel Anne and hearing about her beaus until the sun had gone and night had come. When I came back out onto the porch and found night upon the land, my blood went cold. It was eighty yards up the slope to the cabin where Ma and Johnny waited for me, eighty yards full of the cold rotting hands of Squash Head waiting to suck the stuff out of my bones.

There wasn't a kid in the valley who hadn't heard about old Squash Head. Years before, the redskin had snatched a baby from a farm just up the mountain from ours. He carried the unfortunate child up into the mountains, where he tortured it to death. A posse eventually ran old Squash Head to ground out in the Tintics, but he killed himself rather than let them bring him back where he could do a jig at the end of a rope. Even though Squash Head was dead, schoolyard legend held that his ghost still lurked in the woods around our homes, waiting to snatch another white child. Once, when we were at a barn raising in Lehi, some of us girls climbed up under a canvas in the back of a wagon where Josh Van Orden told us stories about Squash Head cracking the leg bones of white children for the marrow. The stories sent Fannie and Sarah bawling like calves to their folks. Their terror earned Josh a strapping from Pinch Face, which was no surprise. Most things earned Josh Van Orden a strapping.

Anyway, there I was with eighty yards of night to cross. As afraid as I was of Squash Head, I couldn't go back inside and ask for help. Being a Merrell by blood meant that I'd rather have my shin bones turned into flutes than reveal any weakness to Alva in our running feud.

Gathering my meager courage, I started up the slope with my heart in my mouth. The night was alive with menace, as black and full of mischief as a sorcerer's cape. Close to my heart, I gripped the cloth into which Alva had stuck the needle. I stumbled over rocks and low spots in the field, fervently hoping what Josh had claimed that night in Lehi City—that singing "Come, Come, Ye Saints"—was indeed the one thing guaranteed to keep Squash Head at bay. What started as a nervous hum when I left the brick house was, by halfway, a brayed donkeylike solo.

Things might have been different if I hadn't stepped on a chicken. Anyway, that's Pa's explanation. To this day, my own version is that Squash Head found me there in the dark, perhaps attracted by the very racket intended to fend him off, I don't know. I only remember that I stumbled into a patch of milkweed and the night became a flapping, screeching melee. Somehow, I fought myself loose from the clutches of the snaggle-toothed Indian and ran screaming all the way to the cabin. Ma met me in the yard, her arms wide. She hurried me inside and tried to calm me down.

"Ma," I wept, "Squash Head tried to get me. I saw him."

"It's just your imagination, dear," Ma said soothingly, holding me close and stroking my hair. "Squash Head is dead and gone. There's nothing out there but the moon and stars. Hush now."

I disagreed and tried to explain what happened between sobs that threatened to squeeze shut my windpipe. I cried even harder when Ma held up the cloth Alva had given me. The needle was gone.

Needles weren't the easiest things to come by back before the railroad had come to the valley. Oh, you could buy needles at the mercantile in Lehi City, but they were dear and the inconvenience of traveling to town to buy them made the loss worse still. I put my head against Ma and wept my apology.

"We can find the needle," she said. "Don't cry."

Lord, but I loved my Ma. The needle was gone for good. Pinch Face would have beat me with a strap and Alva would have dosed me with Red Jacket Bitters if I had carried on that way in front of them. Ma just rocked me until the sobs ran down into sniffles.

"John?" Ma said, when I calmed down.

I'd forgotten my brother in the extremity of the terror caused by my brush with death. Wiping my eyes, I peered around. Johnny was kneeling on a chair, looking out the window in a dopey attempt to spot Squash Head. When Ma called his name, he turned and gave her a loose, broken smile.

"John," Ma said, "would you please put on your coat and go fetch the needle Rose dropped?"

Johnny nodded. He got off the chair and went for his jacket.

"Ma?" I protested.

I was about to say the needle had fallen into tall grass and besides, it was full night. Ma shushed me, watching Johnny as he laboriously buttoned up his coat. With his tongue between his lips and a demented but studious look to his flat face, my older brother opened the door and tramped fearlessly out into the night without a lantern.

We waited in silence. My childish fear of Squash Head had been replaced by a greater dread of something I couldn't explain. Johnny returned a minute later, smiling shyly. Ma waited while he went through the tedious process of taking off his jacket and hanging it up. Then she held out her hand.

Johnny dropped the needle into it. A bit of grass and dirt clung to the inch or so of white thread still hanging from the eye. I stared at it, stupid with shock.

Ma thanked Johnny and kissed his face. As if what he'd done was no big thing, Johnny went back over to the window and resumed his vigil, still hoping, no doubt, to see this Squash Head about whom he'd heard so much.

Looking at the needle, a whirling sense of despair and wonderment threatened my sanity. It wasn't the feeling you got when a confusing, adult thing occurred to you, but rather when something happened that defied all description. Without the aid of so much as a candle, my feebleminded brother had walked out into the black night, to the very spot where I'd dropped a needle in the middle of a wide field, and returned with it as casually as if Ma had asked him to fetch a bucket of water from the well. He did it by knowing where the needle was to begin with, not by looking around in the dark for it. My mind swam with the implication.

Ma swore me to secrecy, although who I could have told that would have believed me I didn't know. Over the years, I forgot about the needle story from time to time. I think my mind tried to kick it out the back door of my head because it made no sense. I only remembered it when Ma brought it up, usually in the form of a lesson.

With mention of the needle story, all my bitter complaints about Johnny dried up. I felt small and a little grateful that I hadn't been even more vocal in my complaints. I got up, kissed my ma, kissed Johnny on his damp brow and went out to play.

Johnny died three months later.

On that worst of days, Johnny and I were hurrying home from the swimming hole when we encountered Coyle Morgan and Joey Leeks sitting on a log. The two trolls were sharing a cigar and swinging a dead lizard on a string. Friends of the twins, you could always expect trouble out of them. Seeing them now made me groan inside.

"It's Moron and Mutt," Coyle called when he saw us. "Hey, moron, going home to play with your ray-joe?"

"Ray-joe" was a recent invention of Johnny's. He had taken to listening hard to a small, empty tonic crate. Rocking roll, he called it. I'd personally never heard the crate utter so much as a creak, but after the needle incident I steadfastly believed that Johnny did. Pumpkin Ass and Pinch Face believed him too, only they said the sound coming from the crate was probably the voice of the devil.

"Ray-joe?" Joey guffawed, standing up on the log and hitching his pants over his skinny hips. "Hey, what's a ray-joe? Is that like your tally-whacker or something?" He nudged Coyle. "Hey, I bet morons don't even have 'em?"

Coyle and Joey both found that hilarious. With a slow smile, Johnny paused to see what was so funny. I tugged on his hand but he wouldn't budge. I resigned myself to a confrontation, resolving to get in whatever licks I could. I didn't wait, either.

"I've seen you swimming, Joey and Coyle," I fired back at them. "It's general knowledge that you two certainly don't have any. At least not so's anyone could tell."

That cut them off quick. Coyle's face darkened. He climbed down off the log, flicking away the cigar.

"Take that back, Mutt," he said, looming over me. Next to Johnny, Coyle was an evil dwarf. But I was the one who would do any fighting for us Merrells and I looked like a scrawny kitten before him. Coyle's witless henchman, Joey, sidled up alongside his mentor. "You better take that back," Coyle growled, "or so help me..." He doubled up his fists.

"Hey, yeah," Joey said. "You better."

I swallowed hard. That's the problem with playing with boys so much. Do it long enough and they forget you're a girl.

"Won't," I said, wishing I wasn't a Merrell so I could. And because I was Rose Merrell in the bargain, I had to add, "You're both dumber than a sack of cat shit."

Coyle shoved me down in the road. Joey kicked my legs until I cried out in pain. Johnny looked around in confusion, unable to tell if this was a game or something he should genuinely worry about. The empty grin struggled on his face. Coyle solved Johnny's dilemma by tripping him to the road. He fell heavily next to me. Joey drew back his foot and paused when someone shouted.

"Stop!"

I turned and saw Josh Van Orden coming up the road with a fishing pole slung over a shoulder and a can of worms in one hand. Two skimpy fish hung from the pole. Josh's thin face was typically expressionless, but there was something in his eyes then that I wouldn't see again for another year.

"Leave 'em be."

Coyle and Joey turned away from us and advanced on Josh. Josh didn't back up. He tossed aside the pole and the fish.

"Is that right?" Coyle asked. "Who's gonna make us, Van Orden?"

"Hey, yeah," Joey said.

Josh didn't bother to answer them. Instead, he put up his fists. Until the time I met the devil man on the Provo road, I'd never seen anyone so eternally ready to fight as Josh Van Orden.

"Get home, Rose," Josh commanded grimly as Coyle and Joey circled him. "Take John and go."

I scrambled up and helped Johnny to his feet. Coyle took a swing. Josh ducked and gave me a furious look of command.

"Go!"

Joey tried to trip Josh from behind. Josh whirled and kicked him in the face. Joey backed up and said "hey" in surprise at the blood on his face and hands. Then together he and Coyle rushed Josh. Grabbing Johnny's hand, I fled in the direction of our farm.

Fear stretches out time. It seemed forever until we reached the farm. The first person we encountered was Pa, trying to set a new rim on a buggy wheel. Out of breath and crying a little, I told him what happened.

He put down his hammer and hurried off in the direction of the swimming hole. He came back a short time later, leading Josh, whose face had been pounded raw. His lips were already beginning to balloon. Johnny, who normally didn't get too upset about anything, kept pointing at Josh and saying, "Hims face, hims face."

Silla, who was visiting Alva, lit right into her injured son for fighting, saying he was an embarrassment to her just like his no account pa. Pa calmed her down and took Josh up to the cabin for Ma to patch up. I followed to see if he was going to be all right. Also, I wanted to thank him for rescuing us. Pa made me wait outside.

Johnny and I sat on the porch swing. Johnny seemed fretful by what had happened to Josh. He kept trying to go into the house and see, but I knew he'd only get in the way so I made him stay with me. I gave him his ray-joe box, but he didn't seem much interested in listening to it.

"Hims face," Johnny kept mumbling, over and over. "Hims hurt face."

"Yes," I said, impatiently. "Coyle and Joey hurt Josh's face."

Johnny shook his lumpy head. "Not hims."

Perplexed, I asked who he was talking about, but he fell silent, retreating into his strange world. The ray-joe box lay forgotten between his feet.

We waited for a long time, listening through the window to Ma doctor Josh and to Silla telling Pa how Josh was a wayward boy and needed a father to keep him close to the iron rod. If she meant warming his backside with the iron rod, she was wasting her time with Pa. Despite ample opportunity and provocation, he had never so much as cuffed any of us.

I was sitting there thinking how unfair the world was, how it would be nice to have a champion to avenge you when people like Corey and Joey wanted to push you around. Johnny's voice interrupted my reverie. He sounded oddly lucid.

"Angel, Rose. Dark angel. He's coming."

"What?" I said, feeling suddenly cold.

Johnny paused, studying me as if seeing me for the first time. For a split second, he looked as wise as God. I still remember that my brother's eyes were incredibly blue that last day, like the sky in those quiet minutes before the sun.

"The dark angel is coming," he said in a voice as plain and clear as yours and mine. Then his mouth fell open and blood exploded from his nose.

My screams fetched Ma and Pa in an instant. They carried Johnny in and laid him on his bed. Ma did what she could, but everyone could tell this was the worst and last spell my brother would ever have. Ma fought the nosebleed for an hour, wiping his face and pouring cool water on the back of his neck. Nothing worked and Johnny grew weaker by the minute. We prayed and Pa gave John a blessing with the laying on of hands. There was nothing in it about his oldest son staying alive though, just some stuff about the rest of us understanding death.

At the very end, something about Johnny seemed to change. The light in his eyes brightened and he stirred in Pa's blood-soaked arms. Josh, bandaged and emotionless, reached over and took my hand.

"Dark angel is coming, Ma," Johnny said in a waning voice, devoid of its customary clumsiness. "Devil wants him. The devil..."

"Oh," Silla squeaked. "It's an evil spirit.

Pa told Pinch Face to shut up and she started to cry. Most of us were already crying. Everyone except for Ma and Josh.

"He's good," Johnny repeated, looking directly at me. Then he closed his eyes and went back to heaven.

So bad did the death of Johnny hurt me, that I started picking fights with God afterward. I cried myself dry, blaming him for every tear. The world was full of people who deserved death and pain, but it seemed like God only handed it around to those who didn't need it. I swore I'd never forgive God for taking my brother away.

One thing about God taking things from you, he generally gives you something back. You just have to stop crying and cussing long enough to look for it.

After Stuart's Wolf finished killing me, I sort of expected Johnny to come and fetch me along to the Judgement Bar. I even imagined what he'd look like, all dressed in white and looking real normal.

Instead, I came to beside a sputtering lantern. The wick was low and the glass dirty. I was more than a little surprised to find they had Bickwell's Sure-Light lanterns in heaven, and even a little annoyed that someone was doing such a poor job of keeping them clean. Then it occurred to me that given my life's works, this might not be heaven at all. I got scared. I remembered the wolf and looked up.

Fulton Lorings sat on a barrel in the corner of the tack room. The scarf he normally kept around his face lay across his knees. I didn't want to look at his face, but I did. And I was sorry.

Fulton loomed hawkish in the brass light of the lantern. Something was wrong with his profile and it wasn't until he turned and looked at me straight on that I saw why the Indians called him the Ghost Smiler. I swallowed a sour blend of fear and grief. Shadows filigreed the twisted scars across his cheek and neck. I marveled at their evil sculpture. The flesh on the left side of his face was all knotted up in slick purple lines and trenches, exposing permanently a feral gleam of teeth and lending his jaw the undershot profile of an alligator or a wolf. The jawbone itself was dented in on the left, the recipient of a massive blow that seemed to have left it hanging loose on one hinge. The scars razored down across one half of his lips, passing over the point of his chin and disappearing down his neck into the frayed collar of his shirt. It was a confusing sight. The right side of his face was quite normal, belonging to a decidedly handsome man. The left—oh, Lordy, the left—when he turned it toward me, the left side of Fulton's face looked as if it had been crafted by the devil on a terrible day.

For some reason, Fulton Lorings looked less rapacious sitting there in the enormous silence of the barn. After a minute, I decided it was his eyes rather than his face that made him look so terrible. Most of the madness was gone from them now, taking with it the hook of terror from my stomach. In the flat light I regarded him without fear for the first time.

"What happened to you?"

The glow of insanity flared and ebbed in his eyes again, like coals in a forge. When he spoke, his voice was rough and clumsy but devoid of the cruelty that had fired it in the loft. His half mouth said, "Gettysburg."

I'd heard of Gettysburg, a place somewhere back in Pennsylvania where President Lincoln gave a speech. We learned that much in school. I also knew that a battle of some consequence had been fought there during the war.

"Does it still hurt?"

He gave me a predatory flash of teeth. The crippled smile was a frightening thing to behold. It was not the smile of a human being and it made me understand that my insensitive probing was the last thing some men ever did. The smile also convinced me of other things, things I couldn't possibly put into words, things too huge and awful for my mind to grasp completely. I experienced a colossal sense of emptiness, as if that bleak wreck of a smile had sapped all the joy out of my life.

"No," he said.

I could tell it was a lie. He lowered his head and studied the ragged scarf. "Did I hurt you?"

It was my turn to lie. I shook my head and winced at the pain it caused. Tomorrow I would have bruises and a need to explain them away somehow. Folks would get the wrong idea if I told them Fulton scared me into falling through the loft and then saved me by grabbing my throat. I tested my limbs and sat up. It brought us closer together and he grew self-conscious. Carefully, he wrapped his face with the scarf. When the scars were hidden from view, he turned back to me and his eyes softened.

"Sorry."

A single word. Most people don't say it enough. You don't know what it's like to hear someone say it who has dedicated his life to making people sorry. When Fulton offered his apology to me there in the tack room, I saw the barest little sliver of the soul of the man called Red Legs. And what I saw was the dark angel Johnny had told us would come. I saw a man weighed down with a misery so black and heavy and ugly, you could almost hear the devil laugh.

"It's all right," I croaked, close to tears. "I shouldn't spy on folks."

Fulton's answer was to come and lean over me. His hands, surprisingly gentle, inspected my throat and then the knees I'd skinned running to save Eldon. Tucking his arms under my legs and back, he picked me up and carried me out of the barn. We climbed the slope to the cabin. Against the stars and up close, Fulton looked more forbidding than ever.

Fulton tapped on the door. When Ma answered it, he handed me to her and she carried me inside. Putting me on the bed, she washed off my knees and put a salve on them. Then she wrapped a poultice of some wicked-smelling goo around my neck and tucked me straightaway into bed. I wasn't sleepy but I didn't protest my summary banishment. She did it all without a word to either Fulton or me. She wasn't mad, just thinking hard. She turned to Fulton, who had waited silently in the doorway throughout all of this.

"Please come in and sit down, Mr. Lorings."

Ma sounded grim. Fulton hesitated and then came in and sat down at our table. Ma sat across from him and waited. Fulton looked nervous and the silence dragged on. Finally, without a word, he reached up and undid the scarf around his face. It was the only explanation he could think of.

It was the only time I ever saw my ma taken completely off guard. Her mouth parted in surprise and her eyes widened. She looked at him for a long time before getting up and going to the back of the cabin. She returned with some blackberry wine and poured it into two glasses. By then, whatever lecture she may have been fixing to give Fulton had evaporated. She sat again and they had their wine while I watched from my bed.

There in the flickering light of a candle, with the door of our cabin standing open to the cool night, Fulton began to speak in a halting voice. It was clumsy going for him at first. His mouth couldn't pronounce some of the words, but he was stubborn and he gained momentum. Gradually, the killer named Red Legs showed us his real scars.

And I'll tell you, the ones on his soul made the ones on his face seem like kisses from angels.

Virginia born, Fulton Lorings broke a dozen hearts the day he left Richmond for the U.S. Military Academy at West Point. He arrived to climb the wharf road and sign the academy's old register on the same day I was born, 2,000 miles to the west in another world.

The son of a Richmond banker and a Charleston socialite, Fulton's entrance came as the result of a presidential appointment. His and others like it were President Buchanan's effort to appease a growing discontent in the South. As the clouds of war gathered over America, a senator from Virginia shook the hand of this fifteen-year-old boy who stepped aboard the train that would take him to Washington, D.C.; Baltimore; Philadelphia; New York and eventually hell. In Fulton's valise was a bundle of silk handkerchiefs embroidered with the names of some of Richmond's loveliest belles. Tucked through the handles of the valise was the sword his grandfather, Colonel Abner "Night March" Lorings, had used to help drive the British out of America. Hope rode high in his heart.

"My grandfather fought beside George Washington," Fulton told us in a raspy voice full of bitterness. "All I ever wanted was to be soldier just like him." He chuckled without real mirth. "I found out that if God really hates you, he'll give you what you want."

Beyond the wicked bark of his laugh, I saw a younger Fulton, slim and proud, a young Virginia gentleman on his way to the fulfillment of a dream. Judging from what remained of the right side of his face, he must have been something of a dream himself for the Richmond belles. As I listened, I found myself wondering whatever happened to all those embroidered kerchiefs.

Fulton told us how much he loved West Point, how he thrilled to the sound of drums and bugles. Most of all, he talked about cannons, how much he loved the big West Point guns that hurled shot more than a thousand yards. As he spoke, Fulton's broken voice took on the odd quality people adopt when they speak of dead children or the loss of a life's work: a curious lilt that makes you wonder if the grief they feel hasn't left them with the unhinged idea that maybe it was all just a dream.

Fulton studied at West Point for two years. As the eve of slaughter approached, he received a constant stream of letters from his father, outlining in stern detail a native son's obligation to Virginia. Loyal to sire and state, Fulton resigned from West Point on April 22, 1861. Along with five other Virginia-born cadets, he slipped away from West Point on a windswept evening with a cold rain piling in off the Hudson River. Putting away their cadet uniforms for the last time, the boys who would soon be men took a ferry to New York. From there they caught a packet ship south to Norfolk, slipping easily through police cordons thrown up to head off the military talent bleeding away from the Union at an alarming rate.

Two weeks later in Richmond, the boy warriors buckled on the swords of the Confederacy. In a springtime city filled with flowers and hope, two of the former cadets married their fiancées in St. Paul's cathedral. Fulton stood as best man for both. Fulton pledged his own love to a golden-haired girl named Judith, the daughter of an Alexandria lawyer. They were married in St. Paul's on May 6, the day Virginia formally seceded from the United States.

Judith was an angel. She swore undying love to Fulton. The newlyweds went to countless balls and recitals as their days trickled down to an end. Being young and ignorant they made lots of promises they could never keep.

When he talked of those final days before the war, Fulton's face grew hard. His ruined mouth couldn't even pronounce the name of the woman he once loved. He wrote it on a paper so Ma and me would know what it was.

The cadets parted company with a cheery camaraderie that belied their nervousness, boasting how they'd send the Yankees packing at the first volley. Two went into the cavalry, three into the infantry. Fulton followed his love of guns into the artillery. None of the clear-eyed cadets would see Appomattox. Within a year three of them were dead, another dying legless in a Richmond hospital. Only Fulton, by then a merciless warrior with no trace of the eager boy left in him, survived the war—if you can call what happened to him survival.

First there was Manassas, or Bull Run as Fulton said the "damn yankees" called it. Scouting for his battery, Lieutenant Fulton Lorings killed his first man—a round-faced Union courier he shot in the stomach when they stumbled into each other at a crossroads. While the screaming soldier died, Fulton vomited in the ditch at the side of the road. An old sergeant grabbed him and shoved him in the direction of his saddle. If all officers got sick at the sight of dead Yankees, the old sergeant shouted, then the Confederacy was in a hell of a lot of trouble.

"Get used to it fast, boy," the old sergeant told him. "Else you won't have no insides left."

After Manassas, Fulton and fellow West Point cadet Johnny Pelham picked through the body-choked fields and claimed again the old West Point battery they once served, now abandoned by the retreating Yankees. Running his hands along the warm metal of the long barrels, Fulton felt something flicker inside him. He looked at Johnny Pelham and they smiled. It was the start of the Confederate horse artillery and the beginning of a man named J.E.B. Stuart.

During the next two years, Jeb Stuart's cavalry was in the van of the Confederate army and Lieutenant Lorings was in the van of the cavalry, scouting for the horse artillery. Pelham's flying guns opened the battle of Fredericksburg, where Yankees piled their bodies in grisly heaps before the stone wall on Marye's Heights. He lived through McClellan's peninsula campaign, wounded in the right leg by a Yankee ball at a place called Malvern Hill. He fought at peaceful sounding places outside Richmond, isolated spots of horror like Beaver Dam Creek, White Oak Swamp and Mechanicsville. Along the way, he killed more men. Little by little, the boy who only wanted to be a soldier became a man who only wanted to live and go home to Judith. He had two horses shot from under him at South Mountain and received another wound in a skirmish outside Sharpsburg, where he fought like an animal. Despite all he had seen and done since, such were Fulton's memories of America's bloodiest day that he still turned pale when he spoke of them.

Fulton spoke of the Virginia winters, how the horses died for lack of forage and men froze to death on the picket lines. His voice dropped to whisper as he described the way arms and legs of soldiers flew above the smoke from the cannons, how the massed screams of the dying were like the choirs of hell.

Johnny Pelham was killed the following February at a place called Kelly's Ford. After that, only the letters from Judith kept Fulton going, kept him going right up to Gettysburg.

"After Antietam Creek it wasn't a glorious cause anymore," Fulton said, "Johnny was dead and I only wanted to live. But when General Lee said we had to go north, we went. We were soldiers."

Arriving on the final day of the Pennsylvania battle, Fulton was a captain. After a three-day ride around the Union army, Stuart threw his ragged legions between the shattered remains of General Lee's army and blood-soaked Seminary Ridge. The cavalry fought savage rearguard actions against the blue horsemen who threatened the retreat to safety. At Falling Waters, the final crossing of the Potomac River into his native Virginia, Fulton Lorings fell badly wounded.

"Cannon shell," he said, almost in a trance. His hands came up to touch his smashed face as if he still couldn't believe it. "Bright light. Never saw it coming."

The shell exploded in the air above him, killing his horse and four men nearby. The old sergeant carried him face down across his saddle, over the Potomac and into the relative safety of Virginia.

A wagon train delivered thousands of Gettysburg's screaming wounded to Richmond. A rickety wagon brought Fulton back to the home he'd left as a boy just two short years before. With his head encased in bloody bandages, his mother first refused to believe the lice-infested, half-starved body belonged to her son. His father identified him by the filthy lace kerchief embroidered with Judith's name found in one clenched fist.

They put Fulton in a room and slowly brought him back to health. Fevers racked him as infection set in. Judith visited him daily, reading to him from the Bible and telling him how they would have children as soon as he healed. She held his hand and guided him back from the edge of death, unaware of what lay beneath the suppurating bandages.

"Wish I'd died there," Fulton told us. "Because there had to come a day when they took the bandages off."

A family doctor clipped them away. When the last one was removed, Fulton's mother screamed and fainted at the hideous sight of her son. Judith barely made it out into the hall before she was violently sick. Fulton pushed his trembling father aside and sat up, seeing himself in the mirror on the wall, seeing finally what the Yankees had done to him. The smooth face once caressed by Judith's kisses was gone.

"Wanted to kill myself," he whispered.

The face of a monster stared back at him, swollen and red, twisted and leering, leaking pus and tears. A dry hiss was the best he could manage by way of speech. Spitting indecipherable threats, he backed everyone out of the room. Then he sat down and gathered the rags of his resolve, staring at his ruined face until he could stomach looking at himself. He stared all night. By morning, the proud soldier was dead. In his place was a ruthless, hollow shell of a man driven beyond the bounds of pity.

Judith never returned. Unable to cope with the wreck that had once been her beautiful knight, she left Richmond. Fulton's mother kept to the lower floor of the house, sending servants up with his meals. Twice his father tried to visit him, but Fulton snarled him away. Finally, either through fear or because they believed it was the best for him, everyone avoided the silent room on the second floor. Fulton's body gradually healed. He tried a beard but the nerves in his face were so damaged the hair wouldn't grow well over the scars. He gave it up and kept himself clean shaven, an agonizing and bloody chore. Twice during the following week, Fulton told us, he put a gun to his head. Each time, it was hate that made him pull it away.

"Getting even was all I had left," he said.

Eventually, he returned to the world. One night, after the battle of Spotsylvania had poured another army of shattered men into Richmond, Fulton put on a clean uniform and wrapped his face in a scarf. Slipping out of the house, he walked through the streets to a church where a dance was being held for cavalry officers. If he couldn't be a husband, maybe he could still be a soldier. He went looking for General Stuart, for acceptance from his former comrades. He entered the dance and handed his sword and gloves to the servant. Then he stripped off the scarf. Women screamed and fainted. Several officers grabbed him, rushing him back out onto the street.

"They said General Stuart had been killed at Yellow Tavern a few days before," Fulton told us. "Said I wasn't fit company for ladies anymore, that if I had any decency at all, I'd lock myself away."

But Fulton didn't lock himself away. He attended several more balls and social functions, seeking generals who would give him a battery of guns so he could kill more Yankees. The result was always the same—the choking screams, the forced escorts to the street. The officers saw madness in the mutilated captain's eyes and no one would trust Fulton back in the war.

People began to talk about Fulton, about his rude persistence and his lack of decorum. They began to call him the Mad Captain. Stuart's Wolf would come later.

An arrogant newspaper columnist picked up on what he considered a display of poor social graces. He insulted Fulton in print, calling him a "monstrosity of war." Fulton waited until the man attended a benefit for war orphans. There he confronted his insulter and slapped his face. When the man brought out a pistol, Fulton put a yard of steel through his heart in front of Jefferson Davis and half the Confederate cabinet.

The death of the newspaper man attracted the attention of another officer, Major Jotham Darius, who rescued Fulton from the Richmond provost marshal and took him back into the army. He set him to scouting again and gave birth to the legend of Stuart's Wolf.

Fulton's reputation spread like lightning through the Army of North Virginia, eventually reaching the ears of the Union army, who put a price on the head of the ghost who ranged the woods and fields around their army at will, killing frightened Union pickets like so much quail. Although Jeb Stuart had been dead for nearly three months, his wolf was loose again in North Virginia. In some areas the mere mention of Stuart's Wolf was enough to make the Yankees refuse to patrol or even stand guard.

"Two-thousand dollars gold they offered for this ugly face," Fulton's chuckle was like the rattle of river ice, making me cold in my bed. "First time since Gettysburg I felt worth something."

I think Fulton hoped to die in the war. That's why he went back. He wasn't afraid of dying, wasn't afraid of hell, not after what had happened to him. Listening, you could almost understand how much of a blessing death would be for some people. Only it didn't work out that way for Fulton. In the last days of the war, he buried Major Darius and the old sergeant—the last of the people he could call friends. He learned of Appomattox from a passing cavalry patrol. Surrender came and took with it the only reason Fulton had for living. Virginia had no more use for a scarred-face demon whose only talents were killing men and spreading fear.

But Fulton's war wasn't over.

"War was finished, but the price stayed on my head," Fulton said. "In war it's hard to tell which enemy soldier kills your friend or your brother. With a face like this though, they knew who to come after. They knew Stuart's Wolf."

In the days following Appomattox, Fulton learned that his war would never be over. He killed two men who came looking for him one night, brothers, they said, to a Union picket whose throat he had slit more than six months before.

More men came looking for the man with the long red stripes of the horse artillery down his legs, the man with the face of a wolf. The war had refined hate, made a religion out of it for some people. The only valid baptism was in blood and revenge.

He had to get out of Virginia. With other renegades who refused to parole themselves to the Yankees, Fulton went south to Mexico. He fought in a revolution there, killing rebel children who came against him with rifles taller than themselves. In Mexico he became known as Sonria del Diablo, the devil's smile. Mere rumors of his presence vacated entire villages, sending peasants screaming into the desert night.

"Once," Fulton said, explaining his Mexican name, "we liberated this town. Riding in on the train, we were met by the townspeople, all yelling and crying and thanking us for saving them from the rebels. They pressed close to the tracks, swarming us as we jumped down. A pretty young girl ran up to me. She saw my face when she pulled down the scarf to kiss me. She screamed and fainted. Fainted right under the wheels of the train. The soldiers laughed. Said I had kissed her to death."

When the Mexican war ended with the execution of Maximillian, Fulton drifted north. He spent time with the Indians, lived and fought with them. They called him the Ghost Smiler because he could suffer such a terrible wound and return from the spirit world. But the women didn't want anything to do with him, and the children cried whenever he appeared.

He roamed California, seeking a solitary place to settle where his appearance didn't mean anything. Everywhere he went, however, people knew of him and eventually the word would spread that Red Legs or Hash Face was around. Then the guns would gather as men with scores to settle or names of their own to make famous came looking for him.

He wandered into Canada. The Mounted Police found him, recognized what he was, and politely asked him to leave. He came south to Colorado, and it was in Leadville, on a wet spring day in 1868, when Stuart's Wolf realized that his life was all but over.

"Man came looking for me," Fulton said. "Asked if I would kill him. Said he'd pay me."

Taken aback, Fulton refused. The man continued to badger him with the terrible request, offering increasing amounts for the one service he didn't have the courage to perform for himself. Each time, Fulton refused. The man became abusive and then threatening. He pulled open a threadbare coat and showed Fulton the pistol in his belt.

"He went to touch it," Fulton said, "and I put a knife in him." He paused and made a helpless, apologetic gesture with one hand. "After a while, it happens faster than it takes to think. I put my blade through his heart. He just stood there for a couple of seconds like it didn't bother him at all. He thanked me, smiled and fell down dead." Fulton took a deep breath. "Heard later he was wanted for some killings himself."

In spite of all he'd done, the killing of the man in Leadville unnerved Fulton. It was like he'd seen himself, twisted and ugly on the inside as well as the out, traveling down a dusty road where hell waited for him with an eternity of the loneliness he was feeling.

"Man's name was Jeshoneck and he was a Mormon from Utah," Fulton said. "Started working my way over the mountains. Figured whatever it was that made him want to end his life was in Utah with the Mormons. Thought maybe if I could find it, I might be able to fix what was wrong." He shrugged. "Thought if there was a place where I could stop being Hash Face, stop killing, it might be here." He laughed harshly. "Guess I was wrong. Now I'm down to scaring kids in the lofts of barns."

He ended his story and gave us a long look. He stood. There was a finality to his posture that scared me.

"I'm sorry I hurt your daughter, Mrs. Merrell," he said. "I just don't know any better anymore. I'll be gone by morning." He turned and headed for the door.

I opened my mouth to call to him, to tell him that I thought he could be good if he'd just stay and work at it some more. Ma beat me to it.

"Brother Lorings."

Fulton paused and looked back over his shoulder.

"Rose's birthday is next week," Ma said. "We hope you'll be here for dinner."

You could see how hungry he was in the look he gave us both. Not for dinner and cake, but for the company of good people—people who might, if they were good enough, help him be good as well. I think a thousand things passed through his mind in the few seconds before he answered. At least one of them must have been that he might regret staying. He looked at me and then turned back to the door.

"Thank you," he said. "I'd be pleased. Good night."

Things sort of speeded up around our farm after Fulton's confession. The next morning I got up and wandered down to the creek. Thanks to Ma's doctoring, the bruises on my neck never really materialized beyond a faint shadow. I went to the creek because I'd finally decided on a new pet. I'd chosen a frog again mostly because they were easy to care for and the attachment to them was small. A frog wasn't like a dog. No frog had ever put his head in my lap and begged for love the way Herc had. No frog ever fetched a stick or wormed his way into bed with me at night. Frogs I had to drag everywhere and they were always trying to escape. But frogs were safe pets because you didn't cry much when they got killed. On the other hand, it was doubtful a frog would ever miss me if I got killed. Leastways not bad enough to save me from a snake.

The creek bottom was quiet and cool. I waded through the shallows and the cattails with my dress hiked up around my scrawny butt, mud squishing up between my toes. I must have been a sight. I froze when I saw a horse looking at me from under the surface of the water. It took me a minute to realize it was a reflection. Startled, I glanced up.

Fulton Lorings stared down at me from the back of his Appaloosa horse, grim and deathlike as usual. All belted up with his guns and the knife, it looked as if he was fixing to leave us like he said the night before. Standing there with water leaking off my dress and my hair all askew, a sob leaped up my throat. I managed to trap it in time when I saw he didn't have his pack horse.

"Going somewhere?" I asked when I could. His answer was to hold down a hand.

Fulton could have been headed to South America or even the moon.

I never gave it so much as a thought. I sloshed over to him and put my hand in his. He swung me up out of the water and around behind him.

We rode the long way around our farm, down through the woods and into the damp bottoms. After a minute, I got the courage to hang on by putting my arms around Fulton's lean middle. He didn't seem to mind, and once, when his horse jumped a log, the killer's arms even tightened over mine to hold me steady.

"Where are we going?" I asked when the time seemed right for such a question.

Fulton's head turned. An agate eye studied me. "Your birthday?"

"Yes. Well, tomorrow."

He didn't say anything after that. We rode through the woods bordering the river, through the same spot I guess where Gilbert Bair and Philo Hooper got their midnight shaves. After a few minutes we left the trees and rode down into the yard of Slobber Bob's saloon.

I'd never been to Slobber Bob's before. The closest I'd come before was a glimpse of it through the trees one day when Pa took me wood gathering. He'd warned me never to come down here alone. Pa didn't need to worry. Slobber Bob's looks were enough to keep me away. Rumor at school was that whatever had botched up his face was contagious.

Bob's ramshackle brewery squatted toadlike in the trees. Empty barrels, bottles and boards lay scattered around a dusty, fly-filled yard. Two horses hitched to a pole dozed in the sun. A weathered sign nailed to a tree announced: "Bob's Brewery & Drink Emporium. Beer, whiskey, tobacco." It was, I reflected, exactly the sort of sign to make a Mormon sit up and take notice. A yeasty smell hung yellow and heavy over the place.

Fulton helped me off one side and then swung down himself on the other, spurs stamping out a jingle in the dust. The noise must have attracted someone inside because the door banged open and a bearded man carrying a bottle lurched out. Three or four other men flanked him, spilling out on the porch to stare at me like a pack of mean dogs.

"Whatcha want?" the beard snarled around his cigar.

"That's Merrell's brat," someone else said.

"The bishop? What the hell is she doing here?"

"Spying for her pap, I guess."

Worried, I looked around for Fulton. I couldn't see him for the horse. That's when I realized that Slobber Bob's customers thought I was there sneaking around on my own. Fortunately, the Appaloosa backed up a step and suddenly there was Fulton, looking like the masked wrath of God. A collective sigh of fear swept the porch, like wind under the eaves of a deserted house.

"One of the men spoke in a strangled voice. "Godamighty."

Glass shattered as the man with the bottle dropped it. The noise galvanized the men into action. They bumped into each other in a clownish haste to get going. Two men half ran for the horses. The others took off walking up the road, shooting fear-filled glances over their shoulders.

When the porch and yard had emptied as if by magic, Fulton handed me the reins and went up to the door. He poked his head inside and motioned for someone to come out. Slobber Bob appeared, wiping his hands on a rag. Even though Fulton had killed two men in his saloon, and later tacked the bloody ears of two more to his front door, Bob didn't seem the least bit scared.

Like I said before, Slobber Bob was about the ugliest man alive. Born a harelip, he came by his sorry name naturally if you took into account the meanness of normal folks with their own smooth faces. Nobody except someone mean and unblemished themselves would have ever given Bob such a name. He was a short and wide man with a fringe of red hair running around his otherwise bald head. He wore a stained but clean apron and a scarf around his neck like Fulton's. Only Bob's scarf was pulled down low under his chin to collect the spit drooling from a mouth that hooked upward in the center, almost up between his eyes. His nose was almost nonexistent. He looked at me gravely and then back to Fulton.

Oddly enough, Bob didn't seem afraid of Fulton. I realized later that after what life does to some people, the threat of getting killed doesn't hold much water. It wasn't even that, though. Bob and Fulton seemed to respect each other. Two ruined pieces of humanity, I guess, trying to make it as easy on each other as a pitiless world allowed.

Bob babbled something to Fulton that I couldn't even begin to decipher. Fulton said something back to him, low and equally indecipherable behind the scarf. Bob brightened and gave me a hideous smile that displayed the wet insides of his head. Motioning for us to follow along, he went around to the back of the saloon.

The backyard of Bob's saloon was as different from the front as night and day. Roses grew in a profusion that would have made Alva squirm with envy. A wooden bench sat in the middle of an immaculately groomed yard. Birdhouses lined the eaves. Swallows dipped and shot through the shaded yard in pursuit of bugs. At the very back of Bob's private yard, a litter of pups wriggled and flopped over the top of a big yellow dog. Bob paused and made a chirrup sound with his ugly mouth. The pups sat up, a lop-eared collection of wary interest. The ma dog saw us and got to her feet, ready to threaten us off. Bob went over and pulled her to one side, tying her to a large barrel that served as her hut.

Nervous, the pups took a few tentative steps in our direction. When I got down on one knee, I was immediately buried under a landslide of dog. Wriggling and squirming, the pups nipped my hair and my hands. I laughed until I couldn't breathe. While the ma dog growled and showed her teeth, I played with her litter of pups. They were all cute as pie, with wet noses and milk breath sour enough to blind you. I looked around and saw Fulton watching me. It didn't take a genius to figure he'd brought me here to get one of the pups. Guilty thoughts of Herc began creeping in.

After a few minutes, I'd narrowed the litter down to three: two males and a female. One of the males was bigger than the rest. With the exception of two white feet, his coat was a muddy brown. He spent most of his time on top of one unfortunate litter mate or another, chewing ears and necks in earnest but harmless combat.

Fulton saw the big pup, too. He hunkered and sorted through the leaping, yipping mess, isolating the big one from the rest. The big pup wanted back in the safety of the litter, but Fulton wouldn't let him. He started pushing the pup, backing it continually away from the direction it wanted to go. Instead of whining and rolling over in surrender, the pup started to growl. Then it snapped at the offending hand. Fulton picked the pup up, rubbing its freckled belly. The pup wriggled and tried to lick Fulton's hand. He seized the scarf on Fulton's face and pulled it loose. Fulton didn't seem to mind that Bob saw his ruined face. Bob himself acted like he didn't even notice.

Fulton gave Bob ten silver dollars for the big pup, an astronomical sum for a dog. Bob refused at first, but Fulton insisted, giving me a sidelong look that seemed to change the ugly brewer's mind. It took me a long time to understand that it wasn't charity, but rather fair trade for value. Fulton didn't give Bob ten dollars for a pup he could have had for free out of pity for Bob. He did it for me. I had the only ten-dollar dog in the whole damn valley and I'll tell you, I bragged it up plenty in the months to come.

We said good-bye to Bob and rode home with my ten dollar pup peering from a saddlebag like a wizened sage. When he started to yelp for his ma, I decided I didn't like him anymore. He wasn't Hercules and I told Fulton so.

"Give him time," Fulton replied. "He'll end up meaning just as much or more to you. He's a good one. Won't let you push him around. Feel sorry for the weasels and the badgers around here."

"I've got no name for him," I said.

What I really meant was that I didn't much like the idea of thinking up one. Somehow it seemed an unfaithful act. Hercules had been my best friend. My chest still hurt and my eyes got wet just thinking about him. I didn't want him to peek down from heaven and see me picking out a name for the dog taking his place.

Fulton shrugged. "What's in a name?"

I sat there with my arms around the man called Hash Face and knew that what he said was true. But if I had to name the pup I at least wanted something interesting. Folks sat up and took notice when I named my frog after Brigham Young. Alva had a conniption and tried to boss Pa into making me change it, saying it was sacrilegious to name a frog after a prophet. Pa said as long as I didn't call my frog Jesus, he didn't mind much what I named him.

"Does your horse have a name?" I asked.

"Nicodemus."

"From the Bible?"

"Maryland."

"And a pretty girl with a picnic lunch." I chided him. "Bet you liked it."

Fulton's head turned and a gray eye regarded me. I thought I saw the hint of a smile through the scarf. "Yes," he said. "But no picnic."

"What then?"

He paused, thinking. "September '62," he said, taking a long breath as if he could still smell the leaves turning that long ago. He looked across the quiet pastures. "Johnny Pelham and I ran some of General Stuart's guns up on Nicodemus Hill. Killed a thousand Yankees in a cornfield off toward Antietam Creek."

"A thousand?" I whispered, stunned.

He shrugged. "Was a good day."

I shuddered at Fulton's idea of a good day. I turned back to the pup and rubbed his ears. He liked it, cocking his head against the pressure of my hand. He looked stern, even martial hanging there on the butt end of Nicodemus. The sight prompted a reminder of Fulton's long talk with me and Ma.

"Jeb," I said after a minute. "His name is Jeb Stuart."

Through his strong back, I listened to Fulton's chuckle. It was more a growl of appreciation than an expression of mirth, but it let me know that he had once been a boy with a ready laugh. "Good," he said. "General Stuart would be proud to have such a fine dog named after him."

We rode the rest of the way in silence. Periodically, I reached back and rubbed the pup's head. The more I touched him, the less he whined. By the time we arrived home, Jeb Stuart was out of the saddlebag and dozing in my arms.

Fulton helped me off Nicodemus. I put Jeb down to get used to his new home. He whimpered and got under my feet like I was his ma. I knew then that Jeb was what I'd been missing in my life. I looked up at the killer who had healed a part of me. I must have knocked some of the breath out of him when I threw my arms around him and buried my face against his middle. I heard the ring of spurs as he rocked back on his heels in surprise. He smelled of horses and gun oil and hot iron.

"I love you, Fulton," I said through a blur of tears.

Then I was gone, grabbing up Jeb and running for the cabin. When I reached the top of the slope, I turned and looked. Fulton was still standing where I'd left him.

Chapter Eight

Fulton came to my birthday dinner. Before he arrived, Alva set up a table on the porch and put a cake on it with the number "11" scrolled across the top in yellow icing. The family gathered around and sang some songs for me. Then we cut the cake. I kept glancing down at the barn for Fulton. After a while, I decided with considerable disappointment that he wasn't coming. I concentrated on eating my cake and trying to guess what was in the present Pa had brought me from town. Preoccupied, it was few seconds before I noticed that everything had gotten quiet. I looked around, and there was Fulton, standing at the bottom of the steps.

I jumped up and ran down to him, taking him by the hand and leading him up to a chair. Pa got up and said he was glad Fulton had come. Fulton even shook his hand, although it clearly made the lanky gunman nervous.

Fulton sat down across from Laurel Anne and Ma. He fidgeted and kept adjusting his scarf. Alva came over with a nervous smile and a piece of cake. She started to put it in front of him when he looked up and said:

"No, thank you."

Alva jumped at the sound of Fulton's voice. So did Laurel Anne. Pa looked mildly surprised. Everyone thought he was a mute and it gave me great delight to see them so surprised. I was especially pleased that the words sounded almost normal. Fulton was getting better at talking and I knew it was because he'd spent time talking with me.

By the time the cake was gone, most everyone was comfortable with Fulton. He sat off to one side, watching while I opened my gifts. Laurel Anne gave me a bottle of genuine French perfume. Alva gave me a quilt, saying how Ma's cabin was so drafty. Ma got me a book of poetry by a man named Poe. Then Pa helped me unwrap my store gift. It wasn't the skinning knife I wanted, but it was just as good—two dolls with porcelain faces and fancy lace dresses, better even than the ones Perle had.

Just when I thought I'd gotten everything, Fulton leaned over and casually handed me a braided leather collar for Jeb. It had a metal disk hanging from it, on the surface of which was etched Jeb's name. It was beautiful. I located Jeb and put the collar on him. We all got big laughs out of watching him run around in the yard trying to scratch the collar off by diving at the ground.

When the party was over, Fulton got up and left as quietly as he'd come. He walked down to the barn, straight and tall in the golden light of the evening. I think Alva was relieved when he left. I saw Laurel Anne watching him. It was hard to tell what she was thinking. Fulton's presence disturbed both Alva and Laurel Anne, but I suspected it was for different reasons.

The second thing to happen was that Laurel Anne finally got around to deciding who it was that would escort her to the Pioneer Dance. Eldon's behavior on our porch the previous week had sealed his fate. As soon as Henry got back from his patrol, Laurel Anne announced that he would be her escort. When Eldon heard about it, he got mad and swore a blue streak. Then he went out and organized the Dry Creek Vigilance Committee.

We heard about Eldon's vigilance committee when Pa returned from picking up a barrel of horseshoes he had ordered in town. Even though his farrier business had fallen off to the point where he didn't need the horseshoes, Pa's word was his bond and so he paid for them anyway. He told us about the vigilance committee over dinner. Henry du Pont was there to bask in the pleasure of Laurel Anne's recent acceptance.

"Got Leo Poulsen to pound them out some tin badges," Pa said, passing the biscuits. "They're sporting them around and wearing pistols. I tried to tell them they aren't legal lawmen. Eldon told me straight back that citizens have a right to organize any way they please. While I guess that's so, it doesn't seem very bright."

"Who's on the committee, Bishop?" Henry asked.

"Isn't a committee," Pa said, disgusted. "It's a lynch mob in the making. Right now they're just trying to whip themselves up some courage. As near as I can tell, it's Eldon, Hugh Barney, Calvin Averett, Leo Poulsen, Bill Pettus, Bill's eldest son, and a dozen or more of the loafers at Bair's mill, give or take an idiot or two. Sad thing is they seem to have talked Otto into this nonsense as well."

"What're they going to do?" I asked. I had a vision of men storming our farm in the night.

"They'll strut around mostly," Pa said. "They'll make a lot of noise and then one of them will shoot his foot off or something. Then they'll get tired of it and quit." He gave us all a stern look. For once, Alva didn't try and put her horns in. "What we will do is stay close to home and make sure Brother Lorings doesn't need to go into town." His eyes came to rest on me and I could see that despite his casual manner, he was worried. "And we will all be on our best behavior."

Henry tried to get around Pa. "I wouldn't be too hasty about it, Bishop," he said. "Folks have a right to be worried about the situation. After all, your hired hand is a dangerous man. You can't justify what he did to Gilbert."

"And no one is trying to," Pa replied. "But they seem more worried about Gilbert's ear than they are the fact that those two were drunk and trying to break into my home. They could have been killed and no judge would have found guilty the man who did it."

Henry went back to eating. I could tell he wasn't enthusiastic about having Fulton around either. But he wasn't going to argue with Pa in front of Laurel Anne. As it turned out, Pa was right about one thing and wrong about another.

Trying to teach his committee the finer art of pistolmanship, Eldon held regular target practices on the other side of town. During the second practice, Hugh Barney, a red-headed horse breaker from American Fork, didn't get his sawed-off Colt's Dragoon out of its holster in time and managed to blow off a medium to large piece of his own hip. In spite of the demoralizing effects of Hugh's accidental wounding, the committee didn't quit or even slow down. Eldon went right out and recruited more members. Hugh Barney shooting himself lopsided might have been more humorous if it hadn't been immediately followed on its heels by Porter Rockwell's visit to our farm.

I was down in the barn the day Brother Rockwell showed up. I'd been trying to teach Jeb to sit and fetch. So far, the only thing he'd managed to learn was not to do his business on Ma's floor. I needed some help and had a good chance of getting Pa's attention since most of his blacksmith business was gone. Eldon's Dry Creek Vigilance Committee had made it a point to caution everyone about the presence of Fulton and suggest that a good way to make him leave was to take their blacksmith business elsewhere. In the last two days, Pa's only customers had been a couple of freighters with a bent axle and a traveling tinker whose horse had thrown a shoe.

On the afternoon when Porter showed up, Pa and Fulton were in the process of moving his biggest anvil to another place in the shop. First they strapped two poles under the toe and heel, then got down and hoisted it. For someone big like Pa, it was a chore. For someone wiry like Fulton, it looked dang near impossible. Next to each other they looked like a bobcat and a bear. Fulton was game, though, and the cords and veins in his back and arms stood out like rope as he lifted and lugged the anvil with Pa. They carefully lowered it on the block and stood back sweating and panting.

"Now will you help me teach Jeb?" I asked Pa.

Exasperated, Pa turned. He started to say something, but his eyes skipped beyond me, locking onto something else. I turned and there was Porter Rockwell, sitting on his horse just outside the door.

Brother Rockwell was a big man with long hair and a beard mostly gone to gray. He wore a beaded leather jacket and hand-tooled boots. The black handle of a pistol showed through the front of his jacket. I hiccupped in surprise and whirled to look at Fulton.

For his part, Fulton didn't look surprised at all by Porter's visit. His eyes had gone kind of opaque and half-lidded. Long arms hung at his sides, the thumb of his right hand tapping the bottom of a holstered pistol. He looked neither afraid nor ready to fight, just waiting for whatever came.

"Afternoon, Bishop," Porter said to Pa. He motioned at his horse, a scruffy and mean-looking roan. "Seems Albert Johnson here may have a loose shoe. Been favoring a leg. I was hoping you could take a look see?"

Although Porter was talking to Pa, his clear eyes never left Fulton. Pa nodded, not sure what was going to happen. I saw him glance at me before motioning Porter to get on down.

"Can't do it with you sitting on him, Port. Climb down. I'll have Rose fetch you some cool water."

"Thank you," Porter said. "That would be real nice." He swung off and handed the reins to Pa.

"Hello, Fulton," Porter said.

Fulton nodded, offering a single, non-committal word. "Porter."

Pa and I exchanged glances. It was obvious that Fulton and Porter knew each other, but the quality of that knowledge was unclear. Was it hate? Respect? Porter turned and looked my way.

"How about that water, Budge?" he said. His smile was broad and I couldn't tell for sure but it hinted at a keen sense of humor. "I'm awful parched."

Budge? How did Porter Rockwell know Pa's teasing name for me? Porter Rockwell had never said a single word to me in my entire life until now. He had no cause to even know I was alive except that I was standing there where he could see me. Him knowing what Pa called me was surprising. Since then, however, I have known a few men who lived on the wicked edge of life—Fulton, Porter, and my future husband—and every one of them made minute detail their religion.

I turned and left the barn, shivering a little and half expecting to hear the sound of shots before I returned. There was no reason but one for Porter Rockwell to travel all the way out from town just for a blacksmith. Fulton Lorings. I wondered with dread if Porter was part of Eldon's vigilance committee.

I made it to the well and back in record time, lugging a stone pitcher of water. Porter and Fulton were leaning against some boxes, facing each other. I noticed right off there was none of the fidgeting of hands that you get when regular people talk, none of the distracting twitches and tics, no grand gestures and wagging of heads. Fulton and Porter's hands stayed down near their belts, resting easy but never far from the guns. For his part, Pa kept a nervous eye on them while he picked and tapped at Albert Johnson's shoes. My pa was the strongest, bravest man I knew, but there in the combined presence of Porter Rockwell and Fulton Lorings, he was as fidgety and confused as a schoolboy.

Porter saw the water and thanked me. He lifted the pitcher and drank deep, watching Fulton over the rim. "Good water," he said, when he finished. "Merrells were some smart to settle this spot. I thank you, Budge." He wiped his beard and dived right back into the conversation he'd apparently been having with Fulton in my absence.

"Don't suppose you know what happened to Nebraska Jack?" Porter asked. When Fulton shook his head, Porter gave a short laugh and told how this Jack fellow had froze to death up on someplace called the Musselshell, while forted up against some Indians. Porter ran down a list of other names. Fulton indicated with a nod of his head if he knew them. It was disconcerting to hear the two of them passing the time like nothing was wrong, while at the same time expecting them to begin shooting at each other any moment.

"You know the Tulliver bunch is still looking for you?"

Fulton nodded.

"Swifty Boswell?"

"Found me," Fulton said simply. "Denver."

"Dickey James and Lew Moffat?"

"California."

Porter nodded. There was something about Dickey and Lew that silently amused the older gunman while at the same time giving Pa and me the idea that Dickey and Lew, whatever shape they were currently in, probably didn't find it quite so funny.

Pa interrupted them, dusting off his hands. "There's nothing wrong with your horse, Port. Shoes are tight as can be."

Porter nodded, keeping his eyes on Fulton. "Which means I got to get down to the real reason for this visit."

Pa became annoyed. "See here, if Josiah Bair paid you to come out here to start something," Pa said, "I want you to know that—"

Porter gave Pa a look that cut him off. "Nobody paid me for anything, Bishop. I wouldn't take money from that bag of wind if he was giving it out free." He looked back at Fulton. "No. Some folks I do respect asked me to have a look see about this situation. Course, they didn't know Fulton's real name, but I had a good idea who it was once they described the look. I've been over in Nevada helping a friend clean out some rustlers. Didn't even know Fulton was around until I got back yesterday." He stroked his beard and settled back. "We've run onto each other before,

Fulton and me. Bridger's Fort, over on the Humboldt and down around San Berdoo. Never had no reason not to get along. Figured I'd come out and pay him a visit. In our business it pays to look things over before you go making up your mind on the noise of a bunch of citizens." His smile broadened. "Isn't that so?"

Fulton nodded, still waiting.

Porter patted his own knees and straightened up. "But you look good, son," he said to Fulton. "Still got a lot of curly hair on you. I'm damned, though, if you don't look better than I remember you last. Living good for a change, I see.

Fulton gave me a look. "Yes."

"Good, good. Keep it that way. And I guess that concludes my business here." He turned to go and paused. "Oh, one thing." He reached down and took hold of the pistol in his belt.

Fulton tensed but made no visible move for his own pistol. Porter pulled the gun free and offered it to Fulton, butt first.

"Drummer came through selling these new pistols. Made by Sam Colt. Shoots a .44 ball out of a metal cartridge. You can have that one." A clear eye winked at us. "Ignorant road merchant couldn't fill a straight all night. I got me this one and two more." He chuckled.

Fulton took the gun and tested it. The dark, oiled metal seemed to come alive in his hand.

"Barrel's light," he said after a minute.

"That's right," Porter said. "Doesn't feel natural. Too light and airy." He shook his shaggy head. "But it's a sign of the times. Things are changing, son. Come another year won't anybody be shooting cap and ball anymore. What doesn't feel natural now is gonna be regular fare in no time at all." He gathered up the reins of his horse. "I'll leave you some cartridges so you can try her out." He unhooked a heavy cloth bag from the saddle horn and set it on the ground well away from the forge. Then he picked up the reins again and hoisted himself into the saddle.

"A smart man changes with the times," Porter said, looking more grim than before. "A smarter man makes his own time. Was I looking for a place to catch that time, this is as good a place as any." He looked around and then back at Fulton. "But it's you who has to change." He motioned, almost disgusted, off toward town. "Town folks. This is their place. People like me and you can't expect them to stop being scared, bossy, stupid, and general pains in the rump overnight. You understand?"

Fulton nodded.

Porter turned his horse around. "That's good," he said. "I'm not telling you what to do and I'm not saying he didn't deserve it, but if it was me, I'd stop cutting the ears off worthless pissants and try being a little more sociable. It's hard, I know, but not impossible." He nodded in our direction. "Get your friends here to show you how to take off some of that edge. Be seeing you, son." He nodded thanks at Pa, dipped his head to me and rode away.

I breathed a sigh of relief. Fulton got up and left the barn without a word. Jeb tried to follow but I held him back. Pa sagged a little with relief.

"That seems to have gone well," he said to me. I agreed, even though it was a temporary lull. We still didn't know how bad it could get.

The fact that Porter and Fulton parted amiably was a load off our minds. It didn't set well with the Dry Creek Vigilance Committee, however. Upon hearing that Porter Rockwell hadn't killed Fulton or even so much as threatened to shoot him, Josiah Bair stormed up to the tavern Rockwell owned and offered him double the original amount to go back out and do it. Porter declined, saying he didn't think Fulton needed killing and didn't much feel like being killed himself, thank you all the same. After some argument, Bair hinted around that maybe Porter was afraid of Red Legs, whereupon Porter calmly replied that he'd never met a Bair yet worth the cartridge it would take to introduce him to God, but there was always the chance he would and he was saving up for the day. Catching Porter's drift, Bair hurried back to his mill where he could plot in safety.

We heard about the exchange between Porter and Josiah Bair when Brother Knight and Brother Stoddard came to our house for Pa's weekly bishop meeting. Brother Knight said Eldon was organizing the Dry Creek Vigilance Committee to patrol the roads leading to our farm. He'd even posted guards down at Slobber Bob's in case Fulton snuck down for a drink of liquor. There were some valley boys in the committee, but most were tramps, men at loose ends who refused to believe the things they'd heard about Stuart's Wolf.

"Eldon's got maybe twenty men on his committee now," Brother Knight said in his normal wry voice. "He'll probably need another twenty or thirty before it shapes up to a fair fight."

✿

Fulton must have done some serious thinking about the things Ma and Porter told him. It wasn't discernable at first, but I recognized that he was trying to change. He still kept to himself most of the time, but occasionally, when he saw you crossing a field or coming out of the house, he would actually wave before you did. It was a casual wave of the arm, without much feeling or even any expectation of a response. But at least he was trying.

On the morning after Porter's visit, Laurel Anne came up to me in the brick house and held out her hand. I saw the shell comb that I'd given Fulton as a lady's favor.

"I found this on my window sill this morning," she said. "You should stop leaving your things laying around. It's no wonder you lose them."

I took back the shell comb and didn't say anything. While I felt relieved that Fulton had abandoned his knight's vow to guard Laurel Anne, I sensed a loss.

The other thing to happen as a result of Porter's refusal to shoot it out with Fulton was that Josh got fired from the Pettus's cooperage. He came up to our place on noon the day it happened because that's where he knew his ma would be. As usual, Pinch Face was in the kitchen gossiping with Alva. I happened to be inspecting the brick under the window at the time, so I heard what happened when Josh walked in and handed her his final pay.

"Got fired," he said simply.

Pinch Face had a medium-to-large conniption. She demanded to know what Josh had done to get sent packing.

"Pettus said he wasn't going to put money into my pocket anymore because it would only end up in the hands of Bishop Merrell and eventually Mr. Lorings."

"But it's our living," Pinch Face wailed. "It's our earnings, not the bishop's." She became accusatory. "What did you do? I know you did something. You must have done something to make him mad enough to fire you. Tomorrow you go back and apologize. Whatever it is, you apologize for it and beg his forgiveness."

"No."

"Why not?"

"Because he knows you're sweet on the bishop. He won't take me back."

I heard the sound of a slap. Silla began to berate her son. The tone was the same, cruel and injurious. "You're just like your father. You did this to hurt me, to punish me for something that isn't my fault. I've prayed and prayed that you'd be spared his bad blood and now—"

"He left because of you," Josh said. "Because of your nagging."

There was the sound of another slap. Confusion reigned as Silla began screaming at Josh. Alva joined in, trying to calm everyone down by bossing them around. She succeeded only in adding to the pandemonium.

"He's a wicked boy, Alva," Silla said, sobbing, after Josh had left the kitchen.

"He needs a father," Alva replied. "A father to straighten him out and set him on the right path. Let's fry some chicken and potatoes. Afterward we can make a chocolate cake. I know the bishop will like that. You'll see. I think I saw him watching you out of the corner of his eye just yesterday."

"Oh, do you think so?"

I snuck away from the window and hurried around the corner of the house in time to see Josh disappear into the trees. I started after him, Jeb trying to keep up at my heels.

Josh wasn't hard to find. I headed down through the woods toward Indian Rocks. Since it was on our land, not many people came here anymore. No one wanted to risk running into Red Legs. Josh was sitting in the dappled shadows, his back to me as I approached. He didn't even bother to turn around when he heard my footsteps in the grass.

"Go away," he said.

"Won't," I replied. "You're not the boss of me."

If there was anyone who deserved a slap, it wasn't Josh Van Orden. He was a direct boy with little guile and an unnerving way of looking at you that seemed to read all your thoughts at a glance. He worked hard. I knew because I once overheard Bill Pettus tell a dozen folks that Josh Van Orden spent less time loafing and more time working than anyone he'd ever hired. Chances were, if Alva and Silla ever got their prayers answered, Josh would eventually be my brother—the confusing and incomprehensible sort only found in the plural marriages of existing families. Josh had been a distant friend since I could remember. Having him for a brother wouldn't bother me a bit, especially since life would become a lot harder for the twins with him around. But Silla didn't need to be hard on him. She blamed him for their being dirt poor and lonesome when in reality it was her own fault. I moved around to one side and saw his lip puffy from the slap.

A green eye blazed at me from the corner of his head. "I want to be alone," he warned.

"Ma says you spend too much time alone."

"What does she know?"

"She knows enough not to smack me every time I do something wrong," I said. Which was a good thing since I would have been beaten plumb to death long before now if she had.

Josh didn't reply. The look he gave me was barely veiled fury. I knew I had to tread light, but being a Merrell sort of got in the way. We have never been real good at treading light and probably never would be. Jeb, who was Merrell only by ownership, finally caught up with us. When he spied Josh, he wiggled on over to be petted. Josh kicked him away. Jeb yipped and rolled over on his back, peeing in the air.

"Don't kick my dog," I cried.

"Keep him away from me then."

"He's just a puppy," I said, growing hotter. "He doesn't mind very well yet."

"Is that so? Well here's how you teach things to mind." He stood over Jeb and drew back his foot again.

I snatched up a rock the size of my fist. Breathing hard, I took a step forward. "Kick my dog again, you bastard," I said, "and I'll split your damn head with this rock."

Josh thought it over for about two seconds and then booted Jeb again. Actually it was more of a nudge than a boot, a dare to see if I'd carry out my own threat. Jeb yipped again, more out of fear than pain.

I summoned up the most vile curse I knew and pitched the rock straight at Josh's head.

It never arrived.

An explosion slammed through the clearing and the rock disintegrated in the air. Small chips stung my face and hands. Josh fell backwards over the log, where a terrified Jeb tried to wriggle under him.

Speechless, I turned and saw Fulton standing at the edge of the clearing, a cloud of blue powder smoke wafting into the trees beyond him. He had a pistol in one hand. Pointing the gun at Josh, he motioned for him to get up and move over to me. Josh obeyed with haste.

"Both of you get your hands up," Fulton said.

Our hands shot into the air. It seemed a little crazy for someone like Fulton to be robbing two kids, but in a situation like that you do what you're told. Fulton walked over and sat down on the log. He had a pair of heavy saddlebags with him. He set these down between his feet, keeping his pistol out and pointed at the ground between us. A soft thread of smoke curled out of the bore like the spirit of a dead snake.

"I guess this is about the stupidest thing I've seen since I've been here," Fulton said, speaking slowly, trying to pronounce his words properly. "You two fighting when you ought to be best friends."

Fulton's eyes settled on Josh. "You like kicking puppies, do you, boy?"

Josh looked down at his feet, embarrassed. "No, sir."

It was my turn and Fulton's eyes drilled into me like a couple of steel augers. "And I guess you enjoy talking like a trash-fed Yankee."

My face burned with shame. I shook my head, unable to bear Fulton's scorn. His observation on my language hurt me bad. As ugly a reputation as Fulton Lorings had, I never once heard him utter a single curse word. Except for shooting folks in the face and cutting off their ears, the brooding killer had impeccable manners.

"I'm sorry," I said to Josh. "I shouldn't have thrown a rock at you."

"I'm sorry, too," Josh admitted.

Fulton slipped his pistol back into the holster and motioned for us to put our hands down. Jeb, figuring it was safe, bounded out from behind the log and over to me. He changed his mind when he recognized Fulton. He ran over to clamber into the killer's lap.

"What're you doing down here?" I asked when I figured I could without being murdered.

Fulton scratched Jeb's ears. "Practice," he said.

Josh took a couple of tentative steps forward. "What kind of gun was that?" he asked. "A Colt?"

Fulton peered at him, a single look of cold interest that would have sent a ladies' tea circle into screeching flight. "You know guns?"

Josh shrugged. "A little from seeing them. I never shot one."

"His pa ran off when he was young," I explained.

That was all it took. Fulton brought his pistol back out and held it sideways for us to see. It was long and black with worn wooden grips.

"Colt 1860 Army Model," he said. "Six shots of forty-four caliber."

There were other guns in the saddlebags, including the new one Porter had given him. Fulton sorted through them, showing us the tools of his bloody trade. He handed Josh and me a couple of unloaded pistols. Mine dragged my wrist to the ground. For a brief moment, an image of Fulton shooting the screaming corporal in the mouth blossomed in my head, teeth and blood bursting into view. I gave the pistol back to him, feeling slightly ill.

Josh's interest, on the other hand, was intense. Fulton watched him point and inspect the big pistol. After a minute, he reached over and took it away. He motioned for Josh to lift his hands up again and hold them open. Fulton studied Josh's hands with a glance and dug back down into the saddlebags. He came up with a smaller version of the pistol.

"Colt '49 Pocket Model," Fulton said. "Thirty-six caliber. Fit your hand better. Want to shoot?"

Josh's eyes glowed, his fight with Pinch Face forgotten with the possibility of shooting a gun. Oddly it occurred to me that something with great portent was happening here. I felt a little left out. Picking up Jeb, I sat down on the log to watch.

Fulton loaded the gun. He poked little twisted papers containing a lead ball and a measure of powder into each of the six openings of the cylinder. After seating them, he fitted percussion caps onto the nipples. Finished, he handed the pistol to Josh and pointed in the direction of the creek, at a piece of wood on the opposite bank. I stuck fingers in my ears.

Josh raised the pistol and fired. He missed by a mile and a half. Patient, Fulton gave him directions, reloading the pistol several times until Josh got a handle on the idea and was coming close to hitting the target. He hit the target twice with his last six shots, scattering chips in the air.

With considerable reluctance, Josh handed the pistol back to Fulton. "Can I see you shoot?" he asked.

Fulton took out his pistol. He picked up a stone from the ground and tossed it into some tall grass a dozen feet away. Two hoppers whirled up into the sunshine. They disappeared in little puffs of wing parts and bug juice as Fulton shot them out of the air. Then, with his last three shots, he casually snapped the heads off some thistles. It was a remarkable a display of marksmanship and produced something shocking from Josh Van Orden. A smile.

Fulton reloaded. Breaking the gun open, he slipped off the empty cylinder and replaced it with another from his belt. He gathered up his things and when he was done, he handed the smaller pistol to Josh along with a tin of percussion caps and some bullets wrapped in their little paper wads.

"Yours," Fulton said. "Take care of it. If you decide to keep it, practice with it. Nothing more worthless than a gun you don't know how to use."

Josh stared at Fulton in near adoration. I don't think anyone had ever given him anything as substantial as a pistol before. His normally serious face split into another brief smile, one that made my insides feel a queer sort of weakness. He held the gun tight, as if it was his anchor on life. If his ma found out he had a pistol, she'd have a fit. But I don't think Josh or Fulton cared.

"One more thing," Fulton said. "It isn't a toy. "Man who carries a pistol has to be ready to use it. Worse, he has to expect someone will use one on him." He reached up and deliberately pulled down the scarf, exposing his smashed face and the feral snarl of his mouth. Josh paled and swallowed hard at the sight, but he didn't look away.

"There's nothing more serious than the business end of a gun, boy," Fulton said. "Understand?"

Josh, who was about the most serious person I knew, nodded. "Yessir, believe I do."

"Good," Fulton said. He rearranged the scarf and picked up the saddlebags. He turned to me. "Young lady as smart and pretty as you shouldn't say certain words."

My face burned again. After that day I never said another curse word. It took some doing, but it was something I lived by even through the terrible days ahead. I watched Fulton until he disappeared into the trees. Did he really call me pretty? And a lady? Feeling the beginning of a disturbing change, I stood up and brushed off my skirt, scolding Jeb when he tried to climb back into my lap. A little addled by Fulton's visit, Josh and I wandered back to the house.

"What are you going to do with your pistol?"

"Practice. A lot."

"Your ma will near 'bout explode when she sees it."

Josh thought about it for a minute and then asked me if Ma would mind him keeping the pistol at our cabin. The idea of asking her made me nervous. Ma was fair-minded about most everything, but a pistol wasn't something I was sure about. In the end, I agreed to keep Josh's pistol in the bottom of my trunk under my clothes and books and return it to him whenever he wanted to use it. He promised to keep it clean of the sulphur stink.

That's how Josh got his pistol. In the end, I'm glad we lied and kept it hidden away from our folks. As things turned out, the quiet boy who would one day turn the devil's hair white would need all the practice he could get.

❧

Besides shaming me over my language, Fulton taught me a variety of things about the world. During the next few days, Josh and I dogged his heels, pestering him with questions and in general being the sort of nuisances that would have gotten us slaughterd had we been grown men. Instead of fearing him, we found the savage gunman surprisingly tolerant.

Fulton's brooding manner belied a ferocious intelligence. With nothing more to fear from us, he gradually opened up. The things that came out of him were nothing less than slap-your-face amazing. For one, he could talk Spanish, French and some German. Not very well, of course. His wrecked mouth got in the way. But the fact that he knew those languages would have surprised most of the people who figured him for just a common, low-born criminal.

He knew the stars. Lord God, how Fulton knew the night sky. It should have come as no surprise that he did, given his life of solitude. But he knew them right down to the faintest specks of light. At night, sitting on the fence while Nicodemus kept silent watch over our mares, Fulton pointed them out to me. Josh, too, if Pinch Face was staying late in the unflagging hope that Pa would lose his mind and make her Sister Merrell #3. Of all the gifts that Fulton gave me that summer, the night sky was the most awe inspiring. The enormity of the black universe produced a mixture of feelings in me, equal measures of insignificance and promise.

"Hercules," Fulton said one night, pointing overhead at a litter of gems. I looked and wondered if Herc could look down from wherever he was and see me. Fulton's fingers pointed out another chain of light points. "Fighting the great dragon."

Fulton's finger traced the Northern Cross, Antares, Altair, and the

Corona Borealis. There was Scorpio hanging low and twisted at the southern end of the valley, Vega like the eye of some angel keeping watch for God. Sometimes Fulton had to write the names down for us. His mouth still wouldn't let him say the names of some of the things he loved. Like Judith.

There was always a trace of bitterness when he wrote the names, as if he had lost something unbearable in his ability to say the names of those things he found most beautiful. Pondering this to myself, I wondered if Fulton could say "Laurel Anne." I'd never heard him mention her name. Reference to her was always "your sister." Fulton had trouble with Ls and Ts, but he generally pushed his mouth around them if the word was necessary to the conversation. "Sister" had a T in it but he said it anyway. Laurel Anne's name had an L, but Fulton never spoke it, never even tried it out that I heard. Secretly, I thought it was because her name would come out ugly and twisted, unlike Laurel Anne's face and exactly like Fulton's.

None of this meant that Fulton was always a joy to be around. There was still the dark side of him, a place where he retreated when the beauty of something made him feel uglier than he could bear. Fulton's love and fear of beautiful things did not in anyway extend itself to the Creator of those things. Like me, I think he wrestled with the way things were meant to be and the way they turned out, things like Judith and his face.

I thought a lot about Fulton's face. Most of the time he kept it wrapped up. Sometimes, when we were alone, he would take the scarf off. It was the tragedy of his face that got me thinking about the Resurrection. I asked Pa about it one day. He had the time now to give the matter some thought. He hadn't had a real customer since Eldon's committee started patrolling the roads, warning people about Fulton and in some cases even turning them away.

"Pa," I said one evening. "If the twins got their noses chopped off, would they get them back in the Resurrection?"

Pa was reading the Book of Mormon. He leaned around in his chair and looked at me. "Why, what are you planning?"

Insulted, I thought about taking my question somewhere else. "I was just supposing," I said. "Wondering if God really gives everything back."

"Not one hair shall be lost," Pa said, turning back to his scriptures. "That's God's promise to us."

"Even stuff like Gilbert Bair's ear?"

"Yes, even ears."

"Does it say so in the scriptures?"

Pa closed his book. "Well, it doesn't come right out and say ears," he said, "but I think we can trust God to be square. It wouldn't seem right for him to give everyone back their hair and hold off with the ears, now would it?"

"No, but what Gilbert and Philo were doing was bad. Do you suppose God might not give them back their ears since they lost them doing something wrong? It could be like a punishment or a curse, something to remind them of sinning?"

Pa smiled. The flash of teeth in his beard made me aware of how little he'd smiled during the last week. "Everyone gets resurrected, Budge," he said. "Even Gilbert and Philo. Our bodies will be perfect. So it says in the scriptures. If you can't bank on a promise from God, there isn't much use in going on."

I kissed Pa and went off to think about it on my own. What I'd been after all along, of course, was to find out if Fulton would get his face unscrambled in the next life. It didn't seem fair for him to work hard on changing if God was going to leave him like that for the rest of ever.

Up at the cabin, Ma told me pretty much the same thing. With her, I was bold enough to just come right out and ask if Fulton would get a new face come the Resurrection. She said yes.

I suppose I could have gotten another opinion from God but I didn't. If both Ma and Pa agreed about something, praying about it was a waste of time. Besides, my relationship with God and Jesus had deteriorated some over the death of Johnny, Herc and Brigham. And despite a million prayers on the subject, I still didn't have an elephant. The one time I'd prayed for an angel, I got Stuart's Wolf instead. While I was willing to concede that they might in fact not be false-givers, I still hadn't figured God and Jesus for being direct enough to completely trust either. When it came to answering prayers, they were trickier than any of Dan Castello's performing monkeys.

Armed with the good news about Fulton's looks, I went off in search of him down at the barn. I found him mending some harness, sitting on a stool in the doorway where the light was good. If I hadn't been so full of myself, I might have noticed the way Fulton bristled at my approach. Even though he was trying to be nice, there were times when he was still the soulless killer he'd been when he first came to our farm. Later, I understood that the bitterness of his situation affected him most whenever he saw Henry and Laurel Anne together. On this particular day, Henry's horse had been tethered to a porch post for three hours.

"What are you, Fulton?" I asked, skipping up to him.

He looked up from the bridle he was repairing, his gray eyes flat and cold. I should have been paying attention.

"You're not a Mormon," I said. "I already figured that out. So what are you?"

"I'm a nothing," he said shortly.

"No, are you a Methodist or a Lutheran? Something like that."

"My people were Presbyterians," he said, turning his attention back to the bridle.

"Are you?"

"I told you, I'm a nothing." Then he added, "So is God."

When Fulton said God was a nothing, I felt funny inside. "God is too something," I said. "He's our father up in heaven."

Fulton shook his head. "God is something people created so they could do whatever they wanted and blame it on a higher power. There is no God."

That was something for me to think about. I felt weak inside even thinking about there not being a God. But there was. I knew it and one of the reasons I knew it was that I'd always had a case against God. I had never considered God and me good friends. In my head, I kept a running tally of all the things for which I would demand a full accounting at the Judgement Bar. And God, if he was as just as he claimed, had better have some good answers. So, while I figured God for being a lot of things they wouldn't dare teach in church, I always knew he was there.

"Is too," I shot back. "He's up in heaven."

"No," Fulton replied. "It's all in your mind."

"No," I said. "There really is a heavenly father. We're made in his own image. And we're all going to be resurrected someday, too. Gilbert and Philo will get their ears back and won't be able to blame you for anything. And you, you'll..." Here I ran out of steam. Partly because I didn't dare mention Fulton's scarred face to him so directly, and partly because Fulton had looked up from the harness. His eyes were filled with that stomach-weakening light again.

"No god," he said. "Get that through your head, girl. I learned that in the war."

"Is so. And we're all made in his image. Says so right in the Bible and the Book of Mormon and—"

"God!" Fulton snarled. I swallowed hard as my insides froze. He flung the harness away and stood up, terrible as a dragon. "Want to know God, girl? God is a battery of rifled guns on high ground. It's Longstreet behind a stone wall." He leaned close, cracking my bones with a look. "Saw God at Antietam and Fredericksburg. Saw him stack bodies until you couldn't see the fences. Saw men follow flags over their own bloody insides. Saw them killed by flying pieces of bone that used to be their friends." He gave the air a savage chop. "Don't tell me about God." He pulled the scarf away and pointed where white-hot metal had ravaged his face. He gave that rasping bark that passed for a laugh of contempt and smiled hideously, a smile so full of murder it would have sent the devil running.

"If God has a face, it looks like this."

"That's not true!" I said, starting to cry. I didn't know if it was because Fulton said those mean things about God, or if it was because he called me a girl. "You take that back."

"It is true. Next time you pray, tell God he can have his face back. Tell him that being made in his image isn't exactly a glorious experience."

"That's not God's face," I cried, wiping my nose on my jumper. "It's your face. You can't blame God just because you don't like it. He didn't hurt you, the Yankees did. And He can't do anything about it now."

Some of the fight went out of Fulton. He sat down looking tired. "Go away. Just go away and leave me alone."

"Won't."

He looked up at me. There was no threat in his eyes, but I think he meant what he said next: "Good thing you're a girl."

I nodded. "Good for you. Last week you said I was a young lady."

He nodded. "I did. And you are." He turned back to the harness. "Better if I was alone right now."

There was nothing to do then but leave him there. Like Josh, Fulton spent too much of his time alone. It was the only place he felt safe. I thought about what he said, about how being made in God's own image, about how it was no fun. It occurred to me that people never stop getting made. If we were created in God's image, that was just the beginning. Josh, for example, was the way he was because of Pinch Face. Fulton was the way he was because of what happened to him, what was still happening to him. Thinking about it as I left the barn, I vowed to have a hand in changing Fulton for the better.

❋

Fulton wasn't the only one who needed changing. There was Laurel Anne. Since Eldon organized his vigilance committee, my sister complained almost daily about the loss of traffic among her beaus. Stuck some evenings without fawning male companionship, she would sit by herself on the porch, drinking lemonade and watching as Josh and I dogged along after Fulton.

The worship of beauty had built a fence around my sister. I didn't realize it until later, when I was old enough to comprehend such things, that Laurel Anne had done it to herself. After her first family died, and she went to live with Bumpa and Nanna Merrell, she had cultivated her looks as a defense against any more ugliness in her life. She fixed her mind on beauty and manners and adoration, using them to keep additional tragedies from creeping into her life. But now that her adoring audience had dried up, she was left alone with her thoughts. I had no way of knowing if she ever thought about what happened on the Provo road, or if she even considered thanking Fulton for rescuing us, but I knew she was going through some kind of change.

Once, when she was sitting alone on the porch, I saw Laurel Anne wave at Fulton as he passed by all sweaty and hot from carrying a load of fence posts. Surprised, Fulton looked around to see who she might be waving at other than him. When he understood that he was the object of her attention, it addled him. He ducked his head and continued his trudge with the posts, taking the long way around the house in his confusion. Once out of her line of sight, I saw him turn back and peer around the corner of the house, checking to see if maybe he had imagined it all. Seeing him rattled by such a simple thing as a wave from a beautiful woman would have made me laugh if it hadn't been so sad.

One evening, as Fulton, Josh, and me were sitting on the pasture fence watching Nicodemus and the departure of the sun, Laurel Anne gathered enough courage to leave the porch. She pretended to be on an errand to the barn, but she never had any real intentions of making it there. Strolling down the lane, she acted as if she was going to walk right on past us. "Watching for the first star?" she asked as if she really wasn't interested.

"Planet," said Josh.

"Venus and Mars," I added.

Laurel Anne paused and moved closer to us. "Oh? How can you tell the difference?"

Fulton remained leaning against the fence. He didn't turn around and explain to Laurel Anne the locations of Venus and Mars and Saturn the way he would have for Josh and me. He waited to see if she would ignore him and talk to us, or if she would continue on to wherever it was that she had been going in the first place. While he no longer minded talking to me and Josh, I think he was uncomfortable talking in front of her, as if his raspy voice would serve as a sure indication of the real horror under the scarf.

This time, however, Laurel Anne did not move on. I guess she was bored out of her mind enough to find what we were doing interesting. She came over by me, to watch the sun finish dying beyond the mountains. I was sitting on the fence between her and Fulton. I saw her glance at him nervously out of the corner of one eye.

"Fulton says they'll show up in a few minutes," I said. "As soon as the sun gets more down."

"Mars and Venus?"

I nodded. "Fulton says they don't show up together very often. We're waiting. He says Mars is red."

"Red?"

"Yes, and Mars was the Roman god of war. Fulton said so."

Laurel Anne nodded. "It sounds like Brother Lorings knows a lot about the stars."

Laurel Anne's tone of voice was level and colorless. I recognized it as an invitation for Fulton to say something, to talk to her like he'd been talking to us. I glanced at him, wondering if he saw it that way, too.

Instead of replying, Fulton shifted against the fence and checked to see that his scarf was in place. He looked about as ready to talk as a rock. It was up to me to fill in the gaps.

"He knows everything about stars," I said, laying it on a bit thick. "He can make people and animals out of them and he knows all their names. There's a lion, a crab, a bull, and this really big dragon..."

"I know Leo and Taurus," Laurel Anne said. "What's the name of the dragon?" This time, instead of asking the question of us in general, she leaned around me and directed her query straight at Fulton.

I felt Fulton squirm a little. He coughed gently, keeping a hand on the scarf. "Dracos."

The single word was a barely audible hiss. There was a long silence while Laurel Anne digested the timbre of Fulton's voice. I wondered if she was thinking of a scary monster like Beowulf's Grendel, or something along the lines of the frightful things she'd heard about Fulton. I could feel him becoming more agitated, as if he was getting ready to leave. I didn't want him to go off on his own. I wanted him to stay and watch Mars and Venus with Josh and me. Josh apparently did, too, because he spoke up, bridging the sudden silence.

"I'm partial to Orion," Josh said. "The hunter. But he doesn't come out until after midnight. Ma won't let me stay up."

"I like Cassiopeia," I said, pointing to the north where it would come out when it was full dark. "It's like a big W in the sky."

"Oh, I know Cassiopeia," Laurel Anne said brightly. "She was the mother of Cepheus."

"Andromeda," Fulton said.

Laurel Anne's interest sharpened. She was big on mythological stories of beautiful women and handsome warriors. I think it surprised her that someone like Fulton would know more about these things than her. She peered around me at Fulton.

"Do you know much about mythology, Brother Lorings?" she asked.

Fulton acted like he wished he'd kept his mouth shut, like he wanted to squirm up and die. He stayed glued to the fence while Laurel Anne stepped around me and stood close next to him, staring up at the darkening sky.

"They say the Romans and the Greeks named the constellations after their gods," Laurel Anne said. "Chimera, Minerva, Bellerophon, Jupiter...it was such a romantic time, don't you think, Mr. Lorings?"

Fulton didn't respond. He fidgeted some more and kept his eyes on the sky.

I wondered what my sister was up to, acting the coquette, flirting with Fulton as if he was one of her harmless beaus. It wasn't something a careful person did, not if they valued their life. It made me more than a little nervous.

Laurel Anne leaned against the fence next to Fulton and started blabbing on about the Greeks and the Romans, asking Fulton if it was true that there was a bunch of stars named after the son of Apollo—somebody who was part man and part horse and became such a great doctor that Jupiter had him killed because Pluto, the boss of hell, got tired of him cutting down on the number of people dying. If such stuff really was true, I reckon Fulton was one of ol' Pluto's favorite folks.

Fulton just shrugged. His persistent silence didn't bother Laurel Anne. She was used to talking while men listened. She kept right on blabbing about gods and goddesses until I was so turned around about who was which that I got dizzy trying to keep up. No wonder the Romans and Greeks didn't last, I decided. Their gods were all crazier than they were. All this time, I couldn't tell what Fulton was feeling. Laurel Anne was between us. I got to wishing that something would just shut her up so Fulton could continue telling us about the sky.

Josh nudged me. I turned and looked. Twenty yards away, out in the darkening pasture, Nicodemus was growing a fifth leg. It wasn't his fault. One of our mares had her backside presented eagerly to the stud, giving him male ideas. This had been happening a lot lately, taking some of the starch out of the stallion, proof of which was that Josh and me could sit on the pasture fence tonight and not get partially or even fully killed.

While Nicodemus's interest grew more obvious, I watched Laurel Anne out of the corner of my eye. She kept on about Cassiopeia really being the Queen of Ethiopia until she spotted Nicodemus with his male part gone as big as a fence post. The carnal sight immediately derailed her train of thought, turning her such a brilliant shade of red that it was obvious even there in the dark. Embarrassment turned to abject mortification when Nicodemus mounted the mare. He wasn't exactly shy about it, either.

"Oh," Laurel Anne gasped. Recovering quickly, she turned and lamely tried to draw our attention by pointing off at the opposite horizon. "Well, look everyone," she said, flustered. "There's...oh, where Libra is supposed to be."

"Not until spring," Fulton said evenly.

With his mask and the soft tone of his voice, it was hard to tell if he was amused at all by Laurel Anne's discomfiture. If so, he was too much of a gentleman to let on. He continued to listen to Laurel Anne while Nicodemus and the mare snorted and huffed. Josh and I wisely kept our comments to ourselves, but it was hard for me not to laugh. I must not have been doing a very good job keeping it trapped behind my hand, because Laurel Anne discretely reached around and gave me a wicked pinch on the leg.

I sort of lost Fulton after that. He listened to Laurel Anne blab until the sun was gone. Mars and Venus appeared like distant angels over the lake. Following Fulton's directions, we looked through peepholes in our fingers and saw that Mars was indeed red while Venus was a faint blue. Laurel Anne reminded us that Mars was named after the Roman god of war and Venus after their goddess of love and beauty.

"Her name was really Aphrodite," Laurel Anne said, touching her hair. She obviously wanted one of us to draw the comparison between herself and Aphrodite out loud so she could thank us for the compliment. She was used to that sort of thing from her beaus. But Fulton wasn't one of her beaus and if she was waiting for him to do it, she was going to wait a long time. Josh rarely said anything. Me, I was too busy wondering about Mars. If Laurel Anne thought she was a fair representation of love and beauty, was Fulton wondering what the face of Mars looked like?

As night fell full on us, a falling star etched a brief line across the horizon. "Make a wish," Laurel Anne said.

Nobody said anything. You weren't supposed to tell your wish, but I had a good idea what everyone wished for. Laurel Anne wanted to know who she was going to marry, Josh wanted to be free of his ma, and Fulton probably wanted to be normal again. For some reason, I couldn't think of any wishes for myself.

We were quiet for several minutes and then Laurel Anne said goodnight. When she left to go back up to the house, there seemed to be a teasing sway to her hips. I would have passed it off as just my imagination except that I turned around and saw Fulton watching her, too. The look in his eyes before he quickly turned away told me that it wasn't my imagination. Laurel Anne was behaving toward Fulton the same way she behaved toward all men, the only way she really knew how to behave toward them. I wasn't so stupid that I didn't recognize the similarities between what the mare had done to Nicodemus and what had occurred between Laurel Anne and Fulton at the fence. The only difference was that the mare knew what she was doing and was ready for the consequences.

The next day was a scorcher. It began at dawn when the sun came out and drove away the stars. From then on, the heat built up until everything came to a standstill. Pa came down with one of his headaches, Fulton went off somewhere, and Ma had gone over to the Knights to help with a colicky baby. Silla and Alva locked the doors of the brick house, stripped down to their unmentionables, and fanned each other with wet towels.

By midafternoon, the heat was so bad that I was actually able to coax Laurel Anne into coming down to the creek to wade. We cut through the fields and down to a secret part of the creek. When we arrived, the water looked cool and soothing back under the overhanging willows.

"Bet you haven't been swimming naked for a long time," I said.

"It's not something ladies do," Laurel Anne said.

"I guess ladies just stay hot and miserable."

Without arguing the point any further, I fairly tore out of my clothes and ran down to the rock where I leaped, limbs flailing, into the cool shock of deep water. I surfaced, clawing the hair out of my eyes. Laurel Anne stood on the bank watching. I motioned for her to join me. She shook her head.

"Nobody will come," I said.

She laughed nervously, looking around. "That's not the point."

"You're right," I said, spitting water. "Point is you're a scaredy-cat."

Giving me an arch "you'll see" look, Laurel Anne slipped back into the trees and undressed behind a screen of leaves. Muttering to herself, she peeled off yards of hot clothing,

"I must be out of my mind," she laughed, embarrassed by her own daring. She slipped out of her stockings and crept down to the shore, bare naked and nervous as a doe. She tested the water with her toe and peered around at the trees, looking for Indians and night visitors. "What if someone sees us?"

I snorted. If I had a daguerreotype of her naked, I could probably sell peeks of it to the boys in the valley for enough money to buy a dozen circus elephants, maybe even the whole circus. Conversely, the boys I swam with never gave me so much as a second look, naked or otherwise.

"Nobody comes here. But if they did, they'd see you naked up there better than if you're down in the water." Startled by the soundness of this logic, she quickly sat down and slipped off the rock into the pool.

Laurel Anne swam without a ripple, sleek and proud and confident. Her big front lent her a marvelous buoyancy. She never even got her hair wet, just the white ribbon trailing in the water. Next to her I looked like a plucked bird. I was so skinny that the only way to prevent sinking straight to the bottom was to thrash around like some half-crazed waterfowl. We swam in silence, letting the cool water ease the tension from our overheated bodies. After a spell, Laurel Anne stood on the sandy bottom, water dripping from the pink tips of her pillows while she fiddled with the hair ribbon. I could tell she was preoccupied with something. It didn't surprise me when she finally spoke up.

"Rose?"

"What?"

"Why do you spend so much time with him?"

"Fulton?"

She nodded and sank into the water again, pushing off the bottom and drifting back under the overhanging branches. "What's he like?"

"He's interesting."

"How so?"

I thought about it for a minute. True, there was the dark side of Fulton Lorings that piqued my morbid curiosity. I'd never known anyone who actually killed people like bugs, much less done it right in front of me. Fulton was an enigma, as incomprehensible as the Indian hieroglyphs etched into the rocks along the creek. He was like no one I'd ever known. For a people spy like me, he was a precious gem in a litter of dull gravel. But I also suspected him to be of inordinate benefit to me, something so necessary to my own life that I couldn't reach far enough down into my soul to find the words to define it. There was a kinship between us, one that I recognized and valued, and hoped he did as well.

"He doesn't treat me like a child," I said.

"You are a child." Laurel Anne laughed.

I hooked a gob of sandy mud off the bottom with my foot and flung it at her. She ducked and scolded me.

"He talks to me like a grown-up," I continued. "And he called me a young lady." I shrugged. "I can't explain it. He makes me feel like what I think is important. And he's smart. When he came here everyone thought he was just a dumb old mute. He doesn't just know about stars. He knows French and German and Latin. He knows the names of birds and flowers. He even knows—"

"I heard he's deformed, that he was born with a disease from his mother. It that why he wears a mask?"

"His face got hurt in the war," I said with some hesitation. I didn't want to talk about Fulton's face. Especially not with Laurel Anne. I loved my sister, but I knew she was caught up with things being just so. Fulton Lorings was anything but just so, not his face, not his spirit and certainly not the way he moved like a predator through the slow herd of common folks. I'd seen Death portrayed in pictures as a grinning skeleton in tattered black robes. But I knew now that if I ever saw Death for real, he would move catlike with the soft ring of spurs.

Laurel Anne stared at her reflection in the water, touching her hair. "Is it really bad, his face I mean? Do the scars make him look frightful?"

To tell the truth, I rarely thought about Fulton being ugly anymore. After that night in the barn, it was genuinely unimportant to me what he looked like. He scared me sometimes, but it wasn't his face that did that. It was his eyes. I'd seen Fulton at his worst and I can tell you that none of the terrible things he was supposed to have done were half as frightening as the light in the eyes of Red Legs when killing was on him.

"No," I said to Laurel Anne. "Not too bad."

"Well, then," she said. "He should take it off. It's bothersome not to be able to see a person talk. After all, he's among friends. Haven't we shown that? Look at all it's costing us to stick by him. We're Christians. No one's going to mock him here."

I scoffed at that logic. No one mocked Fulton Lorings because he'd kill them if they did. That was the long and short of that nonsense. There was no way to tell Laurel Anne that Fulton's scarf probably saved more people from a bullet in the face than their own good sense and Christian restraint. Despite all that had happened to her, Laurel Anne lived a protected life. She was beautiful and folks went out of their way to dote on her and spare her any of life's routine ugliness. Consequently, she believed things should and could be romantic, like the stories of gods and goddesses. In order for her to understand Fulton Lorings, she would have to understand things like Antietam Creek and Gettysburg. As close as I was to Fulton, these were things I barely understood myself.

I wanted to change the subject, to steer it away from Fulton. Even though I was young, I somehow sensed that only a woman as beautiful as Laurel Anne could hurt him any longer. And I didn't want that to happen.

"Going to the Pioneer Dance with Henry?"

Laurel Anne gave me smug glance from the freckled shade of the willows. She was back on ground where she reigned supreme.

"Yes. I can't tell you why, of course, but Eldon Bair is not even worth speaking to anymore." She smiled, banishing the ugly scene on the porch from her mind. "Henry has promised to wear his best uniform. I think he'll look just dashing."

"I'd go with Lester if it was me. He's more fun. Remember last year when he put that pig in the privy? Old lady Duncan nearly—"

Laurel Anne shook her head. "Courting is no longer a matter of fun, Rose. It's serious business. You can't live on fun these days. I need to find a husband before I grow into an old maid. You don't know this, but Brother Nielsen has even asked Pa permission to court me now—and he has four wives already. Can you just see me married to that old billy goat? I'd die cooped up in that house of his with Prissy Nielsen and her cousins."

"Henry's a gentile," I pointed out. "You swore you wouldn't marry one."

She shrugged, making her pillows wobble. "Maybe I can change that. He has promised to attend services soon."

I frog-kicked out into the middle of the creek. "I'm going to marry Fulton."

Since marrying Fulton had never even been a conscious thought of mine, I don't know why I said it. It just popped out.

Laurel Anne gave me a strange look. "Why on earth would you pick him?" she said. "It's nonsense. He's too old for you and besides, he is not the kind of man a lady chooses for a husband. He has a terrible reputation. Do you know why they call him Red Legs?" She said it as if she knew and I didn't.

"Because a long time ago in the war he had red stripes down the legs of his breeches," I said.

Laurel Anne stared. "Pardon me?"

"The stripes on his legs were for the artillery. That's why." I explained what I knew about the war and a little about how Fulton had come to get the name Stuart's Wolf.

"Well, goodness, you certainly seem to know a lot about him."

I nodded.

"Then you should know he isn't the sort of man a lady marries."

"A lot you know."

"I know—"

"You don't know anything," I said, cutting her off. "If you did, you wouldn't be so scared of him."

"I'm not scared of him," Laurel Anne said.

"You are too."

"I am not."

"Are too."

"Am—oh, this is ridiculous." She swam to the side and started to climb up the bank and out of the water.

The opportunity was too good to pass up. I hooked up another gob of mud and pitched it straight at her backside. She screamed, clutched her bottom, and sat back down in the water.

"Rose Lee Merrell," she cried, furious. "That was a vulgar, vulgar thing to do."

I laughed. "So's what you and Alva have been saying about Fulton. You don't know anything about him."

"What's to know? He has no morals and no manners. He's a gun-man. A lady couldn't be seen talking to him." She seemed to remember then that she had talked to him several times in recent days. "At least not in broad daylight."

Carefully, with great deliberation so she wouldn't misunderstand what I was saying, I told her about the shell comb and Fulton's solemn vow. I told her how he had knelt down like a knight straight out of Ivanhoe and swore a holy oath that nothing bad would ever happen to her. While I talked, Laurel Anne's eyes grew wider. When I finished, she was motionless in the water, her mouth parted in surprise.

"I didn't know."

I shook my head. "That's the kind of man he is. Nobody knows any-thing about him. Just enough to make up their minds to hate him. And that's why they say stupid stuff like what Eldon told you about his mother."

Laurel Anne's eyes narrowed and I knew I'd gone too far. "How do you know about that?" she said.

I stuck out my tongue. "Saw you kiss, too."

With a cry of vengeance, Laurel Anne pushed off the bottom and swam for me. I might have made it to the far bank except I started laugh-ing and accidentally sucked down a lungful of water. Gagging and chok-ing, I couldn't swim very good. Laurel Anne caught me and shoved me down to the mud bottom. I kicked and thrashed and the scuffle degener-ated into a brawl which she mostly won.

Later, when we were dressed and walking back to the house, Laurel Anne asked me again what Fulton was like.

"You need to find out for yourself," I replied. "I guess he's different things to different folks. One thing's for sure, he's not like anyone we've ever known. Just be nice to him. He's trying to change and some folks are making it hard for him."

"Well then," she said. "I shall be nice to him."

She was as good as her word. During the next few days, I saw her speak to Fulton on several occasions. She was polite and kind and seemed genuinely interested. Those times left Fulton reeling mentally, confused by Laurel Anne's sudden apparent interest. Once, when she stopped in the yard to shade her eyes and compliment him on the fine job he was doing fixing the weather vane on top of the barn, the normally agile Fulton Lorings dropped a hammer, a saw and a bucket of nails in rapid succession.

In a different way, Laurel Anne was doing the same thing as Fulton— trying to change her nature. She wasn't a bad person, just a naive one. One thing I learned though, it's almost always harder for good people to change than it is for bad people. I never forgot how I learned that gem of wisdom during the final days of Stuart's Wolf. Over the years I have polished it down until it has became a private and continual prayer in my heart:

God save us all from the best intentions of good people.

Chapter Nine

Sunday rolled around as it always does. We had to go to church in spite of the fact that Eldon's vigilance committee patrolled the road. Being the bishop's family, we would have donned our stuffy clothes and gone off to church in the face of an Indian attack. Besides, Pa said, he wasn't going to let a bunch of idiots think they could keep him locked up on his own farm.

I tried to talk Pa out of church, saying we couldn't leave Fulton alone in case Eldon tried to sneak in and start a fight with him. Pa said Fulton could take care of himself. He pointed out that Eldon was just as much a prisoner out there on the road as Fulton was on our farm. It didn't make sense to me. All I knew was that we were stuck going to church when we had a perfectly logical reason to stay home. There were other reasons why I didn't want to go, all of which centered around being scared.

Ready before the others, I tramped down to the barn to complain to Fulton. I found him bent over a barrel full of water, shaving his scrambled face in a broken piece of mirror. Shaving what little hair still grew from the twisted grooves and ridges of his lower face must have been an agony for him. Blood from a dozen cuts ran in watery veins to the point of his chin. He saw me and straightened up, putting a clean scrap of old sack cloth to his face.

"Church?" he asked, spying my good clothes.

"Church," I said, flopping down on a wooden cask of nails. "You're so lucky."

"How's that?"

"You don't believe in God. You don't have to go to church. You don't have to be bored forever and ever listening to stupid old sermons."

"Your Pa's sermons are stupid?"

I looked around, making sure Pa hadn't followed me down to the barn. "No," I admitted. "But some others are. Edwina Spafford testifies all the time. She's more crazy than anything. It's just boring. I wouldn't go except Pa makes me."

"You don't go to church for your God?"

Talking with Fulton was aggravating sometimes. He was getting better at conversing and once in a while I think he baited a fight out of me just so he could practice.

When I didn't offer to argue, Fulton went back to shaving. I continued to fidget, irritable and out of sorts and wishing Jesus would come again like everybody said he was going to. At least then it would all be over and I wouldn't be troubled with things like school and church and dances.

"What's really bothering you?"

"Boys," I said without thinking.

Fulton's eyebrows went up. With a splintery rasp of the razor, he scraped the last of the whiskers from the undamaged part of his face. Finished, he dunked his head in the barrel and then shook it free of water and soap like a big dog.

"Which boys?" he asked, dragging wet hair back with his fingers.

"All of them. Josh especially. All he does is fool around with that pistol you gave him. He never wants to go swimming anymore, or swinging on the rope. Or—" I was coming to close to the real reason and so I stopped.

"Or what?"

"Nothing."

What really bothered me was the dress Ma was making for me for the Pioneer Dance. It was my first grown-up dress, full length with puffy sleeves and enough lace to make me look as foamy as the bottom of a waterfall. Even Laurel Anne said it was beautiful. Problem was, I had no one to wear it for. Part or even most of the aggravation of going to church was knowing I'd meet up with Sarah and Fannie. I didn't feel like hearing about their alleged beaus and how many dances they were going to have and with whom. I didn't have any romantic interests in boys, despite what I'd told Laurel Anne about marrying Fulton someday, and I sure as hell didn't feel like being teased about it by two prissy smart-mouths like Sarah and Fannie.

"Saw your dance dress," Fulton said.

I turned up my nose. "It's ugly. A pig wouldn't wear it."

Fulton shook his head. "Pretty."

I got to my feet and kicked a pile of hay. "So?" I said. "Who'll care? Nobody is going to be there to dance with me. All my friends have kind-of beaus and they'll dance and I'll just stand around and people will make fun of me and then I'll get in trouble for pouring punch on Eddie Hoffenstetter again. Pa will make me sit in the wagon all night."

It all came out of me in a rush, hot and bitter. Caught between childhood and womanhood, I felt like a molting bird: miserable and ugly enough to be left for dead. My life, I decided, was sorry and frustrating enough to make even God grind his teeth. I sighed.

"Need an escort?" Fulton asked.

"Yes," I said. "Fannie and Sarah are eleven, same as me, and they have them."

Actually, Fannie and Sarah had no such thing. They were going to the dance with their folks just like me, but they had it fixed in their own minds that Randall Leech and Herbert Wallace—two buck-toothed, thirteen-year-old boys with pimples—would meet them at the dance and there act as semi-official escorts. "Fannie and Sarah have store dresses and escorts and everything. I'll have to dance with Pa. Or the twins. I'd rather eat mule snot."

"That's what this is all about? An escort to the dance?"

I shrugged. It wasn't all, it just seemed like all right about now. I'd reached a point in my life where I became frustrated and bored easily. If not for Fulton, I probably would have been driven out of my mind and hung myself before now. Fulton was full of surprises. He was never boring, unless shooting folks was the sort of thing that bored you. As if to prove this point, he stood up straight and bowed forward from the waist.

"Miss Merrell, I'd be obliged if you would attend the Pioneer Dance with me."

"Don't," I said. "I'm not in the mood."

"Is that a no?"

I paused, looking at him. He seemed serious enough. For a second, I had a vision of Fulton at the dance, wearing his guns and the ragged scarf around his face. Men would tremble. Women would faint. Children would scream. It would be perfect.

"Want me to get down on one knee again?"

I blinked, feeling as dumb as a bucket. He was serious. "You want to escort me to the dance?"

He nodded. "With your mother's permission of course."

"You know how to dance?"

Eyes betraying nothing, he nodded. But all belted up with guns and knives and spurs, it seemed an improbability that Fulton would know anything as delicate as a waltz.

A "yes" came out of my mouth in much the same way that my intention of someday marrying a known killer had surprised Laurel Anne the day before.

Fulton nodded. "Don't tell anyone. They might get the wrong idea."

He cocked his head and I heard Pa's voice calling to me. Church didn't seem quite so bad now that I was armed with the thought of having an escort. We'd see what Fannie and Sarah thought of my beau in comparison to theirs.

I started to go, paused and turned back. Fulton looked confident and powerful standing there in the light from the loft. At the same time, he looked strangely vulnerable. I ran back and gave him a hug, scraping my knuckles on the butts of his guns.

"Thank you," I said.

One arm came around and for the briefest of seconds, Fulton actually hugged me back. His touch put a painful knot in my throat. He was changing and for a minute, there was almost a hope that it would be in time and enough.

I ran back up to the house and climbed in the wagon. Pa gave me a perturbed look for making everyone late but I didn't care. I had the best secret in the whole damn world.

We passed a vigilance patrol on the way to church. Eldon and four of his cronies rode by wearing their homemade badges and carrying rifles. I hadn't seen Eldon in a few days and he looked a little too intense now, like the pressure inside him was building up to the danger level. He obviously hadn't gotten over losing out to Henry du Pont. He reined up and tipped his hat to us, especially Laurel Anne. Laurel Anne ignored him, her nose in the air. Pa kept right on driving.

"Morning, Bishop," Eldon called.

Pa ignored Eldon, continuing on as if the vigilance committee had only been a collection of dead skunks in the middle of the road.

Eldon's face darkened. He stood up in his stirrups, shaking his hat at us. "We'll get him, Bishop," he shouted. "Make no mistake about it. We'll get him. He can't hide behind your skirts forever."

As soon as we were past them, the vigilance committee gathered together again and continued down the road that would carry them past our farm. I felt a cold finger of dread. Except for Eldon, they were a sloppy and foolish looking bunch, more like boys on a prank than men trying to flush out a killer. If they weren't careful, someone was going to get hurt. It wouldn't be anything like Hugh Barney shooting his own butt, either. This would be more like the soldiers on the Provo road. Staring at the departing backs of Eldon's vigilance patrol, I had a brief and sudden vision of them lying in the road with splintered skulls, their brains hanging in the trees. I swallowed hard and looked away.

Pa didn't say anything the rest of the way to church. For once, Alva had the presence of mind to keep her mouth shut. The rest of us stayed quiet as well, lost in our own thoughts and fears.

When we arrived, I saw only about half as many wagons, buggies and horses in the churchyard as there normally were for a Sunday meeting. Of those who had come, the Jacksons, the Knights and the Stoddards figured prominently. Noticeably absent were the Hoffenstetters, the Pettus clan, the Bairs and the Poulsens. I sighed. At least we'd get through church without serious incident. When the Spaffords arrived in their wagon, I knew I'd hoped too soon.

With roughly half the congregation missing, Pa had us all sit on the pews up toward the front. It was another Sunday departure from the normal fare of things. After the sacrament was handed around, Pa began preaching a sermon on the gifts of the Spirit and the necessity of keeping an open heart and mind to celestial whispers. He made no mention of our missing friends. The sermon was medium to mostly boring.

At one point during his sermon, I heard Pa falter. He seemed a little confused and then hurried to collect his thoughts, as if he had been distracted. His counselors, Brother Stoddard and Brother Knight, looked mighty uncomfortable too. I tried to figure out what was wrong but couldn't put my finger on what it was. It never occurred to me to look over my shoulder. Instead, I concentrated on just staying awake. After a minute I hit on a method of pinching Lehi under the knee without Ma seeing it. In a couple of minutes I had him mad enough to scream. Red and sweaty, he looked like his head would explode. Ma finally saw what was going on and parted us, making me sit on the other side of her. I was back listening to the sermon.

I thought Edwina Spafford might break out into tongues again. She was nodding at the things Pa was saying and mumbling to herself. When Pa finally finished his sermon, her "amen" was the loudest of the bunch.

We sang "We're Marching on to Glory" and Brother Knight said the closing prayer. He stuttered and kept losing track of what he was trying to say. Oddly enough, he sounded a little scared. Still, he got to the amen part in what I considered good time. As soon as the amens were said, we all got up to stampede for the wagons. Chrissie Spafford made it out into the aisle, stopped short and screamed loud enough to drive nails.

Everyone jumped and turned around. There at the very back, looking dark and forbidding, sat Fulton Lorings.

For everyone but our family, it must have been like turning around and finding the devil sitting behind you in church. It certainly didn't sit well with Edwina. She grabbed Chrissie and pushed her daughter around behind her.

Fulton saw that he was making everyone nervous and stood up. He was wearing a clean shirt and the usual scarf. He held his hat in his hands and I saw that his hair was nicely combed. He'd worn his guns and Edwina Spafford saw them when he got up.

"Oh, Heavenly Father," she whimpered. "He's come to take one of us." She sat down on the bench and pulled Chrissie close. You couldn't have gotten more of a rise out of Edwina with the Second Coming.

Fulton got tired of us staring at him fish-mouthed with surprise. He took two steps and disappeared out the door. I ducked under Alva's arm and ran after him. Outside, I spotted him in the act of swinging up on the back of Nicodemus. I called his name and ran to him. In the saddle, he towered high above me, so high that I had to squint when I looked up.

"You came to church," I said.

I must have sounded a little accusing because he looked down at me and smiled through the scarf. "Your Pa gives a good sermon. I didn't understand much, but it wasn't boring."

"You only came once," I pointed out. "It gets worse. You'll have to come to testimony meeting sometime."

"It doesn't come highly recommended," Fulton said dryly. "But I'm glad I came this time."

I didn't ask him how he managed to avoid the vigilance patrols or how he slipped inside the church during Pa's sermon without a sound. Nothing Fulton did surprised me anymore. I did, however, sense that coming to church represented the greatest effort yet in his attempt to save himself. Behind us, the front steps of the church were filling up with people coming out to gawk at him. Their rapt attention made Fulton nervous again.

"I'll see you back at the house," I said.

"Yes."

He leaned down and touched my cheek in a teasing motion. Then he dipped his hat in the direction of Laurel Anne and the family. He touched Nicodemus with his spurs and rode out of the yard. I watched until he disappeared around a bend in the road. If Eldon's vigilance committee stood in good favor with God, they might be feeling the Spirit right about now to stay the hell off the Merrell Farm road.

When I walked back to the church, everyone was going on about Fulton.

"Just as bold as you please," Lily Stoddard was saying to Sister Knight. "Never heard so much as a squeak of a hinge."

"Thought I'd faint dead away," Sister Howard said.

Floyd Jackson was even more impressed. He fairly hopped with excitement. "Wouldn't have believed it if I hadn't seen it myself. Stuart's Wolf in church! Sakes, they say he's killed five-hundred men."

"Like as not he was after my Chrissie," Edwina Spafford said. "I saw him looking straight at her. No telling what was on his filthy mind."

"All right, all right," Pa said. "Let's go home now. This is supposed to be a day of rest."

I walked back down to where the wagons were parked. I saw several of the boys looking at me with curious interest. Keeping my eye on them, I passed close by the Gormann wagon.

Fannie and Sarah sat inside, perfect angels unless you knew them for what they really were. They giggled and started singing the jump rope song from school, the words altered for the occasion.

"Hash Face, Hash Face, has no nose. He's in love with ugly Rose."

Furious, I snatched a clod off the ground and drew back my arm. Fannie and Sarah shrieked for their ma but it was too late. As they scrambled to take cover, I wound up and let fly. The clod struck Fannie in the back of the head, right between her braids, hard enough to drive sparks out of her ears and knock her half out of the wagon. Of the two, Sarah had sung the loudest and so I stooped and selected a nice sharp rock for her. I drew back again and would have fired it off except Josh caught my arm from behind. He pulled me in the direction of our wagon.

"Leave me alone," I demanded. "They deserved it."

"Yes," he said. "And if you're gonna get them, you deserve not to get caught." He pointed to where Sister Gormann was brushing dirt out of a weeping Fannie's hair while lecturing Alva about me. Sarah, sobbing and sucking snot over her own near miss, stuck out her tongue and hid behind her ma.

Josh made me get in the wagon, climbing in beside me. We were alone while we waited for Pa to get done calming everyone down.

"I'm going to be like him."

I looked at him. "Who?"

"Mr. Lorings," Josh said. "I'm going to practice until I can shoot as good as him."

"It's dangerous," I said, trying to think of other reasons why being like Fulton wasn't such a great idea.

"Yes."

"Then why do it?"

"Because I'm going to be a marshal." He sounded as grim as a graveyard. He looked at me. "There's too many bad people in the world, too many bad things happening. I'm going to do something about it. Someday bad men will break down and cry when they hear I'm coming for them. You'll see."

I didn't know what to say. In all the time we'd known each other, I'd never heard Josh Van Orden express a desire to be anything except away from his ma. I guess maybe Fulton was the first man to pay any kind of positive attention to him, and positive attention was the thing Josh needed most. His desire to emulate Fulton Lorings made me understand just how much of an impact Fulton was having on our lives.

During the ride home, Silla and Alva talked about Fulton showing up at church. Alva was of the opinion that certain people shouldn't come to church until they had repented enough to make the general congregation feel comfortable around them. Proof that Fulton wasn't ready for worship service, she pointed out, was the fact that he'd worn guns inside God's house.

"Good heavens," she blabbered. "What possible need could a body have for guns at church?"

"I agree," Silla said. "No excuse for that kind of behavior."

They both looked at Pa for approval, but he was ignoring them. His eyes were straight ahead on something up the road. I looked and saw two of Eldon's vigilance patrol walking down the road looking a bit forlorn. When we got closer, I saw that it was Clive Wilson and a chunky mill hand I knew only as Graham. Clive and Graham both still wore badges but didn't have a single gun or horse between them. Pa reined up.

"What're you boys up to?" he asked.

Clive paused. He looked mad, fit to bust. Graham, on the other hand, was acting scared enough to pass out. He was sweating and his lips were twitching.

"Afternoon, Bishop," Clive said, disgusted. He tipped his hat to the women. "I'll tell you what we're doing. We're on our way home for keeps. To hell with Eldon Bair." He snatched off his badge and flung it in the general direction of the trees. He thought about it and then did the same with Graham's.

"What happened?" Pa asked. "Anybody get hurt?"

"Nope," Clive said with visible disgust. "That fool Eldon left me and Graham here to watch the fork in the road near your place." He paused and spit to one side. "All along I been listening to the Bairs brag about catching this hired hand of yours. I'm sorry if that offended you, Bishop, but they was paying me and Graham to ride with the vigilance marshals." He grinned. "Shoot, I never figured we'd actually do anything. I never expected we'd run on to your hired man. And I sure never figured he'd turn out to be Satan riding an Appaloosa." Graham shuddered, looking about ready to fall down.

"He took our guns and horses," Clive said. "I never even heard him coming. One minute I was thinking on what a nice day it was, and the next I had me a gun barrel poked in my eye." Clive looked at Graham. "This idjit tried something, I don't know what, and your man poked the barrel of another pistol down his throat and cocked it. Talked in this mean, hissy voice. Said if he caught us hanging around your place again, he'd empty our shoulders."

"Where is he now?" Pa asked.

"Don't know and don't care," Clive said. "I'm going straight home and lock myself inside for a week." He looked at his unhinged friend. "Graham here needs some rest and some new trousers. If you run onto our horses, Bishop, I'd be obliged if you'd let us know." He tipped his hat again and began steering the dumb-struck Graham down the road like a cow to market.

Pa flicked the reins and we started off again. We didn't see any more of Eldon's vigilance patrols. More importantly, we didn't find any of them dead in the road. Fulton must have made it home all right.

Pa was some put out by Fulton's behavior. I heard him tell Ma he'd have to talk with Fulton about being so quick to mistreat folks. Ma said she thought Fulton showed remarkable restraint considering who he was and the fact that Eldon was pushing on him so hard. Only weeks ago, such an encounter would have left Graham and Clive as dead as a couple of Nephites.

"I'm agreeing with you, Colleen," Pa said. "But I'm worried that it's going to keep on until we have more killing. Things have been quiet and I want them to stay that way."

"Then talk with Eldon Bair," she said. "He's the one patrolling our road looking for a fight."

Pa thought about it and said he would.

Surprisingly enough, Alva didn't cram her two cents in. I think it was because she saw how put out Pa was and didn't want to aggravate him further. The danger was too great that Ma would end up receiving him again that afternoon in order to calm him down. Nothing on the face of the earth bothered Alva more than Pa making squeaks with Ma. She pressed her lips flat and said nothing. Pinch Face caught the direction the wind was blowing and kept her yapper shut too.

Back at the farm we found Clive and Graham's horses hitched to the rails of the stock pens. Pa looked at them and shook his head as he drove on up to the house.

We piled out. I wanted to go down to the barn and get Fulton's version of what happened to Graham. Instead, I got an idea and followed Ma up to our cabin. Jeb was waiting for us on the stoop. He came over to be petted, wriggling almost double as his butt failed to cooperate with his front. I looked around for Merlin. It had been days since we'd seen him. Ma said it was possible that he had finally found some more ravens to hang around. Maybe he had gone back to the wild. The thought of anything going back to the wild bothered me.

Inside, I shucked off my church clothes and pulled on my jumper. In one corner of our cabin hung the fancy dress Ma was making for me. In spite of what I told Fulton about it, it was a pretty dress. Ma had spent hours cutting it out, measuring and sticking me with pins, hours more sewing. Years from now, I wouldn't remember exactly what the dress looked like, but I knew I'd remember forever how my ma loved me enough to sit up nights sewing it.

"Ma," I said."

"Yes, dear."

"Do you suppose I might make something for him?"

"Fulton?"

"Yes'm, I want to make him a nice scarf. For his face."

Ma went to the trunk where she kept her yard goods. Down in the bottom was a bundle of white silk brought all the way from China. She took it out and showed it to me. Light as a breeze, it must have cost a minor fortune. She said it would make a soft, gentle scarf for Fulton's face, one that wouldn't chafe him what with the way he was always looking around to see who might be behind him.

That night and most of the next day, we cut and sewed. At first I didn't know exactly what I wanted except for the colors red, white and blue. The design eluded me until Ma was done mixing the colors to dye the silk. Then it popped out of my head. I went over to the bookshelves and tracked down an old Harper's Weekly Magazine. I found what I was looking for inside. In a picture of men charging each other with swords fixed on the ends of their guns was a flag. I studied it, trying to see how to make it work.

I took the magazine to Ma and explained what I wanted. There would be nine white stars on a field of red, bordered by bars of blue and white—a rough copy of the flag Fulton had followed all those terrible years.

While we made Fulton's scarf, we talked a lot. I asked Ma again how she came to America, how she got to be a Mormon and how it was that Alva was younger than her but still Pa's senior wife. I'd heard it all before in pieces, but this time Ma told it to me in one long stretch while we sewed.

"We came over from Ireland when I was not much older than you," Ma said. "Kicked out of the old country because we were poor and we were Catholic, and because the potatoes had all died. The food and the water on the ship were terrible but better than we had in Ireland. I hated the ship. I remember how the gray water and skies stretched for eternity. My mother—your grandmother—died the third week. They sewed her up in a piece of old sail with ballast rocks between her feet. We said a prayer and they dropped her over the rail. Your grandfather was so grief-stricken that I thought he would try and follow her. I was twelve years old and to this very day I still hate ships, Rose. One of the reasons I love this place so much is because it's about as far from an ocean as you can get."

I listened as intently as I could while cutting out the stars for Fulton's scarf. Ma spoke in a soft voice, telling me how she and her brother and sisters and my grandfather docked in New York City on Christmas Day. My grandfather, Connor Bryson got a job tearing down old buildings. Colleen, Alva, Moyle and three-year-old Meredith stayed in a freezing shack on the Hudson River while he worked, often spending entire days under the thin blankets of the only bed because they couldn't afford to buy coal. There was little food.

By spring, tiny Meredith was dead and Moyle was sick with pneumonia. They buried Meredith in a charity plot behind a big church near the Hudson River. Sobbing uncontrollably, Connor Bryson dug the hole himself while a priest stood over him and told him that failure to have his daughter baptized meant she would never be with her mother up in heaven. When Connor finished, patting the dirt gently over his daughter's grave, he handed the shovel back to the priest, gave him a dollar and said the priest would see him in Hell before he ever saw him in church again. That night, he packed up the rest of his children and quit New York City for Pennsylvania.

Two years later, Connor was working for a canal company near Erie. Walking down a muddy street one evening, he heard a Mormon missionary preaching from the back of a wagon. The words rooted him right to the ground as the elder tried to tell a crowd of drunken hecklers that little children were free from all sin. Kicking and cursing, Connor chased away the crowd and pulled the missionary down out of the wagon. Holding the terrified elder by the lapels, Connor demanded to know more about a church that claimed children were blameless in the eyes of God. Before the missionary finished stammering the answer, Connor was ready to be baptized. With one condition.

"Listen, boyo," he growled in the missionary's face, "I find that ye've lied to me about sin and wee children and you'll go back to God carrying your head under your arm."

Grandfather Bryson, Ma, Moyle and Alva became Mormons two days later, baptized in the Le Beouf River by elders genuinely afraid not to. Six months after that they were part of a handcart company en route to the Great Salt Lake to help Brigham Young make the desert blossom like a rose.

"He's either crazy or a great bloody prophet," Connor Bryson declared when he saw drawings of the deserts and mountains they would cross on their long journey to Deseret.

Connor Bryson never made it to Brigham Young's city of the Great Salt Lake. One morning he carried a bucket down to the Platte River for water. When he didn't return, several men took rifles and went looking for him. They found Connor Bryson with an arrow through his neck. The bucket and his suspenders were missing.

Orphans, Colleen, Alva and Moyle were taken in by a family that eventually settled in Salt Lake City. Ma worked in a woolen mill while Alva helped at home, learning to cook and sew.

"One day," Ma said with a smile, "your father saw me walking home from the mill. He followed me and begged to court me." She laughed. "He didn't need to beg. I loved him from the very first minute I saw him."

"Then why'd you let him marry Pump—Alva?"

"On the day we arrived in New York City, I swore to your grandfather that I would take care of my sisters. I failed with little Merry. When your father asked to marry me, I knew right then that Alva would never marry if I left. I made him marry her first. He swore great oaths and said he wouldn't. Brigham Young even heard about it and tried to get your father to marry Alva. They had a terrible argument. Your father even threatened to trounce President Young. He said there was no point of hell in the next life if we had plural marriage here on earth."

I was pleasantly surprised by this colorful revelation. My pa, the most Christian man around, had actually threatened to beat up a prophet of God? Already a giant in my mind, Pa's stature shot higher still.

Ma continued. "I waited for two months while your father pleaded with me. I almost gave in a hundred times. Finally, it was him who gave in. Now Alva has a husband, I have a husband and I have you. We're all happy."

Most of us, I thought. Knowing what I knew about Alva, I bet there were plenty of days when Pa still wanted to beat up Brigham Young.

Being a plural wife might work for Ma. She was strong and knew she was special to Pa. It would never work for me. Nor would it work for Laurel Anne. It wasn't really working for Alva. Pa stayed with her in the brick house and only occasionally stayed with Ma. Then he still had to pay for it by putting up with Alva's bad humor. It was a confusing situation and I only knew that of everyone involved, I felt the most sorry for Pa. He had no more say in who he got married to than Samson had about which heifers we put in the pasture with him. Pa couldn't just go out on his own and choose a wife. If he could, he'd never do it because it really only added to his misery. Ma and Alva had to do it for him, or at least they had to agree on who it would be. With Alva's penchant for attracting women like herself to the family, and Ma's desire to see needy sisters married to a husband who would take care of them, Pa didn't stand much of a chance of rubbing up to any peace and quiet.

It was true that Pinch Face needed a husband and that Josh needed a father, especially since neither of them were much in demand among available husbands and fathers. It was even true that Alva could use a sister-wife that cooperated more with her, and I'd certainly benefit if I had a half brother like Josh to keep the twins in line. But Pa needed a new wife like Josh Van Orden needed another whipping. Trouble was, life always seemed to dish out what you needed the least.

It was inevitable that Pinch Face found out about Josh's pistol. She lacked a lot in the way of useful talents, but when it came to being a snoop she was tops.

Josh had a lot of time on his hands now that he wasn't working like a slave at the cooperage any more. He started wandering off on his own, ignoring his ma's objections. When he came back, Pinch Face told Alva, Josh always smelled like sulphur and his hands were black with soot. Then one day, someone told Pinch Face that her son was off shooting a pistol. Feathers flew at the Van Orden house—Pinch Face demanding that Josh tell her where he'd gotten the pistol and to fork it over, Josh telling her she'd never find it. She tried to beat it out of him but he ran off. Unable to bear the burden of a wayward son on her own, Pinch Face donned her shawl and trudged tearfully in the direction of our place. Pa could irrigate the north pasture with the amount of tears Silla Van Orden had cried on our farm. I was under the porch minding my own business when she and Alva got together to talk about it.

"He's not going to make it to the celestial kingdom," Silla blubbered. "First his father leaving us and now this. I don't know if I can bear it, Alva. The burden is too heavy."

"The boy needs a father," Alva replied. "I've said it all before. The bishop could straighten him out."

"But do you think the bishop will ever marry again?" Silla asked, drying her tears. "I've done everything I can think of to make him notice me."

"Maybe you should talk to him about Josh," Alva suggested. "That might turn his heart to you, to see that you need a husband."

"Do you think so?"

Alva said she did. She went on to tell Silla that Pa had a way with contrary children. "I've had to talk to him a number of times about Rose. Do you know that wicked child once put a lizard in my chamber pot? She has absolutely no respect for adults, Silla. Colleen lets her run wild, lets her read anything she wants."

"I've noticed she's respectful of her father, though," Silla observed. "At least she's that. Does he strap her often?"

"Heavens, no," Alva said, sounding disgusted. "He wouldn't lay a hand on her for fear his precious Colleen might object. She has a spell on that man, I swear. If she wasn't my sister and I wasn't a Christian woman, I'd have a few observations to make on her behavior. But that doesn't mean Rose goes without punishment. He did make her eat some soap for calling me a foul name. But that's it. Mostly he just talks to her. Not enough, in my mind. He didn't even talk to her about the lizard. I got up in the middle of the night and jumped a mile when I felt it. Told the bishop I wanted her strapped. He just laughed, like having a lizard run across your—whatever—was funny."

"Oh, no."

Alva sighed. "That's why I need another sister-wife, Silla, dear. I can't manage the spirit of this family alone. I need some support."

Pinch Face positively gushed. "Oh, I would be that support, Alva. Truly I would. If only the bishop would notice me and..."

I crawled away from under the porch, thinking on looking Pa up and telling him about Silla and Alva. He already knew about it, though. Pa was a lot of things but stupid wasn't one of them. He acted like things went by him without notice, but he knew what was going on. Proof of that came a few hours later when he went looking for Josh.

I was playing with my arrowhead collection when he stopped by the cabin. Ma invited him in for a cool drink. He came in and gave me a kiss. I heard him sigh when he sat down at our table. No matter what Brigham Young and God said about polygamy, I think Pa would have been happiest to live in the cabin with just me and Ma. He made plenty of money from blacksmithing and horse trading, but I think he would have given everything up to move to Mexico with just us.

"Budge?" he said after Ma brought him some cold raspberry tea. "Have you seen Josh today?"

I nodded. When Pa asked me questions in a particular tone of voice, I was always better off answering with nods and single syllables. Past experience had taught me that the less he pried out of me the better off I was. It wasn't fear of a whipping, but rather fear that he'd serve up a lecture once he found out what he wanted to know. Pa's lectures were just awful, long and full of stuff that might have made sense to God or a bishop but were only tiresome and incomprehensible to a kid. If ever offered a choice, I'd take the whipping.

"Where did you see him?"

"Here."

"Did he have a pistol?"

I shook my head. It was the truth. It was me who had the pistol. It was locked in my trunk not five feet from where Pa was sitting. And unless he asked me for it directly, that's where it was going to stay. I'm a lot of things, but stupid isn't first on the list.

After a few minutes, Pa asked me if I'd excuse him and Ma so they could talk over something private. I gathered up my arrowheads, kissed my folks and went outside to play. The spot I chose to sort through my collection again happened to be just under the window. I could hear them both clear as anything.

"I've got to do something about Sister Van Orden," Pa said, sounding weary and out of sorts. "People are starting to talk about her being out here so much. Now she wants me to track down her son and strap him. Seems he's carrying a pistol around like an outlaw bent on murdering folks. Or so she says."

"Lee," Ma said, getting right down to it like she always does. "You keep putting it off. The boy needs a father."

"You mean Silla needs a husband, don't you?"

"That, too, dearest."

"Confound it, Colleen. I said no more polygamy. Why do you insist on pushing the Van Orden woman at me?"

Ma must have come around and sat in Pa's lap because I heard her laugh and then I heard the sound of them kiss. Not the little pecks she gave him when Alva was around, but a long, serious one.

They discussed Josh and Silla some more, Pa arguing against marrying again and Ma telling him he had a moral responsibility to meet the needs of those presented to him.

"Doesn't this trouble you?" Pa asked her. "Doesn't it bother you to live up here in this shack while Alva lords it over you down there?"

"No," Ma said. "I'm happy. Alva can only bother me if I let her. She's not as strong as I am. It's up to me to be gracious. And it's up to me to make a place for you to rest when things get too much for you."

They talked more about it. Alternating Pa's frustrated outbursts with more kissing. After a minute, they got quiet. I held my breath, unsure of what was coming. I'd never actually heard Ma and Pa make squeaks before. I wondered nervously if she'd make noises the way Alva did.

"Rose?"

I jumped a mile, scattering my arrowheads all over creation. Annoyed and a little frightened, I looked up at the window and saw Ma looking out at me.

"Would you be a good girl and run off and play for a while?"

I said I would and she thanked me.

I headed off to look for Josh. Ma and Pa would kiss some more and end up making squeaks. In a couple of hours, Pa would be down at the barn looking like he'd never had a problem in his whole life. Ma knew I'd been listening to them and she sent me away when she wanted some privacy with him. It was all right with me. I didn't mind listening to Alva in the dark, but I was pretty sure I didn't want to hear Ma and Pa.

At loose ends and needing a little excitement, I thought about going down to the brick house and telling Alva where Pa was. The possibility of making her slam her pots and pans around appealed to me. I decided against it, knowing she would only take it out on Pa. Alva didn't mind sharing Pa with Silla, but it drove her crazy that he loved my ma as much as he did. Instead of spreading contention, I went down to the creek.

I didn't find Josh at Indian Rocks, but I did catch a lizard. I put it in the pocket of my jumper and carried it with me back to the brick house. There I found Alva, Laurel Anne and Pinch Face talking about the Pioneer Dance. Laurel Anne was dressed only in her unmentionables while Alva sewed and measured the last of her dress. I sat down in the corner and played with Aaron while listening to the conversation.

The subject of the Pioneer Dance concerned me. Not only was I not pretty enough, I was also going to be escorted by someone everyone was afraid of. And for some reason I didn't like the idea of Laurel Anne putting on airs with Henry.

"Henry is going to wear his best uniform," Laurel Anne was saying.

Alva and Pinch allowed as how that was wonderful, giggling like a couple of simpletons.

"I just know you'll be the prettiest girl there," Silla said.

Laurel Anne blushed. "There will be plenty of beautiful ladies, Silla," she replied. I've seen the dresses you two have been working on. They're lovely."

No one said anything about Ma's dress, which was black with lace cuffs. I'd seen her trying it on and it made her look like a beautiful sorceress.

Alva held up Laurel Anne's dress, lemon yellow with white piping and loops and frills. "I think Henry's uniform will flatter this real nice," she said.

That got them talking about escorts to the dance. Alva told Laurel Anne that she and Pinch Face were trying to talk Pa into escorting Pinch Face alone.

"When I was younger," Alva said, "I had lots and lots of beaus. Why those Salt Lake boys just buzzed around me like flies."

Flies buzzed around a lot of things. I almost mentioned a few of them but decided not to. I didn't feel like being chased off just yet.

The subject of beaus got me thinking. I was now officially eleven. Girls in the valley got married as young as fifteen and sixteen. In another five years, I could actually be married myself, making squeaks and babies with someone I might not even know yet. Thoughts of getting married so young started me thinking about beaus. Except for Fulton, I didn't have a single one, not even the hint of one. It might not have bothered me as much if it weren't for the fact that the girls my age, Fannie and Sarah

Gormann especially, had already started talking about them this summer—how many they had and which of them would be fun to kiss.

Whether it was my age or inclination, I wasn't overly interested in beaus. I had an escort to the dance and that was good enough for now. I thought about what I would do at the Pioneer Dance if it wasn't for Fulton. There were the Hoffenstetter boys, Eddie (of fishhook in the nose fame) Helmut, Karl *und* Paulus. Ranging in ages from eleven to fifteen, they were stolid, blond and boring. Any of the Hoffenstetter boys would have been like dancing with a sack of turnips.

Coyle Morgan and Joey Leeks weren't even worth considering. I'd rather have my legs amputated and dance on the stumps than be escorted by either of them. Not that it made much difference. Word of late had them both banned from the dance for getting caught lifting cigars out of Willoughby's Mercantile in Lehi City.

The Poulsens had a boy, Parley, who was sort of good looking, but as simple as his father. The Rowleys had a son who was a year younger than me, Delbert. He might have been a candidate if not for the fact that he had a hopeless crush on Sarah. Besides, he had warts.

It was almost a useless point until Josh occurred to me. What with Pinch Face hanging around so much, Josh lived so close to our family that I never really considered him as beau material; he was more like a brother. He was nice looking but too distant. Being as standoffish as he was, I started wondering how he would fare at the dance.

"What's Josh wearing to the dance?" I asked Pinch Face.

They looked at me as if I'd crawled out from under the rug. Pinch Face adopted a stern look, hoping Alva would see it and notice that she was trying to teach me something.

"He's not wearing anything, dear," Pinch Face said sweetly. "He's going to be staying home and cutting wood. That's what happens when children don't respect their parents and their elders. Privileges are revoked."

Alva smiled slyly, looking at me out of the corner of her eye, hoping I'd get the hidden message.

"Oh," I said. I got up and walked out of the room, pausing in the hall.

"That one could use some staying home, too," Alva said under her breath.

Silla tittered. Laurel Anne didn't say anything.

It wasn't so much that Josh wasn't coming to the dance, but that I was finally coming to understand how people like Fulton got made. Pinch Face and Pumpkin Ass were like the officers who chased Fulton away from the Richmond dances, like the society women who screamed and fainted when they saw him. Tell someone they aren't good enough, wound their heart deep enough, and pretty soon they'll believe it. And then you've got trouble.

Silla's little knit handbag was on the table near the door. I put the lizard in it.

Tiptoeing out onto the porch, I heard something coming from the direction of the creek. I listened hard and recognized the soft popping of evenly-spaced shots. I held my breath until I realized that it was Josh practicing and not a pitched battle between Fulton and the vigilance committee. The sound made me curious because I knew for a fact that Josh's pistol was locked in my trunk. I decided to investigate. I set off for the creek, noting from the cabin's closed door that Ma was still busy with Pa. Halfway to the creek, I looked back and saw Laurel Anne following me. I stopped and waited for her.

"You can't tell Pa," I said when she caught up with me. "You have to swear you won't say anything about Josh and the pistol."

"Oh, come on..."

"No. You have to swear."

Laurel Anne rolled her eyes and crossed herself between her bosoms like we did years ago when she still played with me. "I promise."

"That's not the same as swearing," I pointed out. Down at the brick house I heard the shrill sounds of Silla screaming. "But it's good enough." I grabbed Laurel Anne's hand and hustled her in the direction of the creek.

"I'm not sure Josh should have a pistol," Laurel Anne said as I towed her along. "He's just a boy."

I didn't say anything to that. Mostly because I disagreed with her and there was no way I could convince her to agree with me. Laurel Anne was used to conducting her life according to regulations. One of those regulations was that people couldn't be adults until they had beards and bosoms. Truth was, life didn't always wait for those things before it set an adult's burden on someone and grew them up almost overnight. Josh had worked a man's job since he was ten years old. Constant harping by Silla had hardened him and forced him to keep most of his thoughts to himself. He had a long way to go before he was fully mature, but right now he was more grown up than plenty of the grown-ups I knew, and that certainly included his ma.

We found Josh firing a pistol at the creek bank near the swimming hole. I recognized the gun he was shooting as the one Porter Rockwell had given Fulton that day in the barn. Fulton himself was sitting on a log nearby, watching Josh shoot. He saw Laurel Anne and stood up. I could almost see his defenses rise around him.

Josh finished his round of shots and stepped back, expertly breaking the gun open and shaking out the copper shells. He held out a hand to Fulton for more cartridges, stopping short when he spotted us. Seeing him there beside Fulton, I realized then how much alike they were. More, I understood finally and completely that the thing that made Fulton a killer wasn't what had happened to his face but what had happened to his heart. Those same things were happening to Josh. For half a second, I felt like snatching the pistol away from him and taking it back to the brick house, where I'd use it on his ma. I learned a secret standing there watching a green-eyed boy whose name would one day make bad men weep with fear. The secret was that killing sometimes wasn't nearly as big of a sin as the daily and countless cruel things it takes to make a killer. In many respects, dying was a minute thing, as inconsequential and temporary to God as going through a door was to us. But God cared about wounded spirits. He cared because they might, if not salvaged soon enough, stay wounded for all eternity. I wondered if there was anything short of a miracle that could undo what had been done to Joshua Van Orden.

Fulton broke the spell by removing his hat. He did it mostly for Laurel Anne, and even though he was my secret escort to the dance, I turned as green as a frog.

"Haven't you practiced enough?" I asked Josh. My voice carried an involuntary note of chastisement which I immediately regretted.

"No," Josh replied. His eyes flashed before he turned to accept the bullets from Fulton. He stuck them in, closed up the gun and turned to blaze at the board set against the bank. Most of his shots blew wooden chips in the air. He was getting better.

Laurel Anne and I watched, our fingers in our ears, our noses wrinkled against the smell of gunpowder. I followed the growing bond between Josh and Fulton with rising irritation. It seemed someone was always trying to take Fulton away from me. I felt like running off to sulk except for the fact that what was going on was so obviously good for Josh.

Ignoring us, Fulton stepped closer to Josh and bent down to say something to him through the scarf. I felt Laurel Anne lean closer, trying to hear his voice. Josh studied Fulton's face, listening intently and nodding at what was being said. Fulton continued to talk, gesturing with his hand at the gun and then at the board. Josh grew confused. Fulton straightened up and positioned his feet so that he was facing the board at an angle instead of straight on. He looked to make sure Josh was watching. Josh tried to imitate him, looking clumsy and uncertain. Fulton shook his head and squatted down to move Josh's feet. The scarf slipped and he grabbed for it.

Fortunately it was the right side of Fulton's face, the relatively unscarred part, that came into view. He got the scarf back in place quick enough, but not before Laurel Anne got a glimpse of what he looked like. He was a mighty handsome man from that angle. I glanced up at Laurel Anne and saw a look on her face that hadn't been there before. Sort of a mix between surprise and interest.

"Turn a bit," Fulton said. "Don't face it straight on. Get hit, want it on the ribs. Might be enough to turn the ball."

Josh did what he was told, but with his next round of shots he missed the board entirely. His face turned red while anger crawled all over him. Fulton got down on his heels and started talking again, patient and slow, while Josh fumbled through a reload. With his mask, the spurs, knife and guns, it would have been impossible to see Fulton as any kind of a father. Everything about him spoke of cruelty—unless you saw him work with Josh. Then Fulton's sharp lines softened and the fog of hate around him receded a little bit. I think Laurel Anne saw it, too. She was watching him without blinking.

"Don't watch the pistol," Fulton said to Josh. "Close work, watch man. Go ahead."

This time Josh banged all his shots straight into the board. It folded wearily in half.

Josh turned to Fulton and I saw him smile through the smoke, bigger than I ever thought he could. Fulton patted him on the shoulder, the sort of touching men do with other men. Josh grew three inches in that moment and I saw his own hard shell slip a little. It surprised me and made my heart skip several beats. I realized with a start that I liked some of what I saw there inside Josh Van Orden. I liked it a lot. I didn't feel it in my head or even in my heart, but right down in the pit of my stomach, and maybe—if the truth had to be told—even a bit lower.

Laurel Anne grew a little bolder herself. "Good shooting, Joshua," she called, patting her hands together in lady-like applause. "Now let's see Mr. Lorings shoot."

Josh became self-conscious. He turned away without a word, doing his best to ignore us. Fulton hesitated, too, looking a little lost. For the fragment of one second, both of them looked young and vulnerable enough to-wet nurse. Then their shells were back up and they ignored us as they reloaded. I dragged on Laurel Anne's arm, hauling her away from the creek before she could say anything that would make those shells thicker. She was mad, though. When we were far enough away, I let go of her and she started straight in on them.

"A couple of stuck ups," she said. "That Josh needs a good whipping."

"He gets whipped too much already," I pointed out.

"Heavens, all we wanted to do was watch them shoot. What gives them the right to be so rude?"

"We're girls," I said.

"Well my goodness, yes," she complained. "What difference does that make?"

I looked up at my sister and wondered how I could ever get her to understand something I knew as instinctively as I knew my own name: that girls—women especially—never really know how bad they can hurt men and boys.

"His ma is a girl," I explained.

"Of course she's a girl," Laurel Anne said. "She's his mother. What—"

"So he's learned not to trust us," I said, cutting her off. "Not what we do or what we say."

I saw the seed of what I was saying go home inside Laurel Anne. As we walked back to the brick house, she kept glancing over her shoulder in the direction of the creek. For a second, I considered telling her about Fulton and Judith. I didn't, though. I think she was finally figuring that part out on her own.

Down in my heart, I hoped that whatever future efforts Laurel Anne made in the interest of Fulton they wouldn't hurt him any more than he had already been hurt. Something told me she was the last person between him and Hell.

Chapter Ten

I gave Fulton his scarf on the day of the Pioneer Dance, exactly two months to the day that he shot and killed Sergeant Bukovski and friends. That morning, Ma wrapped it up for me in some tissue paper and I carried it proudly down to the barn like it was a gift of the Magi.

Pa must have had Fulton off on a chore somewhere because he was nowhere to be found when Jeb and I arrived at the barn. Disappointed, I carried the present into the tack room where Fulton lived and laid it on his rough bed. He'd find it when he returned.

As I stood surveying the present and imagining how pleased he would be to have it, I glimpsed a flicker of color under the folded horse blanket that served as his pillow. When I turned back the blanket, I found Laurel Anne's pink hair ribbon. I understood in a flash that it didn't really matter who Fulton was escorting to the dance, the real Venus of the night in his heart was my sister. An enormous sadness welled up in me as I realized the extent of his hopelessness. Always having to stand outside the circle of a beautiful blessing must have been an agony for him. His loss wasn't something small like praying for an elephant and not getting one. It was like hell.

Ma and I spent the rest of the day finishing my dress. While she pinned and hemmed, I kept thinking about Fulton being my escort and how he would probably much rather be escorting Laurel Anne. I wasn't so dumb that I honestly believed Fulton was in love with me just because he asked me to the dance, but it still hurt a bit to come off second best.

Sometimes the idea of Fulton being my escort sounded dumb and other times it made me want to sing. After finding the hair ribbon under his pillow, nagging doubts about his sincerity kept creeping in. I thought about telling Ma but decided to keep it a secret. That way, if he didn't come for me, I wouldn't look more than just half a fool.

When the dress was finished, I had a nap so I wouldn't be tired by the late night. Ma went down to the house on an errand and I climbed out of bed and said a prayer.

First I apologized to God for not praying as much as I should have in the past. Then I told him I was done asking for elephants and now only wanted him to remind Fulton about being my escort. It wasn't because I'd look foolish waiting in vain if he didn't come, but because I thought Fulton needed to go to the dance. All right, some of both. After I said amen, I waited around for an answer but didn't get one. Still no angel and still no burning in my bosoms. I decided that maybe God needed time to think it over. I crawled back into bed and dozed off hoping that he wouldn't take as long with me as he had the Israelites in the desert.

Two hours later, Ma got me up and made me take a bath. I wanted to look nice for Fulton and so I didn't complain. I'd seen how Laurel Anne got ready for her beaus and I was willing to try any method of success. I asked Ma to put some lavender water in the tub. Then I asked her to wash my hair twice. If she suspected the reason for this unusual behavior, she never let on.

As I got ready, the tension grew until I was about near ready to turn myself inside out. There were a million reasons why Fulton might change his mind about taking me to the dance. Some of those reasons were beyond my control and it frustrated me. There were also reasons that I might be too young to even know about. Despite the intense study I had given courtship from under the porch of the brick house, I was still going about it half blind. There was the distinct possibility that some of the rules had eluded me because of my inexperience and youth. My worry became an obsession. A person could make a complete fool out of themselves if they didn't know all the rules to something.

I sat on my bed and combed my hair while Ma took her bath. Naked, Ma and Laurel Anne were complete opposites. Where Laurel Anne was round and pink and blond like an angel, Ma was slender and dark and sleek, like the trained otters in Dan Castello's circus. Her pillows weren't anywhere near as big as Laurel Anne's or even Alva's, but big enough to notice. It didn't escape me, though, that Ma and Laurel Anne did have something else in common, something that I didn't have any more than a smidgen of bosoms yet. They both had men willing to worship the ground they walked on. I asked Ma if men only loved ladies who had bosoms.

Ma smiled and said having bosoms helped but she didn't believe it was an ironclad requirement. That got me thinking that I might cram something inside the bodice of my new dress as we got ready to leave. I rejected the idea because while I was sure I could fashion some passable bosoms out of wads of cloth, they weren't the sort of things one grew in the course of an afternoon no matter how desperately they were needed. I was also certain that Fulton, given his keen eye for detail, would know that. He was used to me being skinny, and he'd know something was wrong if I suddenly showed up looking like one of the Hoffenstetter dairy cows.

When it was time, Ma and I got dressed and walked down the slope to the brick house; her with her bosoms and me with none. Every little thing about me was an irritation as the tension over Fulton's arrival mounted. What would everyone say if he showed up in a broadcloth suit with a handful of flowers? Courting, I decided, was a useless farce. It seemed an especially mean trick of God's that the continuation of our species required such utter foolishness as love.

When Ma and I arrived at the brick house, Pa had the wagon pulled up in front and everyone was piling into it. The twins were smartly dressed and quiet enough to have been fresh-dosed with Red Jacket Bitters. I had to admit that even Alva and Silla looked nice.

While everyone loaded blankets and Alva's pies and cookies into the wagon, I walked over to the edge of the porch and looked down the lane toward the barn. There was no sign of Fulton. I resolved to wait for him even if it took all night, even if I missed the dance. When Pa called for everyone to climb in the wagon, I turned to Ma.

"Ma," I said, hoping down in my insides that she wouldn't pry into my reasons. I'd never told her that Fulton was my escort. "I'll just wait here and catch up with you later."

Ma smiled. Her eyes glanced briefly at the barn and she nodded. Having a ma able to read my mind like a school primer was sometimes frustrating. Sometimes though, it worked to my advantage.

"That's fine, dear," Ma said, causing Alva to gape at her shocking lack of parental responsibility. "Please come and tell me when you arrive."

Pa might also have had something to say about leaving me home alone, but Ma just caught his arm and he "escorted" her over to the wagon. She looked so beautiful that by the time they reached the wagon, you could have banged Pa on the head with a shovel and he wouldn't have noticed it as anything out of the ordinary.

Feeling more than just a little crazy, I watched the wagon rumble off into the dark. When they were gone, real panic set in. What if Fulton had forgotten me? What if he'd only been joking about taking me to the dance? I had a thousand doubts as I sat in our front room and listened to the sound of the wagon fade down the lane. Why would he want to take an ugly kid like me to the dance when he could have asked someone his own size, someone with bosoms? As horrible of a reputation as he had, surely he could have found a real woman. I sat there wringing sweat out of my hands, just knowing that I'd made a mistake. When the knock came, it surprised me. I leaped up as lady-like as I could and flung open the door hard enough to knock over a chair. I stood rooted in place, mouth open with amazement. If the angel Moroni had been standing on the porch next to Fulton, he would have come in a shabby second. All the stories I'd ever read about princes and knights and highwaymen shriveled in comparison to what I found waiting for me on the porch. It made me realize what a small and measly thing my imagination was.

Fulton Lorings wore a gray uniform decorated with enough brass buttons and gold braid to make it look like he'd been set on fire. He had a sword and pistol buckled over top of a red sash around his middle. Crimson stripes ran down the sides of his trouser legs into boots shiny enough to see yourself in. The stars-and-bars scarf I'd made for him was wrapped around his lower face. Everything about him looked lean and razor-edged and magical. My heart ricocheted around inside my rib cage and I found it difficult to locate a breath.

Fulton held out a gloved hand. "Miss Merrell, you look lovely tonight."

I got all squirmy inside. For a second I was afraid I'd melt right down into a puddle on the floor. Finally, with a fair amount of desperation, I snatched a breath and gave him a curtsey like I'd seen Laurel Anne do for her callers. Then I took his hand.

Nicodemus waited for us at the bottom of the steps. Fresh groomed, he sported a red-trimmed saddle blanket and gleaming harness. He looked like he could gallop to the moon and back.

"I regret, Miss Merrell," Fulton said, still in a formal voice, "that I was unable to obtain a buggy."

Having said that, Fulton stooped and lifted me in his arms. Then he stepped off the porch, into the stirrup and up onto Nicodemus without using his hands. We started off for the dance through the dark woods. Riding along in the moonlight, Fulton thanked me for the new scarf. I got all squirmy inside again and told him he was welcome. After that, we rode in silence. What is there to tell you? All my dreams came true that night, including some I didn't even know I had. We rode through the back fields to avoid the roads and Eldon's patrols. In no time at all we were at the dance, threading our way through parked wagons and buggies. Fulton found a hitching rail and tied Nicodemus to it. He helped me down and offered me an arm exactly like we were courting. Through the wagons was a bower built of fresh evergreen branches hauled down out of the canyons. The night was green with the smell of it. Music and laughter poured out of the lighted interior. I could feel Fulton grow tense as we headed for the dance.

"Don't worry," I said. "We'll have lots of fun. You'll see."

"Yes," he replied tersely. "Fun."

Even though I was trying hard to be a lady, the little girl in me squeezed out when we got closer. I let go of Fulton's arm and skipped ahead where Floyd Jackson was doing duty as a greeter, pointing people in the proper directions for pies, coat racks and dancing.

"Good evening, Budge," Floyd said when he saw me. "You're looking stomp down inviting tonight. Where's that new pup of yours?"

"Left him home," I replied. "He can't dance."

Floyd chuckled and patted my head.

For some reason, being patted on the head tonight irked me. Mostly because it made me feel like something I was trying real hard at that moment not to be—a little girl. Still, I liked Floyd. He never seemed to mind that God fudged and took back one of his arms in the war. He farmed his land with one flipper, came to church with his family and paid his tithing. Outside of Jesus Christ, Joseph Smith, and a rebel general named Sterling Price, Floyd Jackson acknowledged no superiors. He had a fiery temper and a cracker drawl, all the result of having been raised in Missouri, which, as Ma liked to say, was the same as being brought up in a lunatic asylum.

Floyd reached out to pat my hair again. At that moment, though, he looked beyond me and his hand froze.

"Sweet mercy," Floyd gasped.

I turned. Fulton had stepped into the light of the torches, removing his gloves. Blade thin, firelight blazed across the buttons and braid on his uniform. Above the stars-and-bars scarf, the same light bounced in his eyes, like something glorious was alive in them.

Floyd recovered immediately and it was my turn for surprise as the heels of his freshly shined brogans slammed together and his remaining hand leaped to an eyebrow in a salute. It might have looked funny for a one-armed wheat farmer like Floyd to be snapping off army salutes, but I swear that he made saluting Fulton Lorings look as natural as kneeling before a king. My mouth hung open.

"Evening, cap'n, sir," Floyd called, standing so stiff and straight that he was almost vibrating.

Fulton didn't miss a beat. He nodded and returned Floyd's salute with a crisp one of his own. His eyes went briefly to the empty sleeve in Floyd's suit.

Floyd didn't miss the look. His back become even straighter. "Vicksburg, sir," he barked. "Color Sergeant Jackson, Fighting First Missouri. Yankee killers and lady thrillers, ever' one of us, sir."

Fulton's eyes flashed a compliment as he touched Floyd briefly on the shoulder. It was a fraternal gesture, one I'd only seen pass between grown men who had the greatest of respect for each other. Floyd blinked hard and fast, looking ready to cry or bust. Fulton unbuckled his sword and pistol and gave them to Floyd for safekeeping. He tucked my arm through his, just as if I was all grown up and he was my real beau. We started into the dance, me walking on air.

"Begging your pardon, sir," Floyd said with elaborate formality. "But there's a bunch of rabbit-ass Yankees—" He stopped suddenly and gave me a stricken look. "Oh, sorry, cap'n. I sure hope your lady will excuse my poor language, sir—ah, Union officers from the camp in there and, well, sir, are you sure you don't want to keep your sidearms?"

Fulton shook his head. Floyd recovered and beamed his understanding.

"No, sir, I reckon not. I'll just hang on to 'em for you, sir. I wouldn't want to miss the looks on their pasty faces when they see this. An honest-to-goodness officer of our'n! Why they may just soil themselves. Begging your pardon again, Miss Rose."

"It's all right, Floyd." I giggled behind my hand. I didn't know about the other soldiers, but "rabbit ass" fit Henry du Pont perfectly. I also wanted to see the look on his face when he saw my Fulton.

We walked past Floyd and into the dance.

Things might have gone a trifle better if Floyd hadn't followed us on into the bower. As it was, we came up almost immediately on four young army lieutenants: Henry du Pont and three others I didn't recognize. They had little crystal cups of punch in their white-gloved hands and their backs were to us. All eyes were on Laurel Anne, who was waltzing at that moment with Harvey Stoddard. I had to put my hand over my mouth to keep from laughing. With their sparse mustaches and nervous manners, all four of the lieutenants fit Floyd's description perfectly.

"Aten-shun!" Floyd bellowed, scaring the hell out of me and a bunch of others, but especially the lieutenants. They tossed punch in the direction of the crowd as their military training took over and they jerked upright like fence posts.

Some of the dancers faltered and the music slowed as everyone turned to look. The lieutenants peeked at us out of the corners of their eyes. I watched them struggle with the idea of remaining at attention while at the same time trying to cope with disbelief. They looked as paralyzed and stupid as sheep at the first sight of a mountain lion.

"I'll be damned," one of them murmured.

Fulton ignored them. Every eye in the bower followed us onto the floor, where he took me in his arms and then, as natural as the breeze, turned us into the faltering music. It took my breath away. I caught glimpses of Laurel Anne looking our way, her mouth open in surprise. Pa was wide-eyed while Ma had on her knowing smile.

The music recovered. It wasn't the first time I ever danced. I'd waltzed before with Pa and some of my cousins, and one ignominious time with Nephi at the insistence of Alva, but never before had I felt as light as I did in the arms of Fulton Lorings. The music melted right into my bones. We turned and swayed with the rise and fall of those liquid notes. There was none of the clumsiness normally associated in dancing with someone so much taller. My feet barely seemed to touch the ground.

I'll tell you, Fulton Lorings made an angel out of me for a few minutes that night. I wasn't a grubby little girl with skinned knees and flyaway hair anymore. I saw boys looking at me for the first time. Of all the things Stuart's Wolf gave or would give me that last summer of my childhood, I cherish those golden moments under the pine bower the most.

We danced through two waltzes. Other dancers gradually returned to the floor. They gave us a wide berth though, crowding the edges and doing their level best not to brush up against Fulton even by accident. Whenever I looked out from the center of our own dance, I saw them looking at us. I caught images of grim concern, open admiration and even, on the faces of a surprising number of good sisters, veiled interest.

"Dance with Ma," I said when the music paused again. Fulton's eyes smiled. "Your father might have something to say about that."

"Ma is the boss of herself," I replied. "Wait here."

I left Fulton near the punch table and went looking for Ma. I found her talking with Sister Knight. Other women lined the curtained wall, waiting for someone to ask them to dance. That's the problem with Mormon dances, there's always more women than men. The people who like to dance the most are the ones who get to do it the least. I took Ma's hand and pried her away from Sister Knight, dragging her back to the punch table. On the way there, I cautioned her on the various subtleties of Fulton Lorings.

"He's a captain, Ma," I reminded her. "So don't call him Mr. Lorings or Brother Lorings. Oh, Ma, you should have seen it. Floyd even saluted him and he scared the stuffing out of Henry and those other Yankees. He dances real fine and never steps on your feet. All you got to do is just follow him along. It's like flying and it's real fun. He even says stuff in French. He'll tell you what it means if you ask." I ran out of breath.

Ma laughed. "Sure and I'll try and remember all of that."

Fulton bowed forward from the waist when we arrived. Ma curtsied and took his hand. He led her out onto the floor.

If dancing with me had given people pause, Fulton dancing with my ma brought them up real short. At first, nobody took to the floor as Fulton swept Ma around to the strains of a waltz. I saw Pa watching from the other side, his face a confusing jumble of tolerance and anxiety. The good side of him must have won out because he got Alva and went out to dance. A few others followed, but it was obvious that the center of the floor belonged to Ma and Fulton.

Behind me and through the music, I listened to people comment. Several sisters commented on how beautiful Ma looked and how "rakish" Fulton appeared. I heard one or two nervous titters. Others weren't quite so complimentary.

"Is that him? Is that Hash Face?"

"What's he doing here?"

"Some nerve..."

From the back I heard Bill Pettus mumble something that sounded like "a witch dancing with Satan himself." I turned around in time to see him leave, scowling over his shoulder at the dance floor.

After Fulton's dance with Ma, I danced with him again. I didn't get much of a chance after that, but it didn't matter. Everyone knew he was my escort to the dance and they were elaborately polite to me. Otto Hoffenstetter told me I looked like a princess in my new dress. Sister Knight said I was growing up faster than she could keep track. Fannie and Sarah stared at me bug-eyed. Eddie Hoffenstetter only teased me a little bit and I didn't throw any punch on him. Ladies don't do those sorts of things. Being a lady made me feel like I had liquid fire in my veins.

Someone, probably "Color Sergeant" Floyd, got the musicians to play "Dixie." Lots of people danced to it. Pa with Pinch Face, and me with Brother Knight. Fulton danced with Floyd's wife, Lucy, who was from Georgia but right normal nonetheless. Two rebels, Fulton and Lucy put enough energy into their dance to give pause to everyone else. Floyd stood off to one side, whistling shrilly and doing a hoppity jig. At the end of the dance he gave a screechy battle cry that scared Edwina Spafford straight into joining him. Lacking another hand to clap, Floyd pounded a table.

"That was some dance, cap'n," he cried when Fulton brought Lucy back. "Puts me in mind of the old days."

Lucy's eyes sparkled and she blushed prettily when Fulton pressed her hand to the silk scarf covering his mouth.

After that, Fulton was surrounded by people. He was hard to get to but I didn't mind. I watched him be gracious with everybody and knew that the change going on inside him was growing. I made the circuit around the room, raking in the compliments and letting my head swell up. After tonight, after this positive association with good people, I knew Fulton would never be like he was before. I was so happy. And so dumb.

I located Laurel Anne and Henry. Standing off to one side with the lieutenants, they seemed a little subdued, forgotten. Right off I saw what was bothering them. They didn't like all the attention Fulton was getting. More important, they didn't like the fact that the attention had been turned away from themselves. Laurel Anne was doing her best to look like it didn't bother her, but Henry's face was stormy. I couldn't blame them. I think this was the first and only dance within three years and a hundred miles that Laurel Anne had not been the crown jewel. Next to me and Fulton, she and Henry looked like a couple of clods.

"Why aren't you dancing?" I asked.

"There isn't enough room," Laurel Anne said.

"Will you look at people go on over him," Henry complained, staring across the room at Fulton. "Why, he could be arrested for wearing that uniform, dear. It's against the law. Doesn't anyone know that?"

Henry didn't offer any explanation as to why he and the lieutenants didn't go and arrest Fulton themselves. His comments made me see, however, that not everyone was wild about Fulton's appearance or the progress he was making. I thought it best to ignore Henry. He turned and said something to his friends, causing them to laugh mean spiritedly.

"Dance with Fulton," I said to Laurel Anne, causing her to jump.

"What? Don't be ridiculous."

"Why not? You said you were going to be nice to him. That day we went swimming naked—"

Laurel Anne clamped a hand over my mouth. She smiled demurely at Henry when he looked around in mild surprise. Yanking me aside, she took her hand away.

"Honestly," she hissed. "The things that come out of your mouth."

"But you did say that. About being nice to him."

She fluttered her Spanish fan and glanced sideways in Fulton's direction before admitting that she had. "Yes, I did."

"Then why won't you dance with him?"

"Well, because."

"Because why?"

"Because I'm here with Henry. And besides, he hasn't asked me to dance."

"I can fix that," I said and ducked into the crowd.

"Rose Lee!"

Laurel Anne's hand reached out to collar me, but I was too fast. I looked back to see her pinch-lipped and shaking her head. I crossed my eyes and stuck out my tongue before I remembered that I was a lady.

Getting to Fulton proved to be a chore. At one point, I had to pinch Brother Hoffenstetter's leg to move him out of the way. Then I squeezed down through the skirts of a couple of sisters and popped up beside Fulton.

He was nervous. The press of people was still not something he was accustomed to. He looked down at me with relief—until he heard what I had to say.

"Dance with Laurel Anne."

That got everyone's attention. Several people murmured encouragement. The rest just waited to see what Fulton would do, perhaps not wanting him to, but not up to objecting out loud.

I took his hand and led him over. Henry and Laurel Anne saw us coming. Henry and his friends started to look worried. Laurel Anne, on the other hand, looked like she was silently praying that the floor would open up and swallow her.

Once I got him there, I didn't know what to do with Fulton. There was a long period wherein everyone just stared at each other. Henry and his friends studied Fulton's uniform. Laurel Anne swallowed audibly, unable to take her own gaze off Fulton's silk-wrapped face. Fulton was the only one with presence of mind. He looked at Henry.

"With your permission, Lieutenant?"

Henry wanted to refuse. That was plain in the look on his face. Finding the words to do it was another matter. He sputtered a bit and then nodded, more out of not having the current mental faculties to do anything else.

Fulton turned to Laurel Anne and put out his hand. With obvious reluctance, she put her hand in his—and everything seemed to change. I felt a curious sense of loss as Stuart's Wolf led my sister out onto the floor.

Fulton's dance with Laurel Anne fetched the entire bower up short like the blast of a powder keg. Floyd, Fulton's busy squire, had somehow arranged everything again. The band began a timorous rendition of "The Bonnie Blue Flag," growing in strength as those musicians unfamiliar with the tune gradually caught on.

Laurel Anne danced with Fulton alone on the floor. No one else dared go out there with them. The contrast would have been too great and we all knew it. I could spend the rest of my life describing how they looked together and still not do justice to what I saw. For five minutes, the armor fell away from Fulton. I saw the boy he'd been before the war. I saw what he might become if he found someone to love him in spite of the scars on his face and the things he'd done. I had an idea who he wanted that person to be, and for a brief moment, deep in my heart, I hated my beautiful sister.

I don't think anyone else saw Fulton the way I did. Laurel Anne might have. Her face changed while she danced. Some of her reservation about dancing with a killer seemed to melt away the longer she danced. I saw her looking at him with a slight furrow of confusion across her brow. I hoped that meant her heart was changing. The future of Captain Fulton Lorings was in her hands.

Bill Pettus took it upon himself to alert Eldon's committee about Fulton's presence at the dance. After he slipped away from the bower, Bill scrambled up on a horse and pounded away down the road. Two miles south of the dance, in the copse of trees where the road to our farm and the one to town joined up, he found what he was looking for.

Eldon and five members of his committee had waited in vain for Fulton to leave our farm. His vigilance deputies had been complaining all night about missing the dance. Jumpy, they almost shot Pettus full of holes when he skidded his horse to a dusty stop. They listened as he gasped out the opportunity of a lifetime.

Later, after Pa hunted him up and blackened both of Pettus's eyes in a very unbishoplike rage, the cooper said Eldon had received the news of an unarmed and unsuspecting Fulton like a revelation from God.

"We'll be famous by morning, boys," Eldon had cried. "They'll read about us in the papers back East. Come on! Let's get to the dance and finish this."

For several moments after the music stopped, Fulton and Laurel Anne kept dancing. Edwina finally complained in a loud voice about their poor attention. Fulton, embarrassed, brought the dance to a close. He released Laurel Anne and bowed. It took Laurel Anne several seconds to locate the presence of mind to curtsy in response. Fulton took her arm and escorted her back over to Henry and the lieutenants.

"Thank you, Lieutenant," he said to Henry. Then he turned to Laurel Anne and kissed her hand before she could think to snatch it away from him. "Thank you, Miss Merrell," he said.

It was all very formal and yet packed with enough emotion to make your scalp wiggle.

Fulton looked me up, taking my arm in his. "Are you having a good time, Miss Rose?" he asked.

"Yes," I exclaimed. "It's the best night of my whole life." I told him that Sarah and Fannie looked envious enough to kiss my feet while Eddie Hoffenstetter was too scared to do more than cross his eyes at me.

Fulton's eyes smiled. "Shall we get some air?"

I let him lead me out of the bower. It took us a few minutes to shake off people who wanted to say things to Fulton. Some of the men looked anxious enough to meet Stuart's Wolf that I think they would have danced with him. We finally got through the last of them and were headed out the door when I saw Fulton look back at Laurel Anne. Henry was leading her out onto the floor for another dance. She was looking across the bower at me and Fulton.

"You love her," I said to Fulton. "Don't you?"

Fulton's guard came down completely. I saw hope fade in his eyes. With his face and his reputation, he knew perfectly well that we would never let him be like us, that he would never get any closer to Laurel Anne than the dance they had just shared. "It doesn't matter," he said, leading me through the door.

I opened my mouth to say that it did, that his scars didn't matter if it was real love. I didn't get a chance to say anything because at that moment, something struck Fulton, pushing him forward and into the darkness away from the noisy bower.

"Got you now, you scum!"

I whirled and found Eldon standing between us and the bower, flanked by his committee. All of them looked about as scared as they could be, except for Eldon. He looked near about insane. Since Fulton didn't have a gun on him, and there were still people nearby, none of the vigilance committee had pulled their guns out yet. They had their hands on them, though, waiting for Eldon to give them the word.

"You should have stayed on the farm, killer," Eldon snarled. "What you did to my brother is going to cost you plenty now."

Fulton recovered immediately. He put a hand on my shoulder and tried to move me off to one side. I grabbed onto his arm and hung on, refusing to go. Eldon and his friends crowded us further from the bower, pushing us away from the entrance. Eldon's face, white and sweaty, looked demonic in the light of the torch. I tried to peer past the men, tried to find Pa in the milling group of dancers. But there was no one who could help us in time to stop the killing.

Fulton understood what the committee intended. He carefully disengaged my hand from his arm and moved me off to one side where I'd be out of the way. I was terrified speechless. I thought about running to get Pa, but one of the men, a big one with bad teeth, blocked my path. They had Fulton trapped and it was all going to end right here.

"Pa!" I screamed.

Eldon's hand cracked across my face, knocking me against the side of a wagon. When my eyes uncrossed themselves, I saw that Fulton, my sweet, wonderful prince, was gone.

In his place was Red Legs.

In the flat, ugly light of Fulton's eyes I could tell that he had changed back to the great Indian spirit killer, Ghost Smiler; he was Sonria del Diablo again, the bloodthirsty monster whose name reduced Mexican pueblos to ghost towns; he was Hash Face, the butcher of women and children. He was all the things people said about him, and some things too horrible to dream, let alone mention. But overconfident and eager for vengeance and fame, Eldon missed it all.

Still grinning, Eldon reached over to give Fulton a final shove, to push him further away from the bower where their bullets couldn't damage anything or anyone but him. I had a fleeting image of Fulton pushing Jeb the day we got him from Slobber Bob. It was like that now, only Eldon was pushing a rabid wolf.

"Now, you bastard," Eldon snarled, reaching down to his gun. "I—"

Red Legs struck. He slipped around the outstretched hand and plucked Eldon's pistol from its holster, just as easy as flicking your hand at a fly. Too late, Eldon realized what had happened. His hand slapped down on the empty holster. With a cry of rage, he lunged at Fulton. Fulton snapped forward at the waist. His forehead smashed into Eldon's face with a brutal crack of bone. The miller's son flopped on the ground. Blood spurted from his nose, black and shiny in the light from the bower.

The committee reached for their guns, but Fulton's hand popped up full of pistol. They found themselves paralyzed by what they had all planned to avoid by catching Fulton at the dance—a gun in the hand of Stuart's Wolf. They froze in place.

"Take your time," Fulton told them. He deliberately cocked the pistol and pressed the muzzle up between Bad Teeth's eyes. "I'll wait."

In the bower, another waltz started up. Seconds slowed down to hours.

I was scared, real scared, but not so frightened that I didn't under-stand how much ground we'd lost in all our efforts to help Fulton. Seeing those hideous killing eyes again broke my heart.

"N-no," Bad Teeth said. "I don't guess I want to anymore." He held his hand up away from his gun. With the other, he indicated the uncon-scious Eldon. "Was his idea."

Fulton's face stretched into a carnivorous grin behind the new silk scarf. The light in his eyes flared, becoming lethal. I watched in helpless horror as his finger tightened on the trigger. Bad Teeth started to cry.

"Fulton, don't," I whimpered.

The monster flinched. The sound of my voice seemed to call Fulton back from that wild, black place that fury had taken him. He blinked, looking confused. The pistol lowered a fraction of an inch. With a visible shudder, he regained some control.

"Get out of here," he hissed at the committee. "And never forget that your brains stayed in your heads because of this young lady." He gave the unconscious Eldon a savage kick. "Take this with you. If I see any of you again tonight, I'll put you in boxes."

Eldon's vigilance men didn't need any extra coaxing. They gathered up their fallen leader and stampeded around the corner of the bower.

Fulton tossed the pistol into the bushes and headed off toward Nicodemus with long, lunging strides. I ran after him, calling his name, trying to get him to slow down. It was like shouting at a departing thun-derstorm.

Before Fulton reached his horse, Henry and the lieutenants blocked his way. There was none of the frightening eagerness about them that I'd seen in Eldon, only a nervous, swaggering arrogance. Laurel Anne stood behind them looking angry. I ran to catch up.

Henry was already talking to Fulton when I arrived, complaining about Eldon's bloody condition. It seemed odd that Henry would be standing up for Eldon, but then I guess when it comes to impressing the woman you love, any cause will do.

"You fought with him and beat him without cause," Henry said. "Don't bother to deny it. I saw them carrying him inside. His nose is broken."

When no response was forthcoming from Fulton, one of the lieu-tenants, a stocky boy with chin whiskers, said mockingly, "Maybe he doesn't know the war is over, boys." The lieutenants laughed.

Henry nodded, looking disdainfully at Fulton's uniform. He sniffed. "I thought that little fight was over. And as I recall, Captain, your side lost. But I guess you think it still gives you the right to bully people. You must still miss your slaves."

The lieutenants crowded around Fulton, trying to intimidate him with their combined presence. There was no sign of a gun on anyone and I think, like Eldon, they presumed too much on this fact. Standing behind them, Laurel Anne looked torn.

"War's over, Yankee," Fulton rasped. He leaned close to Henry. "Question now is can you win the one you're trying to start?" His voice was the low, cold thing I remembered from that night in the loft.

Stunned by the sound of Fulton's killing voice, Henry backed up a step and fell silent.

"How dare you threaten us, you ruffian," Laurel Anne said, coming through the group. She gave her golden head a toss. "With manners like that it's a good thing you were on the losing side."

"Arrogance cost us that war," Fulton replied. He sounded tired, worn out now. He wanted to be away from us. "You would do well to remember that, Miss Merrell."

I didn't expect what happened next. I don't really think Laurel Anne did either. Fulton probably did, but he didn't try and stop it. My sister reached up and slapped Fulton, slapped him hard, right in the face.

One thing and one thing only made Laurel Anne slap Fulton. She was scared. Not mad like she obviously looked, but scared right down in her soul. I don't think she liked the way she'd felt in Fulton's arms only minutes before, all out of control with fire in her heart and the wind of change in her hair. It was probably the first time she'd been anywhere near a man she couldn't bend around her finger, and that stomach-numbing, swept-away feeling had scared her bad. The slap was a desperate, last-ditch effort on her part to rejoin the safety of the herd. If she sided with Henry and his friends against the predator, she would be back on safe ground and in control. Worse than all of this, though, fear made her incautious. She struck Fulton in the most vulnerable spot he had. She didn't know that behind the silk his ravaged face was all harsh angles and skin stretched taut over the broken lines of teeth and bone. Her slap opened a half dozen cuts in his mouth. Blood spread immediately across the white stars in the silk scarf.

"Oh," Laurel Anne said when she realized what she'd done. "I'm..."

Fulton's fingers touched the scarf. They came away bloody. From the look in his eyes, I think the artillery shell at Gettysburg had hurt him less than Laurel Anne's hand. Then his eyes went flat again and the temperature around us plunged twenty degrees. Fulton reached out and deliberately ran bloody fingers down the sleeve of Laurel Anne's dress.

Henry saw Fulton touch Laurel Anne and got mad. He must have been emboldened by Laurel Anne's successful slap. Otherwise, I doubt he would have had the nerve to do what he did next.

"Unhand her, sir," he cried, just like in the books about knights. He stepped forward and raised his gloves.

I suspect Fulton could have got out of the way of Laurel Anne's slap. She'd never been much for fighting. Heck, even I could win her when it came to dead arm punching. Fulton let her hit him. Henry was an altogether different matter. Fulton blocked Henry's gloves with an effortless wave of his hand.

"Pistols," Fulton hissed. Hate rolled off him like night vapor from the river. "Sunrise, in the stand of oaks by Indian Rocks. Sergeant Jackson?"

Floyd stepped out of the shadows where he'd been watching. He looked grim as he handed Fulton his sidearms. "Sir?"

"Sergeant Jackson will act as my second," Fulton said to Henry. He gave Laurel Anne a bloody look that wilted her. She put a hand to her mouth in fright as Fulton turned back to Henry and said, "Bring your friend, lieutenant." He looked at the other lieutenants. "Bring them all. You'll need someone to carry you home after I shoot out your eyes." He turned and was gone.

All color left Henry's face and he shriveled considerably. In the light of the torches, he looked as pallid and cheesy as a corpse. He knew that he had made a bad mistake, perhaps the worst one in his short life. In spite of the fact that he was a Yankee—and according to Fulton something to be loathed—I liked Henry and I felt sorry for him now. He couldn't back down from a duel in front of Laurel Anne and his friends.

I ran to catch up with Fulton. I found him near the horses, preparing to ride off. He turned when he heard my approach. I saw his hand touch the butt of his pistol and then slip away when he saw it was me. His dead eyes lay on me like a shroud.

"Did you forget about me, Fulton?" I asked.

"No, Rose," he said. "I didn't."

"Are we done dancing?"

He nodded curtly. "I am. Don't belong here. You do. Go back inside. There are boys. Saw them looking."

"I don't want to dance with them. I came with you."

"Mistake. Spoiled it for everyone. Always do. Should have stayed away."

I opened my mouth to argue with him, praying that I could get him to come back inside, but knowing that it would be a waste of breath. I saw his eyes shift beyond me.

One of Henry's friends appeared from the dark. "Sir?"

Fulton waited.

The obviously frightened lieutenant stepped forward. "Sir, it's the matter of balance. With no disrespect to you—-."

"Get to the point, boy. Yankees don't often get this close."

The lieutenant flushed but pressed on, sweating visibly in the cool night. "Well, sir, it's just that you have an unfair advantage. You are a professional gunman while Lieutenant du Pont is a soldier. We, his friends that is, are most concerned, sir, that the duel be a more balanced affair, you understand."

Fulton glanced back to where Henry and Laurel Anne waited. A crowd was gathering, staring at us. His eyes turned back to the lieutenant.

"West Point?"

"Class of '68," the lieutenant said stiffly, coming to attention.

"Very well," Fulton said. His voice sounded weary. "Sabers. Cannons. Knives. Fists. Whatever."

"Sabers will be fine, sir," the lieutenant said, relieved. "Thank you."

The lieutenant turned and started to scurry away. He froze solid when Fulton snarled at him. Carefully, he turned around.

"Sir?"

"This young lady is a friend of mine," Fulton said. "Did you forget your manners?"

The lieutenant gave me a baffled look and then light dawned in his eyes. "Forgive me," he stammered and bowed his head in my direction. "Good evening, Miss Merrell." Then he hurried off, no doubt pleased as punch that he was still alive.

"You didn't have to do that," I said.

"Don't let bad manners go," he said. "Not from Yankees." He started to put his spurs into Nicodemus but reined up when I called to him.

"Are you going to kill him, Fulton?" I asked. "Are you going to kill Henry."

"Yes, girl."

"No, Fulton. Please don't."

He gave me a look that showed how empty it was inside him. "Have to," he said. "Some people need killing. And it's all I have left."

I didn't know what to say. He was wrong, of course. Not about the people he killed, because some folks turned themselves into things that needed to be killed. But killing wasn't a fit way to live. Not for a person like Fulton.

Fulton looked back at the lighted bower, where the good people he had tried to imitate still laughed and danced. He turned the reins, nodded to me and was gone into the night.

"Fulton!"

There was no answer.

Ten minutes later, Ma found me running down the road after him, blind with tears and grief.

We rode home from the dance a somber bunch. Ma had heard about the duel and she knew me well enough to know I would try and sneak away to it in the morning. As she undressed me and got me into bed, she explained that under no circumstances was I to sneak away in the morning.

"Ma," I wept. "He's going to kill Henry. He's going to be bad again."

"Is there anything you can do to change that?"

I thought about it. I couldn't very well offer him anything to not kill Henry. I was a skinny kid with a face and hair like a mouse, certainly nothing a Galahad would want. I couldn't let him kill Henry, though. Not because Henry would be dead, but because of what killing Henry would do to Fulton Lorings. He was going to do it to hurt Laurel Anne as bad as she hurt him. And if he crossed that final line, the line where he could rationalize hurting the one person who could save him from himself, there would be no coming back for Fulton Lorings. Not ever.

I cried late into the night. Ma stayed with me, soothing my tears and keeping good track of me at the same time. Shortly before midnight, someone pounded on our door. Ma got up and opened it. Wearing a nightgown and a shawl, Laurel Anne stood shivering in the doorway.

"I need Rose," she said, her face wet, lips trembling. "I need Rose to talk to him, Colleen. He'll listen to Rose."

"No," Ma said, bringing her inside. "He won't listen to Rose anymore, dear. But I think he'll listen to you. In fact, I think you're probably the only person in the world he will listen to now."

"Me?"

"Yes, you."

Ma sat Laurel Anne down at the table and went to make some herb tea. Judging from her appearance, my sister hadn't slept at all. She put her hands on the table. I watched them twitch and jump.

"It's a nightmare," Laurel Anne said. "Father is down at the house in a rage. He say's he's going to break Brother Pettus's neck. Henry's scared. He's staying in town. When he brought me home, he said good-bye. He knows he's going to be killed but he won't leave, won't even ask for help. He says his honor won't let him run away. It's so stupid and so wrong, and it's all my fault. I feel terrible, like I want to die too. I shouldn't have encouraged Mr. Lorings with a dance." She put her face in her hands and started to cry.

Ma let her cry herself out while she finished making the tea. I felt like telling Laurel Anne that it was her fault for slapping Fulton, not for dancing with him. In reflection, though, it probably was the dance. Being that close to Fulton started her thinking about things, things that scared her. People, when they're scared, get mean. And being that close to Laurel Anne had caused Fulton to lower his guard.

Laurel Anne wiped her eyes. "He's probably down there sharpening his sword."

Ma shook her head. "I think he's down there hoping you'll ask him to spare Henry. He doesn't know it because it's so far inside his heart he isn't aware of it. But if you asked, Laurel Anne, he'd do it for you. It's the only thing he's got left to give. And he's not going to give it up for anyone but you. Not Rose, not Henry, not me. Not even God. Just you."

Laurel Anne wiped her swollen eyes. "Me?"

"Yes."

Laurel Anne looked at me. "What should I do? What should I say to him?"

"He won't talk to you," I said. "Not at first. He'll try to scare you away. You have to be brave. No matter what he does, don't let him scare you away."

It took a long time to tell Laurel Anne and Ma what I knew about Fulton Lorings, what I knew about the wolf in him. By the time I finished talking, night had deepened to its most secret hour.

Looking terrified but determined, Laurel Anne got up and went to the door. Being beautiful can be a curse. It insulates the people it blesses. Laurel Anne was used to people pleading with her, not the other way around. She didn't know how to beg for anything. I didn't envy her now. Having to learn humility at the hands of someone like Fulton could be a terrible thing.

"All I can do is ask," she said. "Or beg."

When she closed the door behind her, it was like she was leaving for her own funeral. I threw back the covers and looked out the window. I watched Laurel Anne's shape fade into the night as she walked barefoot down to the barn, down to a private meeting with the devil. Ma came over and tucked me back into bed.

Twenty minutes later there was more banging on our door. Ma got up and opened it again. This times it was the twins, blubbering as if Squash Head had chased them all the way up the slope from the brick house.

"Aunt Colleen," Lehi cried. "Ma says to come quick. Pa is going over to the cooperage to kill Brother Pettus. She says they'll hang Pa if somebody doesn't stop him."

Ma quickly threw a shawl around her shoulders and left with the twins. I waited five seconds and then flung myself out of bed, reaching for my shoes. Every smidgen of common sense I had was screaming at me to stay in the cabin where it was safe. I didn't because Merrells rarely listen to their common sense, and because two of the people I loved the most in the world were going to collide. I wasn't worried a bit about Pa. It would take Ma all of about a minute to convince him that killing Bill Pettus wasn't worth an eternity in hell without her.

The moon was down and the night was black as I left the cabin. I didn't know what I'd find down at the barn. There was a dark part of my brain that suggested I'd find Laurel Anne dead at the hands of Stuart's Wolf. The rest of my brain didn't know what to think as I cut through the new pens Fulton had helped Pa build. I crept around to the back side of the barn, the side where I knew Laurel Anne would have found Fulton. Long before I reached a point where I knew I could see into the barn, I heard Laurel Anne crying.

"Please, Mr. Lorings. I'm begging you."

Laurel Anne's voice was coming from the tack room where Fulton lived. I slipped along the side of the barn, skidding briefly in some manure, up to where the light of a lantern was coming through the weathered cracks. Too frightened to breathe, I put my face to the wood.

Fulton stood in the middle of the tack room. His uniform jacket was off, and blood from his hurt mouth spattered his white shirt. His face above the silk scarf was as hard and unforgiving as an anvil. In one hand, he held a long saber. Laurel Anne cowered in the doorway, the bright tracks of tears visible on her cheeks. I don't know how long they had faced each other like this, neither of them willing to back away from what they wanted the most.

"I'm sorry I hit you," Laurel Anne said. "I'd do anything to take it back. Just please don't hurt him."

"Get out," Fulton said. He wasn't the friendly Fulton I'd grown close to. He was the mad, cold Fulton from the Provo road. I was suddenly very afraid for Laurel Anne.

"I won't go," Laurel Anne said. She struggled to keep her voice level. "Not until you promise. If you have to hurt someone, hurt me."

Fulton pivoted toward my sister. I opened my mouth to scream as the saber split the air between them, turning the air silver as it struck a wooden post with a ring of steel. Wood chips sprayed through the barn, causing Laurel Anne to jump. She gave a strangled sob but kept her ground, lowering her head and closing her eyes.

I didn't know if the rumors about Fulton killing women and children were true. All I knew was that there was murder in his heart then, and all the fences he had tried to build against killing while living with us were down. Worst of all, Laurel Anne, wearing nothing but a shawl and a thin nightdress, was pressing him harder than any man ever had and lived.

"Told you," Fulton hissed. "Stay away from me."

Laurel Anne swallowed hard. "Not until you listen to me."

The saber came down until it was pointed right at her face. At first, I thought Fulton would kill her. It wasn't until I heard his voice that I understood that what he was going to do to her was much worse. When I heard his voice, a big piece of my heart broke off and tumbled into the abyss of despair.

"How much you give for your Yankee, girl?" Fulton said evilly.

His voice was full of that smothering black menace that I remembered so well from the night he trapped me in the loft. I saw his free hand go to the scarf around his face, and my hair stood out of my head like lightning. I knew what was coming. Most of all, I knew Laurel Anne wouldn't be able to stand up to Fulton's naked face the way she had his saber. What she was about to see would damage her forever. I opened my mouth to yell, to stop Fulton, but nothing came out.

"Money?" Fulton taunted her. "More crying? How about your dreams?"

I watched Laurel Anne as she opened her eyes and looked up. She had changed, too. Facing a man who actually seemed to hate her had unnerved my sister. She was no longer crying, no longer even afraid. In fact, the hopeless resignation in her eyes was infinitely more frightening than the murder in Fulton's. She took a step toward him. In spite of the saber in his hand and the pistols in his belt, Fulton backed up.

"It's my fault," Laurel Anne said. Pleading was gone from her voice now, replaced by an audible numbness. "There's no reason Henry should die for what I did. So"—she took a ragged breath—"I'm willing to pay for it. Myself."

"How much you give?" Fulton said, sounding less sure of himself. The saber still pointed at her face, but the sharp point was wobbling now.

"You...can have me."

Fulton paused, caught off guard. Stunned, all I could do myself was listen to the hammer of my heart against my ribs. For several moments, my brain accused my ears of being twin liars.

Fulton shook his head, as he hadn't heard right. "What?"

"I don't have any money, Mr. Lorings," Laurel Anne said softly. She took another step toward him, backing him toward a corner. "You wouldn't take it if I did. This isn't about money. It's about getting even. If you have to get even with someone, get even with me."

Fulton made a desperate bid to regain the initiative. He started tugging at the scarf on his face, trying to get it loose.

"How much you pay to see the face of the wolf," he stammered. "How much—?"

Laurel Anne let the shawl fall off her shoulders. She caught it with her arms, down near her waist. Time in the barn slowed down to the span of a single heartbeat when I realized that it wasn't just the shawl my sister had shrugged out of. Her nightdress was down around her waist. Round and shining in the brass light of the lantern, her breasts stood out where Fulton could see them pointing at him like a couple of soft white cannons.

"This." Laurel Anne caught a sob in her throat. "You can have this."

When Fulton didn't respond, my sister dropped her night dress to the floor, leaving herself stark naked before him. Despite her obvious humiliation she didn't cringe or try to hide herself. She kept her hands down at her sides and her eyes on the floor, letting Red Legs see exactly what she was willing to give him for the life of Henry du Pont. She stepped out of her night dress and forced herself to look up at him, to meet his terrible eyes. "Please."

Fulton was dumbstruck. He had threatened to show Laurel Anne the face of Satan and she had countered him with the face of God. I don't think anyone had ever gotten the drop on Red Legs the way Laurel Anne had. And God's truth, I think he would have rather been shot dead than see what he had reduced Laurel Anne to. I saw murder leave him as swift as the rush of bats from an old building. With a visible effort, he looked away from Laurel Anne, turning so he could only see her from the corner of his eye. He looked like the meanest of demons cringing from the celestial radiance of an angel.

"Mr. Lorings?"

"Don't," Fulton said. He was shaking now, trembling like a sick dog. "Put your clothes...."

Instead, Laurel Anne went over and sat down on his rough bed, the exact place where he must have spent nights dreaming of just such a thing. She started to cross her arms over her nakedness but forced them back down. A tear fell from her face, a sparkle of falling light.

"I'm not sure I know—" Laurel Anne started to say but stopped herself. "I mean I've never—" Twice more she started to say something but failed to get it out. She leaned back on his bed like it was a blood-stained altar, giving up the last of her secrets to Stuart's Wolf.

A long silence filled the barn while Laurel Anne waited to be claimed, while Fulton tried to marshal the routed remnants of his murderous fury, the only weapon he could rely on in situations like this. He failed miserably.

"Mr. Lorings?"

Fulton's response was a snarl of...fear? Laurel Anne flinched, her breasts bouncing as she recoiled from him. Fulton whirled and lunged out of the tack room, dropping his sword in the process. I heard the ring of spurs as he ran from the only fight in the whole world that he couldn't win. The door at the other end of the barn slammed open and he was gone into the arms of his true lover, the dark night.

Alone, Laurel Anne put her face in her hands and sobbed. I thought about going in to her, to comfort her, but then she'd know I'd seen what had transpired there in the tack room, how she had offered to give herself over like a piece of yard goods or a sack of beans to save Henry. I knew she couldn't bear to know that I knew.

Instead, I ran back up to the cabin, hoping I wouldn't meet Fulton there in the dark. If Laurel Anne knew that I'd seen her undress in front of Fulton, she never would have gotten over the humiliation. But if Fulton knew I'd seen him run away from my sister—well, after all the crazy things that had happened tonight, I wasn't sure that it wouldn't be worth my life.

I made it back to the cabin, thankful to find it still empty. I climbed into bed and shivered there under the blankets. Ma came in a short time later. I heard her whisper my name, to see if I was awake. I pretended to be asleep so I wouldn't have to talk to her. I was too afraid that the things I'd seen tonight might somehow leak out of my mouth and too embarrassed at what I'd done to see them. I spent most of the night wrestling with two big questions: would I have continued to spy on Fulton and Laurel Anne had he accepted my sister's terrible offer of restitution—and would he still kill Henry in the morning?

I realized that it was morning when I heard the sound of a horse go past our cabin in a hurry, heading in the direction of the creek and Indian Rocks. From the sound of the hoofbeats, I knew it was Nicodemus, and from the silver ring of harness, I knew Fulton had his saber with him. It seemed obvious that what Laurel Anne had done last night hadn't worked. I jumped up and ran to the door. Ma caught me before I could get it open.

"I have to stop him," I cried.

"You can't, love." Ma said. "What's done is done."

And that, thank God, was the truest thing of all.

Ma made me swear a holy promise to stay home. When I swore, crossing myself between my future bosoms, she let me get dressed and go down to the brick house. Pa and Alva were sitting at the table looking grim. I heard Laurel Anne crying in her bedroom. It was obvious that she hadn't slept at all last night. It was no wonder.

"Bunch of nonsense this duel," Pa said. He looked mad enough to eat horseshoes.

"Well, why don't you stop it then?" Alva said. "They'll listen to you."

"No they won't," Pa replied. "Not any more than a couple of bulls in the same field would listen. Especially not him."

Whenever someone said "him" in that frustrated tone of voice, I knew they were talking about Fulton. It was plain that Pa wanted to go and try to stop them, even if it meant getting hurt himself. I think he would have gone anyway, except that Ma had made him promise to stay home too. And heaven would fail before my pa broke a promise to Ma.

"They'd just go off and do it somewhere else," Pa said. "Brother Lorings because that's what he is, and Henry du Pont because he isn't smart enough to see how stupid it is to die just to prove that you're brave. All we can do now is wait and see what happens." He put his arm around me and pulled me up into his lap, turning in his chair so we could watch the trees in the direction of Indian Rocks.

We were still sitting there an hour later when Fulton rode out of the trees alone. He didn't even bother to look in the direction of the house. He rode down to the barn and unsaddled Nicodemus. A few minutes later, I heard the ringing sound of him working at Pa's anvil. My heart sank. In a few minutes, the lieutenants would be bringing Henry's body in.

I was right. Only Henry wasn't dead; he just looked that way. His friends rode up to the house around him, occasionally reaching out to steady him in the saddle. When Henry got close, I saw blood on his face. His uniform hung in rags. He looked like he'd had a fight with a bear, possibly even several bears. We all ran out onto the porch, Laurel Anne included.

"Bring him inside," Pa said to Henry's friends as they hauled him down out of the saddle. "Let's get some tonic in him."

Pa had them steer Henry to a chair. Then he went to make a tonic. Pa's tonics were simple: well water and a slug of brandy. I watched him make this one, though, and it was brandy with a slug of water. Henry took a drink and strangled it down, eyes watering. Laurel Anne sat beside him, holding his hand.

"I never want to be that close to dead again," Henry gasped when he had most of the tonic in him. "When I looked at him, I could actually see the bottom of my own grave. It was like having dirt shoveled onto my face." He shuddered. "He was so polite, though. So cold. I never thought dying could be like that."

One of Henry's friends, a nervous-looking lieutenant named Morris, told us what happened.

"Henry is the best swordsman among us," Morris said. The other lieutenants nodded. "But he never stood a chance. Every time he tried to parry, Captain Lorings's sword was at his throat. He tore up his jacket and nicked him a couple of times in the face. It was—awful to see." Morris straightened his collar and looked at Pa. "We're soldiers. We missed the war and as ridiculous as it sounds, we felt bad about it. A war is where a soldier tests himself. However, I think I speak for all of us when I say that if there were any more like Captain Lorings fighting for Robert Lee, I'm very glad I missed it." The rest of the lieutenants murmured their agreement.

"Before we go, there's something I must do," Henry said. He rose to his feet, somewhat more steady, and went outside.

As a group, they led their horses down to the barn where we could hear Fulton working. Laurel Anne, went with them. I tagged along.

Fulton was still working in Pa's shop, standing at the anvil just inside the door. He was stripped down to a ragged shirt, slamming sparks out of horseshoe. He ignored everyone as they gathered around. Henry handed his reins to one of his friends and walked up to Fulton, still wearing his shredded uniform jacket.

"I'd like to apologize to you, Captain Lorings," Henry said. He extended his hand. "I was an unforgivable prig last night. I can only hope you will accept my apology. And my hand of friendship, sir."

Fulton stared at Henry's hand, uneasy. It was a reversal of the duel. Down at the creek with a saber in his hand and killing in his heart, Fulton had been in his element like a hawk riding a desert wind. Here, with the lieutenants and Laurel Anne watching, he was a fish out of water.

"Go away," he said, turning back to the anvil.

"No sir," Henry said. "I'm staying right here until you take my hand and accept my apology."

"Apology accepted," Fulton snarled. "Get out."

"Fulton," Laurel Anne said.

He silenced her with a look. She had already asked more of him than he could give. The look told her that he could still kill Henry, kill them all, if pressed one inch further. Turning, Fulton ignored Henry's hand and walked into the barn.

Henry knew that was as good as he was going to get. He said good-bye to us and got on his horse.

After Henry and his friends were gone, Laurel Anne followed Fulton into the barn. She told me to wait outside, but as soon as she slipped through the doors, I was down off the fence and climbing the ladder into the loft. I snuck over to the edge. Laurel Anne had cornered Fulton in the tack room. This time it was different, though. Laurel Anne had all her clothes on and Fulton wasn't the least bit scared.

"Thank you," she was saying. "You could have killed him but you didn't. Thank you for...everything."

"Mistake," Fulton said. "Didn't do it for you."

"Yes, you did. I know it."

Fulton cut a look at her that two days ago would have sent her screaming to the house. Now, it only made her back up a bit. It was a reminder that the odds had changed since last night.

"You don't know anything," Fulton said.

"And you don't know enough to let me be your friend."

"I'll be gone tomorrow," Fulton said. He turned back to the pack he was loading. "Where I go, friends get in the way."

It took a lot of gumption, but Laurel Anne moved forward. Fulton heard her coming and went still. Carefully, like touching a trap, Laurel Anne put her hand on his back. He jumped, as if the touch had burned him.

"Please," she said. "Brother Lor——Fulton. I'm not sure what's happening to me, but I—"

Before she could finish, Fulton turned around. He reached up and pulled down his scarf. Laurel Anne saw his ruined face for the first time then, saw what she had offered to give herself to last night. She put her hands over her face and turned away. To her credit, she didn't scream, but I could see her breathing hard.

"Still want to be my friend?" Fulton snarled. "Get out and don't come back." He looked up into the dark loft, straight at me. "Both of you."

Chapter Eleven

Fulton left the next morning. From our window in the cabin I watched him load the packhorse and saddle Nicodemus. I cried a lot. There was nothing I could do, nothing I could say to stop him. Between tears, I saw Laurel Anne standing on the porch of the brick house. She was watching him too. I couldn't tell if she was crying.

That was it, I decided. I was quits with God and Jesus for good. Fulton was right. If there really was a God, then he didn't care about us the way they said in church. He was a mean God, cruel and indifferent to the needs and suffering of his children. I vowed never to go to church again, even if Pa beat me with a strap and threatened to sell me to the Indians.

Pa wouldn't. He loved me and besides, he was in trouble himself. The morning after the dance, he rode over to the Pettus place and hit the cooper so hard that it would be three days before Brother Pettus could say his own name. As a result, Pa had been ordered into town this morning to meet with the church superintendent about Bill's black eyes. While there's nothing about it in the Book of Mormon, it's generally accepted that bishops aren't supposed to punch members of their congregations no matter how much they deserve it. Pa stood a good chance of not being a bishop when he came home. Teary-eyed by this tragedy, Alva and Silla had gone with him.

When I could no longer bear the thought of Fulton, I left the cabin and ran down to Indian Rocks where Josh had learned to shoot and Henry had lost his duel. I locked Jeb inside because I didn't want anything to remind me of Fulton while the killer's spirit receded from our farm. Most of all, being gone would mean that I wouldn't have to say good-bye to him when he left. That part would kill me for sure.

Funny about feeling bad. You can't think straight even though you believe you're the only one seeing everything so clear. That works double for Merrells. When we feel mad, we start thinking we're the most logical people in the world. On the way down to Indian Rocks, I was a furious girl. I kicked and swung at anything that got in my way. By the time I reached the swimming hole, I was sweating and breathing hard. I sat down on the same log where Fulton had chastised me for cursing. Across the creek, I saw a tree stump full of holes. Josh's practice target, the place where Fulton put a boy on the trail of something greater than himself.

Seeing the stump made me think about how we had all been affected by Fulton Lorings. Josh had his pistol. Laurel Anne had a new way of seeing things. She would probably never get over the loss of her innocence and would no doubt be the better for it. The rest of my family had learned something about their neighbors and friends. Me, I had learned, after Herc and Johnny and now Fulton, to love and let go. I'd carry pain in my heart forever as a result, but maybe someday I'd be stronger for it.

Fulton. I didn't know if Stuart's Wolf would take anything of benefit from our family. I didn't think so. He was leaving with a memory of people who, despite their moralizing to the contrary, were too frightened and too self-righteous to love him in spite of what he was. They never even tried to see what he could have been. After us, and the poor example we had set for him, I don't suppose he would ever give anyone a chance to love him again. It would be just a matter of time before the loneliness and bitterness waiting for him out there killed him.

I cried some more, knowing I'd never see him again and that he wouldn't know that I'd love him forever. Crying made me hot and messy. When I could control myself, I got up and took off my dress and waded out into the water. Wrapped up in my self pity, I wondered if I'd be able to hold myself underwater long enough to drown. I tried it, falling forward and hanging onto some roots at the bottom. I held my breath. If there really was a God, and if he really did love me, I wanted to see if he'd get me out of this.

I held by breath until it started to hurt and water began leaking in my nose. It wasn't long enough because I was still alive. I pressed on until my lungs started to burn. Just what I thought: God didn't care. The blackness behind my shut eyelids started to turn a sickly yellow color.

Just when I was set to take a deep breath of water, a hand latched onto my hair and dragged me up out of the creek. Even before I clawed the hair out of my eyes, I knew it wasn't God or Jesus or even an angel. It was a strong hand and the grip it had on my hair hurt. Gagging and coughing, I glimpsed Fulton's determined eyes as he pulled me up onto the bank. Backing off, he squatted down on his heels to watch me suck air back into my lungs. He was wearing all his guns and knives and the cannon soldier trousers with the red stripes down the legs. Beyond him, I saw Nicodemus and the packhorse.

"I came to say good-bye," Fulton said when I stopped choking. "Looks like I was almost too late." There was none of the fury in him from the day before. It was there though, hiding bloody and awful somewhere just around the corners of his eyes.

I rolled over and retched up some creek water. "It was because of you," I said when I could.

He shook his head. "You're the craziest young lady I've ever known. What am I going to do with you?"

"You can stay and wait for me," I said, feeling thoroughly miserable now. "When I grow up we'll get married."

I got up on my hands and knees and crawled over to him, putting my head against his knee, shivering. I wanted to tell him that I wouldn't always be a skinny, ugly little girl who tried to drown herself in creeks. The words were inside me, but I didn't have the smarts or the experience to get them out.

"I don't belong here, Rose," Fulton said. "I'll end up killing more. Keep moving, maybe I can stay ahead of them."

He was right, sort of. There was nothing I could say to make that part of his life any different. I felt his hand warm on the side of my neck. Desperate, I played my last card. I loved him enough to give him to someone else, just so he would stay forever.

"Laurel Anne loves you."

He took his hand away from my neck. I knew the words had gone home in his heart, but he was too much of his old self now to believe them. Just like your body, you can hurt your heart until it's just numb and useless.

"She does," I insisted. "She isn't sure yet and it scares her, but she does." I sat up and looked at him. Wearing his guns and knives, he looked scary enough to freeze water. But for a brief second, I saw the good Fulton down there in his soul behind the eyes of the wolf. "Come home with me," I pleaded. "Just long enough to say good-bye to everyone. Please? I won't make a fuss when you leave then. Only just don't leave us like we were nothing to you." Tears were running down my face. He reached over and pushed them off my cheek. He nodded.

"All right," he said. "Long enough to say good-bye."

I got up and hobbled over to get my dress. Grabbing it up, a heavy piece of old rope spilled out at my feet. I thought it was a snake and I jumped, shrieking. I had a brief, illogical flash of Herc jumping in to protect me. I turned to give Fulton an embarrassed look. He was on his feet drawing a gun. A buzzing sound seemed to slow everything down. I realized the old rope really was a snake the moment its needle fangs sank deep against the inside of my knee, numbing it to the bone.

I dropped my dress. Panic robbed me of reason as images of Herc slobbering to death welled up in me. Fighting a terror so black it threatened to smother me, I took a single running step in the direction of home. The snake struck me again in the calf.

"Ma!" I screamed.

I heard the boom of a shot and knew Fulton had killed the snake. With his other hand, he reached out and grabbed me by the hair as I ran past, spinning me around and throwing me to the ground. The sword knife flashed in the sun, licking fire across the places where the snake had bit me.

I fought Fulton, hitting and scratching at him as he tried to hold me down. All I could think of was Ma, that dying wouldn't be so bad if she would just hold me. Fulton's hand swung brutally against the side of my head. Suddenly I was laying in the grass, my head ringing and my chest heaving with sobs. Through the foggy edge of consciousness, I felt Fulton sucking hard on the bites and spitting blood away into the grass.

I don't know how long Fulton worked on me. His ruined mouth, still swollen by Laurel Anne's slap, made it hard for him to suck the poison out of me. Between breaths, I heard him stammering something that I could have sworn was a prayer. But if anyone was listening, it was the devil who put a hand in first.

Coyle Morgan and Joey Leeks appeared on the opposite bank of the creek. Mounted on the Morgans' mule and holding fishing poles, they had obviously sneaked through our fields and down to the creek for a little fishing. Their faces registered the sort of shock you might expect to see on someone confronted by the likes of Fulton crouched with a knife over a bloody girl.

Fulton whirled on them, his face a red mess of scars and blood. "Get help!" he roared. "Go!"

I understood Fulton's ruined voice but Coyle and Joey didn't. All they saw was the monster called Hash Face and me laying butchered at his feet. Dropping the poles, they kicked the sides of the old mule and fled, screaming in terror. Frightened by the noise, Nicodemus and the packhorse trotted away into the trees.

Fulton turned back to me. By now, I was starting to twitch uncontrollably. Either because of shock or the snake's poison, my vision had begun to darken. I remember only fleeting images, bits and pieces of Fulton arguing and threatening someone who wasn't there. Later, I realized that it was his first prayer.

Fulton went back to drawing the poison out of me and spitting it into the grass. When he did as much as he thought he could, he wrapped me in my dress, picked me up and started running for the farm.

As I bounced along in Fulton's arms, I knew what had happened to me was bad. I remembered Herc again and the way he had jumped between me and the other snake. Most of all, I remember the way Herc died. I fully expected to go the same way, gasping and slobbering for my final breath. I knew I was dead. I only wanted Fulton to hurry, to get me home to my ma so I could die with her arms around me. I didn't know that what Fulton had already done for me had saved my life—and that what he was doing by taking me home would cost him his own.

Eldon and his Dry Creek Vigilance Committee learned of Fulton's departure from a couple of good sisters who passed by our farm earlier in the morning and saw the killer loading his packhorse. Wearing a plaster bandage across his smashed nose, Eldon rounded up every member of the committee and rode out to reclaim our farm for the Lord and the law. Even Otto Hoffenstetter came, carrying a shotgun and trying to talk some sense into Eldon. But Eldon wasn't in the listening mood. Outwitted, out-waited, and eventually out-fought at the dance, he was thinking only of murder now. The committee rode into our yard and demanded to know in which direction Fulton had gone.

Josh replied that if they told, half the committee would be dead by sundown. That got some of them thinking about going home. Not Eldon. He took out his pistol and pointed it at Josh, telling him that if he didn't supply them with information, he'd be dead in five seconds. Ma said later that it was obvious to everyone but the committee that Eldon was crazy. Josh didn't care. Already beginning to imitate Fulton, he was getting ready to tell Eldon to go to hell when Coyle and Joey came belting up out of the trees, whipping their lathered and frightened mule.

No one understood them at first. I learned this part from Laurel Anne. It took a few minutes for Ma and the more reasonable members of the vigilance committee to calm them down. When Coyle blurted out what they'd seen, Ma's face went white.

I knew it," Eldon shouted, pointing his finger at Ma. "Your husband wouldn't listen to me and this is your due." He waved for the committee to follow him and they headed for the creek at a gallop. Ma, Josh and Laurel Anne ran after them.

All I remember of Fulton's run to our farm was the ring of his spurs on the road and the sound of his threats against God. I wanted to tell him that it was all right, that dying wasn't all that bad. I couldn't because I was shivering so hard. Someone kept calling to me from off to one side of the blackness threatening to close over me. As incredible as it seems, it sounded like Johnny. I couldn't make out the words.

Near the farm, the committee rode down upon us. I think Eldon would have started firing immediately except for the fact that Otto yelled to him that I was in the way. Fulton stopped as the horses ringed him. He stared up into the muzzles of a dozen shotguns and pistols.

"What'd you do to her," I heard someone cry.

"Snake bit," Fulton said, gasping from his run. "Needs help."

"Yeah, she does, you murdering bastard," Eldon said. "And we're it. Put her down and back away."

"Needs help," Fulton said. His voice sounded weak and confused.

Several of the committee climbed off their horses and while the rest kept Fulton covered, they came over and dragged me out of his arms. He tried to stop them and someone hit him from behind with the butt of a rifle.

It still might have been a fair fight, except for the fact that in the process of saving my life, Fulton had risked his own. Laurel Anne's slap from the other night had opened a dozen deep cuts in his damaged mouth. Some of the snake venom he pulled from me had entered him and the run from the creek had pumped it through him. Unsteady, he stared up at the committee.

"Needs a doctor," he said, his breath laboring. "No time for this."

Eldon jumped off his horse, pistol in hand.

"I'll tell you what we have time for," he said. "We got time for a hanging."

I tried to tell them what happened. My voice was weak and everyone was shouting at Fulton, calling him vile names for what they thought he'd done to me. With a burst of relief, I saw Ma and Laurel Anne and Josh running up the road. I held out my arms for her. She ran to me and took me away from the committee. Between hugs and sobs, I managed to get out what had happened.

"We're not even going to bother with a trial, you scum," Eldon was saying. "You'll swing right here."

Laurel Anne tried to push through the men, yelling at Eldon to stop. The committee held her back. Eldon looked at her.

"You're sticking up for him after what he did to your sister?"

"He didn't do anything," Laurel Anne. "He's just trying to leave." Her voice broke on the last word.

A few members of the committee looked like they might back away. Eldon raged at Laurel Anne, calling her something vile and telling her to stay out of a man's business.

"I don't want any trouble," Fulton said. He looked sick and ready to drop.

"You got it anyway," Eldon said. He cocked his pistol and pointed it at Fulton. "You're going to pay for everything you've done."

I don't know why he did it. Fulton turned away from a fight for the first time since the war. It might have been because he thought God expected it of him, to turn the other cheek. I doubt it. More, I think it was because he was still doing things for Laurel Anne. Stumbling a little, he pushed his way through the committee. As delirious as I was, I saw him looking at my sister when Eldon shot him in the back.

A piece of me died when Fulton fell in the road. I heard Laurel Anne scream.

"I did it," Eldon shouted, leaping up and down. "You all saw it. I killed Stuart's Wolf."

But Fulton wasn't dead. Bleeding heavily, he raised himself on his arms and slumped back into the dirt.

"Out of the way," Eldon shouted. "He's still alive. He's still dangerous."

"Eldon," Otto Hoffenstetter said. "Dot's enough. You shot him in der back."

"So what," Eldon cried, nearly foaming at the mouth. "You can't give an animal like this a chance. You have to put it out of his misery. Everyone get back."

Ma and Laurel Anne screamed again at Eldon, but the committee used their muskets to hold them back. The men might not have agreed with Eldon's methods, but no one was going to help the dying Red Legs. Eldon deliberately cocked his pistol again and pointed it at Fulton's head.

"This is for Gilbert, you scum," Eldon said. "It's over for you."

The shot that made everyone jump didn't come from Eldon's pistol. A hole appeared in his tin badge. The miller's son stared down at it. Wobbling, he looked around at us in surprise. I think he thought Laurel Anne had shot him. But it was Josh.

Calmly holding his pistol like Fulton had taught him, Josh thumbed back the hammer, steadied his aim and shot Eldon again, straight through the heart. Eldon fell on his face in the road. That's when the blackness swept over me for good.

For two weeks we fought death for the life of Fulton Lorings. Or I should say Laurel Anne did. As soon as Ma got Eldon's bullet out of him, Laurel Anne pushed everyone out of the cabin. She moved a chair to the edge of the bed and except for the necessities of life itself and occasional visits from Ma, never left it.

Ma and I stayed down at the brick house with Alva and Pa and the twins. No one dared suggest that it was unseemly for Laurel Anne to stay alone in the cabin with Fulton. We had moved beyond those things.

I missed most of the official maneuvering that happened as a result of

Eldon shooting Fulton and in turn being shot to death by a twelve-year-old boy. During that time, my leg swole up and turned black and green. I had fevers and nightmares of blood and hate. Periodically, I heard doctors whispering to Ma about amputating my leg. I heard enough to know that any amputating would be done over Ma's dead body and so I didn't worry too much. I concentrated on trying to get better and praying for Fulton.

All my defenses were down. My prayers had become devoid of any argument. I wasn't in a position to make deals with God over the life of Red Legs or elephants or anything. I had nothing to trade, nothing left to promise. My bargaining position was less tenable than Laurel Anne's the night she offered herself to Fulton. Miserable, I broke down and pleaded nightly for my Father up in heaven to spare the life of a man who had rarely spared anyone himself. The irony didn't escape me. I hoped, however, that God, who seemed to specialize in ironies, would listen to someone like me. I didn't hold out much hope. The daily reports on Fulton's progress weren't good. They dragged me deeper into depression. Fulton was going to die just when things could have gone so right.

One night, while my leg throbbed and burned, and the ghosts of Bukovski and French Pete haunted my bed, I fell asleep. Or at least I thought I was asleep. I remember that my leg still hurt. I don't know if what happened that night was a dream or an answer from God. One minute I was crying silently in the dark and the next there was someone standing at the foot of the bed. I wiped my eyes and saw that it was Johnny.

"Hello, Rose," he said in a voice that spread warmth through me. He was handsome and tall and intelligent looking, not like the Johnny I remembered.

"The dark angel came," he said. "You did well."

"I didn't," I wept. "I did everything wrong. He's dying and Josh is going to prison. Everything went wrong."

Johnny didn't say anything. His smile wasn't slow and stupid anymore. There was nothing about him that I remembered except the love he had for us. It came off him like sunshine in the spring.

"What will we do now?" I asked him.

"Get well," Johnny said. "There's still much to do."

I nodded, not understanding what he meant. He turned to go and I saw Herc, Bumpa and Nanna Merrell standing in a place so beautiful it made me frantic to get out of bed and go with them. Johnny smiled at me over his shoulder and Herc barked as everything closed down to black. When I opened my eyes, the dream or whatever it was had taken away most of my bitterness. I concentrated on getting better.

The one bit of good news was that the official verdict in what would become known as the Indian Rocks shoot-out eventually cleared Josh and Fulton of any wrongdoing. The testimonies of Otto Hoffenstetter, Leo Poulsen, Laurel Anne and Ma carried considerable weight. They smothered the bitter objections of Josiah Bair. A week after burying his son, Josiah sold his mill to a Danish immigrant and moved what was left of his family to San Francisco.

Fall whispered its own advent. By the first of September, the mornings had grown cooler, tickling your nose with the frigid promise of things to come. Even as Fulton coasted toward his own death, I skipped handily away from my own. I got out of bed for the first time on the morning of our first frost. Pa wrapped me in a blanket and carried me up the slope to the cabin where Fulton lay dying. He laid me on Ma's bed, kissed Laurel Anne and then left us to talk.

Laurel Anne looked awful. Dark circles ringed her eyes and her hair was pulled back out of the way, making her normally beautiful face look severe. Her dress was wrinkled and stained with old blood.

Fulton looked worse. He'd lost weight and his ruined face was sunk in even further. He lay on the bed like an old man, his breath ragged and labored.

Laurel Anne looked at me, as empty as I'd ever seen her. "He's going to die. I've been praying and crying and working and he's still going to die."

"What will you do if he doesn't?" I asked.

The look she gave me told me what she would do, even if she wasn't yet ready to admit it out loud. She leaned over and gently wiped his half face.

"I don't know what it is, Budge. There's something about him. Nothing around here has been the same since he arrived. He's changed all of us, including me. I've seen him do terrible things." She looked down at the shine of sweat on his ruined, tortured face. "He certainly is no dandy, but he's got a hook deep in my heart. I could have any man in the valley for a husband, but I don't want them. I never saw anything in any of them but dances, a home and children. Now, for the first time I can see the angel inside the man. And he's lying right here at death's door where I put him. I know he's killed people, but most of them were devils and I guess they deserved it. My sin is greater." She looked at me with a shine of tears in her eyes. "Rose, what will God do to me if I killed an angel, even one of his dark ones?"

"If I was you I'd think more about what Fulton was going to do when he comes around. We hurt him awful bad, Laurel Anne, and he's got this far in life by not forgiving. He hasn't got but one cheek to turn."

Laurel Anne bowed her head and wept. Later, when she was through, we said a prayer together for Fulton.

I don't know what Laurel Anne promised God for the life of Fulton Lorings. Whatever it was, it must have worked. Word came down one morning that he was awake. Pa brought it to us. He was still a bishop after whacking Bill Pettus. The superintendent knew Bill Pettus and decided that looking like a raccoon suited him. Other than Fulton, our lives had returned pretty much to normal. When Pa gave me the news, I jumped up. As fast as my stiff leg would allow, I ran up the slope to the cabin. Jeb ran at my heels. Josh trailed along behind us.

Laurel Anne let me in. She looked marginally better, cleaned up at least. I hurried past her to the bed where Fulton lay. He was propped up on some pillows, the ragged blue scarf wrapped back around his face. I saw the butt of a pistol underneath the blanket near his hand.

"Hello, Fulton," I said.

His eyes recognized me but that was all. They weren't the eyes of a friend anymore. They were the flat gray, dead things I remembered from the Provo road. Killing eyes.

Laurel Anne came up behind me. "He hasn't said a word. The first things he wanted were the scarf and a gun," she said. "I figured those out by following his eyes." She sounded afraid.

Fulton's eyes came back to rest on me. The scarf moved as he whispered, "Should have never come back."

I couldn't tell if he was talking about coming back to the farm with me to say goodbye or coming back from dying. I didn't know what to say. Everything he had tried to do for us had come back to hurt him.

I sat on the edge of the bed and tried to take his hand. He rolled away from me. A black despair welled up in my heart. To be rejected by someone you love is the worst hurt there is. It's the only thing that can kill all of you, body and spirit. I realized then how Fulton had lived his life—moving from one place to another, rejected every time he trusted someone enough to take down his mask. What I felt sitting there next to him on the bed scared me. There were men whose time on earth was measured in the days and minutes it would take between now and the moment they encountered Stuart's Wolf.

Looking at Fulton's scarred back, I think I saw myself and what I could be if the hurt I was feeling became a way of life. And a way of death. I got up and left him, feeling deep down in my heart that we had finally managed to do what no one had ever been able to do who tried—kill all of Fulton Lorings.

Fulton got better. Laurel Anne continued to stay with him in the cabin. Except for the fact that Fulton never said a word to her and that they slept in separate beds, it was almost like they were married.

Gradually, he started to move around some. Laurel Anne tried to help him out of bed one day. He snarled her away. When he crashed to the floor because his legs wouldn't support him, he hissed her back and slowly crawled toward the bed himself. He made it. After that, it was only a matter of time.

By October, Fulton was ready. He left the cabin and moved back down into the barn. Looking pale and deathlike, he wouldn't last a winter in the open. But his mind, or what was left of his mind, was made up. No one dared approach him.

No one had reckoned on Laurel Anne.

On the day he rode away from our farm, I was waiting for him at the bottom of the lane. He couldn't leave without passing by me. My heart was breaking as he came down the lane to the road, looking like a messenger from Satan again. A left turn would take him north to Salt Lake City and the Immigrant Trail. Beyond that was California and hell. He held my gaze as he rode closer.

"Good-bye, Fulton," I said. "I still love you."

He didn't say anything, but I knew he heard me. He started to pause and then moved on, not willing to trust even me. It made my eyes blurry with tears.

"You can't stop me," I shouted at his back. "I can love you all I want and there's nothing you can do about it."

He kept moving, taking a big piece of me with him, taking all the wrong pieces of us, too.

"I'm going to start cussing again," I yelled after him. "I'll say the baddest words I know all the time."

Pa came up to stand beside me. He put an arm around me and I cried harder. "Don't let him go, Pa," I wept. "Make him stay."

"Hush," Pa said. "It hurts but there's nothing we can do."

Fulton was near the bend in the road, about where I thought I'd see him for the last time, when another rider joined him. It took Pa and me a minute to recognize who it was.

Wearing one of Pa's old coats and carrying a valise, Laurel Anne fell in beside Fulton. Fulton stopped and pointed back at the farm. I saw my sister shake her head. When Fulton put his spurs into Nicodemus, Laurel Anne turned her horse in behind him.

"Oh, Lord," Pa said, his face growing pale.

I jumped down off the fence and ran. Pa couldn't keep up with me. Fulton moved Nicodemus into a trot, trying to leave Laurel Anne behind. Together, they disappeared around a bend in the trees.

I ran hard on my snake-bit leg. It started to ache way down in the bone but I didn't care. I'd run until it fell off. I cut through the trees, down across the creek and out over a field. Pa lagged farther behind me with each step.

Through the trees on the far side of the field, I burst out onto the road again. Fulton was off his horse, reaching for Laurel Anne to drag her down. I ducked back into the bushes, hunkering low.

"You can't," Fulton was saying. "Get down."

Laurel Anne tried to rein the mare away from his reaching hands. "No!"

Fulton lunged and caught her arm, pulling her from the saddle. Laurel Anne fought her way clear of him, standing in the road with fists clenched at her side as he slapped the horse's rump, sending it back in the direction of the farm.

"I'll walk," Laurel Anne told him defiantly. "I'll follow you. Wherever you go."

He couldn't shoot her. And judging from the look on my sister's beautiful face, that was about the only way Fulton would be able to stop Laurel Anne. I saw his shoulders sag. Laurel Anne saw it too and she moved toward him. He backed up against the side of Nicodemus, who had the good sense to stay put, blocking Fulton's escape.

"I love you, Fulton," Laurel Anne said, putting a hand on his chest. Fulton looked like he'd rather be shot again, but he didn't say anything. Laurel Anne faltered. "If you don't love me, that's fine. I'll follow until you do. I'll beg you to love me."

Laurel Anne almost broke down. I watched as she shook her head, trying to gather her resolve so she could save Fulton, and herself.

"I know what kind of man you are." Laurel Anne said. "And I know what kind you can be. And I know what kind of a woman I'll be without you. So if you leave, I'm going with you, no matter where you go."

Laurel Anne reached up and pulled the scarf away from Fulton's face. She didn't flinch from the awful sight. During the time she had nursed him, she'd gotten used to it. More importantly, I don't think she even saw the scars anymore. She gazed up at him, studying him intently. Waiting.

Fulton tried to take a step back, tried to hide his face in the collar of his shirt, but he was stuck between Nicodemus and Laurel Anne. Under my sister's calm, beautiful eyes, Stuart's Wolf cringed like a yard dog. It was terrible to see and I wept silently for him. His hands came up to block the sight of his face but Laurel Anne caught them in her own, holding them tenderly, refusing to let him go or to retreat another step.

"No," Fulton begged.

"I want you to come home with me," Laurel Anne said in a rush. "I want you to speak to my father. But first, Fulton, first I want you to kiss me. And then I want you to say my name."

"No," he said, his voice breaking.

She held onto the front of his shirt and said fiercely, "Yes. I love you, Fulton. Please."

He tried to tear himself away from her. He almost made it, too. I think if he had, there would have been nothing left between him and death but empty miles and lonely nights. Indeed, he had already accepted that fate. I saw clearly the look on his face and knew he would still rather murder hope, shoot it in the face, than let it get close enough to hurt him again.

Fortunately for all of us, Laurel Anne was a Merrell. She swung an arm around Fulton's neck and before the monster named Red Legs could do a thing to stop her, she was kissing him hard and fast. The radiance of her face overwhelmed the wreckage of his, a startling contrast of heaven and hell. It was the sort of kiss I'd seen Ma sometimes give Pa, a kiss where the giver surrenders one more piece of their soul. My hair stood on end and a wild feeling pierced the very center of me. I knew then that the most binding thing between men and women isn't love or even making squeaks, it's when their hearts find each other and make a whole person out of two imperfect halves.

The kiss finally ended but Laurel Anne stayed locked against Fulton. "I love you, Fulton."

Fulton was staggered. A personal appearance by Jesus couldn't have shocked him more.

"Say my name, Fulton," she said.

He mumbled something garbled, eyes rolling wildly. After a moment, when he seemed more certain of himself, he tried it again. "Lora-anne."

"I love you, Fulton."

I crept away through a silver blur of tears. I looked back once and saw Fulton Lorings with his arms around Laurel Anne, his ruined face against her neck. I heard muffled calls of my sister's name while she cradled a wild head against her and gently rocked Fulton through the fires of his own private Appomattox. I have never seen my sister more beautiful. Far off down the road that led to California and death, I fancied I saw the dim and furious gray spirit of Stuart's Wolf, sharp-toothed and alone, moving hard and eventually gone forever.

Epilogue

I'm fifteen years older now. I have two kids of my own, one-year-old Stuart and three-year-old Annie, who loves to chase frogs and skinny-dip with the boys. I don't feel much smarter than I did on the day our valley stood still when Laurel Anne got married to Fulton. Pa married them in the shade of a pine bower built by the valley men who had vied for my sister's hand. Ma cried happily. Alva, of course, bawled buckets. Henry du Pont, a damn Yankee, stood up next to Fulton as best man, proving to me and Floyd Jackson that with God all things are possible.

Most of the valley couldn't understand why a beautiful woman like Laurel Anne would marry a scarred-up killer like Red Legs. Me, I couldn't see why a man like Fulton would marry a snooty and simpering woman like Laurel Anne. Fulton and Laurel Anne know and I guess that's good enough for them and God. They moved west to Warm Springs, where they raise horses and children in what seems to be equal numbers.

People hurt Fulton Lorings bad. That's why he swore to Laurel Anne he'd never become a Mormon or put away his guns. Fortunately, God and time have a way of making liars out of some people. That's probably why Laurel Anne, who swore she'd never marry a gentile, got hitched to Fulton Lorings anyway. And it's probably why, three months after Laurel Anne and Fulton got married, Pa drove up to Salt Lake with Silla Van Orden, where they were hitched by Brigham Young.

Me, I grew up and fell in love, both as patient and natural as the turn of a season. I found my own wild spirit to claim. I chased U.S. Marshal Joshua Van Orden until he caught me and dragged me to the altar. In this territory he's God's own particular curse on rustlers, murderers and thieves. I'm never really afraid for Josh, but I know my green-eyed seraph well enough that there are times when I find myself saying little prayers for the men he hunts in the desert and the saloons. Sometimes Josh hitches up the wagon and we drive west to visit Fulton and Laurel Anne.

The years have mellowed Stuart's Wolf. He still wears the scarf I made for him, although now I think he wears it for the people who might be frightened by his scars, and not because he's ashamed of them. They're good folks out there in Warm Springs. I doubt any of them care much one way or the other what Fulton looks like.

Warm Springs never knew Fulton Lorings as a blink-of-an-eye killer and he sure never gave them cause to find out. They accepted him right off for what Laurel Anne and me and Jesus helped him become. The change must have set well with what remained of the wolf in Fulton. I guess that's why he eventually put away his guns. Like I said, time and God make terrific liars out of some people.